DAVID GIBBINS has worked in underwater archaeology all his professional life. After taking a PhD from Cambridge University he taught archaeology in Britain and abroad, and is a world authority on ancient shipwrecks and sunken cities. He has led numerous expeditions to investigate underwater sites in the Mediterranean and around the world. He currently divides his time between fieldwork, England and Canada.

CRUSADER GOLD is David Gibbins' second novel. His first, ATLANTIS, was published in 2005 and was translated into twenty-seven different languages. It was a massive international bestseller and became one of the biggest debuts of the year.

CRUSADER GOLD

DAVID GIBBINS

headline

First published in Great Britain in 2006
by HEADLINE PUBLISHING GROUP

First published in paperback in 2006
by HEADLINE PUBLISHING GROUP

3

Cataloguing in Publication Data is available from the British Library

0 7553 2424 2 (ISBN-10)
978 07553 2424 8 (ISBN-13)

Typeset in Aldine 401BT by Avon DataSet Ltd,
Bidford-on-Avon, Warwickshire

Printed and bound in the UK by
CPI Mackays, Chatham ME5 8TD

Headline's policy is to use papers that are natural, renewable and recyclable
products and made from wood grown in sustainable forests. The logging
and manufacturing processes are expected to conform to the environmental
regulations of the country of origin.

HEADLINE PUBLISHING GROUP
A division of Hodder Headline
338 Euston Road
London NW1 3BH

www.headline.co.uk
www.hodderheadline.com

Acknowledgements

With huge thanks to my agent, Luigi Bonomi of LBA, to my publisher, Harriet Evans, and to the entire team at Headline. To Tessa Balshaw-Jones, Gaia Banks, Jenny Bateman, Alison Bonomi, Sam Edenborough, Mary Esdaile, Nicki Kennedy, Rebecca McEwan, Tony McGrath, Amanda Preston, Rebecca Purtell, John Rush, Poppy Shirlaw and Ann Verrinder Gibbins. As with my previous novel, *Atlantis*, the settings in this book are based on first-hand experience, and I owe much to those who have made this possible. To my parents for many trips to Hereford Cathedral as a child, and for accompanying me years later on a memorable study tour in Rome. To the British Institute of Archaeology at Ankara for a travel scholarship that allowed me to study the Golden Horn in Istanbul, and to the Chair of the NATO Life Sciences and Technology Committee for inviting me to Kiev. To the crew of *RV Akademik Ioffe* for taking me into Ilulissat icefjord in Greenland, a truly unforgettable experience, and to Parks Canada for opening the L'Anse aux Meadows site. To Steve Aitken and Tom D'Entremont for my first dives under ice, at the very outset of my diving career, and to my brother Alan for diving with me in the Yucatán and for his technical expertise. To Angie and to Molly with much love for our trips to Stamford Bridge and the holy isle of Iona, and to LNG for having been there too.

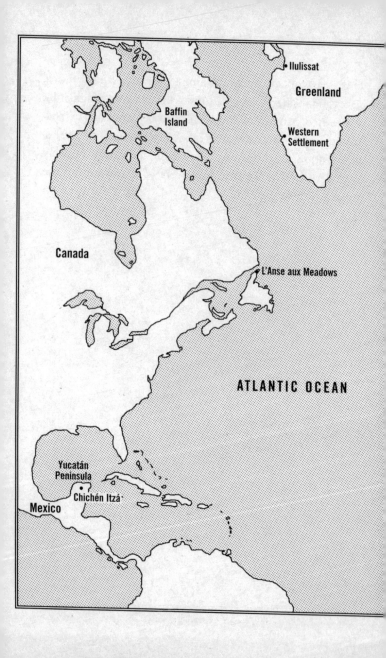

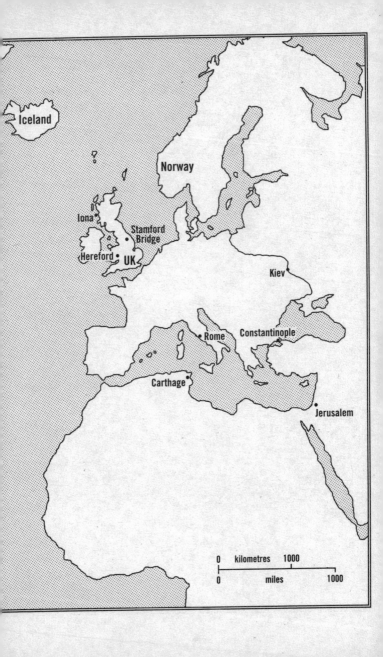

The spoils in general were borne in promiscuous heaps; but conspicuous above all stood out those captured in the Temple at Jerusalem. These consisted of a golden table, many talents in weight, and a lampstand, likewise made of gold, but constructed on a different pattern from those which we use in ordinary life. Affixed to a pedestal was a central shaft, from which there extended slender branches, arranged trident-fashion, a wrought lamp being attached to the extremity of each branch; of these there were seven, indicating the honour paid to that number among the Jews . . . The triumphal ceremonies being concluded and the Empire of the Romans established on the firmest foundations, Vespasian decided to erect a Temple of Peace . . . into that shrine were accumulated and stored all objects for the sight of which men had once wandered over the whole world, eager to see them severally while they lay in various countries. Here, too, he laid up the vessels of gold from the Temple of the Jews . . .

Josephus, *Jewish War* VII, 148–62

Prologue

The two golden eagles swept in low over the city from the west, their wingbeats slow and deep as they flew unswervingly towards the podium. In the pastel light of dawn their shadows seemed to undulate and magnify across the temples and monuments of the forum, like two denizens of Hades come to take their rightful place at the table of victory. At the last moment the eagles dipped their wings and veered north along the line of the Sacred Way. The man with the laurel crown who stood alone on the podium felt the brush of their wings, saw the purple streamers issuing from their talons and the speckly radiance where their plumage had been brushed with gold. They were his prize pair, descendants of mighty eagles he had brought back to Rome for another triumph half a lifetime ago, snatched from their desolate mountaintop eyries on the northern fringes of the empire. Now as he watched they rose majestically over the very heart of the city, their wings lifted as if on an updraught from the massed exhalation of the people thronging either side of the Sacred Way far below. At the highest point they seemed to hang motionless, as if Jupiter himself had reached down and seized them in his embrace. Then with a raucous screech they flapped upwards and dived down on closed wings, swooping low over the Capitoline Temple and out of sight back towards the massed legions waiting on the Field of Mars.

In the tremulous silence that followed, all eyes strained towards the podium. The man drew his cloak up over his head in the customary way and raised his right arm for all to see, palm facing outwards. The omen had been propitious. The greatest triumph of all time could now begin.

As the thudding drumbeat of the procession began to echo from the Field of Mars, a slave mounted the podium and proffered his hand.

'Fresh from the mint, *princeps*.'

The man took the coin and quickly turned back, impatient not to miss any of the spectacle. He held the coin up so it was framed by the triumphal arch at the beginning of the Sacred Way, the place where the procession would appear. He could see that the coin was a silver denarius, minted from the spoils of war brought up from the river port at Ostia only the day before. He squinted and read the inscription around the edge. *IMP CAESAR VESPASIANUS AUG*. Imperator

Caesar Vespasianus Augustus, holder of tribunician power, consul for the third time, pontifex maximus. He had been emperor for less than a year, and the words still sent a tremor through his heart. He saw the image in the centre and grunted. It showed a heavy-set, balding man, advanced in years, with jutting chin and hooked nose, deep creases round his eyes and mouth and lines on his forehead. It was not a pretty sight, but his was a grunt of satisfaction. He had ordered his portrait deliberately made in the old fashion of the Roman Republic, warts and all, in contrast to his reviled predecessor Nero, whose effeminate Greek-style images were being torn down and erased all over the empire. Vespasian was tough, gritty, honourable, a man close to the earth. A Roman of the old ways.

He flipped the coin over and held it high so the first rays of the sun behind him glinted off the silver. In the centre was a bowed, weeping woman, her hair done up in the Eastern fashion. Beside her was a Roman legionary standard, identical to those that lined the Sacred Way today. Below her was the word he had ordered put on all his coins, the word that made this day his crowning triumph.

IVDAEA.

Judaea captured.

At that moment the crowd, hushed by the flight of the eagles, erupted in a huge crescendo of noise. The insistent drumbeat which had been coming up from the Circus Maximus suddenly became a thudding boom. Through the arch emerged an enormous African elephant, its trunk swaying from side to side almost to the hands of the spectators who were reaching out to touch it. Astride the elephant sat two immense Nubian slaves, their heavily muscled arms beating in unison on drums slung to either side. Immediately behind came the six Vestal Virgins, their hair in braids and their white robes shimmering as if they were emissaries from heaven itself. Then came a cohort of the Praetorian Guard, resplendent in their black breastplates and plumed helmets, giants among men recruited from the finest warriors across the Roman Empire. Then the first in a long procession of men and boys, senators and equestrians and members of Vespasian's own family, all dressed in purple togas interwoven with gold. Between them at close intervals came wagons piled high with fabulous riches, some resting on biers and pedestals and others held aloft by slaves from all corners of the empire.

Vespasian watched as the wagons trundled slowly by, each new wonder bringing a gasp of awe from the crowd. There were magnificent statues of gods in gilt bronze, sumptuous royal treasures from the kingdoms of the East, wild-haired slaves wearing heavy gold neck-torques from Gaul and Germany, mounds of emeralds and diamonds from beyond the Indus, shimmering silk tapestries from the far-off land called Thina. All the wonders that men had previously travelled the world to see were here today in this one place, this eternal city.

Only Vespasian knew that many of these treasures were being seen for the last time. Beside him on the podium was trumpets. Through the archway came two horsemen riding side by side, both bedecked in crimson and wearing laurel diadems just like the emperor. The crowd erupted in thunderous applause, and Vespasian felt a surge of nostalgia as he watched his sons Titus and Domitian receive the acclamation. The next spectacle had the crowd dumbstruck, and Vespasian himself felt his jaw drop. Following the horsemen came a succession of immense travelling stages, each drawn by a team of white-garlanded bulls and carrying a vast scenic backdrop that towered to the full height of the arch. Each was a living tableau of scenes from the war, with prisoners and legionaries playing their part. One showed a countryside laid waste and its occupants put to the sword. Another depicted Roman siege engines battering a huge wall, the city's occupants valiantly defending from above. Others showed scenes of utter destruction. Enemy soldiers annihilated on the battlefield. Whole families committing suicide in a clifftop citadel rather than surrendering. A great temple ripped down and destroyed in a conflagration, its priests locked inside. A triumphant legion marching through a ruined city, shackled prisoners and carts of booty in tow. Scenes of desolation so chastening that even the bloodthirsty Roman crowd was cowed to silence, and roared its approval only after the last tableau had been hauled past.

The triumph was heading inexorably towards its climax. Next came the prisoners, men, women and children, hundreds of them chained together and corralled between lines of spear-carrying legionaries. Following time-honoured practice, they were well dressed in purple robes, a way of concealing their wounds and making them seem more formidable adversaries. Vespasian leaned forward and eyed them keenly. These were a different breed from the wild-eyed savages he had brought back from Britain thirty-five years previously. His Jewish informant Josephus had told him his people believed their God came with the Romans to purge their temple and blot out their city, as punishment for corruption. Yet these seemed a proud people, their heads held high, not captives broken by remorse. In their midst was the rebel leader Simon, shackled between two legionaries, a handsome bearded man struggling to walk tall and seemingly contemptuous of his fate. As he came level with the podium he flashed his dark eyes up towards the emperor, and for a second Vespasian felt his soul pierced, a fleeting moment of disquiet that he quickly put aside.

Another blast from the trumpets signalled the climax of the procession. Vespasian turned from the prisoners and looked towards the arch. Josephus had told him about the spoils from the Temple and he was eager to see them. Now they came, not heaped extravagantly on carts like the earlier treasures, but carried individually so they could be properly viewed. First came the sacred curtain that screened the sanctuary from the rest of the Temple. Then came the vestments of the high priests, heavy garments dyed in precious Tyrean purple and bedecked with brilliant jewels. Next the scrolls of their ancient testament, the sacred laws that Josephus called the *pentateuch*. Then a long procession of ritual objects from the sanctuary, cups, platters, ablution vessels, all in solid gold, followed by a heavy golden table carried by four legionaries, wreathed in smoke from incense burners attached to each corner. As the heady aroma of cinnamon and cassia wafted over the podium, Vespasian felt himself transported back to his early days of soldiering in the East. When he opened his eyes he was met with an apparition that left him gaping in awe.

Through the swirling smoke that lingered in front of the arch came a treasure like nothing seen before in Rome. Josephus had described it well but Vespasian had not expected such an immense weight of gold, so burdensome it took twelve legionaries to heft it on their shoulders. As they emerged slowly into view he began to make it out, a glowing object the height of a man or more. Rising from a two-tiered octagonal base was an ornate tapering column, and on either side were branches extending upwards symmetrically to the same level. It was like a huge golden trident of the sea god Neptune, only here the tips of the prongs were fashioned into ornate lamps, seven in all. As the bearers cleared the arch a slave emerged with a burning torch which he used to light incense in each of the lamps, sending thick white smoke tumbling down over the throng on either side of the Sacred Way and enveloping them like a dawn mist.

Vespasian knew this was the menorah, the most sacred symbol of the Jewish Temple. Josephus had told him that the number seven held special significance for his people, and harked back to the days of their earliest prophets. He said that robbing the Temple of the menorah would be like an enemy stealing the statue of the she-wolf from the Capitolium, an unimaginable desecration that would tear out the heart of Rome itself.

A sudden commotion to the right drew the crowd away from the menorah. They had drunk their fill of treasure and were now baying for blood. Vespasian knew what was coming next, an act fixed in ritual since the days of Romulus and Remus. Far up under the Capitoline Hill he could see where the crowd had parted to form a wide circle around an ugly gash in the ground, the swaying mob held back by a detachment of the Praetorian Guard, their swords drawn. Here had gone Jugurtha, enemy of the Roman Republic, Vercingetorix the Gaul, the British chieftains Vespasian himself had dragged to this spot. He could see where the Jewish prisoners had been formed up around the edge of the circle, their chains removed but motionless and silent. In the centre the bearded man was being tormented like a dog, baited and prodded by the surrounding guards like a beast in an amphitheatre. He was doing all he could to remain upright and dignified, but offered no resistance as his tunic was torn off and a noose was thrown violently round his neck. The crowd jeered as he was jabbed at spearpoint towards the hole. Suddenly he tumbled out of sight. At that moment the scene was lit by a blinding beam of light, the sun having risen above the Temple of Mars, the war god, behind Vespasian, and reflecting dazzlingly off the menorah and the other golden spoils assembled in the forum.

The crowd erupted. It was yet another good omen.

Vespasian remembered those dark eyes, and set his face impassively to the west.

Let this be an end to it.

For a few moments there was a hushed silence, like the silence when the eagles had flown over, then a hooded man emerged from the pit holding up something in his hand. The crowd roared. Now it was the turn of the other prisoners. Vespasian watched dispassionately as the children were separated from their parents and led forward. A woman fainted and was held up by the hair and decapitated on the spot. A man broke free to stagger after his child and was stamped to a bloody pulp by one of the Nubians. The children were pushed to the edge of the pit in groups of three and had their throats cut, their little bodies hurled into the chasm. Then the women, then the men. The men were beheaded, gladiators with masked helmets bringing their giant curved swords down in unison, each sweep of steel accompanied by a single drumbeat as if they were oarsmen in a galley. Bodies piled upon bodies. Steel flashed up and down in the glare of the sunlight. The crowd swayed, gorging on blood. Vespasian glanced again at the menorah. The seven prisoners he had ordered spared hung from posts on the far side of the pit, their naked bodies sprayed crimson. They would go home to their compatriots in the desert of Judaea and bring news of the vengeance of Rome, of the submission of their most sacred object to the vaults of the victor. As long as Rome held the treasure of the Temple they would never dare rise against her again. Any trouble and their guiding light would be extinguished for ever. It was the Roman way.

The executioners had done their work. Now the triumph could begin in earnest, days of feasting and games, piety and acclamations. Even before the crowd had shouted their exaltation, the bulls which had drawn the carts of treasure had been led up under the Temple of Jupiter, and already the altar and the statue of the she-wolf were spattered with blood from the first sacrifice.

Vespasian turned to leave the podium, still fingering the coin. He shrugged off his purple cloak and donned the crimson robe held out for him by two slaves. He would join his sons Titus and Domitian on horseback at the rear of the procession, leading a line of priests to the altar below the Temple of Jupiter, where he would perform his customary rituals as pontifex maximus. Before leaving he glanced one last time at the marble plan and made a silent vow. The age of conquest would end. His would be an age of reconstruction, a return from decadence to the virtues of his ancestors. On this very spot where he stood he would build a Temple of Peace, a temple greater than any other. Here he would store for all time the treasure of this vanquished people. He remembered those dark eyes again. He would do all in his power to ensure that the menorah was never again paraded in triumph through the streets of Rome. He turned

1

'I think we've hit pay dirt!'

Jack Howard looked up from the chart table to the minarets of Istanbul on the skyline, then down to where the excited shout had come from the foredeck below. He quickly replaced the nautical dividers he had been using and swung out of the bridge door for a better view. He had been on edge all morning, hoping against hope that today would be the day, and now his heart was racing with excitement. When he saw what was happening he turned and slid down the metal handrails three flights to the walkway on the port side of the ship. Seconds later he was mingling with the crew on the foredeck, his dark blue fisherman's jersey conspicuous among the overalls bearing the logo of IMU, the International Maritime University.

'Right. What have we got?'

Before the crew chief could reply, one of the divers surfaced in a tumult of white water off the port bow. Jack leaned over the bulwark railing to watch as the diver spat out his regulator mouthpiece and injected a blast of air into his stabilizer jacket.

'It's Venetian,' he called up breathlessly. 'I'm sure of it. I saw the markings.'

The diver vented his jacket and disappeared back beneath the waves. Jack watched the slew of bubbles that rose from his exhaust and that of the three other divers who were guiding the lifting platform to the surface. It was a potentially treacherous operation, with *Sea Venture* maintaining position against a five-knot surface current. A slight wobble in the current and the divers and their precious cargo would be swept off into one of the busiest shipping lanes in the world.

Jack narrowed his eyes as the sunlight glinted off the waves, his rugged, tanned features creasing as he kept his attention glued on the spot where the diver had disappeared. Behind him the machinery on the foredeck clunked and whirred into action and the crane dipped with the weight of its load. Slowly, inexorably the cable rose from the sea bed thirty metres below, groaning alarmingly as the current took hold. The crew lining the railing seemed to hold their breath as the cable creaked upwards inch by inch. At last the spread of chains holding each corner of the platform appeared and Jack knew they were safe. *Sea Venture* had been positioned with her port side in the lee of the current, facing the shoreline of the old city, and the lifting platform would now be protected by the deep draught of the vessel.

From the murky depths an oblong form began to take shape. Jack felt the familiar tug of excitement, the burst of adrenalin he always felt at this moment. Despite being present at some of the greatest archaeological finds ever made, he had never lost the thrill that came with every new discovery. Even the most mundane object could open a whole new window on the past, give reality to momentous events only obscurely remembered in myth and history. As he watched intently, his hands gripping the rails, the four divers emerged at the corners and the platform was winched clear of the waves. When they saw what lay in the middle the crew erupted in a ragged cheer. Months of planning and days of round-the-clock effort had paid off.

'Bingo.' The crew chief grinned at Jack. 'You were right again.'

'Couldn't have happened without your hard work.'

It was a great gun, a gleaming bronze cannon at least two metres long, its upper surface washed clean of the accumulated grime of centuries and shining like gold. Jack could immediately see it was an early type, its ornate cylindrical breech tapering to an octagonal fore end. He had seen guns like this of sixteenth century date from King Henry VIII's flagship *Mary Rose* in Portsmouth, and from shipwrecks of the Spanish Armada. But this one looked

15

older, much older. After the crane had slowly swung its load over the railing and deposited it on the foredeck, Jack strode over for a closer look, the crew crowding eagerly behind. He ignored the spatter of mud from the cleaning hose as he crouched down and stretched his hand reverently towards the gun.

'The Lion of St Mark's,' he said. 'It's Venetian all right.'

He pointed to a raised casting near the breech end of the gun. The image was unmistakable, a winged, forward-facing lion wreathed in a leafy garland, one of the most potent symbols of medieval Europe. He traced his fingers over the emblem and trailed them towards the rear of the breech. Suddenly he raised his other hand to order the crewman holding the hose to avert the flow.

'There's a foundry mark,' he said excitedly. 'In front of the touch hole.'

'It's a date.' The crew chief leaned over Jack, shielding his eyes from the glare. '*Anno domini*. Then Roman numerals. I can barely make it out. M, C, D . . .'

'1453,' one of the others exclaimed.

'My God,' Jack said quietly. 'The Great Siege.' He had no need to explain that date; its significance had been drummed into the crew during his many briefing lectures. *1453*. The year of the greatest ever showdown between East and West, a clash of titans at this crossroads between Europe and Asia. The year of the last dying gasp of the Roman Empire, its domain shrunk to this one defiant promontory from its heyday fifteen hundred years before, when Rome had ruled the greater part of the known world. For a moment Jack felt a frisson of energy as he pressed his hand against the cold metal of the gun. He glanced along the line of the barrel towards the city, its minarets and domes rising like a studded jewel from a mirage. He was touching history itself, drawn into the past with an immediacy no textbook could ever convey.

After a moment he stood up and arched his back, his tall, lean frame towering over most of the crew. 'It's a field piece, a siege gun, much bigger than the anti-personnel breech-loaders carried on ships of this period. My guess is we're looking at one of the guns used by Sultan Mehmet II and the Ottoman Turks to pound the city defences.' He gestured towards the shoreline where the fractured remains of the Byzantine sea walls were just visible, their impressive stature further reduced by earthquake and modern development. 'The Ottomans would have used any gun they could lay their hands on. This one was cast in Venice earlier that year, then maybe captured in battle or by pirates, then used against the massed forces of Byzantium behind those walls, including the Venetians themselves. The Turkish media are going to love this.'

As the crew dispersed back to their jobs, Jack looked again at that emblem on the gun. Like his own forebears in England, sea captains and explorers who had touched the furthest reaches of the globe, the Venetians were maritime adventurers who had spread their tentacles across the Mediterranean world, even installing a colony of merchants here in Constantinople. Theirs was a world of trade and profiteering, not imperialism and conquest. Yet they had been responsible for one of the greatest crimes in the history of civilization, a crime which had drawn Jack to this spot and which he was determined to fathom before the expedition was out.

Back on the bridge Jack resumed his seat behind the chart table and rolled up his sleeves. It had been a cool early summer morning but the sun was beginning to bear down as the sea mist burned off. He looked over at Tom York, IMU's senior captain, a neatly attired, white-haired man who was conferring with the ship's second officer, a newly appointed Estonian who had come with impeccable credentials from the Russian merchant marine academy. York glanced keenly at Jack and inclined his head towards the bridge window where he had been watching the scene on the foredeck below.

'I'd say mid-fifteenth century, from a distance.' York had begun a distinguished career in the Royal Navy as a gunnery officer, and since then had developed an expertise in early naval ordnance which had proved indispensable on IMU projects. 'I can't wait to take a closer look. Right at the dawn of naval gunnery. But too late for us.'

Jack nodded. '1453, to be precise. Almost two hundred and fifty years too late. We're looking for something way before guns were used at sea. It's a terrific find and I didn't want to deflate the crew, but we've got a long way to go before we reach the Crusades.'

Jack gazed pensively towards the shore, his view momentarily obscured by an overcrowded ferry that passed perilously close to the excavation. In the shimmer of phosphoresence left in its wake the city behind seemed to be floating on a cloud, like a heavenly apparition. It was one of the supreme images of history, a palimpsest of the greatest civilizations the world had ever known. To Jack's eye it was like a cross-section through an archaeological site, only instead of layer built upon layer, here everything was jumbled, the threads of history all interwoven and nothing clear-cut. At the lowest level were the cracked and fissured remnants of the walls of Constantinople, first planned by the emperor Constantine the Great when he moved his capital here in the fourth century AD and abandoned Rome to decline and ruin. Above the walls rose the slopes of the much older Greek acropolis of Byzantium, a name which survived as the term for the Christian empire of the Middle Ages based in Constantinople which traced its roots back to Rome. Above that rose the sprawling splendour of the Topkapi Palace, hub of the city the Ottoman Turks renamed Istanbul after they defeated the Byzantines in 1453, and shining heart of the most powerful state in the medieval world. Higher still, above the few remaining wooden houses of old Istanbul, rose the minarets and cascading domes of Hagia Sofia, once the greatest of all Christian cathedrals in the East, but after 1453 a holy site of Islam. And somewhere, Jack knew, it was possible, just possible, that the sprawling mass of the city concealed evidence of a migration at the very dawn of history, of settlers from a precocious civilization who had fled their citadel of Atlantis as it was inundated by floodwaters far to the east in the Black Sea.

He could hardly believe it was six months since he and Katya had lost themselves in the labyrinthine back ways of the city. It had been a time of supreme exhilaration, basking in the discovery of a lifetime, but a time also of emptiness and loss. For Katya it had been the devastating truth about her father's evil empire, a revelation that weighed heavily on her despite all Jack's efforts, and led her to return to Russia to spearhead a renewed effort against the illegal antiquities trade. For Jack the sense of personal loss had been more acute, and he still felt it now. They had been together when the search for Peter Howe had finally been called off. Howe had been a friend since boyhood and Jack was reminded of him every time he saw Tom York, his limp a legacy of the same gun battle. Jack had insisted on staying with *Sea Venture* over Atlantis until the search had finally been called off. For many days afterwards he felt that his ambitions had become entombed in the Black Sea with the wreck of *Seaquest*, that he had no right to risk the lives of others in his search for adventure. It was Katya who had nursed back his confidence as they became absorbed in the history of Byzantium during their long days together exploring Istanbul. She had persuaded him to reawaken a schoolboy dream he had cherished with Peter Howe, a dream of a fabulous lost treasure which had become all-consuming after Jack and Katya had parted ways at the airport, a dream which had led Jack back to where he was now.

'I've done it!'

Jack snapped out of his trance and hurried over to the source of the noise in the navigation room behind the bridge. In the darkened interior he could see where the radar and position-fixing consoles had been stacked on either side to make way for a complex array of electronic gadgetry surrounding an outsized computer screen. In the midst of it all, oblivious to his presence, sat a swarthy, dark-haired man with a rugby player's physique, his eyes glued to the screen and his head clamped in earphones festooned with antennae.

'Good thing you finally lost some weight,' Jack said. 'Otherwise we'd be excavating you out of this.'

'What?' Costas Kazantzakis shot him an impatient glance and reverted to the screen. Jack shouted the words at him again.

'Okay, okay.' Costas lifted off the headset and leaned back in what little space he had. 'Yeah, well, it was scraping my way through that underwater tunnel that did it. I've still got the scars. If anything good came out of that project it was the gods of Atlantis warning me to pull back on the calories.'

Costas craned his neck round and took in Jack's mud-spattered sweater. 'Been playing again?'

'Siege gun. Venetian. 1453.'

Costas grunted then suddenly snapped the headset back on as the screen erupted in a kaleidoscope of colours. Jack looked on fondly as his friend became absorbed again in his task. Costas was a brilliantly inventive engineer, with a PhD in submersibles technology from MIT, and had accompanied Jack on many of his adventures since the foundation of IMU over a decade ago. His hard science was a perfect foil to Jack's archaeology. Not for Costas the complex interwoven threads of history and the uncertainties of interpretation. For him the only significant problems were those that could be solved by science, and the only complexity was when things failed to work.

'What's going on?'

Another figure had appeared at the doorway and squeezed in beside Jack, his frame definitely on the bulky side. Maurice Hiebermeyer seemed to be in a permanent sheen of sweat, despite his baggy shorts and open shirt. Jack turned and nodded in greeting.

'I think Costas has finally got this thing to work.'

Jack knew what was coming next. Hiebermeyer had flown in by helicopter the night before from the Institute of Archaeology in Alexandria, like a bird of prey pouncing on its target, hoping that Jack would be looking ahead, having found the problems of excavating in Istanbul's harbour insurmountable. They had last spoken on the deck of *Sea Venture* six months ago when Hiebermeyer had mentioned another extraordinary find of ancient writing from the necropolis of mummies that had produced the Atlantis papyrus, and since then he had been bombarding IMU with phone messages and emails.

He fumbled with a folder he was carrying. 'Jack, we need to . . .'

'It will have to wait.' Jack flashed a good-natured smile at the portly Egyptologist. 'We're on a knife-edge here and I have to concentrate. Sorry, Maurice. Just hang on till this is over.' He turned back to the screen and Hiebermeyer went silent.

'Yes!'

The screen rippled with colour, and the two men moved up behind Costas for a better view. They were looking at a video image, a floodlit grey mass with a mechanical pincer arm extending into the middle.

'We're now almost sixteen metres below the sea floor, fifty-one metres absolute depth from our present position.' Costas removed the headset and leaned back as he spoke. 'In a few seconds the imaging will automatically revert to sonar and the ferret should be back on line.'

'Ferret?'

Costas glanced apologetically at Hiebermeyer and handed over a plastic model he had been holding like a talisman, an odd cylindrical shape that bore a passing resemblance to the remote-operated vehicle they had used to explore the Neolithic village in the Black Sea. 'A combination remote-operated vehicle, underwater vacuum-cleaner and sub-bottom sonar,' he enthused. 'It's controlled from here via an umbilical and can burrow through sediment with pinpoint precision, sending back images as crisp as an MRI scan. At the moment it's digging through terragenous sediment, land

23

runoff, tons of it. We're at the edge of the channel swept by the Bosporus, but even so there's vast quantities of sediment, several metres per century. We need to go deep if we're to stand any chance of finding what we want. The weight of that chain is going to bury it further still.'

'Ah, the chain,' Hiebermeyer murmured. 'Remind me.'

Jack shifted over to a yellow Admiralty Chart of the Istanbul approaches pinned to the wall beside Costas. Their position was clearly marked at the outer edge of the estuary that cut through the city, its sinuous scimitar shape defining the promontory of Byzantium and forming one of the greatest natural harbours in the world. To the ancient Greeks this was Chrysoceras, the Golden Horn, as if a giant mythical bull had embedded itself in the Bosporus as it strained towards the Black Sea, a significance not lost on the three men with the bull imagery of Atlantis still fresh in their minds.

Jack picked up a pencil and traced a faint line over the entrance to the estuary. 'During the Byzantine period the Golden Horn was closed off in times of emergency by a giant boom almost a kilometre long, huge links of roughly forged iron held up on pylons and barges. It was attached here, on a tower near the extremity of the city walls where the estuary meets the Bosporus, and here, about three hundred metres away from us on the Galata shore. The chain is first recorded in the eighth century AD and had a famous role in the Great Siege of 1453, but we know of only two occasions when it may have been breached. The first was in the eleventh century, when a gang of Viking mercenaries supposedly got their longships over it. The second is more definite, in 1204, when Venetian galleys broke it with a ram. The chain was rebuilt, but a severed section may have been lost on the sea bed. If we can find it, then we've hit the layer with the loot and we're in business.'

'The first link in our story.' Costas' pun scarcely concealed his anxiety, his fingers quietly drumming the desk and his eyes flitting over the screen. The image had gone dark and the only indication that the ferret was operational was the depth gauge in the corner, cycling with agonizing slowness through five-centimetre increments.

'So how can you be so certain about the location?' Hiebermeyer had put his own quest on hold and was becoming absorbed in the project.

'It's always been contentious, but a fifteenth-century manuscript unearthed in the Topkapi archive last year gives an exact position-fix between known monuments on the shoreline.'

'I don't like it.' Costas glanced at the wall clock and shifted uneasily in his seat. 'If that gun was from 1453, then we've got at least five metres of compacted sediment to dig through before we're anywhere near the target layer. And we've only got twenty minutes before *Sea Venture* has to shift position.'

Jack shared his concern, and pursed his lips. This project was like no other they had worked on, a constant game of cat and mouse in one of the most overcrowded waterways on the planet. They had a six-hour window each day authorized by the port authorities, but even so they had to shift repeatedly to let a ferry or cargo vessel past, some with draughts so deep their screws churned up the bottom sediment. Jack had every confidence in Tom York's ability to trouble-shoot the navigation, and *Sea Venture*'s dynamic positioning system meant that she could reacquire precise co-ordinates with ease. But there was no protection for the excavation on the sea bed, or, more importantly for Costas, any guarantee that his prize creation would not become enmired for ever with all the other detritus of history.

Hiebermeyer sensed the tension and persisted with Jack. 'So what's this childhood dream of yours?'

Jack took a deep breath, nodded, and beckoned Hiebermeyer over to a computer console on the far side of the room. It was a story he had told a hundred times before, to the crew, to the press, in his repeated attempts to gain backing for the project from the IMU Board of Directors and the Turkish authorities, but it never failed to send a shiver of excitement up his spine.

'The Great Siege of 1453 was one of the defining moments in history,' Jack began. 'The death knell of the biggest empire the world had ever seen, the event that gave Islam a permanent foothold in Europe. But for the city of Constantinople a far more calamitous event took place two and a half centuries earlier. Desecration and rape on a colossal scale, a horrendous atrocity even by medieval standards. And the perpetrators were not infidels but Christians, Crusaders of the Holy Cross, no less.'

'The Crusades,' Hiebermeyer said. 'Of course.'

'The time they didn't quite make it to the Holy Land.'

'Remember what Professor Dillen drummed into us at Cambridge,' Hiebermeyer murmured. 'That the greatest crimes against Christendom have always been caused by Christians themselves.' The two men had been contemporaries as undergraduates, and when Jack had returned to complete his doctorate after a stint in the Royal Navy they had studied early Christian and Jewish history together under their famous mentor.

'The date was 1204,' Jack continued. 'Pope Innocent III had called for a fourth Crusade, yet another doomed expedition to free Jerusalem from the infidel. How the noble knights of the Crusade came to be diverted from their cause to sack the greatest treasure house of Eastern Christianity is one of the most appalling sagas in history.'

The small screen in front of them suddenly flashed up an image recognizable the world over, four splendidly wrought horses in gilded copper standing together in front of an ornate architectural backdrop.

'The Horses of St Mark's,' Hiebermeyer said.

'A few tourists would drop their cameras if they knew the truth about how these sculptures reached Venice.' Jack was in full stride now, his words tinged with anger. 'The leaders of the Crusade needed someone to ship the knights and their equipment across the Mediterranean to the Holy Land. And who better than the Venetians, the greatest maritime power of the day. But the Venetians had other ideas up their sleeves.

The Byzantine Empire based in Constantinople had begun to encroach on territory near Venice in the Adriatic Sea, and the Venetians didn't like it. Venetian merchants in Constantinople had been murdered. The Venetian doge Dandolo had been imprisoned and blinded by the Byzantines years before and was secretly bent on revenge. Then the Crusaders proved unable to come up with the cash for their passage after they had embarked, virtually enslaving them to the Venetians. Add to that a claimant to the Byzantine throne among the Crusader ranks, and the stage was set. Pope Innocent III found himself unwittingly sponsoring the sack of the second city of Christendom, the focal point of the Eastern Church. Once they arrived at Constantinople, the Crusaders forgot the Holy Cross and behaved like any other marauding army of the Middle Ages, only with a ferocity and barbarism unparalleled even for that period.'

'What happened?'

'Imagine if an army out of control landed in London and stripped all the public statues, desecrated Westminster Abbey, emptied the British Museum, burned the British Library. All the symbols of nationhood and the treasures of empire lost in a single blood-soaked rampage. In Constantinople the holy warriors applied their much-vaunted Christian zeal to the great churches, Hagia Sofia foremost among them, looting the hallowed relics of a thousand years of Christianity. They destroyed the libraries, descendants of the ancient libraries of Alexandria and

Ephesus, an incalculable loss for civilization. They stripped the hippodrome, the ancient racing circus that was the focus of the city, leaving only the fragments of sculptures you see there today and a few monuments too large to pillage.'

'The Egyptian obelisk of Thutmose III,' Hiebermeyer said, nodding.

Jack gestured at the screen. 'We know that Constantinople was the inheritor of all the greatest treasures of Western Civilization. Priceless artefacts that had once been in Egypt and Greece and the Near East were first brought to Rome as the empire expanded. Then, when Constantine moved the capital, many of these treasures moved with him, shipped across the Mediterranean from Rome to Constantinople. The Horses of St Mark's may originally have been fifth century BC Greek creations, perhaps embellishing the famous sanctuary at Olympia. Five centuries later they're in Rome, on top of a triumphal arch of Nero in the forum, part of a sculptural group showing the emperor drawing a four-horse *quadriga*. The arch was destroyed by Vespasian but the image survives on Nero's coins. Four centuries after that they're here in Constantinople, perhaps in the hippodrome beside that obelisk. And remember Constantinople had never been sacked before 1204. The treasures we know from eyewitness accounts were plundered by the Crusaders can only hint at what was there. Some of the loot was melted down for bullion and coin. Others treasures, like the Horses of St Mark's, were shipped back to Venice and the Crusader homelands, France, Spain, the Low Countries, England, where the relics of this crime may still lie secreted away in the great cathedrals and monasteries. And other objects, especially antiquities with pagan symbolism, were desecrated and hurled into the Golden Horn.' He paused. 'When Peter Howe and I first became obsessed by this story we were convinced that one of the greatest troves of ancient art anywhere in the world may lie on the sea floor below us now.'

There was a sudden commotion behind them as Costas drew his chair up to the video screen. Hiebermeyer's eyes remained pensively on the image of the horses and he put his hand on his friend's shoulder.

'You say anything from ancient Rome could have been brought here,' he said quietly. 'Last year after our little adventure on the Black Sea I was called to Rome to translate an Egyptian hieratic text found on the site of Vespasian's Temple of Peace, near the spot where the fragments of the marble plan of the city were found. It proved to be one of a series of bronze plaques attached to the public colonnade of the precinct, each with an identical text in all of the main languages of the Roman Empire. Latin, Greek, Egyptian, Aramaic, you name it. They were proclamations listing Vespasian's victories and Rome's triumph. Their subject was the Jewish War.'

Jack turned from watching Costas and looked Hiebermeyer full in the face, his dark eyes fathomless. The other man spoke haltingly.

'Are you thinking what I'm thinking?'

Jack remained silent.

'My God.' Hiebermeyer's German accent became more pronounced, and his voice was wavering. 'The Jewish treasures of the Tabernacle. Vespasian had them consigned to the Temple of Peace, never to be paraded again. They passed into legend.' His voice became a whisper. 'Could they have been secretly shipped to Constantinople before Rome fell?'

'The thought had occurred to me,' Jack said quietly.

Hiebermeyer took off his little round glasses and mopped his forehead. 'The sacred vessels of the inner sanctum. The golden table. The menorah.' He seemed to have difficulty getting the last word out, a hoarse gasp. 'Do you have any idea what we could be getting into?'

'Yes,' said Jack.

'We're not just talking fabulous treasures here. We're talking major present-day ramifications. The menorah is the symbol of the modern state of Israel. Any hint that we're on to the lost treasure of the Jewish Temple and the result could be explosive. Literally.'

'It doesn't go beyond these four walls,' Jack said.

At that moment there was a whoop and a joyful string of Brooklyn expletives from the other console. Jack and Hiebermeyer quickly returned to their positions behind Costas, and the ship's second officer appeared beside them. Jack glanced curiously at the man and then reverted to the screen. They could immediately see why Costas was jubilant. The screen had transformed into a fantastic multi-coloured image, the lines and contours of the scan as sharp as a 3-D computer drawing. In the centre were unmistakable signs of human agency, a dark twisted mass embedded in the sediment. It was an immense metal link, at least a metre long, a figure-of-eight shape crudely welded at the waist. A second link was looped through it and extended offscreen to the right, but the loop to the left was scarred and buckled where the adjoining link had sheared off.

'Fantastic!' Jack clapped Costas on the back. He was overjoyed, his mind already racing forward to the next stage of the search, but his eyes remained glued on the screen as the camera panned forward to the edge of the exposed metal. Wedged into the final loop was a fragmentary mass of wood, evidently ship's timbers, a section of overlapping hull strakes with lines of regularly spaced dark protrusions where the iron rivets had been preserved for more than eight hundred years in the anaerobic ooze. Jack and Hiebermeyer both gasped as they realized what was interwoven in the link, a mass of white that looked like denuded branches from a tree. It was a crushed human skeleton, its arms pinned at grotesque angles through the metal, the skull distorted and barely recognizable but still covered with a rusty brown stain where there had once been a close-fitting conical helmet with a nose-guard.

'There's your chain, and one of its casualties,' Costas said. 'Now it's time to get out of here.'

Costas activated a control to cast off the umbilical just as the ship's engines began to throb. Jack left Hiebermeyer with him and stooped out of the navigation room to join

York on the bridge. He would broadcast the news of the discovery to the crew during the hour that *Sea Venture* would have off-site before the shipping lane was accessible to them again. He looked out of the window beyond the ore-carrier waiting to ply the passage and to the low arches of the Galata Bridge, its road bustling with morning traffic and its balustrades lined with hopeful fishermen, oblivious to the true treasures that might lie beneath them. The choppy waters once plied by the pleasure barges of emperors and sultans now shone again, a result of the massive cleanup operation of the past decade. As Jack looked beyond the bridge to the radiant skyline, he felt again the allure that had drawn him and Katya to seek out its deepest secrets. For all its chaos and dark history, this city had come to symbolize hope, the place where Jack had revived his passion for the mysteries of the past that had driven him since childhood.

He looked down as the sparkling waters off *Sea Venture*'s bow erupted in turmoil from the vessel's water-jet stabilizers. He was exhilarated beyond belief that they had made the discovery that could vindicate his dream, a stepping stone to even more sensational finds over the coming days. The chain put them right at the key moment in history, and showed they were at the outer limits of the harbour where the spoils from the sack of Constantinople were dumped. All they had to do now was work their way into the Golden Horn and they should hit pay dirt. But as usual Jack's jubilation was tempered by anxiety. The pressure was now on. They still had a long way to go. He knew they

2

Maria de Montijo shifted almost imperceptibly on her stool and briefly shut her eyes. It had been their longest day in the cathedral precinct so far, and despite the adrenalin that had sustained her hour after hour she knew her concentration would soon begin to wane. Outside, the dull grey English afternoon was beginning to darken, and she could hear the insistent patter of rain on the window panes. She straightened her back, blinked hard and raised the palette with her cleaning tools to the edge of the frame. In the utter silence of the room, time seemed to stand still, and all attention was focused on the intricate pattern of ink revealed by the microlight only inches from her face. She breathed slowly and deliberately, at the end of each exhalation bringing her brush to bear with a steadiness born of years of experience. After fifteen minutes she rocked backwards and handed the palette to her assistant.

'That's it,' she said. 'We're finished.'

She carefully pulled back the angle-lamp to reveal the entire inscription, the product of more than a week of painstaking labour. With the patina of centuries removed, the letters stood out crisp and black as if they had been applied only days before.

Tuz ki cest estorie ont. Ou oyront ou lirront ou ueront. Prient a ihesu en deyte. De Richard de haldingham o de Lafford eyt pite. Ki lat fet e compasse. Ki ioie en cel li seit done.

The unfamiliar spelling of the Old French only served to deepen the mystery of the man who had composed it. After a moment of contemplation Maria turned encouragingly to her assistant, a willowy young man with steel-rimmed spectacles, who eagerly leaned forward to make the translation.

'*All those who possess this work, or who hear, read or see it, pray to Jesus in his godhead to have pity on Richard of Holdingham and of Sleaford, who made it and set it out, that he may be granted bliss in heaven.*'

It seemed appropriate that Richard's last words should also be theirs, that they should finish their task at the spot where the scribe had last lifted his quill from the parchment almost seven hundred years before.

★

Twenty minutes later Maria stood in the centre of the room and gazed one last time at the map before it was sealed behind its protective glass covering. With the spotlight now removed, the low-intensity glow of the room seemed to accentuate the age-old appearance of the vellum, the shadows and undulations showing where the calfskin had shrunk and buckled with the passing of the years.

Normally the job of cleaning manuscripts would be left to her technical staff at the institute in Oxford. But when the call came for a new programme of restoration on the Mappa Mundi in Hereford Cathedral, the temptation proved too great. It was the chance of a lifetime, the opportunity to work on the greatest extant thirteenth-century illuminated manuscript, to touch with her own hands the most important and celebrated medieval map in the world.

As her eyes adjusted to the gloom, the familiar form began to take shape. Almost filling the immense squared parchment was an orb more than four feet wide. At the centre was Jerusalem, and below it the T-shape of the Mediterranean dividing Asia, Africa and Europe. Squeezed in at the lower left were the British Isles, and in the exergue beyond was the inscription she had been cleaning. Everywhere on the map were hundreds of miniature drawings with captions in Latin and French, some illustrating biblical stories and others depicting bizarre creatures and mythical places.

It was a cornucopia of fact and fantasy, the supreme

expression of the medieval mind. Yet it was also hemmed in by ignorance. In its order and confidence the map seemed the last statement on the world of men, yet beyond the thin strip of ocean that encircled Christendom lay nothing at all. To Maria the figure of Christ in the gable above seemed to be sitting in judgement not only on the dead but also on the living, on men with the hubris to think that the myriad wonders they had crammed into their *mappa mundi* represented anything like the entirety of God's creation.

'Dr de Montijo. You must come at once.'

The dapper figure in the clerical robe caught up to Maria as she made her way briskly across the cathedral forecourt, her umbrella raised against the perennial English drizzle. She was due back in Oxford that evening and had little time to spare if she was going to catch the train.

'This had better be good,' she said, her slight Spanish accent giving a lilt to her voice. 'I'm scheduled to give a seminar on Richard of Holdingham at my institute in about three hours and need time to prepare.'

'That may just have to wait,' the little man wheezed excitedly. 'The workmen in the old chained library have just made an extraordinary discovery. Your assistant is already with them.'

Together Maria and the cleric approached the north porch of the cathedral. With its soft honey hue the weathered sandstone of the buttresses made Hereford seem less forbidding than many of the great cathedrals of England, yet even so the effect when they entered was awesome. Maria glanced down the nave to the altar and up at the cavernous space in between, her view framed by the massive pillars on either side that rose to the smaller arches of the clerestory and the spreading fans of the ceiling vault far above. As she followed the cleric up the north aisle she was assailed by the smell of damp stone and a faint hint of decay, as if the sickly reek of putrefaction which had permeated the cathedral for so long had left a lingering aura long after the last burial vaults had been sealed.

The nave had changed little since Richard of Holdingham last passed this way. She brushed against a pillar and felt a sudden thrill of intimacy, as if she had reached back in time to shadow the great man's footsteps. In his day the ponderous masonry of the Normans had been in place for only a century, yet a minster had stood on this spot since the time of the Anglo-Saxon kingdom of Mercia. It had been the Cathedral Church of St Ethelbert, the King of East Anglia who had been foully murdered nearby. In Richard's day it also attracted pilgrims who came from far and wide to pay homage to Thomas Becket, the archbishop martyred at Canterbury, whose enamel reliquary had also survived through the centuries, another of the cathedral's great treasures alongside the Mappa Mundi.

After passing the north transept they reached the choir aisle where the map had been displayed over the past century before being moved to its present home in a purpose-built museum outside. Immediately opposite the blank space on the wall was a low doorway into the outer structure of the cathedral. Through it the beginning of a spiral staircase could be seen.

'The reconstruction work is almost complete,' the cleric said. 'This is just a precaution.' He passed Maria a yellow safety helmet and put one on himself, its appearance incongruous above his brown clerical cassock. As she followed him up the steeply corkscrewing steps, his words resounded with a muffled echo.

'A sandstone cathedral is like a wooden ship,' he explained. 'Keep an old hull in service long enough and all the timbers will need to be renewed. Like HMS *Victory*. Sandstone isn't the most durable building material. When we moved the library we took the opportunity for some much-needed stone replacement.'

They were nearing the chamber which had once held Hereford's world-renowned chained library, a fabulous collection including rare *incunabula*, books printed before 1500, as well as 227 manuscript volumes, beginning with the priceless *Hereford Gospels* of the eighth century. Both the books and the cases to which they had been chained were now reconstituted in the museum which also housed the Mappa Mundi, itself once also stored in the library.

After ascending to the clerestory level, they squeezed past a stack of freshly quarried blocks and stood at the entrance to the chamber. In the thin rays of daylight cast through the slit windows they could just make out the lighter patches along the walls where the bookcases had once been. Instead of a library, the chamber now looked like a medieval stone-mason's workshop, with cutting tools and fragments of decayed masonry piled all over the floor.

At the far end a group of workmen were huddled over a patch of bright light in the wall. It came from a hole where two blocks of masonry had been removed, leaving a space just wide enough for a slender form to get through. At that moment a head appeared upside-down, its tousled blond hair and glasses caked in dust.

'Maria! You're not going to believe this.'

Jeremy Haverstock had been her best-ever doctoral student, a virtuoso in early Germanic languages, but had been cloistered in Oxford writing his dissertation and was clearly revelling in the sense of adventure. She had invited him along to Hereford to give him a break, and to share in the unique experience. Since his arrival from America she had encouraged him to travel widely to visit early monastic libraries, yet he still had the infectious enthusiasm of a tourist touching history for the first time. She smiled in spite of herself as she and the cleric picked their way across the debris and pulled down the dust-masks from their helmets.

'It's your career on the line,' she said. 'Anything less than an Augustinian Bible and you'll be doing the seminar single-handed.'

'It's better than that. Far better.' As they approached she could see his face was streaked with sweat despite the chill of the room. He heaved one of the blocks aside and withdrew out of sight into the wall.

'Follow me.'

Moments later Maria was squeezed in beside him, her wavy brown hair and leather jacket covered with dust. Any irritation she may have felt instantly evaporated when she saw what lay before them. The workmen had broken through into a space about a metre wide within the massive exterior wall of the cathedral. From Maria's hunched position she could see they were squatting above a ruined spiral staircase, a relic of some previous building phase which had long ago been blocked off. Three steps below them the well of the staircase was clogged with debris, jumbled chunks that looked like eroded sandstone covered with a pall of red dust. With her body bent double Maria sidled down for a closer look, the spotlight angled directly behind her head.

'*Es estupendo.*' The words of her native Spanish came out involuntarily as she stared open-mouthed in disbelief.

'See what I mean?' Jeremy slid down eagerly beside her. 'It's like Aladdin's cave.'

The debris was not discarded masonry but a great mass of brown and yellowed parchment, some compacted like papier mâché but much of it well preserved with letters still plainly visible.

'It looks like a clean-out of the library,' Jeremy said. 'Torn fragments, books damaged beyond repair. It's all hand-written manuscript and none of it looks later than thirteenth century. The architectural historian reckons this staircase became redundant and was sealed up some time before the completion of the north transept in the fourteenth century.'

Maria shifted sideways and pointed to the spot where her head had obscured the centre in shadow. She was suddenly trembling with excitement.

'Look,' she exclaimed. 'It isn't all fragments. There's an intact folio volume.'

Jeremy reached over with his longer arms and carefully extracted the leather-bound book from its bedding of parchment fragments. While he held it Maria gently blew off the dust and opened the hoary brown cover.

'*Historia Ecclesiastica Gentis Anglorum.*'

She read out the words slowly, her mind reeling in astonishment. 'The Venerable Bede's *Ecclesiastical History of the English People*. And in Latin, which means one of the original copies. Ninth, maybe eighth century.'

Jeremy peeled off a sheaf of parchment that had become stuck to the back of the volume. With the musty leaves balanced on his hands he began humming quietly to himself, his eyes darting to and fro across the writing. Maria watched bemusedly as he suddenly became silent.

'What is it?' she asked.

'Incredible,' he whispered. 'A twelfth-century continuation of the *Anglo-Saxon Chronicle*. It mentions King Henry II and King John. It must be the latest document anywhere in

Old English, the language the Normans tried so hard to suppress. It clinches my thesis once and for all, that the Anglo-Saxon tradition was kept alive in the secret scriptoria of the cathedrals well into the medieval period. If this doesn't get me my doctorate, nothing will.'

Maria surveyed the scene in front of them, noting several more intact volumes poking out where they had removed the Bede.

'This was more than just a clean-out,' she asserted quietly. 'It's always been a mystery why these two seminal works of Anglo-Saxon history were missing from the Hereford library, in a collection with liturgical manuscripts going back to the eighth century. It may have been an overzealous librarian keeping up with the times, making space for more recent works. But it may have been more than that, a deliberate culling of works of Anglo-Saxon history from the library, an attempt to conceal anything the Norman aristocracy saw as subversive.'

She carefully closed the book and cradled it in her arms, at the same time looking with concern at the fragments of parchment which had broken off and crumbled where Jeremy had extracted the volume from its resting place.

'We'll take the Bede and those pages of the *Chronicle*,' she instructed. 'But everything else must remain *in situ* and the entrance resealed until we can assemble a full conservation team. We can't afford to expose any more parchment to air.' She peered again at Jeremy, who was cleaning his glasses with a serious look on his face. 'And I forgive you,' she grinned. 'You may just have stumbled on the greatest treasure trove of early English history ever discovered.'

As they swivelled round to go, Jeremy caught sight of an anomalous shape protruding from the sea of parchment fragments. It was one end of a wound scroll, something that might be even older than the bound manuscript volumes. He was unable to restrain himself and leaned back to extract it just as Maria was beginning to crawl out.

He cleared his throat suggestively and Maria looked back towards the bright tungsten light. She saw his guilty expression and then the metre-long scroll perched on top of the *Chronicle* pages.

'We must leave it,' she said sharply.

'Not if you still want to do that seminar this evening.'

Maria's curiosity was piqued and she turned back towards him. Jeremy had unravelled about ten centimetres of the scroll and was holding it so she could see. The radius of a large inscribed circle was visible, and within it she could make out faint forms that looked like outline drawings and tightly written inscriptions.

She knew what she was looking at even before she reached him. In her own doctoral thesis a decade earlier she had argued that the Hereford Mappa Mundi was a copy, the work of a remarkable artist but not a scholar. It was the only way to account for its most glaring error, the word *AFFRICA* written across Europe and *EUROPA* across Africa. The Bishop of Hereford had commissioned the map from Richard of Holdingham, who had prepared a blueprint in his home cathedral of Lincoln, but the final version had been completed in his absence by an artisan at Hereford skilled in calligraphy and illumination but not very literate or accurate. His ignorance was revealed in the finer detail, from small licences he had taken for aesthetic purposes at the expense of credibility to peculiarities in the spelling and geography.

Now to her astonishment she knew she was looking at the sketch prepared by Richard himself, the cartographer and monk whose vision of the world had fascinated her since student days. She stared with reverence at the precise, confident hand which had created captions all over the map. Just below Jeremy's left hand where he held the wound scroll were the faded letters *EUROPA*, correctly placed over France and Italy. Beside his right hand where he had pulled the scroll open was the elongated form of the British Isles, with Hereford and Lincoln prominently displayed.

As Jeremy moved the fingers of his right hand to the edge of the parchment she noticed something odd.

'My God,' she breathed. 'The exergue. It's missing.'

The elaborate decoration which filled the space between the orb of the world and the square edges of the parchment on the finished Mappa Mundi had clearly been the creation of the artisan alone, a place for decorative features of less interest to Richard, embellishments which could have been tailored to the whim of the cathedral authorities. It explained the bizarre parade of images, from huntsmen and clerics to references to the Roman emperors, which the artisan must have drawn together haphazardly from other maps and manuscripts he had seen.

In the corner Maria saw that the dedication she had so painstakingly cleaned on the Mappa Mundi was missing, so must have been the work of the artisan rather than the master himself. Richard must have visited the cathedral to discuss the commission but had clearly not been present at the dedication. It solved the mystery of how the misnamed continents had been allowed to remain, mistakes Richard would surely never have countenanced. She felt a pang of disappointment as she looked at the blank space, a sense that Richard was no longer so securely in her grasp, that he had stepped back into the shadowlands of the past.

As Jeremy shifted slightly, she realized that the mottled brown and yellow of the parchment where the dedication should have been held a defined shape.

'Angle it towards the light,' she said. 'There's something here.'

The faded image of a drawing came into view. It was another landmass, an irregular image not much larger than the British Isles wedged into the corner of the parchment.

'It's beyond the outer ocean surrounding the world, so it can't be part of the map,' she said. 'It must be Richard's sketch for one of the continents. Look, you can see where he used his knife to scrape away the ink to try to erase it.'

Jeremy was craning his head over for a better view, his lank blond forelock hanging directly in front of Maria's face.

'I'm not so sure,' he murmured. 'It's somehow vaguely

familiar, but not from the Mappa Mundi. Perhaps if I saw it the right way up I might get a better . . .'

As his words trailed off they both looked up at each other in astonishment.

'*The Vinland Map*,' Maria whispered.

With her heart racing, she pulled out her magnifying glass and began scrutinizing the lines. Only a few weeks earlier they had attended a conference at Yale University on the latest dating evidence for the famous Vinland Map, a drawing now thought to have been a forgery but based on a lost map that pre-dated Columbus by some fifty years, a map that showed a shoreline said to have been discovered by the Vikings centuries earlier to the west of Greenland.

'It's incredible,' she exclaimed. 'It's exactly the same. There's the river leading to the lake and the large inlet lower down. And the legend looks identical, in medieval Latin.'

With the magnifying glass the faint smudge at the top became legible: *Vinlanda Insula a Byarno repa et Leipho socijs*.

'Island of Vinland,' Jeremy murmured. 'Discovered by Bjarni and Leif in company.'

'It proves the authenticity of the image on the Vinland Map beyond doubt.' Maria was flushed with excitement. 'But if this is truly the hand of Richard of Holdingham, then it dates more than two centuries earlier than the Vinland Map. You can forget early English history for a while. You may just have discovered the oldest known depiction of North America.'

They stared at each other in blank amazement. The Mappa

Mundi and this sketch dated from the thirteenth century, almost three centuries before the first European voyages of discovery to the New World, hundreds of years before the first maps of the American shoreline were thought to have been drawn.

'There's more writing further down.'

Maria had been focused on the upper part of the depiction and had failed to register a second faint inscription beyond the drawing. She moved her magnifying glass a few inches lower.

'This definitely isn't on the Vinland Map,' she said. 'It's in the Roman alphabet, but it isn't Latin or French. It looks like Old Norse.'

She passed Jeremy the glass and took the map to hold it for him, tacitly acknowledging his greater expertise in the language of the Vikings.

'There's a curious rune here,' he murmured. 'It's set at the beginning of the inscription like the illuminated letter of a medieval text. A single stem with branches on either side, angled up. It looks symmetrical. Five, maybe seven branches altogether, including the stem. Very odd.'

'Can you make out anything else?'

'*Harald Sigurdsson.*' He paused and looked up. 'That's Harald Hardrada, Harald Hard Ruler, King of Norway. Killed at the Battle of Stamford Bridge in his attempt to take the English throne in 1066, only weeks before the Norman Conquest.'

'It's not possible,' Maria whispered incredulously. 'Go on.'

'*Harald Sigurdsson our King with his thole-companions reached these parts with the treasure of Michelgard,*' he slowly translated. '*Here they feast with Thor in Valhalla and await the final battle of Ragnarok.*'

He looked up and eyed Maria with disbelief.

'Isn't Michelgard the Viking name for Constantinople?'

For a moment she was too stunned to speak. Then she let the scroll roll up and passed it over.

'Guard this with your life. Don't breathe a word of it to anyone.' She picked up the Bede and scrambled hurriedly towards the wall, extracting her cellphone as she went. Just as she was about to crouch through, Jeremy called out excitedly.

'That rune,' he said. 'I knew I'd seen it somewhere before. It's not a rune at all. I can't work out why on earth it should be here, but there's only one thing it can be. It's the symbol of the Jewish menorah.'

he would be needed to provide technical backup for another IMU field project currently off Greenland. For Jack the decision had come only the previous evening, following the extraordinary phone call from his friend Maria de Montijo in Hereford. He had summoned an emergency meeting of the excavation staff and had asked Hiebermeyer to take over the archaeological supervision, knowing that Maurice would be secretly delighted to accept a role well beyond his usual remit in the deserts of Egypt.

'You'd better make it quick.' Costas extracted a cellphone from his oil-spattered overalls and checked a text message. 'They're due in any time now.'

Jack nodded and made his way from the patio where they had been sitting towards the open door of his office. He paused to look back over the broad sweep of Carrick Roads, the sinuous estuary which led out from the tip of Cornwall towards the English Channel and the Atlantic Ocean. From here generations of his ancestors had set sail to shape the destiny of England and make their fortune. Howards had fought with Drake against the Spanish Armada and under Nelson at Trafalgar, had brought back the riches of the Indies and had mapped the furthest reaches of the oceans.

Jack felt a surge of certainty as he surveyed the scene, knowing that he was maintaining a family tradition that stretched back a thousand years to before the Norman conquest of England. It was Jack's father who had decided to donate the Cornwall estate to the fledgling International Maritime University, but IMU had been Jack's dream and he had seen it to fruition. With generous financial backing from Efram Jacobovich, an old friend who had become a software tycoon, the mansion and outbuildings had been transformed into a state-of-the-art research facility that rivalled the best of the world's oceanographic institutes. Beside the estuary the old shipyard had been expanded into a sprawling engineering complex, complete with a dry dock facility for the IMU research vessels as well as an experimental tank for submersibles research. On a wooded hill adjoining the complex was the elegant neoclassical building of the Howard Gallery, one of the foremost private collections of art in the world and also a venue for travelling exhibits from the IMU Maritime Museum at Carthage in the Mediterranean. Only a few weeks earlier Jack had inaugurated one of their most stunning exhibits yet, a dazzling display of finds from the Bronze Age Minoan shipwreck they had excavated the previous year. A banner advertisement showing the golden disc and the magnificent bull's head sculpture from the wreck adorned the wall facing Jack as he entered his office, a former sixteenth-century drawing room which was now the hub of IMU research and exploration all over the world.

A few moments later he was back outside with a map of Europe which he unrolled and pinned down on the patio table using their coffee mugs. Costas drew his chair up as Jack swept his hand from Scandinavia to the Black Sea.

'The Byzantines called them Varangians,' Jack said. 'Tall, blond, terrifying barbarians from the north who served as mercenaries in the Byzantine emperor's legendary Varangian Guard, the successor of the Praetorian Guard of ancient Rome. In Hardrada's day the Varangian Guard were mainly Vikings, Norse warriors from Scandinavia whose behaviour fully justified their reputation. They pillaged and burned their way around the Mediterranean, thinly disguised as standard-bearers for the Christian emperor but in reality pagan heroes who returned to their homelands in the north full of tales of bloodlust and booty. By the time they were wiped out by the Crusaders during the Sack of Constantinople in 1204, many of the Guard were English, descendants of Anglo-Saxon warriors who had fled England following the Battle of Hastings in 1066 when William of Normandy defeated King Harold of England.'

'You mean the other Harold?' Costas queried.

Jack nodded. 'There was Viking blood in all the contestants to the English throne in 1066. The Normans were north-men, descendants of Vikings who had settled in France the century before. King Harold of England's Anglo-Saxon ancestors were themselves migrants from Denmark and northern Germany. But the only thoroughbred Viking among the contestants in 1066 was Harald Hardrada, King of Norway. He was the most feared of them all, and had learned his trade decades earlier as chief of the Varangian Guard in Constantinople.'

Costas measured the distance with his hand and shook his head. 'That's over two thousand miles from Norway.'

'Just as the Vikings were beginning to explore west, to the

British Isles and beyond, they were also going east,' Jack explained. 'From as early as the eighth century AD Scandinavian traders were penetrating the rivers of central and eastern Europe, from the Vistula on the Baltic to the Dnieper on the Black Sea. They were seeking untold wealth, the fabled treasures of the Orient, a hunt for silver and precious stones that took them to central Asia and deep into the world of Islam. Eventually they founded the Viking kingdom of Rus, the origin of modern Russia. From their stronghold at Kiev they were within striking distance of the place they called Michelgard, the Great City, a perilous journey down the Dnieper but the key to riches beyond their dreams.'

'That's how they got to Constantinople?' Costas said.

Jack smiled. 'It's true. If you don't believe it, you only have to look at Viking treasure hoards discovered in their Scandinavian homeland, full of Arab silver coins which the Vikings acquired in exchange for furs and slaves and amber.'

Jack could see Costas looking dubiously at the distance between Norway and present-day Istanbul. 'If you still need convincing, take a look at this.' Jack passed over a black-and-white photograph showing a polished marble railing, its surface covered with ancient graffiti. 'Those linear symbols on the edge? They're runes, Viking letters, probably eleventh century. They're too worn to decipher completely, but a name can be made out. "Halfdan was here", or something like that. Any guesses where it is? Thousands of tourists pass within touching distance of it every year. It's in an alcove high above the nave of Hagia Sofia, in the heart of ancient Constantinople. Halfdan was almost certainly one of the Varangian bodyguard, and given the date, he could even have been one of Harald Hardrada's men.'

As he finished speaking, a thudding noise from the east that had been increasing in volume became a reverberating clatter, and a Lynx helicopter appeared out of the clouds and descended towards the helipad near the shoreline. 'I'll take your word for it.' Costas grinned and handed back the photograph. 'Right now I think we need to greet our guests.'

A few minutes later the two men stood at the edge of the helipad as the twin Rolls-Royce Gem turboshafts powered down and the main rotor of the Lynx shuddered to a halt. The first figure to step out of the passenger compartment was a strikingly attractive woman wearing a leather jacket and jeans, her long brown hair swept back into a loose bun. Maria de Montijo was one of Jack's oldest friends, part of a close-knit group including Maurice Hiebermeyer and Efram Jacobovich who had first met as students at Cambridge. Maria and Jack had helped each other through difficult times and had forged a close bond. He had involved her in the Golden Horn project from the outset, and it made sense that he was the first person she would call with news of the astonishing discovery in Hereford Cathedral.

Maria's dark Spanish features creased into a smile as she embraced Jack and Costas in turn. 'Jack, you've met Jeremy, my American graduate student.' The lean young man who loped behind Maria swept his blond hair from his face and proffered his hand. They had met several weeks earlier when Jack had visited the Institute of Medieval Studies in Oxford to have the newly discovered Topkapi manuscript translated, the eyewitness account of the Crusader siege of Constantinople that contained the crucial position-fix for the chain across the harbour. Jack had been impressed by Jeremy's facility with the medieval Greek, and had no reason to doubt Maria's enthusiastic judgement of his potential.

'How long have you been out of the States?' Costas asked amiably.

'Three years.' Jeremy peered down at the shorter man through his glasses. 'I've got a fellowship waiting for me at Princeton, but I just don't seem to be able to get away from this place.'

'I know the problem,' Costas said. 'I keep trying, but every time I do he finds some reason to keep me here.' He jerked his head towards Jack and grinned. 'Luckily working for an international outfit means I'm not trapped in English drizzle all year long.'

'Gentlemen, allow me to introduce Father Patrick O'Connor.' Maria gestured towards the helicopter and they turned to watch the figure being helped down by the pilot. In startling contrast to the flight suit and helmet of the crewman, he was wearing the distinctive black cassock of a Jesuit priest, and was carrying two battered leather briefcases. After nodding to the pilot, he strode confidently across the helipad, dropped his cases on the tarmac and shook Jack's hand firmly. 'Dr Howard. Delighted to meet you at last. Maria's told me all about you, and of course I've seen you on TV following your remarkable discoveries last year.'

Jack eyed the other man keenly. The accent had a hint of Irish brogue, but could as easily have been Boston. He guessed that O'Connor was a youthful fifty, his remaining hair grey and cropped close but with the weathered face and fit body of a man who had not spent his entire life in the cloisters.

'Maria tells me you have a PhD in early Church history,' Jack said.

'Trinity College, Dublin, then Heidelberg,' O'Connor replied. 'Then I found my vocation. Twenty years in Central America, mainly Mexico, doing what we Jesuits do best, building schools, ministering to the sick, trying to bring humanity to places where there's sometimes hardly any left at all.'

'And then you found academia again.'

O'Connor nodded. 'Five years ago. I'd done my tour of duty and applied for a vacancy in the Vatican library. To my delight they offered me a tailor-made position in the Antiquities Department, as inspector of early buildings and archaeology. My remit covers everything in Rome under Vatican control up to the time of the Renaissance, with plenty of time for my own research. I was in Oxford to hear Maria's seminar on Richard of Holdingham and the Mappa

Mundi, one of my special areas of interest. I believe I may have something to offer.'

'That's the reason we're here now,' Jack said. 'Let's get down to business.'

After a quick coffee on the patio, Jack led them into his office. Almost the entire length of the old drawing room was occupied by a massive wooden table, its gnarled oak surface made from timbers reputedly salvaged from the ships that had brought the Norman invaders to England. Every time Jack sat at the table he felt the power of his own ancestry, as if his forebears who had plotted wars and voyages of discovery from this very table were keeping him ghostly company and egging him on. Now, instead of nautical dividers and parchment charts, the table was covered with the instruments of twenty-first-century exploration, computer workstations and communications consoles. To these Maria added a large black manila folder, which she laid at one end of the table, and at the other end Jack raised a video screen linked to a laptop he had opened up beside the folder.

Costas arrived breathlessly after a rushed visit to the engineering complex, and Jack closed the door behind him and dimmed the lights. Maria and O'Connor sat down at the end of the table, with Jeremy on one side and Jack and Costas on the other.

'There was something I didn't tell you on the phone, the reason why I wanted to show you this in person.' Maria spoke slowly, her hands laid flat on the edge of the manila folder. 'Father O'Connor was in Oxford when I arrived from Hereford the night before last, and I took him immediately into my confidence. He is the world's leading authority on what you're about to see.'

Just as Maria was about to raise the cover of the folder, O'Connor put his hand on hers. 'What we discuss here must remain secret,' he said quietly. 'The time may come when this story will be headline news, but until then even the slightest leak could jeopardize everything. And I'm not just talking about archaeology. Lives are at stake here, perhaps countless lives.'

He released his grip and looked at the others, who all nodded in turn. Maria glanced at him again and then lifted the cover, folding it back to reveal a protective sheet of tissue paper over a hard white board. She slid away the paper and they saw the image that had transfixed her in the lost chamber of the cathedral two days before. Costas let out a low whistle as he and Jack stood up and craned over for a better view. The vellum was about a metre square, and had been rolled out and pressed under a transparent poly-urethane sheet. Even after seven hundred years in the dusty cathedral chamber the ink was still dark and clearly preserved the outline of the map.

'Fantastic,' Jack murmured. 'I haven't seen the Mappa Mundi for ages, but this is all familiar. You can clearly make out the T-shape of the Mediterranean and Red Sea dividing the continents, with Asia at the top and Jerusalem in the centre. And Europe and Africa are even labelled correctly.'

O'Connor nodded. 'I've no doubt this is Richard of Holdingham's exemplar. His sketch made in Lincoln and then copied and embellished by the illuminator in Hereford. Now look at the lower left corner.'

Jack had already seen the delicate lines of text and drawing Maria was pointing at, but had wanted to take in the whole map first. Now he peered closely at the image beyond the western rim of the world, an image so different from the dedication inscribed in this place on the finished map.

'My God, they really are runes,' he said excitedly. 'I'm a little rusty, but this must be it.' He pointed at the smaller of the two inscriptions and glanced at Jeremy, who nodded and recited from memory.

'*Harald Sigurdsson our King with his thole-companions reached these parts with the treasure of Michelgard. Here they feast with Thor in Valhalla and await the final battle of Ragnarok.*'

'Ragnarok is the mythical battle at the end of time, when the warriors in Valhalla will seek final glory,' Maria said. 'The second inscription and the drawing are virtually identical to the Vinland Map, showing the coastline discovered by Leif Eiriksson beyond Greenland around the year AD 1000. Sigurdsson was the family name of Harald Hardrada. The implication is that Hardrada and his companions actually reached America, a generation or two after the first Vikings blazed the trail.'

'With the treasure of Michelgard, of Constantinople,' Jack murmured excitedly. 'That's why we're here. I only wish I knew what he'd taken. It's hardly likely to have been a shipload of classical bronzes.'

'Look closely at those runes,' O'Connor said. 'Then you'll see the real reason we're here.'

Jack scanned the text from the bottom up, from the clearer ink of the lower lines to the more faded inscription above. The symbols seemed to be a standard version of the *futhark*, the Norse runic alphabet named for its first six letters. He could see nothing exceptional until he came to the faded symbol at the beginning, a symbol that had been drawn slightly larger like the first letter of an illuminated manuscript.

He took the magnifying glass offered by Jeremy and leaned over to peer closer. 'That's definitely an odd one,' he said. 'It looks like the *futhark* symbol for the letter F, with the arms angled up on the right side, only here it's got three arms instead of two and it's repeated symmetrically on the other side.'

Jeremy shook his head impatiently. 'Forget runes for a moment. Think outside the box.'

Jack looked up and stared at Jeremy without expression and then looked down again. Suddenly his mouth opened and he nearly dropped the magnifying glass.

'*The menorah.*'

'It was Jeremy who first noticed it,' Maria said after a silence. 'I was completely wrapped up in that extraordinary map.'

'An understandable distraction,' Costas said, smiling at her.

'My father's ancestors were Sephardic Jews,' she replied quietly. 'Expelled from Spain by the Christian king not so long after your Crusaders were trying to save the Holy Land. One of the great ironies of history.'

Jack slowly sat back, his face a picture of stunned incomprehension. O'Connor pulled the laptop towards him and loaded a CD into the drive. 'Forgive me for jumping in,' he said. 'But if we're talking about the menorah, we need to know something of its history. It so happens that the mystery of the lost Jewish treasure of the Temple is another special passion of mine.'

4

Moments later a spectacular vision of ancient Rome appeared on the screen at the far end of the table. In the foreground a perfectly proportioned marble arch towered several storeys high, its eroded surface embellished with relief carvings. They could make out trophies, banners, laurel wreaths and winged victories standing on globes. In the background loomed the vast tiered façade of the Colosseum.

'The most enduring legacy of the Flavian dynasty of emperors, Vespasian and his sons Titus and Domitian,' O'Connor said. 'The Arch of Titus straddles the Sacred Way in the centre of Rome. The Colosseum was financed on the spoils of the Jewish War, and inaugurated by Titus in AD 80. It was built next to the Colossus of Nero, a monstrous gilt-bronze statue that gave the amphitheatre its name.'

'But not until the medieval period,' Jeremy interjected. 'The name Colosseum first appears in the Venerable Bede's *Historia Ecclesiastica Gentis Anglorum* in the eighth century AD.' He looked sheepishly at the group. 'Another of our finds from the Hereford library.'

'The Jewish War,' Costas said. 'Another excuse for rape and pillage on a colossal scale?'

'It was pretty ghastly, even by Roman standards,' O'Connor replied. 'Probably a greater proportion of the Jewish population was annihilated in the war of AD 66 to 70 than during the Nazi Holocaust, either killed in battle or put to the sword in an orgy of retribution that lasted for another three years. But the story's more complex than you might think. The Jewish state had enjoyed an unusual degree of autonomy under Rome, and there were close links with the emperors. King Herod Agrippa of Judaea was educated in Rome and was a friend of the emperor Claudius. A generation later the Jewish historian Josephus became a confidant of Vespasian, having switched sides to Rome during the rebellion. He has a bad press because the Jews never forgave him, but his writings are invaluable as the only eyewitness account of the war and the triumph in Rome in AD 71.'

'And the arch?'

'Built on the site of an earlier arch, exactly the spot where the triumphal procession would have first become visible to the huge crowd waiting in the forum.' He tapped a key and zoomed in to an inscription on the attic of the arch above the passageway. '*Senatus Populusque Romanus,*' he read. '*The Senate and the People of Rome, to Divine Titus, son of the Divine Vespasian, Vespasian Augustus.* This shows that the arch was dedicated by the emperor Domitian, who succeeded his brother Titus in AD 81. With a few notorious exceptions, like Nero, the title Divine was only bestowed on emperors after they'd died. The sculpture on the ceiling of the passageway even shows the apotheosis of Titus, riding heavenwards on the back of a great eagle.'

'The triumph was a family affair,' Jack added, his composure now close to normal again after the shock of seeing the menorah symbol. 'According to tradition, Vespasian was the main celebrant as emperor at the time, but the Roman Senate voted a double triumph to acknowledge Titus as victorious general. Domitian was enhancing his own prestige by honouring the glorious achievements of his brother and father.'

O'Connor scrolled through a succession of views, each one bringing them closer to the arch as if he was walking them along the Sacred Way from the direction of the Colosseum. Through the passageway under the arch they could make out the heart of ancient Rome, the jumble of ruins in the old forum with its shattered columns, vestiges of law courts and temples and the stark brick walls of the Senate House. Beyond the forum lay the Capitoline Hill, where the foundations of the Temple of Jupiter lay submerged under the medieval palace built by Michelangelo and the extravagant Vittorio Emanuele Monument which dominated Rome's modern skyline.

'And now the incredible part,' O'Connor enthused. 'This is where ancient history really comes alive for me, even more than in the arena of the Colosseum. Standing under the arch it's as if those few moments at dawn two thousand years ago are endlessly re-enacted, imprinted in the marble. You can sense the exaltation of the victors, the pent-up frenzy of the crowd, the terror of the condemned. You can hear the drumbeat, feel the pounding vibration of the procession. It never fails to send a shiver up my spine.'

He stopped at an image of an eroded relief panel. 'On the wall of the passageway through the arch on the right-hand side, facing the forum,' he explained. 'You can see Titus in a *quadriga*, a four-horse chariot, led by the goddess Roma. The priests behind him are carrying long axes, *fasces*, which they'll use to sacrifice bullocks on the steps of the Temple of Jupiter.'

He tapped the key again. 'And this is on the left-hand side.' O'Connor sat back as they absorbed the scene. It was fragmentary and worn, but the central portion was clear enough. It was one of the masterpieces of Roman relief sculpture. On the right-hand side was a triumphal arch in three-quarters view, with two *quadrigas* on top. In the background were placards borne aloft like standards, with blank spaces where there had once been painted inscriptions naming cities and peoples defeated in the war. Below them was the image which for almost two thousand years had fuelled the ardour of a people determined to rebuild their holiest temple, and of their enemies sworn to do all in their power to prevent that happening. It showed a procession of tunic-clad soldiers crowned with victory wreaths carrying two biers, each supporting an ornate object hefted high for all to see. On the right heading towards the arch was a table decorated with trumpets, the great altar of the Jewish Temple. On the left in the foreground was an extraordinary but unmistakable shape, a tapering column with three arms on each side curving upwards in concentric semicircles, each arm terminating at the same level and capped with an elaborate finial shaped like a lamp.

Costas let out a low whistle. 'That's some candlestick.'

'The menorah.' O'Connor spoke with barely suppressed excitement. 'The most revered symbol of Judaism, placed immediately in front of the sanctuary in the Temple. The menorah represents the light of God, and harks back to the ancient symbol of the seven-branched Tree of Life. The Temple menorah was one of the most sacred treasures of the Jewish people, second only to the Ark of the Covenant.'

'How old was it?' Costas asked.

'There are those who believe the Temple menorah was the Tabernacle menorah itself, divinely ordained when God instructed Moses on the Mount,' O'Connor said. 'Rabbinic tradition has it that God showed Moses the menorah drawn in fire, and that divine light was radiated in pure gold. The earliest mention of the menorah is in the *pentateuch*, the Jewish Old Testament. In the Book of Exodus God instructs the Israelites on the form of their wilderness sanctuary, their Tabernacle, the basis for the Holy of Holies in the Temple built by King Solomon in Jerusalem a thousand years before the Romans arrived.' He closed his eyes and recited from memory. '*And thou shalt make a candlestick of pure gold. And there shall be six branches going out of the sides thereof; three branches of the candlestick out of the one side thereof, and three branches of the candlestick out of the other side thereof. And thou shalt make the lamps thereof, seven; and they shall light the lamps thereof, to give light over against it. Of a talent of pure gold shall it be made.*'

'A talent.' Costas stroked his chin thoughtfully. 'How much was that?'

'The biblical talent was about thirty-four kilograms, seventy-five pounds,' O'Connor replied. 'But don't take it at face value. A talent was the biggest unit of weight in common use, and was probably used in the Old Testament figuratively, to represent the largest weight that people could readily quantify.'

'It took at least ten Roman soldiers to heave the menorah, five on either side.' Costas was peering at the image on the screen. 'The base looks at least a metre across, and I'm assuming that was gold too. If the arch was carved only a decade after the triumph then many people in Rome would have seen the original, so the sculpture's probably not an exaggeration. With the base, my guess is we're looking at three hundred, maybe three hundred and fifty pounds of gold, four or five talents at least. That's millions of dollars at today's bullion rates.'

'It's priceless,' O'Connor said tersely. 'A symbol of nationhood, of a whole people. Nobody would ever value the menorah solely in monetary terms.'

'But that's surely the point.' Jeremy turned and looked at O'Connor, his voice nervous but persistent. 'The Vikings couldn't care less about symbols of nationhood. Costas is right to see it in cash terms. In the Viking homeland, silver was the main bullion, and gold was at a huge premium. You hardly ever find it in Viking hoards. Three hundred pounds of gold would have assured Harald Hardrada's place as the most powerful man in all of Scandinavia. So given the chance for a quick loot, he and his companions opted for the largest gold object they could lay their hands on. Substitute Vikings for Romans carrying the menorah and you've got a snapshot from one stormy night on the Golden Horn almost a thousand years later.'

Jack nodded as Jeremy spoke, his respect for the younger man's knowledge increasing. 'An extraordinary image. But before we get to the Vikings, let's work out how on earth the menorah found its way to Constantinople.'

Half an hour later Jack stood with Maria and Jeremy in front of a building the size of an aircraft hangar, a stone's throw from the edge of the estuary. O'Connor had asked for a break to search the IMU database for some key references, and Jack had taken the opportunity to give the other two a brief tour of the campus. They had reached the engineering complex just in time to see the door of the main loading bay roll open and a strange contraption appear on a flat-bed truck.

'My latest baby,' a voice yelled out. 'Come over and let me show you.'

They looked into the cavernous interior and saw Costas directing a team of workmen behind the truck, his overalls smeared with a fresh layer of oil and grime. He had excused himself from the meeting at the same time as O'Connor and was now fully engrossed in his work. The hangar was a fantastic jumble of technical projects, some on the drawing board and others clearly at the experimental stage. Through the flash of a welding torch Jack could make out the battered form of the ADSA, the Advanced Deep Sea Anthropod, which had saved him from the wreckage of *Seaquest* only six months before. Ranged on either side were the Aquapods, the one-man submersibles in which he and Costas had first seen the silt-shrouded walls of Atlantis, their metal carapaces still streaked yellow from the sulphurous waters of the Black Sea.

'We're nearly ready to roll,' Costas called out. 'A final systems check and that's it.'

Jack and Maria weaved their way towards him through piles of hardware and semi-finished projects, Jeremy bringing up the rear. Costas put up his hand to order a generator switched off and the unearthly din subsided. He beckoned them over to the contraption on the truck, his face beaming with excitement. 'You may have seen something like this in our pictures from the Golden Horn,' he said to Maria and Jeremy. 'The ferret, the sub-bottom borer we're using to dig through the sea bed to the medieval layers. I haven't got a name for this one yet, but it does a similar job. Spot the difference?'

'Let me take a look.' Jeremy craned forward, peering intently at the forward end of the contraption. He grunted, stooped down to look under the cradle and then straightened up, ignoring the streak of grease he had acquired on his tweed jacket. He pushed his glasses up and squinted at Costas. 'It cuts through ice.'

'Very good.' Costas raised his eyebrows and winked at Jack. 'Go on.'

'It has an electrical element around the rim,' Jeremy said. 'I'd guess a superheated element using semiconductor materials, probably in a ceramic matrix. And that box behind looks like a high-energy laser device.'

'I'm impressed. Pretty good for a medieval historian. You're in the wrong line of business.'

'When I applied for my Rhodes Scholarship, it was either engineering or Anglo-Saxon, Norse and Celtic. My school was very conservative.'

'You drew the short end of the straw.'

'I disagree,' Maria said. They all laughed and Jeremy looked ruefully at the contraption. Costas slapped an oily hand on Jeremy's back and turned to Jack.

'We're air-freighting it out this evening,' he said, his demeanour now serious. 'I had a call from James Macleod a few minutes ago and he said the ice conditions are perfect. Another day or two and the summer melt could make it too risky. I'm flying out to Greenland tomorrow morning to oversee the setup. And there's something else. He mentioned a local, some old guy, who claimed to have seen some old ship's timbers in the ice. Something to do with a European expedition way back, before the Second World War. Macleod was adamant that you should see the guy, and soon. Apparently he's on his last legs. I know it's a bit of a diversion on the trip back to Istanbul, but you might just want to tag along.'

Back in the office, Jack clicked off his cellphone and swivelled his chair back to face the conference table. After a conversation with Maurice Hiebermeyer and Tom York on *Sea Venture* he felt reassured that the excavation in the Golden Horn could carry on for another forty-eight hours without him. The greatest prize, he now knew, might lie elsewhere, in a place they could never have imagined, but the Golden Horn could still contain treasures of inestimable historical value. The team were riding on a wave of euphoria after the cannon and chain discoveries and had already begun to use the probe to penetrate the harbour sediments, but it was hit and miss and could be days before they came up trumps.

'Right,' he said. 'What have you got?'

O'Connor sat with a small green-backed book pressed open in front of him, Greek text visible on one side and English on the other. Costas had excused himself but

Maria and Jeremy sat expectantly at the table with Jack.

'In his book *The Jewish Wars*, Josephus tells us that Vespasian had the treasures locked away in the Temple of Jupiter,' O'Connor began. 'But we know they were transferred to the Temple of Peace when that was completed, a few years into Vespasian's reign. After that there's no mention of the menorah for hundreds of years.'

'But surely the emperor would have wanted to display his loot at every opportunity, at parades and festivals in the city,' Maria protested.

'Vespasian was the supreme embodiment of the Roman imperial virtues,' Jack interjected. 'Conquest, stability, building. As a young man he had commanded a legion in the conquest of Britain, and as emperor he oversaw the conquest of Judaea. Then he stabilized the empire following the disastrous reign of Nero. Now his focus was entirely on building. The Temple of Peace, the monuments in the forum damaged by the great fire of AD 64 under Nero, above all the Colosseum. He didn't need to shout about his triumphs any more.'

'There may be more to it than that,' O'Connor said cautiously. 'You know, it's an odd feature of Josephus' account of the triumph that he only mentions the execution of Simon, the charismatic Jewish leader who'd been brought in chains to Rome. There's nothing on the fate of the hundreds of other Jewish captives, men, women and children. Some of us now believe there was an orgy of murder at the end of the procession, a scene so appalling

Josephus couldn't bring himself to describe it. After all, these were his people, and he never forsook his Jewish faith. When Vespasian saw it, he too was repulsed. The emperor was a tough old soldier, as ruthless as any Roman to his enemies, but was well known for his hatred of gratuitous bloodshed. Perhaps he contrived an ill omen as an excuse never to celebrate the Jewish triumph again, secretly instructing his priests to keep the menorah under lock and key for all time.'

'And then the trail goes cold,' Maria said.

'All we have to go on is Procopius.' O'Connor gestured at the book in front of him. 'He was an eyewitness to the last great attempt to reunite the Roman Empire, when the Byzantine general Belisarius recaptured Rome from the Vandals and Goths who had overrun the western provinces in the fifth century AD.'

'It amazes me that the menorah survived for so long in Rome without being looted,' Jack said. 'Those weren't exactly centuries of peace and harmony. Think of Commodus, the demented son of Marcus Aurelius. He thought he was the god Hercules, and melted down most of the imperial treasure to pay for gladiatorial contests. Or the anarchy of the third century, when there were more than thirty emperors in fifty years. The Temple of Peace was a well-known repository for the spoils of war, and its treasuries would surely have been thrown open to find gold to pay for the mercenary armies of each new claimant to the throne.'

'Absolutely.' O'Connor paused, then looked piercingly at

Jack and lowered his voice. 'I must ask you again to keep what I say within these four walls. The answer is staring at us in that image of the Arch of Titus. In the 1970s a sonar survey by a conservation team revealed a hidden chamber in the attic, behind the dedicatory inscription.'

Jack's jaw dropped. 'You're not suggesting the menorah was hidden away inside the arch?'

O'Connor hesitated again, then reached inside his cassock and pulled out a brown envelope. 'Few realize that the Arch of Titus is under Vatican control, one of many ancient monuments in Rome consecrated by the Church in the Middle Ages as a way of stamping papal authority on everything pagan. My predecessor in the Vatican Antiquities Department tried endlessly to have the chamber opened, but every time his application was rebuffed by the cardinals. I believe his persistence was the main reason for his dismissal from the Vatican. I finally managed it last month during the current programme of restoration work on the arch. One evening the chief conservator and I were alone on the scaffold inspecting progress, and a stone abutting the chamber gave way. An accident of course, you understand.'

Jack raised his eyebrows as O'Connor extracted a photograph from the envelope and slid it across the table, his hand remaining on it for a moment as he looked at Jack. 'It's not only my job that's on the line here. It's more, much more.'

Maria and Jeremy craned their necks as Jack took the picture. It showed a flashlit image inside a small chamber, its smooth walls discoloured by streaks of brown and green. On the floor were mounds of decayed matter, peppered with fragments of wood and fabric. It looked like an Egyptian pharaoh's tomb, opened for the first time after having been looted long ago in antiquity.

'I managed to reach in and take a handful of that stuff, which I had secretly analyzed,' O'Connor said quietly. 'The wood's shittim, acacia, the hardwood mentioned in the Old Testament. It was probably used for making a bier, something that required a lot of load-bearing strength. And the fabric's silk, coloured with Tyrean purple, the prized dye derived from the murex shell found off the coast of Lebanon.'

'My God,' Maria murmured. 'The Temple Veil, the sacred curtain of the Holy of Holies, used to conceal the sanctuary from the rest of the Temple.'

O'Connor nodded. 'Probably used by the Romans to wrap up the menorah and the golden table.'

'So they were inside the arch all that time, directly above the symbol of the menorah on the relief carving.' Jack shook his head in amazement. 'The priests must have had them moved under cover of darkness from the Temple of Peace, only a stone's throw away.'

'And then hundreds of years later one of the custodians let the secret out, maybe using the treasure as a bargaining chip to save his own skin when the barbarians invaded,' O'Connor said. 'Rome was devastated by the Goths under Alaric in AD 410, and then again by the Vandals in 455.

According to Procopius, the Vandal king Giseric seized the Jewish treasures and took them to Carthage in North Africa, and after the Byzantine general Belisarius captured Carthage from the Vandals in 533 he had the treasures shipped to Constantinople. Procopius tells us that the Byzantine emperor Justinian was overcome by piety and had the treasures returned to Jerusalem, but I don't believe a word of it. There's no reliable record that the treasures of the Temple were ever again in the Holy Land.'

'So the menorah really was in Constantinople.' Maria looked keenly at O'Connor. 'Could the story of their return to Jerusalem have been a cover-up, a false trail?'

'It's very possible,' O'Connor replied. 'Procopius became Prefect of Constantinople, and was a member of Justinian's inner court. The rituals and superstitions of pagan Rome continued well into the Christian period, and emperors of the golden age were revered. Perhaps Vespasian's instructions to conceal the menorah still had potency through the centuries, and the story of the return of the treasures to Jerusalem was a way of keeping their presence in Constantinople secret. And just because the Byzantines were Christian doesn't mean they were any more sympathetic to the Jews than the Romans of Vespasian's day. I believe the menorah was locked away for another five hundred years, perhaps deep in the vaults of Justinian's new cathedral of Hagia Sofia in Constantinople.'

'There are some who believe the Jewish treasures never made it out of Rome at all, that they were secretly taken by the papal authorities and lie hidden to this day in the Vatican.' Jack looked penetratingly at O'Connor, uncertain how much the other man might reveal. 'Even before the barbarian invasions, the Church had begun to appropriate temples in Rome and cleanse them of their artefacts, from soon after Constantine's conversion to Christianity in the fourth century AD.'

O'Connor paused for a moment before replying, his voice hushed but deliberate. 'It is true that the Vatican conceals untold treasures, priceless works of art unseen for generations. There are sealed passageways in the catacombs under St Peter's even I haven't seen.' He looked solemnly at Jack. 'But I can assure you the menorah is not among them. If it was I wouldn't be here now. I would have been sworn to secrecy by the papal authorities. Remember our history. The treasures of the Jewish Temple would represent the ultimate triumph of Christianity, retribution for the complicity of the Jews in Christ's death. If we held them it would have to be the world's best-kept secret. Any word and there would be war.'

'War?' Jeremy said sceptically.

'Total breakdown in relations between the Vatican and Israel. Age-old animosities between Jews and Christians reignited across the world, fuelling anti-Semitism and ultra-Zionism on a horrifying scale. And if the treasure was ever returned to Jerusalem it would spark the final showdown in the Middle East we have long feared. Some orthodox Jews believe the restoration of the menorah to Jerusalem would be the first step in rebuilding the Temple, on the site now occupied by the al-Aqsa mosque, one of the holiest sites of Islam. The menorah would give Israel total confidence in its destiny, empowering fundamentalists and persuading waverers. And the Arab world would know once and for all that their demands would never be achieved by negotiation.'

'It's curious that the Nazis never came looking for it in Rome,' Jack said.

'The Second World War was a dark period for the Church,' O'Connor said grimly. 'The Pope never gave Hitler an excuse to plunder the Vatican. But there have been plenty of others knocking on our doors since then. Zionist fantasists, conspiracy theorists, treasure-hunters who believe they're halfway to finding the Holy Grail. I can assure you they have all been on a dead-end trail.'

At that moment there was a bustle of activity outside and Costas burst into the room. 'Sorry to interrupt,' he said breathlessly. 'But I thought you should see this.' He hurried over and handed Jack a piece of paper. 'Remember those timbers with the chain in the Golden Horn? You thought they looked a little odd.'

'Overlapping strakes, attached with iron rivets.' Jack struggled to take his mind off the menorah and focus on their remarkable find of the day before. 'More in the north-west European tradition of shipbuilding in the early medieval period. Odd for a Venetian galley of 1453.'

'Well, there's your answer.' Costas leaned forward

excitedly, his hands on the table. 'The sample we brought back's just been analyzed. It's Scandinavian oak. And it's from the prow of a longship, not a Mediterranean galley. It looks as if it broke off in the chain, probably without sinking the vessel. And check out the tree-ring date.'

'1042, plus or minus a year,' Jack read, his mind reeling with astonishment.

Jeremy let out a whoop and stood up, unable to contain himself. 'It fits perfectly! Harald Hardrada fled Constantinople in 1042. His ship could have been built the year before, on the shores of the Baltic. You haven't found the chain from the Sack of Constantinople of 1204 at all. You've found the chain sunk by a band of Viking mercenaries a century and a half earlier, as they powered their longship out of the Golden Horn.'

Costas glanced at the image of the soldiers burdened with loot in the triumphal procession on the arch. 'And now we know what could have given their ship the weight to smash that chain.'

'The menorah.' Jack shook his head and then grinned broadly at Costas. 'I've got to hand it to you. Another one for science.'

5

Jack peered out of the window beside him as the aircraft banked to starboard and the full expanse of the ocean came dramatically into view. It had been a cloudless early morning, and the sun shimmered off the waves more than thirty thousand feet below. For half an hour since their refuelling stop at Reykjavik they had been out of sight of land, but after passing over the Arctic Circle the sea had become increasingly speckled with white. Some of the shapes were huge, great slabs of white surrounded by turquoise where the iceberg continued for hundreds of metres underwater. Now the bergs were joined by sea ice, a fractured mosaic of white that extended as far as the eye could see, and Jack could make out the first fingers of land ahead of them to the west. He leaned towards the occupant of the seat opposite him and pointed through the window.

'You can see the Greenland icecap.'

'It's breathtaking.'

Maria's face was ablaze with excitement, and Jack again felt certain he had been right to invite her along. After O'Connor had left for Rome three days before, Jack had put in a call to James Macleod to follow up on Costas' account of a discovery in the ice. There was more, much more, an exciting development over the last few days that now made Jack's visit imperative. The ice-corer had turned up a sample that made the account of a ship buried in the ice far more than just a local legend. Jack had also learned of another extraordinary find that would call upon Maria and Jeremy's expertise, and they had both leapt on the chance to join him for a few days on IMU's premier research vessel in one of the most extraordinary projects they had ever undertaken.

Now they all sat in the forward compartment of a customized Embraer EMB-145XR, the sleek regional jet IMU used for personnel transport around the world. Across the aisle Jeremy was hunched behind a sea of paper and books, tapping quietly on a laptop. Jack closed the introduction to Old Norse he had been reading and stared out of the window. For the past few days he had absorbed himself in Harald Hardrada, reigniting a boyhood passion. On his mother's side Jack's family had come from coastal Yorkshire, tall, blond people whose accent even retained a Scandinavian lilt, and Jack had always felt a strong affinity with his Norse ancestors. Harald Hardrada was the greatest of all the Viking heroes, yet his was a life unfulfilled. A man who would be king, whose destiny seemed too great even for him to reach. At the flip of a coin Harald could have won the Battle of Stamford Bridge, and the history of England, of the whole world, would have been different. Jack had driven alone to the battle site near York the day before, had slogged around the muddy fields feeling for the spot where Harald had wielded his battleaxe for the last time. He had felt close, had almost felt a presence, yet had come away strangely unsatisfied. Something was not quite right.

Opposite him in the aircraft Costas was slumped over, snoring fitfully, his head slowly descending to his chest and then jerking back up again. He had been up all night in the engineering lab perfecting the ice probe, and was still wearing his favourite tattered IMU overalls. With his stubble and tousled hair he looked more than ever like his grandfather, a Greek sponge fisherman who had made a fortune in shipping but had insisted that his family remain close to their roots. It was a legacy that Costas had unwittingly developed to a fine art in his appearance.

Jack grinned across at Maria as Costas snorted and stirred, and the two of them reverted their gaze to the window. The coastline of eastern Greenland appeared as an irregular line of rock between the sea and the icecap, the bare outcrops of granite girding inlets filled with shattered slabs of white. Soon they were directly over the icecap itself, a carpet of brilliant white that undulated to the horizon, its surface dotted with pockets of meltwater that shone like turquoise gems in the morning sunlight. It was one of the world's most forbidding landscapes, yet it had a compelling beauty that drew out the explorer in Jack, that made him understand what drove the Norse adventurers who first sailed to these shores a thousand years ago.

'There's one thing I don't understand.' Costas had suddenly jolted awake, as if there had been no hiatus in the conversation they had been having an hour before. 'Harald Hardrada was killed in England, in 1066. Right? Then how come the map inscription suggests he died somewhere out here?'

Jack gave Costas a bemused look and they both peered at Jeremy, who was ruffling a sheaf of papers and seemed completely preoccupied by his work.

'Jeremy?' Maria said.

'Huh?'

'The Battle of Ragnarok in the map inscription. How does that fit in with Harald's death at Stamford Bridge?'

'Oh, the wording was probably just figurative,' Jeremy said dismissively. 'All Viking warriors slain in battle went to Valhalla, where they served Odin and awaited the final showdown against evil at Ragnarok. Valhalla was perceived as being in the west, beyond the rim of the world. The inscription doesn't necessarily imply that Harald and his men met their fate there.'

'And the treasure of Michelgard?'

'Can't help you there, I'm afraid.'

'Jeremy, do you have my copy of Sturluson?' There was an edge of irritation in Maria's voice as Jeremy held out a book without looking at her, his attention again completely focused on his computer. She took the book and held the cover towards Costas. It showed an image of a knight on horseback clad in chain mail, wearing a close-fitting open helmet with a nose-guard and carrying a large kite-shaped shield.

'Looks like a Crusader,' Costas said.

'Not far off,' Maria replied. 'This is from a tapestry in Norway dating from the twelfth century, a hundred years or so after Harald died. But in the absence of any kind of portrait of him it gives a pretty good idea of what Harald and his men would have looked like. The Varangian bodyguard in Constantinople were Vikings by birth and upbringing, and carried the dreaded war axe of the Norse. The axe was the stuff of legends, man-high, single-bitted, terrifying in battle. The Varangians cashed in on the reputation of their forebears, Vikings who had raped and pillaged their way around western Europe, and had even sailed into the Mediterranean to terrorize Italy and France. But the Varangians were also pretty cosmopolitan characters who had spent their adult lives in Constantinople, the most sophisticated city in the medieval world, serving the Byzantine emperors. Their armour and finery wouldn't have looked out of place in the Crusades, and they would have spoken Greek as well as Norse. Harald Hardrada even campaigned in the Holy Land.'

'In the Holy Land?' Costas sounded incredulous. 'But I

thought the Crusades didn't begin until the end of the eleventh century. That's a generation after Harald died!'

'You could call Harald Hardrada the first Crusader,' Maria said, her eyes shining with enthusiasm. 'He was born a pagan, and certainly wasn't seeking redemption for his sins, but he did serve the interests of the Christian Church in the Holy Land. You have to understand, Costas. The Crusades as we know them were only part of the story, told from a Western perspective. The Byzantine Church and its warriors had been trying to wrest control of the Holy Land from the Arabs for centuries. In the year 1036 the Byzantine emperor Michael concluded a treaty with the Arab caliph of Egypt to allow the restoration of the Church of the Holy Sepulchre, the shrine raised over the site of Christ's grave in Jerusalem. A year later Harald Hardrada led the Varangian Guard to escort the Byzantine craftsmen to Jerusalem. The scene could have been straight from the Crusades, tall, blond horsemen weighed down with armour sweeping across the desert, except Harald was actually successful in pacifying the Holy Land. All of the towns and castles of Palestine surrendered to him without a fight, and he cleared the roads of robbers and brigands. He gave treasure to the shrine of the Holy Sepulchre, presumably on the instructions of the Byzantine emperor. He even bathed in the river Jordan, like any good pilgrim.'

'You can shore up the case even further.' Jeremy had abandoned his work and was now fully focused on Maria. 'After Jerusalem, Harald Hardrada campaigned for three years on behalf of the Byzantine emperor in the central Mediterranean, in Sicily and Italy. At the time, Sicily was an Islamic emirate, captured by the Arabs in the great jihad which saw Muslim armies take the Holy Land and sweep as far west as Spain. Harald was leading an army under the banner of the cross against the infidel, to reclaim lands for the Church. The Byzantines called their enemy Saracens, the same opponents the Crusaders faced a few generations later. Harald's war was one of Christian against Muslim, the first major flaring of the conflict that ignited the Crusades and is still with us today. Hardrada was the most feared leader of all the Christian forces, even more so than Richard the Lionheart or Baldwin of Flanders in the Crusades. To the Arabs Hardrada was Ra'd Shamaal, the Thunderbolt of the North.'

'This was some guy,' Costas murmured. 'And you say he was from Norway originally?'

Maria waved the book she had taken from Jeremy. 'This is our main source, *King Harald's Saga*, written by the Icelandic poet Snorri Sturluson in the early thirteenth century. It's part of the *Heimskringla*, a history of the kings of Norway. It gives us our only description of what Harald looked like: immensely tall, fair-haired, with a fair beard and long moustache, a classic Viking. It shows that he was born Harald Sigurdsson in the year 1015. Later he acquired the name Hardrada, literally "Hard Ruler", Harald the Ruthless. His indoctrination into the ways of war came early, at the age of fifteen, when he fought alongside his half-brother King

Olaf the Saint at the Battle of Stiklestad against a rival Norwegian army. Olaf was killed and Harald fled east into exile, first to Sweden and then to Novgorod and Kiev to serve as a mercenary of King Yaroslav of Rus.'

'How did he get to Constantinople, then?' Costas asked, looking at the map.

'Well, the pickings were richer there. At the age of eighteen, Harald arrived in Constantinople to join the Varangian Guard. He quickly rose to be *atrologus*, chief of the Guard, and for nine years plundered his way across the Mediterranean in the name of the Byzantine emperor. In 1042 he fled Constantinople. He was laden with booty and reclaimed the throne of Norway. Twenty-four years later, years in which he ravaged Denmark and ruled Norway with an iron fist, his ambition drove him to the fateful encounter with King Harold of England at the Battle of Stamford Bridge. It was a career drenched in blood from beginning to end, but along the way Harald secured his birthright and became one of the wealthiest and most feared rulers in the medieval world.'

'It's plausible that he should have visited Vinland,' Jack murmured. 'Iceland and Greenland were predominantly Norse settlements, discovered by Norwegian Vikings, and a king like Harald Hardrada would have wanted to exert his influence. Also there's the kudos factor. A voyage to Vinland would have been a daring feat, further shoring up his reputation as a fearless warrior and adventurer.'

'He wouldn't have been the only big man to try,' Maria said. 'The Icelandic annals mention a Bishop of Greenland, who set off for Vinland. He vanished for ever, disappeared from history.'

'It doesn't add up.' Jack sounded troubled. 'If Harald made the voyage to Vinland then he obviously did survive it, returning to Norway in time for 1066. He would have had everything to gain from proclaiming his success, asserting his claim over the western Viking settlements and extolling his courage. It's the stuff of sagas, yet there's nothing about it in the *Heimskringla*. All we've got is a secret reference on a map in Hereford Cathedral. It doesn't make sense.'

'His treasure, the stuff he looted with the Varangians,' Costas said. 'What do we know about that?'

'It's a fantastic story.' Maria flicked through the book to find a page and then held it open. 'Listen to this: *His hoard of wealth was so immense that no one in northern Europe had ever seen the like of it in one man's possession before. During his stay in Constantinople, Harald had three times taken part in a palace-plunder: it is the custom there that every time an emperor dies, the Varangians are allowed palace-plunder – they are entitled to ransack all the palaces where the emperor's treasures are kept and to take freely whatever each can lay his hands on.'*

'I guess that's the price you pay to keep the loyalty of mercenaries,' Costas said.

'It means the Varangians not only had as much as they could carry from the palaces each time an emperor died, but also must have known the location of treasures that remained out of bounds. After all, their main job in Constantinople was to guard the Imperial Treasury. But Snorri's account of palace-plunder is undoubtedly exaggerated, something that would appeal to his Viking audience. The greatest treasures must of course have remained under lock and key.'

'You're talking about the menorah,' Costas said.

Maria nodded keenly. 'But wait for the rest of the story. It gets even better. By 1042, after more than a decade in the service of the emperor, Harald had had enough of campaigning. He'd got all the fame and plunder he wanted, and was now bent on reclaiming Norway. So on his final return to Constantinople from the wars he resigned from the Varangian Guard. The emperor Michael Calaphates was a weak man who seems to have been okay with this, but the empress Zoe was furious. She already had a grudge against Harald. Apparently he'd asked for her beautiful niece Maria's hand in marriage, but Zoe had refused. The story later put about by the Varangians was that Zoe herself wanted Harald, and this was the real reason she was so upset about his departure from Constantinople.'

'A love triangle,' Costas chuckled. 'The Thunderbolt of the North had finally met his match.'

'Harald was thrown in prison, but was released by a mysterious lady, maybe another lover. The story goes that Harald summoned his Varangians and they exacted terrible revenge on the emperor, blinding him in his bed. That same night Harald broke into Maria's apartment and kidnapped her. This is what Snorri says happened next: *They went down to the Varangian galleys and took two of them. They rowed to the Bosporus, where they came to the iron chains stretched across the*

Sound. Harald told some of the oarsmen to pull as hard as they could, while those who were not rowing were to run to the stern of the galleys laden with all their gear. With that, the galleys ran up on to the chains. As soon as their momentum was spent and they stuck on top of the chains, Harald told all the men to run forward to the bows. Harald's own galley tilted forward under the impact and slid down off the chains; but the other ship stuck fast on the chains and broke its back. Many of her crew were lost, but some were rescued from the sea.'

'That's it,' Jeremy said excitedly. 'What I was saying yesterday. The timbers you found in the chain in the Golden Horn were from Harald's second ship. Snorri doesn't say it actually sank, which explains why you only found the wood broken off in the chain. The skull with the helmet must be one of the drowned Varangians.'

'What happened to your namesake?' Jack asked Maria.

'According to Snorri, Maria was released unharmed when they reached the Black Sea, and even given an escort back to Constantinople. Maybe her kidnapping was Harald's way of cocking a snook at Zoe, but he'd already moved on and was planning to marry King Yaroslav's daughter Elizabeth, probably a girlfriend of his in Kiev before he joined the Varangians.' Maria smiled at Jack. 'But others think Maria remained with him, and was his mistress and true love to the end.'

'So you think the menorah was stolen on the same night?' Costas persisted.

'Yes. If the Varangians had time to kidnap Maria, they also

had time to snatch the greatest forbidden treasure they knew of in Constantinople.'

'That maybe explains the menorah symbol on the Hereford map.' Costas stared into the middle distance for a moment, lost in thought. 'If the Vikings were only interested in the treasure as gold bullion, then it seems odd that the shape of the menorah should still have meaning years later when Richard of Holdingham wrote down that runic inscription. Maybe the fact that it was forbidden treasure, not palace-plunder, gave the menorah added significance. It could have become a symbol of Harald's prowess, his manliness, a spoil of victory like in Roman days, to be endlessly trumpeted by the Vikings in sagas and feasts. When they got back home the story of that final night in Constantinople must have kept the Varangians in free drinks for the rest of their lives.'

They all turned to Jeremy, who averted his gaze and glanced down at his computer, then looked Costas full in the face. He paused for a moment before speaking, his tone oddly troubled. 'You're probably right. But that may only be part of the story.'

At that moment the pilot's voice came over the cabin speakers to announce that they were beginning their descent into Kangerlussuaq, the former US air base that now served as Greenland's main international hub on the west coast. Jack looked out of his window and saw that they had crossed the edge of the Greenland icecap and were now approaching the Davis Strait, the wide channel of ocean between western

Greenland and the Canadian Arctic. Below them lay sinuous fjords and expanses of green that suddenly made the Viking settlement of these shores seem plausible, an inconceivable thought on the barren east coast. As the aircraft banked sharply and turned back east they came in line with the longest inlet of them all, Søndre Strømfjord, with the bleak and sparse settlement of Kangerlussuaq scattered over the valley at its head. A few minutes later the undercarriage dropped and Jack could make out two aircraft parked in bays of the former military airfield in the centre of the valley, the first an Antonov AN-74 transport jet which had preceded them with Costas' precious gear and the second a Lynx helicopter bearing the distinctive logo of the International Maritime University.

'We're coming over the icefjord now. Take a look out to port and you'll see the tips of icebergs through the mist.'

James Macleod took his hand momentarily off the cyclic and pointed past Jack at the jagged pinnacles of white that appeared like peaks of distant mountains through the clouds. In the passenger compartment behind them, Maria and Jeremy leaned forward to follow his gaze. With the three-hour time difference from England it was still early morning, and the sun had yet to burn off the sea mist caused as the cold air tumbled off the icecap and met the warmer air rising from the sea. In the summer sun it was actually warmer at three thousand feet than on the surface of the icecap, but even so the temperature was a few degrees below zero and they all wore fully insulated flight suits as well as helmets, a precaution against turbulence as the helicopter encountered thermal updraughts over exposed land and water along the coastline.

'We've got fifteen minutes until the helipad's clear. Time for a quick sightseeing tour.'

Macleod had met them on the tarmac at Kangerlussuaq when they landed and had escorted them straight to the waiting Lynx helicopter. It had taken them just under an hour to fly due north to the Ilulissat icefjord, on Greenland's west coast, almost two hundred and fifty kilometres north of the Arctic Circle. They had been following a heavy Chinook transport helicopter, based out of the remaining US air base in Greenland at Thule, a welcome part of the US Government's contribution to the IMU project. Costas had decided to fly in the Chinook to oversee the transfer of his equipment, and Jack could imagine the other man's gnawing anxiety as he sat in the loading bay watching the fruit of months of labour suspended in a cargo net above the void. A few moments earlier they had watched as the Chinook descended into the sea mist at the head of the fjord.

'This is where the iceberg came from that sank the *Titanic*,' Macleod said, his thick Glaswegian brogue enhanced by the intercom. 'It's one of the fastest-moving glacial icestreams in the world.' He swung the helicopter round to the east, facing inland, and flew at maximum speed for a few minutes until they had cleared the mist and could see the Greenland icecap rising ahead of them in a vast stark dome. 'The Ilulissat glacier's the main pressure outlet for the icecap, where the glacier flows down to discharge ice into the sea. You can see where the ice flow begins now.'

Macleod worked the controls and swung the Lynx in a wide arc back towards the sea. As they peered out they could see where the seamless undulations of the icecap began to fracture and crenellate, forming a corrugated flow that seemed to ripple off towards the west.

'Believe it or not, that thing's flowing at an incredible rate, almost eight miles a year,' Macleod said. 'The crevasses are caused by the pressure of the glacier as it moves against the bedrock, in places almost three thousand feet below. It's like a river flowing through rapids. And now for the fun part.'

He dipped the nose of the helicopter and they were suddenly hurtling towards the glacier, its fractured surface looming up at them in gigantic folds and fissures. At what seemed like the last moment Macleod levelled out, and almost immediately they were enveloped in sea mist, the glacier only fleetingly visible as the rotor swirled away the mist to reveal patches of white and yawning crevasses of deep blue.

'We're actually more than five hundred feet above the glacier,' Macleod reassured them. 'Remember how huge those features are.' For a few minutes he flew by instruments alone as they continued to hurtle through the mist, and then he eased back on the cyclic and dropped down until the altimeter read only two hundred and fifty feet above sea level. 'Here we are.'

As he brought the Lynx to a hover the mist parted and a spectacular image materialized before their eyes. It was a vast wall of ice, towering almost as high as the helicopter and extending on either side as far as they could see. Rather than a sheer face of compacted ice, it was a fragmented mass of towers and canyons, fissured with streaks of blue where meltwater had flowed down from the surface and frozen again. The whole mass looked unbelievably fragile and precarious, as if the slightest nudge would bring it all cascading down.

'The leading edge of the glacier,' Macleod announced. 'Or rather the mass of icebergs that have sheared off it and jammed up the head of the fjord. The edge of the glacier itself is more than five nautical miles east of us towards the icecap, back the way we came.'

'It's awesome.' Jeremy's voice came cracking over the intercom, and for once he seemed at a loss for words. 'So this is where the North Atlantic icebergs come from?'

'Ninety per cent of them,' Macleod replied. 'Twenty billion tons every year, enough to affect global sea levels. That wall of ice may seem pretty static, but it's sped up recently and is actually moving towards us at nearly five metres an hour. Some of the large bergs will be pushed out more or less intact, but almost all of them calve, producing smaller bergs and vicious little slabs called growlers. Almost ten thousand big bergs make it out of the fjord every year into Disko Bay. They process anticlockwise with the current around Baffin Bay and then float as far south as the Grand Banks of Newfoundland and as far east as Iceland.'

'One of them's calving now,' Jack said suddenly.

Without warning a vast slab of ice had cracked off the precipice immediately in front of them, the wrenching noise audible even above the din of the helicopter's rotor. The slab of ice slipped straight down into the water and disappeared completely, then erupted upwards almost to its full height before settling down again, bobbing up and down until only a jagged pinnacle was visible above the slurry of ice fragments in front of the bergs.

'I see what they mean about icebergs being mostly underwater,' Jeremy said, his tone still awestruck. 'The bigger ones must scrape along the bottom of the fjord.'

'That's exactly what happens. Sometimes they drag along the sea floor, sometimes they tumble over.' Macleod flipped down a small video screen from the cockpit ceiling and tapped a keyboard, revealing an image of the fjord bathymetry.

Jack whistled. 'Pretty deep.'

'Over a thousand metres.'

'That underwater ridge on the image, across the mouth of the fjord,' Jack said. 'I assume that's where the ice tongue reached its maximum extent?'

'The Danes who settled here in the eighteenth century called it Isfjeldsbanken, the threshold,' Macleod replied. 'A huge sill of sediment bulldozed by the glacier. The tip of the threshold's only about two hundred and twenty metres deep, so the bigger bergs get stuck on it. Until recently it marked the edge of the ice tongue, the congestion of bergs that choked the fjord.'

'But now the breakup occurs several miles closer to the icecap, where we are now?'

'Correct.' Macleod tapped the screen and another image appeared, showing a satellite photo of the fjord. 'Courtesy of NASA, a composite image from the Landsat satellite. The sequence of red lines across the fjord shows the retreat of the calving front of the glacier between 2001 and 2005. At the same time the glacier has accelerated dramatically, almost doubling its velocity. And airborne laser altimetry measurements have shown a thinning of the glacier by up to fifteen metres a year.'

'Global warming,' Jeremy said.

'Bad news for the environment, but good news for us.' Macleod snapped back the screen and re-engaged the cyclic, pulling the helicopter round on a westward bearing and flying through the mist away from the ice face. 'Bad news because it suggests global warming has a more dramatic effect on the icecap than many have feared. Good news because it allows us to work in the fjord itself, to carry out research that's never before been possible.'

'And now we're into summer,' Jack said. 'I'm assuming that increases the rate of calving and ice disintegration along the glacier front?'

'That's why I wanted you here now,' Macleod replied. 'A

few more days and we're closing shop. We're working on the edge in more ways than one.'

Twenty minutes later he eased back on the cyclic and the Lynx began to descend over the jagged line of icebergs near the head of the fjord. Jack's heart began to pound as he saw a ship's superstructure appear out of the mist to seaward. Macleod reached over to the ship-to-shore intercom, but before pressing engage he turned and looked at Jack.

'And now it's time to let you know why I dragged you halfway round the world to this place.'

6

The man in the prison cell slowly raised his head and listened hard for any signs of life, but heard nothing. He had heard nothing but the sounds of his jailers for more than five years now. He closed his eyes and breathed in slow and deep, immune to the aroma of faeces and urine and vomit that had long ago impregnated the fabric of the prison. He had been sent to serve out his sentence in his grandfather's homeland, in an empty prison left over from the Gulag, saving them the trouble of putting him in solitary confinement. But sensory deprivation held no fear for him, his training having taught him to exclude the reality of confinement and live in a world of his own creation. He slowly bent his head from side to side and then leaned again over the chessboard, the only indulgence he had asked of his captors. He lowered his elbows to the table and raised his hands together in their fingerless mitts, rubbing them against the damp chill that pervaded the cell all year round. For the thousandth time he reached down and picked up a little white pawn, shaped like a Viking warrior with chain mail and a shield, and placed it in front of the Christian king.

'Checkmate,' he said quietly.

He leaned back on his stool, with the exaggerated slowness of a man whose tiniest movements have become his main preoccupation, his way of filling the solitary hours of yet another day. He lifted his left hand slowly to his face and drew his index finger along the scar that ran from his eye socket to his lower jaw, testing himself against the pain he felt every time. From his jaw he moved his hand to the wall beside him, and began to trace his finger along the lines of incised graffiti, his hourly ritual, quietly reciting the words like a scholar with a holy text. '*Paul Kruger,*' he murmured. '*Hauptsturmführer, Leibstandarte Adolf Hitler. Kurt Hausser, Sturmbannführer, Panzergrenadier-Division Das Reich. Otto Lehmann, Brigadeführer, Panzer-Division Wiking.*' He knew the names by heart, names of the true heroes of the Great Patriotic War, crusaders in the struggle against the East, the captured survivors of Kharkov and Kursk and countless other battles, sent here more than half a century ago by the Russians on their last stop before the squalid execution chamber at the end of the corridor. Names like his grandfather's. Only his grandfather had been luckier, for a while.

He shut his eyes and raised his hand to the jagged runes that cut across the names, knowing exactly where to place his two fingers to draw them down, then up, then down, lines so deeply carved the Soviet guards had given up trying to erase them decades ago. They were the graffiti he liked to trace his fingers over best, the symbol of his grandfather's order, *Schutzstaffel*, the SS. He dropped his hand slowly as his fingers fell away from the lines and pressed his ear against the clammy wall, feeling he was truly communing with the knights of the past, brothers in arms who had left their last imprint on this wall to give him strength, to guide him in his quest to find their holiest treasure, to put to rest all who had gone before him and failed.

'Anton Poellner.' The man awoke from a well of blackness as the voice spoke loudly through the slot in the door. He pushed himself upright as the bolts were drawn and the door clanged open. An official in a peaked cap stood silhouetted between two guards against the harshly lit corridor behind.

'Anton Poellner.' The official repeated his name, and the man in the cell held his hand up against the glare before slowly replying in English.

'What do you want?'

'By order of the International Criminal Tribunal for the Former Yugoslavia,' the official said, speaking in Lithuanian. 'Case number IT-99-37b, the Prosecutor of the Tribunal against Anton Poellner, former paid mercenary of the Bosnian Serb Army. Indicted under Article 7 on the basis of individual criminal responsibility, for genocide and crimes against humanity.' The official paused, then raised a document he had been carrying. 'Under the amnesty convention signed last year in the Hague, your case came up for review in the Appeals Chamber.' The official lowered the paper, and spoke with obvious distaste. 'You are free to go.'

He snapped his fingers and the two guards heaved the man to his feet, throwing an old Soviet greatcoat around him as they did so. The man blinked furiously against the light as they shoved him through the cell door, then shackled his feet for the last time and jostled him down the corridor. He was the final occupant of a condemned prison, and as the echoes of his chains resounded through the empty cells it was as if the ghosts of the past were urging him on, knowing he was their last hope that any would escape.

At the final door they unshackled his feet and thrust him wordlessly into the outside world. It was drizzling and unseasonably cold for early summer, but the man raised his pallid face upward and smiled as he let the rain course over his skin. He picked up the bag that had been dropped beside him and began to walk slowly towards the open outer gate and the road beyond, falling into the easy stride of a man accustomed to route marches. Outside the gate he shouldered the bag and thrust his hands into the greatcoat pockets, waiting for the car he knew would come. Minutes later a dark Mercedes drew out of the shadows, its rear passenger door swinging open as it stopped in front of him. Without looking once at the prison he stooped down and got in.

'Welcome back,' a voice said in English from the front seat. 'Your instructions.'

An envelope was thrust into his hand as the car drew away. The man felt the sheaf of papers inside, but first reached in and pulled out an object lying loose at the bottom. It was a golden ring, lustrous with age, and as he raised it he felt his lips brush against the symbol as they had done since childhood, a symbol so different from the one in his prison cell yet so familiar. He slipped the ring over the index finger of his right hand and pulled out the sheaf of papers. On top of them was a newspaper image imprinted in his brain for more than five years now, showing an old man with a swastika armband lying in a pool of blood. He looked at the dead face and then out at the lowering sky, and whispered to himself: 'Payback time.'

'There she is now,' Jack said excitedly. 'It's the first time I've seen her on the open sea. It's like meeting a long-lost friend, born again.'

Seaquest II had been commissioned only three months before, and the west Greenland ice-core project was her first official outing as a deep-sea research vessel of the International Maritime University. Ever since her predecessor had been lost in the Black Sea six months ago, Jack had been determined to find a replacement, and had decided to rename a vessel already on the stocks for IMU in the yards in Finland. Whereas the original *Seaquest* and her sister ship

Sea Venture had been derived from the Akademik-class Russian research vessel, designed originally for acoustic submarine surveillance during the Cold War, *Seaquest II* was an entirely new concept planned from scratch to IMU specifications. Her state-of-the-art navigational features included dynamic positioning system, using lateral thrusters and ballast control to maintain stability in virtually any sea conditions, vital for position-keeping and search tracking as well as to maintain a level platform for laboratory work. She could launch remote-operated vehicles and submersibles, using either deck cranes or an internal docking berth which allowed underwater egress. Like all IMU vessels she had a defensive capability, with a gun pod retracted below the foredeck. And, crucial for polar research, the ice-strengthened hull allowed her to plough through the shattered sea-ice which choked the coastal waters north of the Arctic Circle even in early summer.

Jack was still casting a critical eye over her deck arrangements as the Lynx bounced on to the helipad and the rotors shuddered to a halt. While the awaiting crewmen secured the undercarriage to the deck, Jack eased off his helmet and released his seatbelt harness. The sun was burning off the sea mist and ahead of him he could see the entire length of the superstructure, gleaming white in the pellucid Arctic light. He was in his element again, and his excitement showed as he leaned back and grinned at Maria and Jeremy. 'Welcome to *Seaquest II*. This is where the fun really begins.'

★

James Macleod led them directly from the helipad through the hangar entrance and down a steep gangway into the bowels of the ship. They were joined by Costas, who had been winched down from the US Air Force Chinook fifteen minutes before and had been busy uncrating his cargo on the stern deck. He looked as if he needed about a week's sleep, but with his sleeves rolled up his burly forearms and fresh smears of grease on his beloved overalls it was clear he was not going to waste a moment getting the equipment operational.

They reached the lower deck and Macleod ushered them through an open door into a brightly lit lecture room, gesturing for them to stand beside a projector screen to the right of the door. Ranged in front of them on plastic chairs was a motley group of about thirty men and women, some talking intently among themselves and others hunched over laptops and sheaves of printout. They all looked up as Macleod entered, and Jack could see several bearded blond men with the Danish flag on their parkas, a couple of native Greenlander faces and a number of men and women wearing the navy blue sweaters of the US Air Force. Among the IMU contingent he nodded courteously to a man in the front row splayed languidly on his chair and stroking his sideburns, so lost in thought that he failed to catch Jack's gesture. Lanowski was a brilliantly adaptive engineer who had been indispensable to IMU since they had poached him from MIT, but he had a manner calculated to irritate almost everyone who came across him.

'People, you should all be familiar with Jack Howard, my colleague at IMU. At least from the TV news.' Jack looked distinctly uncomfortable, and Macleod gestured to the other three. 'Dr Maria de Montijo and her graduate student Jeremy Haverstock from Oxford, though he's originally from the States. Costas you already know.'

They gazed with evident curiosity at Jack, a face familiar even to those who did not know him personally. Costas grinned at a few old friends, several of whom had got to know him very well when he had attended the project briefing several weeks previously at the IMU campus in Cornwall.

'We're an international team, as you can see,' Macleod said. 'Officially the project's a collaboration with NASA and the Geological Survey of Denmark and Greenland, and there are also a couple of guys from the International Ice Patrol. We're all doing our own thing, glaciology, biology, palaeoclimatology, but we're pooling basic resources. IMU provides the research vessel, NASA the satellite imagery and GSDG the aerial photography and laser altitude measurements. A lot of the work's just monitoring, making sure the ice conditions are safe enough for us to get the samples we need. With the summer melt almost in full swing we're working against the clock. I wanted you here for a quick greet and meet. Any questions now, fire away.'

'I don't want to detain anyone, so just a few,' Jack said.

'The Greenland icecap, the inland ice. Can we have a swift rundown on its age and significance?'

'Most of it dates from the last two hundred and fifty thousand years, and most of the ice at Ilulissat is from the last hundred thousand years,' Lanowski said, brushing his shoulder-length hair from his face. 'It's an outstanding survival from the last glaciation of the Quaternary.'

'Meaning?' Maria asked.

'Meaning the Ice Age we all know about, the one that ended ten thousand years ago when the ice sheets receded,' Lanowski explained, sighing impatiently. 'Quaternary is a geologic term encompassing the recent Ice Age, beginning about one point eight million years ago, involving many episodes of advance and retraction in the ice. We've been in one of those warm spells for the last ten thousand years.'

'So what makes Greenland so special?'

'There are plenty of glaciers around the world dating from the Ice Age, and of course there are the polar icecaps,' Macleod said. 'But the Greenland icecap is the last remnant of the continental ice sheets that covered the northern hemisphere until ten thousand years ago. It's a fantastic window into the past, as exciting to me as any of your archaeological discoveries.'

'Which brings us to why you're here,' Jack said.

'It's still early days, but the results are very promising,' one of the Danish scientists said. 'We're mostly looking at air bubbles trapped in the ice as it formed, preserving a detailed record of atmospheric conditions in the Ice Age. The calving front is now exposing areas of ice formed very recently, in a cold snap just prior to the Great Melt ten thousand years ago. It's an unparalleled opportunity, the first time any research like this has been possible.'

'Global warming has its uses,' Costas remarked wryly.

'We can't turn back the clock now, so we may as well get all the science out of it we can,' the Dane replied.

'One question,' Maria said. 'You wouldn't get me going anywhere near that calving front we just saw on the glacier. How do you get your samples?'

'We drill cores, just like a sedimentologist or an oil prospector on land,' Macleod said. 'Each band of ice represents a cold spell, sometimes hundreds or thousands of years. It's a bit like dendrochronology, tree-ring dating.' Macleod turned and looked intently at Jack. 'Which brings me to why you're here.'

'I'm still baffled,' Maria persisted. 'You've still got to get close up to the ice to drill a core.'

'All will be revealed.' Macleod beamed at her and started towards the door, nodding his thanks to the assembled group and turning to Jack. 'Follow me.'

Seaquest II was marginally smaller than her predecessor, more economical on space to maximize fuel efficiency and endurance, but with a displacement of a little over seven thousand tons she was still one of the largest research vessels afloat, and it took them a good five minutes to reach the upper accommodation deck. Without stopping Macleod pointed at a line of cabins with their names pinned on the doors, their bags already visible inside. At the end of the corridor they walked into a room that occupied the entire forward end of the accommodation block, directly below the navigation room and wheelhouse. The layout had been Jack's idea, providing a dedicated control and observation room for project staff, avoiding the problems of sharing bridge space with crew which they had recently experienced in *Sea Venture* in the Golden Horn. The room had a director's chair set on a dais in the centre, a duplicate of the bridge radar screen, four computer workstations arranged in an arc radiating from the dais and viewing seats with high-powered scopes set up against the window, a continuous sloping screen that wrapped around the front and sides of the room. With the mist now lifted completely it gave them a dazzling view of the sea to the west, a deep blue expanse dotted with fragments of white, the low form of Disko Island just visible off the starboard bow and the Canadian shore of the Davis Strait somewhere beyond the horizon.

They had been followed from the lower deck by the shambling form of Lanowksi and by one of the Greenlandic scientists, an Inuit woman of striking appearance who pointed to the coffee machine as they entered the room. Macleod grunted, then nodded, and proceeded to pour them each a drink and hand round steaming mugs. Jack shook hands with the captain, who had bounded down the stairs from the bridge to greet them, a former Canadian navy officer who had spent a lifetime carrying out maritime patrols from the Arctic to the Gulf of Mexico. Jack would have time later to do the full rounds of the crew, many of them old friends and veterans of the first *Seaquest*, people with whom he shared a special bond.

The Greenlander woman sat down beside Lanowski at the computer workstation on the right-hand side of the room, positioning her laptop on the available corner of the desk and moving her papers and books neatly on the floor to give the others space to stand. From the body language it was clearly an uneasy alliance, with Lanowski hunched directly in front of the main workstation screen surrounded by his papers, making no concession for her.

'I knew I should have brought my own hardware,' Lanowski grumbled. 'Someone should have given these things a trial run before they installed them. I may as well crunch the numbers by hand.'

Jack raised his eyes at the woman and she forced a smile. 'I'm interested in sea-bed biology; Lanowski does the simulations,' she said. 'James paired us at the beginning of the project.'

She cast Macleod a malevolent glare, and he quickly turned to the others. 'I'm sorry. I should have introduced you. This is Dr Inuva Nannansuit, with the Geological Survey. She's a native of Ilulissat, the town on the headland, so she grew up with the glacier in her backyard. She's been a fantastic addition to the team.'

'So what have we got?' Jack said.

'It's behind the stern, but the captain's swinging the ship round to give us a broadside view to starboard. It'll be a few minutes yet. We're using the dynamic positioning system, as we don't want water movement from the main screws to disturb what you're about to see.'

'That berg out by the island, dead ahead of us now,' Maria said, pointing towards the ship's bow. 'It's got a streak of black on the top. Is that ancient sediment from the glacier?'

'Well spotted, but no,' Macleod said. 'If you look at the berg, it's smooth and rounded, like a sculpture, quite different from the jagged and fissured bergs we saw when we flew over the fjord.'

'It must have rolled,' Costas said.

'Correct. We watched it happen last night. One of the most awesome sights you can imagine, a quarter of a million tons of ice doing a somersault in the water. You don't want to be anywhere near one of those babies when that happens.'

'Of course,' Maria exclaimed. 'That smear is from the sea floor!'

'Exactly. When we arrived two weeks ago that berg was butted up against the threshold on the north side of the fjord, but we already knew from side-scan sonar that the submerged part had become eroded and lost much of its mass. It was only a matter of days before it would roll, and we kept well clear. Some of the bergs make it out that way, others get pushed upright over the sill. You can always tell from whether they look like Henry Moore sculptures or Disneyland ice castles.'

'You mean like that one,' Jack said.

They followed his gaze to starboard as a vast wall of ice came into view, about a quarter of a mile distant and clearly taller than the superstructure of the ship. It had the same contorted and jagged face as the front of the glacier, riven with veins of deep blue where meltwater had frozen inside crevasses, except for a wide flat area in the middle where it sloped down smoothly from the summit. The berg was immense, at least half a kilometre across, and blocked a large stretch of the entrance to the fjord along the line of the underwater threshold.

They stared in awe, and Macleod broke the silence. 'Remember, three quarters of that thing's underwater. You're looking at a cubic kilometre and a half of frozen water, at least a million and a half tons.'

Costas let out a low whistle. 'That'd keep all the bars in the world in ice well into the next century.'

'A single day's outlet from this glacier would be enough to supply New York with water for a year. Twenty million tons a day. We're talking global impact here.'

'Tabular bergs of this size are pretty rare in the Arctic,' Inuva said. 'We think it's atmospheric warming again, resulting in the glacier receding to a point where larger fractures occur. It's the biggest berg I've seen here in my lifetime.'

'Why hasn't it broken up?' Costas said.

'It's had one major calving event, where you can see that smooth face,' Macleod said. 'But the core's unusually compact, solid glacial ice you'd only crack with explosives. It's ideal for us. That face calved back to the core ice, so it's relatively safe to work under. If you look closely you'll see a couple of Zodiacs with the drilling team out there now.'

'I don't understand it.' Jeremy had been quietly absorbing everything since arriving on the ship, but had now recovered his normal inquisitiveness. 'What's to stop that thing tumbling over and crushing them?'

'That's where the conditions really work in our favour,' Macleod said enthusiastically. 'Without the pressure of the ice tongue behind them, bergs trapped on the sill are a lot safer to work on. The glacier itself is way too dangerous for coring, especially now that it's flowing at such a rate. Bergs floating down the fjord are out of the question because they're moving, and once they're beyond the fjord they're not only moving but are more liable to tumble. So a relatively fresh berg trapped on the sill is ideal for us. It's a unique opportunity, but the window is closing fast.'

'How long has it been there?' Jack said.

'About three months. Lanowski's run a simulation showing it processing down the fjord and jamming against the threshold. Any chance of seeing it?'

'You'll be lucky.' Lanowski muttered irritably to himself as he tapped a sequence of keys, and then visibly relaxed. 'Finally.'

The screen showed a 3-D isometric simulation of the fjord, with the glacier at one end and the arc of the threshold at the other. The berg was shown perched perilously on the sill, its vast underwater bulk now visible but with the sea bed dropping off to even great depths on either side.

'You can see the scour channel,' Inuva said. 'That groove in the sea bed leading up the threshold. As they grind along the bottom, the bergs pulverize the sea bed, crushing everything to powder. It creates a sterile biotope, devoid of life. But the sampling we've been able to do here shows something else, that it actually benefits the diversification of species, allowing life to regenerate like a forest after a fire. And there are other pluses. James said you saw a berg calving as you flew in. Each time that happens, the upwelling brings a host of nutrients. These were incredibly rich fishing grounds for my ancestors.'

'A biologist,' Lanowski muttered. 'Just what we needed.'

Inuva glared at Lanowski, and Jack quickly moved on. 'How stable is that thing?'

'I created a simulation of ice conditions in the fjord over the planned period of the project, from two weeks ago ending tomorrow,' Lanowski said. 'Everything's happened exactly as I predicted. This should give you an idea of what we're looking at.' He pressed a key and they watched as the screen sped through several dozen images on the same backdrop, showing the glacier receding alarmingly and a procession of bergs tipping over the threshold.

'A few years ago that would have been a whole season. Now it's two weeks.' Lanowski pushed up his little round glasses and peered rheumily at Jack. 'At the moment, the berg's fine. There's diurnal fluctuation in the grounding line, of course, about three metres as the tide goes up and down, and eventually the abrasion will knock off enough ice at the bottom to unbalance the berg. Right now the worst-case scenario is a major calving event, losing a lot more ice underwater than above, making the berg top-heavy. Then, say at high tide, we get an earthquake, or a storm, or ice from the glacier coming down the fjord and pressing from behind. That could push the berg against the sill and topple it.'

'What are the odds?'

'We're not predicting any big ice coming down the fjord for at least a few days. An earthquake's pretty well out of the question. A storm's a possibility. There's a local freak storm that could affect water movement against the threshold.'

'A *piteraq*,' Inuva said quietly.

'A what?' Costas said.

'A *piteraq*. Caused as cold air tumbles down the icecap and meets the warmer air of the sea.'

'Of course. James mentioned it as we flew in.'

Lanowski ignored them and carried on. 'But there haven't been any storms of the magnitude needed for almost seventy years. The last one recorded was in 1938.'

'What about calving?' Jack said.

'That's where the simulation runs dry,' Lanowski said. 'I just can't predict it.' He looked at the floor in consternation, as if the limitations of science were his own personal failing, then relaxed his shoulders and gave Jack a defeated look. 'All I can say is that the chances increase with the summer heat, especially now with the twenty-four-hour Arctic summer daylight. Forty-eight hours down the road I'll be recommending that all work at the berg cease, and advising the captain to reposition the ship at least two miles further offshore.'

Macleod turned to Jack with a sense of urgency in his expression. 'All the more reason for us to get on.' He nodded thanks to Inuva, handing her a two-way radio from the command chair which she took out of earshot through the side door on to the deck wing. 'While Inuva sets up the final part of your tour, I think we're now ready to show you what this is really all about.' He tried and failed to catch Lanowski's attention, then led them to a workstation on the other side of the room where a large man in a check shirt and jeans was positioning a long metal tube like an oversize map case.

'Don Cheney, senior glaciologist from NASA,' Macleod said. 'Don, show us what you've got.'

They quickly shook hands and stood in an arc behind the table and computer monitor. Cheney carefully pulled out an inner cylinder partway from the case and laid it on the table in front of them, a transparent plastic tube about a metre long and ten centimetres in diameter. He sat down at the workstation and leaned forward on his elbows, tapping the tube with a pencil and speaking in a low Texan drawl.

'For anyone who hasn't seen one, this is an ice-core,' he began. 'Came out of that berg yesterday. Mostly glacial ice, the cloudy-looking stuff with tiny bubbles in it, but also bands of clearer blue meltwater ice. We've got one meltwater band with modern contaminants in it, atmospheric hydrocarbons from factory and engine emissions. Some time in the last century that glacier opened up, then snapped shut pretty quickly. It happens. We've traced the fracture line up to the surface of the berg, the one relatively weak point in the core.'

'We thought of using explosives to crack the berg along that line, then pretty quickly ditched the idea,' Macleod said. 'It would probably have destroyed what we've found.'

'Which is?' Costas said.

Cheney drew the tube about a metre further out of the casing and pointed at it. 'We were about to pull the corer out yesterday and wind down the project, but then one of my NASA guys spotted this.'

The final part of the core was totally different from the bands of ice, a mass of black and brown fibrous material about half a metre long.

'It's nothing to do with sea-bed sediment this time,' Macleod said.

'It's wood!' Costas said.

'Correct. Embedded in an ice layer about a thousand years old, from another sealed-up crevasse. The structure's very compacted, and some of it even looks carbonized, whether through burning or decay we can't tell yet. But we think we've got about a thirty-year tree-ring sequence. I had another core from the same spot air-freighted back to Cornwall in the Embraer that brought you in this morning.

We should have the results from the IMU dendro-chronology lab this evening.'

'It couldn't be natural, a local tree trunk,' Costas said, shaking his head. 'There's no tree growing anywhere in Greenland this big, let alone finding its way on top of the icecap.'

Macleod eyed Cheney keenly. 'Don, show them the scan.'

Cheney nodded and swivelled the workstation monitor so they could all see it clearly. He tapped a command and an image like an ultrasound scan appeared on the screen, with bands and patches in different shades of grey that flickered in and out of focus.

'A high-resolution still taken from the sonar,' Cheney drawled. 'It shows the upper part of the berg, just behind that calved front. The shades of grey are mainly differences in ice density, between glacial ice formed during the Quaternary and ice formed by meltwater, surface snow and ice that melted and poured down fissures in the glacier to freeze again. But there's something else in there, and it's big.'

He tapped a key, and another scan came on the screen, this time dominated by a darker mass in the centre. He scrolled slowly through a series of stills, giving them different angles as the sonar moved from the side to the top of the glacier. At the final still Jack nearly dropped his coffee mug in amazement.

'You must be kidding,' he whispered.

'It's the real deal,' Macleod said. 'I told you about the wood on the phone yesterday, but we only just realized what this image was when we processed the data a few hours ago. We've run the sonar over the berg again this morning, and each vertical scan gives this identical image.'

'My God,' Costas said. 'It looks like a ship!'

'We can't see what else it could be. It's about twenty metres long, wide-beamed with a symmetrical stem and stern. From the horizontal scan it looks flattened, probably no surprise under all that ice.'

'That halo you see around it is frozen meltwater, surrounding the thing like a cocoon,' Cheney said. 'It's the weirdest damn thing you ever saw.'

'Maybe it was on fire when it got embedded in the ice,' Jeremy said quietly.

'Yeah, right,' Cheney replied. 'Whatever it is, I've never seen anything like it before.'

'You sure the wood came from there?' Jack's eyes remained fixed on the image as he spoke.

'Absolutely,' Macleod said. 'Dead centre. The keel, if that's what it is.'

'And it's a thousand years old?'

'The frozen meltwater around it is a thousand years old, yes,' Macleod replied.

'Then we may have the first ever Viking longship discovered in the Western hemisphere,' Jack said, his heart pounding with excitement. 'I'd hoped against hope for this when you told me about the wood. This could be fantastic, one of the most amazing shipwreck finds ever.'

'I told you I was right to get you here,' Costas said.

'I never doubted you.'

'I knew how fascinated you were by Viking exploration,' Macleod said. 'By the possibility of finding a Viking wreck in the New World.'

'The Inuit natives here didn't build wooden ships, and there's no other design from Europe at that date that looks like this,' Jack said. 'It makes total historical sense with the Norse settlement of Greenland at that period. But how a vessel could have ended up in a glacier, formed miles inland, is completely beyond me.'

'One reason we need to take a closer look,' Macleod said suggestively.

'Let me see.' Costas stroked his stubble and leaned over Cheney, peering at the scale on the scan. 'That's about three hundred metres into the berg from that calved front, and about fifty metres below present sea level, right? I'd guess the core would be pretty solid against tunnel collapse, but we'd want to go in underwater to avoid introducing air pockets into the berg.'

'Our thinking exactly.'

'What are the risks?' Jack said. 'I mean, the odds against collapse?'

'Lanowski's the man for simulations, and he's pretty well said it all,' Macleod replied. 'All I can add is that it's now or never. Once that thing's rolled over the threshold and is out at sea, there's no chance. Everything's in place; we just need your go-ahead.'

'Thank God I don't have life insurance,' Jack murmured. 'Imagine trying to sell this one to your broker.'

'It's probably no more dangerous than diving inside an active volcano,' Costas said ruefully.

'No. You can't. It's crazy.' Maria's face froze in horror as she realized what they had planned, and she looked from one to the other for some sign that it was all just a joke. Jack looked apologetically at her and then cast a familiar gleam at Costas, who gave him a crooked smile in return.

'Okay. That's good enough for me.' Macleod glanced at Inuva, who had returned the radio receiver and was waiting patiently behind them. 'While the team at the berg are getting your gear into position, we're taking a quick trip ashore.'

7

An hour later the mighty form of the iceberg loomed before them, a jagged wall of white cut by bands of translucent blue and green. Jack zipped up his orange survival suit and adjusted his lifejacket, glancing back at the sleek lines of *Seaquest II* receding behind their wake. Beside him Maria tightened her grip on the safety line, and Macleod gave her a reassuring glance from the opposite pontoon.

'It's a wee bit of a rollercoaster ride, but Henrik here's an expert. He's been playing in these waters all his life.'

The Danish crewman grinned and stood up in front of the Evinrude 120 outboard, holding the line of the painter taut in one hand and the throttle in the other. He began to drive the Zodiac like a chariot through the slew of brash that covered the sea, effortlessly swinging the big engine from side to side to avoid the growlers that lurked treacherously just below the surface. After five minutes of weaving through the ice debris they reached a pair of red buoys, the entrance to a floating boom that kept a large area in front of the berg free of ice. As they slowly drove the last few hundred metres to the berg they watched a pair of men ascend the huge face in front of them using crampons and ice axes, their forms diminutive against the vast bulk of the berg. Already they could feel the cold radiating off the ice, a chill aura that sent a shiver through Maria. She had insisted on joining them on the trip, but now she felt unnerved, as if she had strayed too far into a world beyond her experience.

'It's like a living thing,' she said. 'Almost like it's breathing.'

'The cold exhalation actually shows it's melting, and fast,' Macleod said. 'Soon even the calved face in front of us is going to be too dangerous to work.'

They drew up alongside a floating dock about twenty metres off the berg, the bobbing form of an Aquapod submersible visible on one side and two Zodiacs on the other. A twisted mass of cable was being lowered through the dock into the sea, and a group of men stood by wearing black IMU E-suits, all-environment dry suits that would prolong their survival even in these frigid waters should something go wrong. After a few moments the cable halted and a familiar form disengaged himself from the group, waving back at them and walking over the platform towards the Zodiac.

'Good work, guys. I've done all I can here.'

With an agility belying his stout frame, Costas leaped from the platform on to the Zodiac, landing with a crash on the floorboards in front of Jack. He had preceded them to the berg by half an hour, and had clearly been on overdrive. He staggered up and stripped his E-suit down to the waist, sat down and cooled off for a moment, then slipped on the orange windbreaker and lifejacket passed to him by the crewman.

'I'm good to go.'

The crewman pushed the Zodiac off and swung it back towards the line of the boom, driving slowly out to sea and then veering right once they had passed the buoys at the entrance. Five minutes later, the boom now out of sight and the northern edge of the berg behind them, Macleod motioned the crewman to drive a short way into the fjord and then ease back on the throttle and cut the engine. With the noise of the outboard gone everything suddenly seemed preternaturally still, an illusion of serenity, as if by crossing over the underwater threshold they had entered a fantasy world of ice, had become one with the towering crystal palaces that surrounded them.

'Don't be deluded,' Macleod said. 'There are titanic forces at work here.'

As if on cue the silence was rent by a tremendous bang, followed by a percussive shockwave through the air and an immense rushing sound as a wall of ice slid off the glacier far away on the edge of the icecap. The noise seemed to resonate off all the bergs caught in the fjord, an eerie chorus of competing echoes that seemed to pummel the Zodiac from every direction and then trailed off like a long sigh. In the unearthly silence that followed, the bergs around them seemed even more awesome, their own stature more puny and impotent.

'The sea's often this placid in the summer,' the crewman said. 'But it's also the most active time for the glacier. And the warmer it gets down here, the more likely you are to get a clash with the cold air coming off the icecap. It can happen very quickly.'

He pointed up the fjord to the eastern horizon, to a band of sky over the ice that could have been dark blue or dark grey, but their attention quickly shifted to a growler the size of a car just ahead of them. It had suddenly begun to rock from side to side, an alarming sight that seemed to defy reason on the glassy sea. It rocked more and more aggressively and then tumbled over, revealing a surface sculpted smooth and sending a ripple coursing out into the fjord. The brash surged around them like a slurry of broken glass, and other growlers reared up uncomfortably close out of the depths.

'That was frightening,' Maria said.

'You haven't seen anything yet,' Macleod replied. 'When a big berg rolls, you might not feel much out here, but a ten-metre tidal wave can hit the shore. You don't want to go beachcombing around here.'

'Don't speak too soon,' Costas said. 'We want our berg to stay nice and quiet for at least the next twenty-four hours.'

Jack gazed back at the creaking mass of ice, and then down the fjord towards the glacier. Outside the threshold the bergs seemed to glide majestically towards the open sea, but inside it was as if they were inchoate, shackled and straining to go, their jagged edges still raw and fresh from the violence of their birth. The power of the place was all the more awesome because so much of it was invisible, convulsions of energy that pulsed unseen through the depths each time a slab of ice fell into the sea, a steady unleashing of power seen nowhere else like this on earth. For Jack it was a new measure of human frailty in the face of nature, an envelope he seemed to be stretching further and further with each new project.

Macleod nodded at the crewman, who pulled the starter cord and fired up the engine. The Zodiac turned back in the direction of the open sea and then accelerated towards the shore, its wake rocking the brash that extended out from the fjord in long tendrils of white. The crewman found a patch of clear water and opened the throttle wide, planing the Zodiac in a wide arc towards the rocky promontory that marked the northern edge of the fjord. Jack held on to the safety line and leaned back from the pontoon where he was sitting near the front of the boat, letting the freezing spray lash his face and relishing the tang of salt in his mouth. It had been several months since he had dived and he had missed the taste of the sea. He saw Maria smile at him as she clung on beside him, and he watched as Macleod and Costas ducked down and held their hoods against the spray. He remembered his last dive with Costas, deep in the bowels of the volcano six months before, a dive that had reawakened his worst trauma. The dive they had planned now was even more confining, and would be one of the most extraordinary they had ever undertaken. The fears were still there, but under control, and all he felt now was a sense of over-whelming elation. The Golden Horn project had reignited his passion for archaeology, but it had been directed from the bridge of a ship, one crucial step removed from revealing history with his own hands. He was itching to get underwater again, to be the first to see and touch fabulous treasures lost for centuries in the ocean depths.

As the engine powered down, the roar of the outboard was replaced by an eerie chorus of howling and yipping, and they realized that the valley ahead was dotted with dogs chained to posts, some of them baying with hunger and others gorging on hunks of meat left for them in their muddy pens.

'The Greenlanders still use dog sleds in winter,' Macleod said, his hood now pushed back. 'Much of the terrain's too rugged for snowmobiles, and the icecap's a long way from fuel. They keep the dogs chained up all summer long and shoot them when they get too old to work. It's not everyone's cup of tea, but then they're not pets.'

'I seem to recall that when they excavated the last abandoned settlements of the Norse Greenlanders, they found dog bones with cut marks on them, their final meal,' Jack said. 'Ancestors of these dogs.'

'Maybe that's why they're howling,' Costas said.

Maria stared apprehensively at the dogs after the others had scrambled over the bow on to the pebbly beach, and it took Jack proffering his hand to persuade her to join them. Macleod quickly led them to higher ground, above the danger zone from berg displacement, then responded to a call on his two-way radio and handed it to Maria. She stopped and spoke briefly into it, then passed it back to Macleod and resumed her place beside Jack.

'That was Jeremy,' she said. 'He stayed on board to finish analyzing the Mappa Mundi inscription. He thinks he's got something else. It could be really exciting, but he needs a bit more time.'

'Should be just ready for us when we finish our dive,' Jack said. 'We'll need to sit down and work out where we go from here.'

'I still can't believe you're doing it,' she said, gazing at him with concern. 'Sometimes I think you have a death wish.'

'This is your first time with IMU in the field,' Jack grinned. 'As James said, you haven't seen anything yet.'

Despite the warmth of the summer sun, they kept their survival suits zipped up against the insects, and followed Macleod from the beach escarpment up an eroded path towards a low saddle in the valley. There was no vegetation standing more than a few feet high, but the bleak rock of the surrounding ridges was offset by lush beds of moss and grass that carpeted the valley floor.

'The ruins ahead are ancient Sermermiut,' Macleod said. 'A sacred place for the local Inuit. People have lived here for at least four thousand years, since the first Greenlanders made their way across the frozen sea from the Canadian Arctic. The town of Ilulissat is over the ridge to the north, but it was only founded in 1741 with the modern Danish occupation of Greenland. The Danes called it Jacobshavn, but the Greenlandic name is a little more appropriate.'

'What does Ilulissat mean?' Costas said.

'Icebergs.'

Costas grunted, and they trudged off the path over a marshy depression towards the ancient site, waving away the clouds of midges that seemed to rise from the bog like mist. 'What about the Vikings?'

'To the Norse this whole stretch of coast up to the polar icecap was Norðrseta, the northern hunting grounds, a forbidding place where hardly any Viking remains have ever been found.' Macleod stopped, waiting for Costas to catch up. 'The Norse only settled permanently where they could have some hope of a traditional Scandinavian way of life, stock-raising and basic agriculture. In Greenland that meant the fertile fjord valleys near the southern tip, where Eirik the Red arrived with his family in the early eleventh century. Most of the colonists came from Norway and Iceland. Eventually there were hundreds of homesteads, a population that peaked at several thousand, and they even built crude stone churches after they converted to Christianity.'

'What happened to them?' Costas asked.

'One of the most haunting mysteries of the past,' Macleod said. 'They clung on for generations, trading walrus ivory and furs back to Europe, but the last known contact was in the fifteenth century. When the Catholic Church sent an expedition to Greenland in 1721 to check that they were still God-fearing Christians, they found no sign of them.'

'Believe it or not, the Crusades were probably a factor,' Maria said.

'Huh?' said Costas. 'The Crusades?'

'In 1124 the Norwegian king Sigurd Jorsalfar established an episcopal see in Greenland. That meant the Church could impose taxes on the Norse settlers, adding greatly to their hardships. Sigurd was known as "The Crusader", one of a number of Scandinavians who joined the Crusades in the twelfth century. He had the gall to exact a special tax for the Crusades from Greenland, of all places. They paid it in walrus tusks and polar-bear hides.'

'That'd be handy in Jerusalem,' Costas muttered. 'The Crusades really were a global madness.'

'The Church was undoubtedly an economic burden,' Macleod said. 'But others think the Norse in Greenland were wiped out by the natives, or by English pirates, or even by the Black Death. I think environment was the biggest factor. The so-called Little Ice Age of the medieval period blocked off the sea routes that were their lifeline back home, with sea-ice remaining all summer long round the coasts. The cold would also have ruined their agriculture, and maybe they were unable or unwilling to adapt to the native way of life and survive by hunting and fishing.'

'So the last of the Vikings were done in by climate change,'

Costas said. 'Not exactly a glorious end for a warrior élite, was it?'

'Let's wait and see,' Jack murmured. 'It could be that the real warriors among them got further west than this.'

The ruins of the ancient site were barely recognizable, humps of turf and low circles of unworked rocks set close into the ground, some of them nearly swallowed up by the alluvial soil and others exposed in patches of peaty bog. On a slight platform towards the seaward edge was a low, dome-shaped tent about fifteen feet across, its frame of whalebones covered with layers of sealskins and musk-ox hide. A thin wisp of smoke rose from a hole in the centre.

'Some of these stones are tent circles, used to batten down tents against the wind,' Macleod explained. 'You see them all over the Arctic, the main evidence of ancient habitation. People haven't lived in this place for generations, but it's hallowed ground for the Inuit of Ilulissat. Sometimes the elders who remain close to the old ways come here to prepare for death. Their families erect traditional tents inside the sacred stone circles of their ancestors when they know the time is close.'

A team of lean white huskies had been chained to stakes surrounding the tent, and as Macleod led the others forward the dogs strained at their fetters and slavered menacingly at them. Maria held back uncertainly, but Jack led her forward, careful to keep outside the radius of the chains. The growling had alerted the occupants of the tent, and a flap opened, revealing a Greenlander woman wearing a traditional sealskin parka, her dark hair tied back and embellished with beads. As she looked up they recognized Inuva, who had left *Seaquest II* by Zodiac an hour before them. She hushed the dogs and beckoned to Macleod, who kneeled down and exchanged a few words with her before the flap closed again.

'Inuva's the old man's daughter.' Macleod turned back to the others and spoke quietly. 'He knows Danish but will only speak Kalaallisut, the local Inuit dialect, so Inuva will translate for us. His name is Kangia, which is also their name for the icefjord. He's well over eighty years old, a great age for these people. They have a tough life. In his youth he was one of the most renowned hunters of Ilulissat, venturing hundreds of miles along the edge of the icecap with his dogs, paddling his *umiak* far beyond the last settlement to the north.'

They stooped under the flap as Macleod held it open, then he followed them in. Jack's eyes smarted from the acrid smoke rising from the hearth, fed by slabs of dried musk-ox dung. Macleod motioned for them to sit down below the smoke on a ring of hides arranged around the fire. As their eyes grew accustomed to the gloom, they could see that the far side of the tent was occupied by a wooden sled, its rails dark with age but beautifully carved with flowing animal shapes. Sitting on the edge, draped in blankets, was an old Inuit man, his face leathery and gnarled and his long white hair flowing free over his shoulders. As he looked at them they could see that his eyes were dimmed by snow-blindness, and his skin had the grey pallor of approaching death. With great effort he began to speak, and Inuva translated the soft clicking sounds of the native Greenlandic every time he paused.

'My father says that since time immemorial his people have lived here, and outsiders have come and gone,' she said softly. 'Now it is nearly time for him to leave and join the dog sleds of his ancestors, as they speed across the icecap for all eternity.' The old man extended a wizened hand out of the blankets and picked up a worn photograph on the sled beside him, nodding silently at Macleod as he passed it to him.

'This is why we're here,' Macleod said. 'Inuva told him about our research ship in the fjord, and it was she who summoned me to Kangia two days ago. Take a look at the picture.'

Macleod passed the photograph to Jack, and Maria and Costas shifted closer to get a better view. It was a faded black-and-white image of a group of men dressed in full polar gear, standing beside wooden sleds laden with equipment and surrounded by dogs.

'Some time before the Second World War, judging by the gear,' Jack said. 'Nineteen twenties, maybe thirties.' He paused, then peered more closely. 'That older man in the centre. Isn't that Knud Rasmussen? I know he was born in Jacobshavn.'

'Kangia was one of his dog-handlers. He's the boy on the left.'

'So Kangia knew Knud Rasmussen!' Jack looked in awe at the old Inuit, then glanced at Costas. 'One of the most celebrated polar explorers, half Danish, half Inuit. The first person to make it all the way across the Greenland icecap.'

'Rasmussen was a father figure to Kangia, and encouraged him to keep the old ways. Kangia revered him, and admired his respect for native traditions. Which is more than can be said for these characters.' Macleod took a waterproof photograph sleeve out of his inner jacket pocket and passed it over. 'Kangia also gave me this.'

'*Ahnenerbe*?' Jack's expression suddenly became grim.

'Correct. I scanned the picture and did some research before you arrived. A German expedition came to Jacobshavn in 1938, a year before the war. They needed dog-handlers, and Kangia was an obvious choice.'

The photograph showed two European men standing against a backdrop of rock and ice. From the shape of the promontory the setting was clearly Sermermiut, near where they were now, but the line of the icebergs formed a continuous wall along the threshold of the fjord, as it had done more than fifty years ago before the glacier began to recede. Both men were dressed in the standard expedition gear of the day, thick sweaters, heavy woollen jackets and plus-four trousers tucked into knee-high socks. The man on the right was tall and handsome, perhaps in his mid thirties, with a shock of blond hair, but was standing slightly apart as if reluctant to be photographed. The other man was small, dark-haired, with pinched features, with one leg bent and his right hand on his knee, staring imperiously into the camera. With his left hand he was holding a pair of measuring calipers over the head of a young Inuit man sitting awkwardly on a rock in front of him, easily recognizable from the previous picture as Kangia. It was like a hunter posing with his trophy, only it was far more chilling than that. On his left arm the man was wearing a red band bearing the black symbol of the swastika.

Jack glanced at Costas. '*Ahnenerbe* meant "Ancestral Heritage". It was a department of the SS set up before the war by Reichsführer Heinrich Himmler, Hitler's deputy. Devoted to the investigation of the ancestral origins of the Aryan race.'

'What on earth were they doing here?'

'Believe it or not, probably searching for Atlantis.' Jack gave Costas a wry look. The Nazis thought the Atlanteans were the original Aryans. In the late 1930s the *Ahnenerbe* sent expeditions all over the world, to Tibet, to the depths of Mesoamerica, to the Arctic. They believed they could find the purest descendants of the Atlanteans in the remotest regions, in areas cut off from the rest of humanity. One of their techniques was phrenology, measuring heads for so-called Aryan features. That's what this moron is doing in the picture. The science was medieval, but the genuine anthropologists conscripted by the *Ahnenerbe* had to bow to the Reichsführer's demented obsessions. They even called it Himmler's Crusade.'

Macleod nodded. 'Yes,' he said. 'And the expedition to

Greenland was doubly bizarre. The Nazis were also obsessed with *Welteislehre*, World Ice Theory, a cosmological fantasy cooked up by an insane Austrian at the turn of the century. It was one of the many weird theories that gained adherents after the First World War, that seemed to offer order and explanation in a world gone mad. According to the theory, everything about the universe was a perpetual struggle between ice and fire. The Aryan master race was born in a realm of ice, and had been scattered across the globe by floods and earthquakes. Where better to find evidence of the original Aryans than the Greenland icecap, the last great remnant of the Ice Age.'

'It would be laughable if it wasn't for the poisonous racism underlying everything the *Ahnenerbe* did,' Jack said. 'Because they only told Himmler what he wanted to know, their activities helped to solidify his views about Aryan superiority. Remember he was the chief architect of the Final Solution, the liquidation of the Jews.'

'So these two guys were Nazis.' Costas had picked up the photograph and was scrutinizing it with Maria.

'According to Kangia, the greasy-haired one with the armband was a thoroughly nasty piece of work, constantly ranting on about Hitler and treating the Greenlanders like dogs,' Macleod said. 'But the other guy seems to have been more reasonable, apparently attempting to befriend Kangia and pulling his weight on the expedition. He was fascinated by the oral traditions of the Greenlanders and promised to visit them one day by himself to record them. Apparently he became a decent dog-sledder and earned the Greenlanders' respect. The two Germans loathed each other and hardly spoke.'

'Do you have any idea who they were?' Inuva spoke quietly from the bedside where she had been listening, her hand on her father's brow.

Macleod turned to her. 'Records of the expedition disappeared mysteriously from the *Ahnenerbe* headquarters at the outbreak of war, so this picture and Kangia's memory are all we've got to go on. I emailed the scan back to the IMU library yesterday. They couldn't identify the smaller man with any certainty, a face that blurs with a thousand other thugs, but the other guy has quite a history.'

'Of course. Now I recognize him,' Maria suddenly exclaimed. 'The blond one. Surely it's Rolf Künzl, the renowned archaeologist?'

'Correct.'

'One of the founders of Viking archaeology,' Maria enthused. 'His doctoral thesis on the Norse settlement of Greenland remains a benchmark for the subject. A precocious career cut short by war.'

'Then you know what happened to him.'

'The von Stauffenberg conspiracy,' Maria replied.

Macleod nodded. 'One of a raft of genuine scholars forcibly recruited into the *Ahnenerbe* to shore up Nazi fantasies about a Norse master race. Künzl had little choice but to play the game, even though he was openly contemptuous of the lunatic fringe who ran the *Ahnenerbe*, mostly crackpots and failed scholars who owed their careers to the Nazis.'

'The lunatics were running the asylum,' Costas murmured.

Macleod nodded again. 'But Künzl was never inducted into the SS because he was from an old Prussian military family, a reserve officer in the *Wehrmacht*, and managed to wheedle his way out of Himmler's tentacles when the war began. He fought for two years under Rommel in the desert, reaching the rank of colonel and winning the Knight's Cross, but then was recalled to Berlin and given a menial job. Himmler seems to have singled him out for special bullying, repeatedly accusing him of having stolen records of the Greenland expedition and concealing what they'd found. But Himmler must have given up on him by September 1944, when Künzl was arrested and strung up with piano wire alongside von Stauffenberg for attempting to assassinate Hitler.'

'One of the good guys,' Costas murmured.

'None of the conspirators were saints,' Macleod replied. 'Künzl had been one of the most effective panzer commanders in the Afrika Korps, and had plenty of Allied blood on his hands. He knew about the racial policies of the Nazis from his *Ahnenerbe* days and had apparently done nothing. But he detested Hitler and wanted the war finished before it destroyed Germany. If you look at the other man in that picture you can see where Künzl's loathing for the Nazis came from.'

Kangia suddenly began to speak, the soft clicking tones filling the tent as if a gentle wind were ruffling the sealskins. He reached out for the photograph and Costas handed it to him, and they watched as he jabbed his finger at the image of the taller man. Inuva leaned over intently as the old man spoke, and then looked back at the others.

'Three days into the expedition they'd reached the edge of the icecap, due east from here, and found a way up the ice to the top. After a day of hauling the sledges across the ice they were suddenly pinned down by a *piteraq*, a wind storm.'

Kangia heard his daughter repeat the Greenlandic word and suddenly became animated, the shadows of his arms arched high against the tent wall as he gesticulated in the flickering firelight.

'It was a ferocious storm, the worst my father had ever seen,' Inuva said. 'The expedition was at the northern edge of the glacier, where a tributary ice stream begins to flow towards the fjord. The two Germans insisted on crossing on to the glacier and seeking shelter behind an ice ridge, one of the undulations where the glacier had buckled. But the Greenlanders refused, knowing it was too dangerous, and braved it out with their dogs on the exposed icecap, huddled behind their sleds.'

The old man put his fists together, pulled them apart while making a cracking sound, and then spoke again to his daughter. 'There was a mighty noise,' she translated. 'The glacier had pulled apart and the Germans had disappeared into it. I, Kangia, was the only one courageous enough to crawl through the wind to the edge of the crevasse, where I looked down through the swirling snow and saw an incredible sight.'

The old man had been following his daughter's intonations and nodding emphatically, but suddenly he coughed painfully and lay back on the pile of furs, his face grey and drawn.

'He has not got long now.' Inuva gently caressed her father's arm, and then looked up apologetically at Macleod. 'I think it might be time for you to go.'

Macleod nodded slowly and began to get up, but the old man held out a wavering arm and spoke once more, his words now almost inaudible. His daughter leaned close and then translated again.

'It was far below, as deep as the icebergs in the fjord are high.' Macleod sat back down as she spoke. 'At the bottom of the crevasse was the prow of a ship, curving up to a fearsome face, its timbers blackened and old. I, Kangia, knew what it was as soon as I saw it. Legend passed down told of giants sheathed in steel, *Kablunat*, who arrived from across the sea and set one of their great ships alight on the ice. I, Kangia, heard the story as a boy from my grandfather, inside this very tent circle.' The old man stopped and coughed, and Inuva looked at the others. 'Our Inuit ancestors, the Thule, arrived here from the Canadian Arctic to settle about eight hundred years ago, after the native people who lived here before had died out. But Thule hunters had already been coming here before that, and had encountered the bearded giants who lived in stone houses in the south of Greenland. My ancestors called them *Kablunat*.'

'My God,' Jack whispered. 'A ship in the ice. It couldn't be.'

'Wait. There's more.' Inuva held her hand up and listened again as the old man spoke. 'The ice began to move beneath me,' she translated. 'I, Kangia, threw down a rope and hauled up the two men. The crevasse closed with a crash just as they came out. The ship had disappeared in the ice. The *piteraq* continued for many days and we returned to Ilulissat. That was the end of the expedition. The Germans sailed away and we never saw them again.'

The old man reached under the blankets Inuva had laid over him and pulled out a package wrapped in white sealskin. With trembling hands he held it out and Macleod took it from him, bowing his head gravely as he did so. In full view of the old man he passed it on to Jack, who cradled the soft leather in his hands and looked questioningly at Macleod.

'This is why you had to come in person,' Macleod said. 'When I spoke to Kangia two days ago he said he had an object he wished to pass on. I told him you were our boss, and he said only you could receive it from him.'

Jack looked at the old man and bowed his head solemnly, and then carefully began to unwrap the package. Maria and Costas shifted closer for a better view as the folds of calfskin fell away. Maria gasped, her face pale with excitement.

'It's a runestone!'

The object was a polished slab of dark green a little longer than Jack's hand, roughly squared at the corners and with a flat upper surface. Crudely inscribed on it were three lines of runes, several of the symbols immediately recognizable to Jack as he angled it towards the light.

'It's fantastic,' Maria murmured. 'The runes are Old Norse, no doubt about it. There are some odd symbols and I don't recognize the words, but Jeremy should be able to help.'

'My father told me the story, but never showed this to me,' Inuva murmured. 'There's one just like this in the museum at Upernavik, about a hundred miles north of here, found on a remote burial cairn at a place called Kingigtorssuaq. It's the most famous Viking find in Greenland, the most northerly runestone ever discovered in the Arctic.'

'Wait till you hear where this one came from,' Macleod said. 'When Kangia rescued the two Germans from the crevasse they were struggling over something, but the smaller man slipped and nearly lost his hold. Kangia had seen him slash at the other man with a knife but drop it into the crevasse. He was in a fury about something else he'd lost, but with the storm raging it became a matter of life and death to get them out and the struggle was forgotten. Before they left the icecap Künzl gave this stone to Kangia for safekeeping. He said it came from the ship in the ice. Künzl apparently told the Nazi he'd dropped it in the crevasse, but the smaller man suspected he still had it and was rifling through his belongings in the night. Künzl told Kangia it was a sacred stone, that he must never let the other man know he had it. Kangia loathed the Nazi and was only too happy to oblige.'

'Künzl must have translated it,' Maria murmured. 'He was the best runologist of his day, an expert in all the Norse scripts. In those few desperate moments in the crevasse he must have read something that made him determined never to let it fall into the hands of his despised SS colleagues in the *Ahnenerbe*.'

'Künzl told Kangia that if he was unable to return to Greenland Kangia must keep the stone secret for the rest of his life, and only pass it on to another who in his heart he could trust. The war sealed Künzl's fate, and now you are that man.'

While they were talking, Kangia's arm had fallen back over his chest and he had begun to breathe in shallow rasps, his eyes half closed and staring at the ceiling. Inuva turned and looked at them with urgency in her expression. 'Now it is truly time.'

Macleod nodded and they all got up to leave, ducking in single file under the flap at the entrance to the tent. Jack remained to the last, and before going he turned back and kneeled down beside the old man, talking quietly to him and then saying a few words to his daughter. He touched Kangia's hand before getting up and following Maria out into the bleak ruins of the old settlement.

'What did you say to him?' Maria asked.

'I wished him and his dogs Godspeed across the ice,

wherever their journey should take them. I told him that he had been right to pass on his treasure to us, that we would hold his trust sacred.'

Inuva appeared at the tent flap to bid them farewell.

'What will happen to him?' Maria asked, her voice soft.

'After the shaman comes we will help him to the high cliff overlooking the fjord, to the place we call Kællingekløften. We will leave him there, and tomorrow he will be gone.'

'You mean suicide?' Maria said in a hushed voice.

'At Kællingekløften we gather every year to watch the sun appear for the first time over the glacier after the weeks of winter darkness, and at that same place those who are tired of life leap into the icy depths of the fjord to join the spirit world. It is the traditional way. My father has finished here now, and is eager to go on his next journey.'

She lowered her eyes and backed into the tent, closing the flap behind her. High up on a crag a dog raised its head to the west and howled, and then strained on its chain as it saw them, flattening its head like a hyena and baring its teeth in a snarl. Maria shuddered and pulled her coat around her, drawing closer to Jack as they made their way down the rocky path towards the sea.

'What is it?' he said.

'An ancient Norse legend.' She paused as they negotiated a boggy patch. 'The dread wolf Fenrir, one of a monstrous brood produced by a giantess, brother of the world-serpent Jormungard and the creature Hel, guardian of the dead. Odin heard a prophecy that the wolf and his kin would one day destroy the gods, so he chained Fenrir to a rock. *Thar liggr hann til ragnarøks*, there he waits till Ragnarok, till the final showdown at the end of the world, when he will wreak his vengeance on the gods.'

'It's a sled dog, not a wolf,' Jack said.

'I know. It's irrational.' Maria glanced back at the distant figure of the dog and turned quickly back to the path. 'But I feel as if we've reached the edge of that world of myth, a threshold between the world the Vikings knew and a world that even their gods couldn't control. The Vikings who came here must have felt the same, a sense of foreboding as they looked over the icy sea to the west, wondering whether the horizon held riches and a new life or the nightmare of Ragnarok. It's as if we're being warned that others have been this way before us and not returned.'

Jack put his arm round Maria and gave her a reassuring hug. 'I take it as a good sign. If Fenrir is here, then we must be on the right track.' He smiled and passed her the swaddled package he had been given by the old man. 'Anyway, ancient legends will have to wait for a while. You've got your work cut out for you. The sooner we can have a translation of these runes, the better.'

'The Greenland Norse saw those storms, you know, the *piteraqs*,' Maria said. 'There's a haunting fragment from a poem called *Norðrsetuðrápa*, about these northern hunting lands. It goes something like: *Strong blasts from the white mountain walls wove the waters, and the daughters of the waves, frost-nurtured, tore the fabric asunder, rejoicing in the storm*. It's virtually the only writing to survive from Norse Greenland, preserved in an Icelandic saga.'

'Don't worry,' Jack said. 'We'll be careful.'

A few minutes later they reached the shoreline and clambered into the waiting Zodiac. It was early evening now, but in the perpetual sunlight of the Arctic summer it was impossible to gauge the time of day, an effect Jack found vaguely disorientating. After he had helped Maria over the bow and they were all settled again on the inflatable pontoons, Macleod gave the crewman a signal and the Evinrude roared into life. They zipped up their survival suits and donned their lifejackets as the crewman reversed out and then swung round the bay in a wide arc, the propeller churning up the brash as he searched for a passage between the floating slabs of ice. As they rounded the promontory at the head of the fjord the iceberg came dramatically into view, dwarfing the flotilla of Zodiacs that were drawn up alongside it laden with equipment and technicians. Costas anxiously scanned the scene as they sped towards *Seaquest II*, then visibly relaxed and looked over at Jack. He gave a thumbs-up signal and then shouted against the engine and the wind, his words lost but the excited refrain familiar to Jack over the years.

'Time to kit up.'

now seemed like another place and time, and they listened as the last of the Zodiacs carrying the crewmen sped off out of the danger zone and back towards *Seaquest II*. They were almost on their own now, their final human contact awaiting in the Deep Submergence Rescue Vehicle nestled against the berg thirty metres below. Costas tightened his straps, scanned the instrument panel and gripped the controls. With its bubble dome and tubular ballast tanks on either side, the two-man Aquapod was not unlike a small helicopter, an impression enhanced by the multidirectional waterjet propulsion system which gave it even greater agility than its counterpart in the air.

'You can wave goodbye to the surface now,' Costas said.

'At least it'll still be daylight when we return,' Jack murmured. 'That's something to look forward to.'

Costas opened up the ballast tanks and a geyser of water erupted on either side of the Aquapod, settling to a bubbling ferment as the submersible slowly trimmed down in the water and became negatively buoyant. For a few moments as the sea level rose up the dome in front of them they were looking at two worlds, both awesome in their magnitude. Above them was the towering form of the iceberg, familiar now yet still breathtaking, its hues of green and blue refracted through the flecks of brash that plastered the dome. Below them was a world as different as outer space, a place nature never intended them to broach. The Arctic waters were astonishingly clear, with visibility extending a hundred metres or more in every direction, and the sheer wall of the berg dropped below them as far as they could see into the frigid depths of the fjord. It was a stupefying sight, and for a few moments they stared in stunned silence as the dome slipped under the surface.

'Holy shit!' Costas exclaimed suddenly. 'Taking evasive action!'

Costas gunned the main thruster and swung the Aquapod down towards the berg. Out of the corner of his eye Jack could see what Costas had sensed just in time. It was a rhythmic commotion in the water from within the fjord, a slow-motion whirling that was advancing relentlessly towards them. The deeper they dropped the larger it loomed, like some nightmare tormentor from which there was no escape. Jack fleetingly remembered Maria's warning about the wolf Fenrir and the edge of the world, about forces even the gods could not control. They jetted down until they were nearly vertical, plummeting straight into the blackness of the abyss.

'Brace yourself!' Costas yelled.

A scything wall of white suddenly appeared out of the tumult, an apparition that bore down on them with horrifying speed and then swept past the front of the dome with inches to spare. They were jolted violently to one side and Costas fought to keep the Aquapod from spiralling out of control, then righted the submersible and brought it to a standstill. Above them they caught a glimpse of the giant slab of ice as it tumbled on towards the open sea, swirling away until nothing but a mist of bubbles was left to mark its progress.

'That was close,' Costas said.

'I thought all this was supposed to end six months ago,' Jack said plaintively. 'A quiet life of contemplation, tending the garden and writing my memoirs.'

'Yeah, right,' Costas replied. 'Anyway, we needed some excitement to kick-start the adrenalin for what we're doing next.'

Now that the water was calm again they looked around, and both men fell silent. They had plummeted to a depth of nearly a hundred metres, and the DSRV was now far above them, with two divers just visible outside and silvery trails of bubbles cascading up the ice towards the surface. The immense face of the berg filled the view in front of them, only at this depth with all colour lost except blue. It had a surreal tint, an azure glow that made it loom at them like a mirage. They could see huge concavities where the current had eroded the ice away, and a vast skid-mark of sediment and rock fragments where the berg had scraped against the side of the fjord. And below them, far below, barely discernible in the darkness, they could just make out a sepulchral landscape of boulders and undulations, a shadowy ridge that dropped off into an infinity of blackness on either side. It was a savaged and rutted seascape, pulverized by ice, and they knew it was one of the most dangerous places in all the oceans.

'The threshold of the icefjord,' Jack murmured. 'We must be the first people ever to see it.'

'Awesome,' Costas whispered.

'Not a place I want to go,' Jack replied.

'Roger that.' Costas turned his attention to the instrument panel and injected a blast of air into the buoyancy chambers, bringing the Aquapod towards the berg until it was directly under the DSRV. 'Ben, this is Aquapod One, safe and sound. We'll be with you in five minutes. Out.'

The Deep Submergence Rescue Vehicle that equipped *Seaquest II* featured a small internal dock, an open pool that allowed the dome of an Aquapod to rise into a chamber at the rear of the submersible. As Jack looked up at the belly of the DSRV, he watched the dock door slide open, and saw the wavering form of a figure staring down at them from inside the chamber. Two divers appeared on either side of the Aquapod and hooked on four anchoring cables that slowly drew them up. As they broke surface and the dome opened up inside the cramped space, they were met by the welcoming face of Ben Kershaw, a former Royal Marine who had been at the centre of the action in the Black Sea six months before, and had recently taken over as chief security officer on *Seaquest II*. Jack reached out and took the hand proffered to help him up, then shook it warmly once he was on the narrow gangway that ringed the dock.

'Thought it'd be a while before I saw you back inside a submarine.'

'All in a day's work.' Ben looked serious. 'Everything okay?'

'A small brush with a growler.'

'We noticed. We thought you were goners. The fjord's become more active in the last twenty-four hours, with more big chunks of ice like that calving off the glacier.'

'I want you away from here as soon as we're gone,' Jack said.

'What happens if you need to bale out?'

Jack was firm. 'We can surface and fire a flare. We've got the radio buoy. I don't want anyone in the danger zone if this berg shifts. I want the DSRV back at the ship. We've had too much loss already over the last year, and I don't want to put anyone else's life on the line.'

'What about me?' Costas gave Jack a look of mock indignation as he lurched out of the Aquapod and crouched down beside them.

'Oh, you're expendable. You should know that by now.'

'Yeah, there's always Lanowski to take my place.'

Jack grimaced and the two other men laughed, a noticeable easing of the tension they had all felt. 'Okay, point taken,' Jack said. 'I promise I'll look after you like a father to a son. Now let's get this show on the road.'

Jack followed Ben through the bulkhead hatch that divided the docking chamber from the main compartment of the DSRV, his tall frame stooped almost double in the confined space. Around the floor ring where the DSRV could dock with a stricken submarine were two identical arrangements of diving equipment, and Costas stooped down behind them to do a quick inventory. Jack followed Ben a few metres further to the command station at the front of the submersible, and Costas joined them moments later. They nodded to the crewman who was sitting in the pilot's chair, a battery of monitors and instrument panels in front of him, then squatted down on either side of Ben behind the navigation console as he activated the screen.

'We've plotted a best-fit route,' Ben said. 'Ideally we'd have you go in shallower, but we're protected here by a ridge in the ice from any calving off the berg. We'll put you in breathing nitrox, which will give you a longer bottom time than air at thirty metres.'

'Umbilical?' Jack said.

'Right. We'll hook you up to the cylinders in the DSRV. That way you'll conserve the gas you're carrying with you.'

'It's crucial we avoid exhausting gas inside the berg,' Jack said. 'Lanowski was clear on that one.'

'Have no fear,' Costas interjected. 'A little gizmo I've been playing with at HQ. There's no problem with exhaust when you dive down into a wreck, right? You can prevent it pooling and damaging whatever you're diving into by putting it through a tube that's buoyed upwards, venting the exhaust above the wreck. The difficulty comes the other way, when you're going up into a structure from below.'

'You pump it out.'

'Right. We'll be hooked up to two hoses, one bringing us the nitrox and the other extracting the exhaust and venting it outside the berg. Not sure how it's going to behave in the cold.' Costas rubbed his hands in anticipation. 'Should be fun to try.'

'Let me guess. You haven't tested it yet.'

'You don't get icebergs in the English Channel.'

Jack turned from Costas and pointed at the screen, which showed an isometric computer simulation of the DSRV against the iceberg, with a dotted red line running up at a forty-five-degree angle from the DSRV and then levelling to a horizontal line that ended at a dark mass near the centre of the berg.

'I take it we reach ten metres below sea level as quickly as we can, then ditch the umbilical and switch to rebreathers,' Jack said.

'Correct,' Ben replied. 'We'd love to kit you out with the latest IMU closed-circuit mixed-gas rebreathers, but there's too much danger of freezing and too much to go wrong. This is one time when the old technology is best. You've got our tried and tested semi-closed rebreathers, with an oxygen nitrox mix configured to give you maximum endurance at that depth. The carbon dioxide will be absorbed but not the nitrogen, so there will be a buildup in the counterlung that you'll need to vent. But the nitrox fraction is small and that shouldn't happen till you're out of the berg again. You won't be producing any exhaust inside.'

'Just make sure you stay above ten metres,' Costas added. 'We'll be breathing over eighty per cent oxygen, and the mix becomes toxic at that pressure. Stray any deeper and you won't know about it, you'll convulse and be gone.'

'You'll have the standard trimix package in the cylinder consoles on your backs, giving breathable mixes down to one hundred and twenty metres,' Ben said. 'The regulators have an antifreeze cap on the first stage, so should be safe. But that's an open-circuit system, producing exhalation inside the berg. Strictly for emergencies.'

'Okay,' Jack said. 'Now tell me about your ice-borer. Nothing technical, I just want to know how to drive the thing.'

Twenty minutes later Jack and Costas sat kitted up on either side of the docking pool, like divers preparing to go through a hole in the ice. The Aquapod had been driven away ten minutes earlier by the two divers who had assisted them into the dock. Now the only crew members remaining were Ben and the pilot, and they had already begun finalizing systems checks in preparation for departure.

'We'll be here until you drop the umbilical,' Ben said. 'Then you're on your own.'

Jack nodded as he sat festooned with diving equipment, his dark hair tousled where he had tried on his helmet. Opposite him Costas ballooned as he struggled to control the inflator on his E-suit, and Jack tried to suppress a smile at his friend's appearance. Over their E-suits both men wore compact rebreathers slung like small rucksacks on their chests, and on their backs were streamlined yellow consoles containing three high-pressure cylinders with oxygen, nitrogen and helium, as well as integrated weights. Ben finished his second complete check through all their equipment and then squatted beside the pool between the two men. 'I have to level with you, Jack. It's my obligation as security chief. Those timbers could just be some old whaler's boat. The risk might just be too high.'

'I know where you're coming from, Ben, and I appreciate it,' Jack said. 'But it's a calculated risk. We can laugh at Lanowski, but I trust his judgement on this one.'

'Okay, it's your call.' Ben glanced at Costas, who nodded firmly at him. Without further discussion Jack and Costas put on their yellow Kevlar helmets, and Ben went to each in turn locking the neck seals, activating the twin headlamps on either side and checking that the rebreather and trimix feeds were in place. Jack and Costas pulled on their gloves and checked that the watertight seals were secure, then pressed the temperature control consoles on their shoulders to ensure that the chemical heat connection to their hands was functional. Finally they pulled on their fins, disturbing the wisps of mist that swirled off the frigid pool as it met the warm air of the compartment. Just as they were about to flip down their visors, the face of the other crewman appeared through the hatch.

'Message from *Seaquest II*. For you, Jack. Something to do with tree rings.'

'Read it to us, will you?' Jack said.

The crewman kneeled down and held up a printout. '*From IMU Dendrochronology Lab, 0212 GMT. Ilulissat Fjord wood sample is Scandinavian oak, possibly Norwegian. Extensive carbonization present from burning. Match to north-west European tree-ring sequence indicates felling date of AD 1040 plus or minus ten years.'*

'Yes!' Jack punched his gloved hand into the air. 'There's your answer. I knew it in my gut all along. This could be one of the archaeological finds of the century.'

Looking down at the water, Jack pursed his lips, then gazed across at Costas with a gleam in his eye. He was looking forward to seeing the surface above them and the sunlight as they dropped out of the DSRV, a respite from the niggling sense of claustrophobia he always felt, but now he was itching to get inside the berg and probe its secrets. He reached down and picked up the umbilical that was coiled by his side, the twin hoses twisted together as a single mass, and plugged it into the remaining open port below the chin of his helmet. He watched as Costas did the same, then the two men clamped shut their visors and switched on the intercom. Jack eased himself off the bench and sat with his legs suspended over the abyss, the astonishing clarity of the water making him feel like a parachutist about to exit an aircraft. He and Costas were already in a world apart, their intercom only audible to each other. Jack gave an okay signal to Ben and a thumbs-down to indicate he was descending, and then looked at Costas.

'Good to go?'

'Good to go.'

9

The man in the black cassock walked confidently towards the main entrance of the Apostolic Palace, his trappings as a Jesuit priest entirely in keeping with the other applicants milling around the doorway. He had left the crowd in St Peter's behind him, and had already passed the first security cordon at the bronze doors leading off from the Square. Now he was approaching the very heart of the Vatican, the headquarters of the College of Cardinals, the hub from which the Holy See exerted its influence far beyond Rome to every corner of the globe.

Ahead of him two Swiss guards stood resplendent in their finery with halberds crossed in front of the door, an image that could have been straight from the Renaissance except for the Heckler & Koch sub-machine guns slung discreetly over their backs. An officer of the guard took the Jesuit's ID and proceeded to scrutinize him, comparing the black beard and expressionless eyes with the photo on the card. Despite the heat of the early summer, the face was pale and pinched, but it was a scholarly visage all too common inside the closeted walls of the Vatican. The officer turned to a secretary beside him, and they checked the level of authorization on a palm computer. The officer grunted in surprise and immediately handed the Jesuit back his card.

'You are free to enter.'

The guards raised their weapons and the Jesuit passed through, avoiding the usual body search and metal detector. He walked straight along a wide corridor on the ground floor, then turned left at the end and carried on until he came to the ornate door of a private chapel, its entrance marked by trays of dedicatory candles on either side. He knocked once and pushed the door open. In the candlelit gloom he saw another man kneeling before the simple altar at the far end of the chapel. The man crossed himself and stood up, then turned towards the door. He was tall and aquiline, with white hair, and wore the full episcopal vestments of a cardinal, with a golden cross hanging in front of his scarlet cassock. He had the benign, ageless face of one who had spent many years in holy orders, but with a hard edge to his eyes. It was an expression appropriate for a man such as him, a man whose ambition had brought him to the very threshold of supreme power in the Catholic Church.

'Eminence.' The Jesuit bowed slightly, then closed the door behind him.

'Monsignor.'

The two men spoke in English, the Jesuit with a clipped drawl that could have been South African, the cardinal with a hint of north European in his accent.

'He is here?'

'The second one present at the opening of the chamber. We suspected, and he confessed. The Holy See has techniques of persuasion refined over the centuries.'

'And the other?'

'He is your next task.'

The Jesuit walked forward and kneeled in front of the cardinal. The cardinal quickly drew off the holy ring from the middle finger of his right hand and replaced it with another, a heavier, flat-faced ring that glinted in the candlelight as he held it out. The Jesuit took his hand and kissed it, closing his eyes as his lips brushed the familiar shape, and with his other hand felt his own ring hanging round his neck under his cassock. He got up, made the sign of the cross and backed reverently towards the door, then stopped for a moment and held up his right hand towards the cardinal, whispering words in a language that sounded unearthly, words never before uttered in this holy place, that seemed to blaspheme against all that it stood for.

Hann til ragnarøks.

The Jesuit closed the door of the chapel behind him and began to walk down the long corridor, his footsteps echoing off the walls of the palace. He emerged into an open courtyard, raising his hands in prayer as two officials passed in the opposite direction, then made his way towards an unassuming entrance partway along the other side. The bells of St Peter's suddenly began to boom across the still air of the city, asserting the sovereignty of the Holy See as they had done since the dying days of the Roman Empire. Above him the walls of the courtyard framed the sky, two huge birds of prey circling far overhead, and he could hear the dull rumble of the city outside. He ducked through the entrance and looked quickly behind him, then gathered up his cassock and mounted the stairway to the first floor. The corridor ahead was lined with statues, bulletin boards and posters advertising exhibits, but was empty of people, today being a holiday for the museum staff. The Jesuit reached a door with a light on inside, just where he had been told it would be, and saw the word *Conservatori* above the lintel.

He paused, not out of hesitation but to relish the moment. In the shadows he stood with his head bowed, his fists clenched. Sixty-five years earlier his forefathers had failed to breach these walls, had stopped short of taking the Vatican in their triumphal sweep through Rome. Now he would make amends, he would make his mark. He unclenched his left hand and raised it to his face, drawing his index finger down the ragged scar that pulsated beneath his beard, pressing it hard until he flinched in pain. He slipped his left hand back under his cassock, and with his other hand knocked three times on the door.

'Enter,' a muffled voice said in Italian.

The Jesuit pushed the door open and closed it behind him. The room was crammed with books and manuscripts, with a computer workstation at the far end. In the foreground was a fragmentary stone relief sculpture on a pedestal, and in front of it sat a middle-aged man in jeans and a casual shirt, hunched over a notebook.

'Monsignor.' The man finished what he was writing and looked up, his expression alert and intelligent. 'I had not expected to be interrupted today. What can I do for you?'

'You are the Chief Conservator?' The Jesuit spoke in Italian.

'I am.'

'You were present at the discovery of the secret chamber in the Arch of Titus, along with Father O'Connor?'

The other man suddenly looked deflated, and tossed his notebook on the floor. 'Now everyone seems to know. We kept it secret for the good of the Church. I wish we had never found it.'

'So do I.'

The silenced Beretta coughed twice and the man jerked back on his stool, an expression of horrified surprise on his face. He tottered over and fell heavily to the floor, coming to rest with his arm splayed awkwardly over his front, his eyes wide open and uncomprehending in death. The Jesuit pulled his left hand out of his cassock, and slowly raised it to his face. He drew his finger down the scar on his cheek, again and again, as hard as he could, grimacing with pleasure as he watched the blood seep from the man's chest and pool on the cold stone slabs beneath him.

There would be more.

'Activating ice probe now.'

Costas turned to Jack as he spoke through the intercom, and the two men gave each other the okay sign. For about the fifth time Jack cast a critical eye over Costas' equipment. Once they shed the umbilical they would be absolutely reliant on their breathing systems and on each other, with no bale-out option, no emergency escape route to the surface. The IMU equipment was state of the art, with a rock-solid computer system which took the job of calculating their breathing mix and ascent rate entirely out of their hands. It had been tested in conditions of extreme heat, six months before inside a submerged volcano, but this was the first time it had been deployed in water that was as cold as it could be without turning to ice.

'Take up your position.'

Jack swung in from where he had been hanging by one hand and gripped the metal bar beside Costas. They were like two climbers on a vast ice wall, dwarfed by the immensity of the berg. Below them the ice dropped off hundreds of metres into the abyss, where the slope of the threshold sheered off to unimaginable depths, to a place of freezing blackness no human had ever dared enter.

'There's only one safety drill,' Costas said. 'Any sign of

movement in the ice and we switch to trimix. If this baby rolls off the threshold we're going down. Remember, the trimix gives us breathable gas to one hundred and twenty metres. That should at least give us some margin.'

Jack gave another okay sign and checked the three hoses which fed into the ports in his helmet. The nitrox they were breathing now was the best option at this depth, its reduced nitrogen load providing more bottom time than compressed air, but the increased oxygen load making it more toxic below thirty metres. It was fed through the umbilical hose which drooped below them and led back to the DSRV, its reassuring bulk still in position a few metres behind them. The second hose led to the rebreather on his chest, a self-contained system they would activate when they reached ten metres depth. With its integral high-pressure oxygen cylinder it could sustain them for several hours, and was the ideal shallow-water gas. Like the nitrox umbilical with its venting system, the rebreather would produce no exhaust inside the berg, all exhaled gas being recycled through the system. The third hose led to the trimix cylinders on their backs, a variable gas system that substituted helium for nitrogen and could extend their depth envelope to the maximum possible for breathable gases.

But trimix was their fallback option, and would produce exhaust inside the berg. In truth they knew their safety drill was a forlorn hope. If the berg moved off the threshold, the vast bulk of it would slip underwater, its base plunging hundreds of metres into the depths. If the movement of the

the umbilical bringing in their nitrox and sucking out their exhaust, their lifeline to the world outside. Jack raised his head and watched in fascination as the borer carved a perfectly smooth tunnel through the ice, proceeding upwards at a forty-five-degree angle at a rate of more than two metres per minute. He had no sense of the water temperature in his E-suit, but the changing thermostat readout on his environmental regulator reflected the blast of warm water that was being ejected from the borer and driving the machine into the ice. Ahead of them their lamps lit up the wall of the tunnel, a dazzling spectacle of white, yet Jack knew that without artificial light they would be entering a world of total blackness, hemmed in on all sides by unimaginable quantities of ice which had blocked out the last vestiges of the sun's rays far above them.

'Okay,' Costas said. 'We've reached ten metres external water depth. I'm going to level out and disengage.'

Costas adjusted the heat output controls on the panel in front of him, easing off on the lower elements so the borer would melt more ice above and gradually become horizontal. Jack watched their progress on the LED screen, a 3-D isometric image of the berg identical to the one Lanowski had shown them earlier that day. The image had been generated by the surface team using ultra-high-frequency sonar, created from thousands of data points where the sound waves had met differential resistance from frozen cracks and fissures in the berg. Lanowski had plotted a best-fit point of entry and route to minimize the chance of following a frozen meltwater fissure and rupturing the berg, and so far his plot had held true. The ice they had passed through had all been the cloudy white ice of the glacier, as hard as rock, formed a hundred thousand years ago in the depths of the Ice Age.

Costas reopened the external channel on his intercom receiver. 'Ben, this is Costas. Do you receive me, over?'

'Costas, this is DSRV, we receive you loud and clear, over.'

'We've reached the disengagement point, over.'

'Roger that. We've got you on screen as long as you're hooked up. Be advised, we have a meteorology warning from the captain of *Seaquest II*. There's some thermal disturbance on the edge of the icecap, a cold air mass moving in from the east. It may be nothing significant, but the captain's pulling back another mile from the fjord as a safety precaution. You have the option to abort. Over.'

Costas and Jack looked at each other through their visors. 'We're carrying on,' Costas replied. 'We're only fifty metres from our target, and we're not going to hang around. We'll be out of here within the hour. But you must leave now. Over.'

'Roger that. Send up the radio buoy when you're clear of the berg and we'll pick you up. Standing by to receive umbilical. Over.'

Costas flipped a switch on the control panel in front of him and pulled out the power cord from the ice-borer. For an alarming moment the device went dead, and Jack could almost see the water around him beginning to freeze up.

Then the LED screen and forward light array reactivated as the battery came on line, and the water began to shimmer again.

The two men turned towards each other in the narrow confines of the ice tunnel, their visors only inches apart. Costas talked them through the procedure they had practised repeatedly before leaving the DSRV, each man visually checking the other as they worked methodically through the steps.

'Engage rebreather.'

Jack copied Costas and opened the outlet valve of the rebreather on his chest, then turned the knob under his helmet that activated the flow of gas into the silicon rubber skirt that sealed over his nose and mouth. The first lungful of oxygen sent a tingle down his arms and legs, an invigorating effect he relished every time they used rebreathers. He grasped the umbilical hose with his right hand and with his other hand closed the nitrox port on his helmet, his body wedged awkwardly on his elbows against the wall of the tunnel and pressed up against Costas.

'Disengage umbilical.'

Simultaneously the two men pulled out the nitrox hoses from their helmets and dropped them to the floor of the tunnel, and Costas released the power cable he had been holding. As they sucked on their rebreathers they watched the coiled mass of the umbilical slither off behind them and disappear over the bend in the tunnel, dropping down their entry route towards the open sea. The microfilament tendrils keeping the tunnel liquid wavered and undulated as if they had been caught in a breeze, then gradually became more stable, spreading out over the entire width of the tunnel.

'Ben, we're disengaged. We'll be out of communication range once we hit that mass of meltwater ice. Looking forward to a hot brew when you return. Over.'

'Roger that. Good luck. Out.'

They were now completely cut off from the outside, dependent solely on each other and the array of equipment that festooned their bodies. As Jack watched the umbilical disappear he had felt a pang of unease, a warning sign of his secret vulnerability as a diver, the lurking claustrophobia he was constantly battling to suppress. Years before he had nearly died in a submerged mineshaft, his life saved only by buddy-breathing with Costas, and the trauma had been reawakened in the labyrinth of Atlantis when his wound had left him weakened and exposed. He knew Costas was aware of his battle, and the unspoken bond between the two men was a source of strength. Jack gripped the guide rail behind the probe and forced himself to concentrate on the excitement ahead.

'We're dead on target,' Costas said. 'Check out the screen.'

Directly ahead of them the LED display showed an anomalous form, the image created by the sonar data points around the mass of meltwater in the heart of the berg that had mystified Cheney and the NASA team. Even the ultra-high-frequency sonar had failed to penetrate further, and from this angle there was no sense of the extraordinary shape which had been so clear from the vertical sonar images. In the centre of the dark mass was a red cross-hair where the ice-corer had picked up the timber sample, and slightly above it a green cross-hair which marked their objective.

'Remember, we're taking pictures, grabbing anything we can, then leaving,' Costas said. 'No time for science today.'

'For once I'm with you,' Jack said. 'Now we've got the tree-ring date, all I need is to confirm what it is and prove its origin. A couple more wood samples and we're out of there.'

'While you're doing that I'll use the probe to melt a pool above the target zone, just wide enough to turn this baby round and head for home. I can already taste that brew Ben's got going for us.'

'Let's do it.'

The two men hung side by side behind the rail as Costas reactivated the element, and seconds later it began to carve out the tunnel towards the target zone. The borer was now an autonomous vehicle, free of any tether to the outside world. It was drawing them along like a slow-motion underwater scooter, pressing further and further into the heart of the berg. Costas concentrated on keeping them above the ten-metre threshold for oxygen toxicity. As they progressed onwards Jack experienced a rush of elation, as if the oxygen and the adrenalin he had needed to overcome his anxiety had filled him with an overwhelming exhilaration. The tiny bubbles that gave the ice its milky opacity were fizzing in the meltwater, and he suddenly realized that the only life-sustaining properties around them had been released from the depths of the Ice Age. The air was the same as that breathed by their most distant human ancestors, hunter-gatherers who had roamed the edge of the ice sheets thousands of years before civilization. Jack had known he would feel a frisson of excitement as their objective neared, but this was an unexpected sensation, the extraordinary feeling of swimming through a tunnel in time that would be impossible to experience anywhere else on earth.

'This is it.' Suddenly the white ice ahead of the borer gave way to a wall of ice as clear as glass, refracted deep blue as their headlamps shone into it. 'Meltwater ice,' Costas said. 'It's the first we've encountered. This must be from one of those crevasses in the glacier Lanowski was on about.'

He drove the probe forward another two metres until the clear ice was all round them, and then came to a halt. As the swirl from the waterjet subsided, Jack realized they were over a dark mass just beneath the ice, and he could see it curving off to either side through the blue haze. He sank down to the floor of the tunnel for a closer look, his headlamp pressed directly against the ice.

'Well I'll be damned.'

'What is it?' Costas released his hold on the probe and dropped down beside him, their bodies up against each other in the narrow space.

'Timbers,' Jack said excitedly. 'A huge mass of them. It's the side of a boat, a wooden ship. I can see rivets, rows of rusted iron rivets along planks. And the planks are overlapping, clinker-built. That does it. We've got ourselves a Viking longship.'

'Awesome,' Costas said, his eyes glinting through his mask at Jack. 'And they're black, carbonized, just like the sample they analyzed from the ice-core. There's charring across this whole section of timber. This boat burned.'

'A burning ship on the ice,' Jack murmured. 'Remember Kangia, his story of the ancient Inuit legend?'

'It explains the clear ice that cocoons this thing, the image they got with the sonar,' Costas said. 'It's not just meltwater from a crevasse that filled up and froze. I think this boat was burning when it sank into the ice. The ice and snow falling on the timbers must have put the fire out pretty quickly, but not before the heat melted this cavity in the glacier.'

'Before we pull out I want to get some sense of the dimensions,' Jack said.

'The target point's eight metres ahead. That should give you what you need. Once there I'm turning straight back.'

Moments later Costas came to a halt again. The edge of a huge blackened timber had appeared on the left side of the tunnel, and he adjusted the course of the probe to avoid colliding with it. As they passed alongside they could see that it curved upwards, and was superbly carved with writhing animal forms and abstract interlinked shapes in a wide strip along the edge.

'Urnes style,' Jack said excitedly. 'Thank God Maria gave me a refresher course on Viking art last night. I'm certain this is Norwegian, a new style developed around the mid eleventh century.' He rolled over and looked up through the ice where the timber extended above them. 'It's the stem post. Take a look at that.'

Costas followed suit and aimed his headlamp through the ice at the top of the timber. He let out a low whistle through his regulator as he saw the carving at the top, a dark shape frozen in the ice at the limit of their visibility, a snarling head with flattened ears that protruded at least a metre in front of the curved prow of the ship.

'It must be Fenrir, the wolf-god,' Jack said in hushed tones, remembering Maria again. 'He seems to be the guardian of this place.'

As they flipped back over and progressed slowly forward, a fabulous image unfolded beneath them, as if they were floating over a full-scale diorama of a shipwreck in a museum exhibit. The image was stunningly clear, and on either side they could see for at least five metres until the ice became too blue. Some sections of timber were remarkably intact, others charred and crushed by the ice that must have fallen on to the hull before the meltwater froze up and protected it. Jack took photographs continuously with the digital camera integrated into his helmet, and murmured the technical descriptions as each new element of ship structure came into view.

'It's classic west Scandinavian construction, completely consistent with the eleventh century,' he said after a few minutes. 'More a deep-hulled, broad-beamed sailing vessel than the Hollywood image of a longship, but then you wouldn't have wanted an oared warship out here. They were fine for skimming the waves at high speed and landing raiding parties, but they had a low sheerline and swamped easily in heavy seas. You wanted a ship that could transport people and supplies across the north Atlantic, sometimes spending weeks at sea.'

'It's been repaired,' Costas said, staring through the ice. 'There's a section near the bow where planks have been replaced, where the carpentry looks different. Maybe they hit an iceberg. And look, there's an oar.'

'It's a steering oar, a side rudder,' Jack said, looking down at the perfectly preserved oar on the warped deck planking beneath them. 'The Vikings didn't have fixed rudders, so a broad oar was attached to the stern of the ship. It looks like this one was stowed inboard deliberately, near the bow, not the stern. This ship wasn't at sea when it went down. And there's more. Take a look at that. It's incredible.'

As they passed beyond the bow area they began to see shapes that were not timbers, but items which seemed to have been arranged in a pile leading up to a dark structure in the centre of the hull where the mast-step should have been. There were amorphous masses clearly identifiable as skins and furs as they went over them, and wooden platters and utensils placed alongside. Costas quickly adjusted the setting as the ice-borer narrowly missed the top of a large pottery jar that lay shattered over the middle of the furs.

'An amphora.' Jack picked up a rim sherd off the lid which had come out in the meltwater, and stowed it in his E-suit.

'An east Mediterranean wine amphora, of the Byzantine period. In Greenland. It's bizarre.'

'I guess they had to keep warm in those cold Arctic nights,' Costas said. 'Anyway, I thought the Vikings were beer-drinkers.'

'Some of them were pretty widely travelled, remember, and must have picked up peculiar foreign habits.' Jack's mind was racing, and he was beginning to think the unthinkable. 'I may be wrong, but I'm wondering . . .' At that moment another object appeared inside the tunnel meltwater beneath them, a long wooden shaft with its head still embedded in the ice. Costas stopped the waterjet to give the element time to melt more ice around the object, and Jack carefully drew it out and held it in the narrow space between them.

'Holy shit,' Costas said.

It was a huge, single-bitted battleaxe, hafted to a thick handle at least a metre and a half long. The head shone with gold and was embellished with ornate engravings on both sides.

'It's gilded,' Jack murmured, his voice hoarse with excitement. 'That's what preserved the iron from corrosion. Standard technique for making a weapon look like gold, but keeping it functional with the harder metal underneath.'

'I've got symbols on my side of the blade,' Costas said.

'So have I.' Jack turned his side flat so Costas could see. The surface was engraved with a large pendant shape that respected the lines of the axe head, a wide stem dropping to symmetrical extensions that filled the width of the metal above the blade. The outline form was simple but it was elaborately decorated inside, with swirling curvilinear designs and garish animal forms, most prominently the snarling head of a wolf at the apex of the shape. Jack pointed to a line of symbols just above the axe blade.

'Mjøllnir.'

'What?'

'The letters are Greek, but the name's Norse. The most potent symbol of the Vikings, the invincible weapon of their greatest god, their one hope of defeating evil at the Battle of Ragnarok. Mjøllnir, Thor's hammer.'

'What's the bird above it?'

Jack peered closer. 'I can't believe I'm seeing this. It's the double-headed eagle. One head signifies the old Rome, the other the new Rome, Constantinople. It's the imperial symbol of the Byzantine emperor.' He paused, then looked through his visor at Costas, his eyes lit in wonder. 'We've just found one of the most famous weapons in history, a battleaxe of the Varangian Guard.'

'That makes sense. Look at these.' Costas twisted the axe round so Jack could see the other side.

'Runes!' Jack's heart was racing, and he was sucking the oxygen hard from the rebreather. 'And not just any old runes. I'm not an expert, but I happen to know these like the back of my hand. They're identical to the ones in the church of Hagia Sofia in Constantinople. It's the signature of Halfdan, the Viking who inscribed his pagan symbols into the holiest cathedral of eastern Christendom some time in the eleventh century.'

'So we've found Halfdan's war axe.' Costas' voice was deadpan, but his expression was incredulous. 'In an iceberg off Greenland. This guy sure got around.'

'There's one final thing I need to check,' Jack said. 'There should be a simple mast-step and crossbeam in the centre of the hull, but instead it's some kind of rectangular structure. I've now got a pretty good idea what it is, but I need to see it with my own eyes. Then we're out of here.'

'Roger that.' Costas reactivated the waterjet and they began to move up and over the dark structure a few metres ahead of them. Jack held on to the axe for a moment, scarcely believing what they had found, and then fed it over his shoulder under the straps of his trimix cylinders, carefully pushing the shaft back until the gilded axe head was wedged safely away from his regulator manifold. He turned back and clasped both hands on the guide rail, watching closely as the edge of the rectangular structure appeared beneath them and they began to see what lay inside, a shadowy, sepulchral form that seemed completely different from everything that had gone before. At the foot of the structure Jack suddenly saw another fantastic pile of artefacts, a gilded conical helmet on top of a coat of gilded chain mail, and below them a folded scarlet cloth with gold embroidery, evidently a cloak. Just as they were about to pass over the middle of the structure, Costas flipped the control handle and the probe came to a halt.

'I'm getting a warning reading on the seismograph,' he said. 'Probably just a wobble in the machine, but I need to stop to make sure.'

Jack looked with sudden unease at the red light flashing at the bottom of the screen. He could sense nothing unusual, but the microfilaments trailing behind them seemed to flutter longer than usual after the waterjet had shut off.

'There's definitely something going on,' Costas said.

Just then there was a horrifying creaking noise, followed by a series of wrenching vibrations that set Jack's teeth on edge and sent an uncontrollable tremor through his body. The water began to vibrate, until all he could see of Costas and the ice probe was a shapeless blur.

'Holy Mother of God. We're…'

Costas' words were drowned out by a terrible shrieking noise, as if they were being assailed on all sides by demented banshees. Splinters of ice began to shear off the tunnel walls, rocketing through the water like shrapnel. One piece wedged itself in Jack's left thigh, slicing through the Kevlar exoskeleton like butter and embedding itself in his flesh. All he felt was numbness, and he watched in shock as the water filled with swirling tendrils of red. Then there was a grating lurch and the ice probe went dead, its entire fore end crushed beyond recognition by a seismic shift in the ice.

Everything went silent. Costas frantically tried to reactivate the probe, but to no avail. The space had become narrower, their bodies pressed against each other with hardly any scope for movement. Jack's torso was twisted on the bottom of the tunnel with his face mask hard against the ice above the mysterious rectangular structure embedded below them.

With the probe now dead, the only light came from their headlamps. With superhuman effort Jack managed to turn his head to peer back down the tunnel. What he saw confirmed his worst fear. The tunnel was completely cut off, sealed shut by some tectonic shift in the ice. The space they were in was only about a metre longer than their bodies, and was shrinking fast. Jack watched in horror as the water froze up around his feet. The icy brash that seemed to appear out of nowhere refracted his view into a kaleidoscope, with Costas fragmented into a thousand shapes and colours. Jack tried to move his hand towards his friend but there was already too much resistance. A terrible wave of certainty passed through him. They would be frozen into the ice before they were dead, a living nightmare of the worst kind.

'We're rolling!' Costas shouted. 'Switch to trimix!'

Jack had barely registered the movement, but it suddenly became huge, bigger than anything that had gone before, a gigantic lurching that pressed him hard into the brash against the tunnel wall. With all his strength he heaved his arm up through the solidifying slurry and reached for the valve under his helmet, feeling Costas' hand trying to do the same. With agonizing slowness he twisted it open while Costas shut off his rebreather, then Costas withdrew his hand and reached for his own valve. Seconds later the first bubbles of exhaust crackled through the brash, some pooling mid-water, trapped under the forming ice, and the rest erupting upwards to form a pocket of air against the ceiling of the tunnel. The pocket quickly enlarged as Costas began to breathe out, and Jack slowly rose into it as the berg rolled. The instant he broke surface the sheen of liquid on his mask froze, a mix of water and blood that gave his view a surreal tint. He was now almost completely immobile, unable to move his limbs, and with each breath the compression of ice against his chest made it harder to inhale. He knew he had only moments left. He strained to the right, but there was no way he could see Costas. The intercom indicator inside his helmet was dead, and all he could hear was the suck of his own breathing and a terrible tearing and grinding far away, the noise of titanic forces within the berg that had entombed them with no hope of escape.

As Jack began to black out, he glimpsed something on the ceiling of the air pocket, then realized it was a reflection of his own form on the ice. His breathing became shallower, quick and rasping, and he became light-headed, flitting in and out of consciousness as his body starved of oxygen. The form above him began to take on a wavering, surreal shape, as if it were something more than just a reflection. Through the blood-streaked sheen of his mask he saw a flowing red robe where there should have been an E-suit, and instead of a diving helmet there was a bearded face framed by long golden hair. The eyes were dark shadows, sunk beneath the grey pallor of the face, but they seemed to be boring into him. In his delirium Jack saw one arm extended, a blackened hand shining with gold, beckoning him closer. Jack had found what he had been searching for, the ancient warrior who had passed out of time inside this ship, a wraith of Valhalla come to take him in his embrace. He shut his eyes on the image as a mighty crack rent the ice, seeming to throw him far beyond the present into merciful oblivion.

brotherhood. As the three men began to descend, the damp rock seemed to exude an essence of the past, as if the porous limestone preserved within it the exhalations of their revered forebears, a commingling with the spirit world that seemed to draw them to the very gates of Valhalla itself.

At the bottom of the stairs they entered a circular chamber, their inner sanctum. At first they were overwhelmed by the aura, dazzled by a dozen burning torches evenly spaced on pedestals around the edge of the chamber, the flames sending wisps of black smoke curling to the vaulted dome above. Then they began to make out the surrounding wall, an arcade of twelve pillars cut from the rock with an encircling passageway beyond. On each pillar was a fearsome battleaxe, girded to the rock with twisted thongs, the blades radiating the light in flashes of gold. Above each axe hung the chain mail and conical helmet of an ancient warrior, the visors with their empty eyes flickering in and out of shadow as the torchlight leaped up the wall. On the floor in front of the pillars stood twelve identical chairs, their heavy oaken frames carved with swirling animal shapes and runic inscriptions, and in the centre of the chamber was a massive circular table, its timbers smoothed and blackened with age. Inlaid on the table was a twelve-spoked sun-wheel, continuing the symmetry of the room to a carved symbol obscured in shadow at the very apex of the design.

The three men passed silently inside and took their places behind chairs at different points around the table, clasping their hands in front of them and bowing their heads before sitting down. All of the chairs were now occupied except one, directly opposite the entrance, the pillar behind it lit up by a double torch and the axe glinting as if it had been freshly sharpened.

The hooded figure seated to the left of the empty chair stood up slowly and raised his right hand, revealing a deep scar that ran across his palm. He spoke in English, his voice gravelly and deep. 'Herr Professor. Your Excellency. Mr President. Welcome. The *félag* is nearly complete.'

He sat down and placed his left palm on the table. On his index finger was a luminous ring, a twisted band of gold with a signet, its surface impressed with a linear symbol similar to the runes on the chair behind him.

'For thirty generations now we have kept the fire of Thor burning for the return of our king,' he said. 'Now the forces that would destroy us again threaten the sanctity of the *félag*. We will unleash all the powers at our disposal to safeguard our treasure, to find our inheritance from the king of kings.' He gestured towards the empty seat beside him. 'But before the council begins we must complete our circle.'

A hooded figure emerged from the dark recess of the passageway behind the empty chair. In the flames of the double torch his robe seemed ablaze, glowing with the deep orange of a hearth. His hands were clasped in front of him and his face was concealed inside his hood.

'You have carried out your appointed task?'

'It has begun.'

'Come forward.'

The man stepped out beside the pillar until he was level with the axe, its shimmering blade only inches from his head. He raised his right hand to his face, pulling his hood back slightly to reveal his pallid skin and thin lips. A jagged white scar ran across his cheek from his eye socket to his chin.

'You are sworn to avenge your grandfather, our thole-companion who last occupied this chair,' the man at the table said. 'The blood-feud will not end until the last of our enemies are dead. You will seek to know what they know, and extinguish their knowledge with them. You will exact terrible vengeance. You will honour the *félag* and earn your place at this table.'

The man beside the pillar drew his finger hard down the scar on his cheek, wincing slightly. He bowed towards the table, and the shadow of a smile passed across his lips. The eleven others watched as he turned to the axe. He raised his right palm to the blade and drew it down sharply, pressing hard into the steel until his blood welled out. He reached his bleeding hand down into his robe and pulled out a golden ring, identical to the one worn by the man at the head of the table, then walked forward and sat down. The others raised their hands in unison, revealing identical rings and scarred palms.

A channel of fire suddenly ignited under the table, lighting up the symbol in the centre. Around it the flames shone through the embedded glass that made up the sun-wheel, an orange light that pulsed over the hooded figures to the wall beyond, illuminating the axe blades and the empty helmets in a flickering orange glow. They had been joined by the spirits of the departed *félag*, the sacred fellowship, warriors called from their eternal feasting in Valhalla once again to occupy their armour in readiness for battle.

The symbol was their tree of life. Seven-branched, it would light their way until the final showdown at the end of days, when they would at last wield battleaxes shoulder to shoulder with their king.

The twelve hooded figures all reached forward until their rings touched, the blood of the one anointing the others, dripping in rivulets down their sleeves and over the symbol in the centre of the table. When their fists were all touching the figure who had spoken first spoke again.

'*Hann til ragnarøks.*'

Jack seemed to be waking into his worst nightmare. He first realized he was conscious when he recognized the sound of his own breathing, a rasping, sucking noise followed by the rush of exhalation from his regulator exhaust. He gradually became aware of his body, the dull ache of the old gunshot wound in his side and a sharper pain in his leg. He seemed to have been in limbo for an eternity, hovering between a dream world and some kind of reality, but as he opened his eyes and saw the digital time display inside his visor he realized it had only been a few minutes. The view beyond seemed pure hallucination, a fragmented, kaleidoscopic pattern drawn in tendrils of red. He shut his eyes and instantly confronted another image, one etched on his mind that refused to go away. The wraith-like form of a man was laid out in front of him, as if Jack were floating above his own shrouded body entombed in the ice. The image receded from him as he seemed to float higher above it, bringing an overwhelming, narcotic sense of relief, but something within him was fighting desperately to pull back, as if the image of his own death was his only lifeline.

The rushing sound of his exhaust became a bubbling maelstrom and then a high-pitched hiss. Jack opened his eyes and saw a diagonal line running across the centre of his visor. He realized he was lying half in and half out of the water, and that the view he had seen a few moments before was his headlight refracting through a slurry of brash interspersed with his own blood. The lamp now shone above water and he could see a wall of ice only inches from his face. Cautiously he turned his head to the right, angling his lamp until he could see the length of his body. He was inside a cavity about the size of a small car, the upper part an air pocket created by his exhaust. Instead of the smooth surface of the tunnel created by the ice-borer, the walls were jagged and fractured, great slabs of ice that seemed to have compacted violently together. Some of the slabs were cloudy and others nearly transparent, creating the illusion that the chamber extended off in fissures and tunnels around the white ice.

For a fleeting moment Jack's mind wandered again and he

felt cocooned and safe, as if the chamber that had opened up and protected him from the crushing impact of the ice would be his ultimate salvation. Then reality kicked in and he felt a cold dread. Somehow the ice had cracked as the berg rolled and he had been given a reprieve, but it could only be temporary. As more water was displaced by his exhaust he could feel the slurry of brash around his lower body thicken, immobilizing his legs. To his horror he realized he was being frozen alive all over again, only this time there would be no quick end, but a long, lingering agony half in and half out of the air pocket, as his breathing gas gradually expended and he suffocated in his own exhaust.

A noise crackled around his head and jerked him back to life. The intercom whined and then settled to the sound of grunting and straining. It seemed unbelievable, little short of a miracle. 'Jack, can you hear me?'

'Costas.' Jack's voice sounded peculiar, oddly distant to his own ears, and then he remembered the trimix contained helium. 'Where the hell are you?'

'I can see you, but you can't see me. Try to turn over. You have to get yourself out of the water, otherwise we've had it for good this time.'

Costas' voice was a reassuring measure of reality, calm and collected despite the desperate situation. Jack marshalled all of his energy and heaved himself up on his elbows. He could swivel his torso slightly to the right and his arms were free, but his feet and lower legs were nearly frozen into the ice. It was like fighting against clinging mud, and each time he pulled he only seemed to embed himself further.

'It's no good,' he panted. 'I can barely move my legs.'

'Can you reach your cylinder pack?'

'Just.'

'Okay. Pull out that axe and lay it on the ledge beside your head.'

Jack did as he was instructed, laboriously extracting the wooden haft of the axe hand over hand from where he had slid it behind his cylinder straps. He could scarcely register what he was holding, a Varangian battleaxe from a Viking longship, a discovery that now seemed pure fantasy. By the time he had finished withdrawing the axe the surface of the slurry had frozen solid around his waist, and the moisture in his exhaust had caused a sheen of ice to form over his visor.

'I can't see any more,' he exclaimed, trying to remain rational and collected, to stave off panic. 'The pressure's going to build up in here now there's no more water to displace, and the moisture from my exhaust is freezing my upper body too. This could be over quicker than I thought.'

'Lie back and push the shaft of the axe as far as you can above your head. The ice-borer's embedded in the cavity, and I can see the filaments of the coil frozen in the ice below you. If we can reactivate the battery then we might be able to melt you out.'

Jack held the bit of the axe and pushed it as far as he could, along a shelf of ice that angled slightly upwards above the slurry. At first he felt no resistance, but at the limit of his reach the base of the haft hit something solid.

'Okay. That's it,' Costas said. 'Now try about six inches to your left.'

Jack strained again and prodded the haft along. Suddenly he felt something depress, and a green aura became visible through the ice on his visor.

'Good. You've done it. The main element of the corer was crushed when things went haywire back there, but the coil is operated from a separate battery pack that looks intact. All we have to do now is wait.'

'How are you doing?' Jack spoke as he slumped back, forcing himself to think beyond his surroundings.

'Just great. Trapped in the Ice Age. Follow Jack Howard and see the world.'

'Seriously. I can't see you.'

'At first I couldn't work it out. If the berg had flipped we'd be hundreds of metres deep, crushed to oblivion. Then I saw the ice probe and realized. We've rolled a full three hundred and sixty degrees and come back upright again. Whatever force was behind this thing made the berg somersault right over on the threshold. My guess is it's still stuck on the outer edge of the sill, but has slid down deeper than its original position. My depth gauge reads one hundred and twenty-three metres, just about the limit for our trimix gas. If the berg was floating out to sea it would have flipped again and we'd be way beyond that depth, gone for good. That could happen any time.'

'A reassuring thought.'

'Before we rolled. Did you see what I saw?'

'It was Halfdan. The guy whose runes are on the battleaxe. We were directly over the bier in the centre of the longship, where his body was meant to be burned. We must be the only people alive to have seen a Viking warrior in the flesh. Fantastic.'

'Yeah, fantastic. It spooked me. Let's hope we're not joining him.'

'Got any plans?'

'Let's do this step by step. The first thing is to get thawed out.'

In the lull that followed, Jack noticed the utter stillness of the berg, broken only by the noise of their breathing, in contrast to the deafening cacophony of a few minutes before as the ice sundered and cracked. Somehow the stillness accentuated the sepulchral quality of the chamber, and brought home the full enormity of their situation. They were trapped deep inside an iceberg, hemmed in by a million tons of rock-hard ice, at the limit of their survivable depth and with every prospect of a fatal tumble into the abyss. Jack began to feel unnerved, and as he stared at the ice only inches from his head he began to feel the old claustrophobia nagging at the edges of his consciousness. Lurking beneath the surface was a fear that he would be gripped by panic, as had so nearly happened when Costas had kept him going in the tunnels of Atlantis six months before. He knew Costas' banter had kept his mind focused, that his friend knew him too well, and he forced himself to concentrate on little things, on the small steps that might eventually lead to their salvation.

'I've got movement,' Jack said. 'I can move my feet.'

'Excellent. Try to swivel round in my direction.'

The sheen of ice on Jack's visor was beginning to drip away, and he could now see the slurry more clearly. The coil of microfilaments from the probe was doing its work, and the surface was beginning to liquefy. He arched his back and flexed his legs, causing a stab of pain and a sudden spasm of shivering. For the first time he inspected the injury in his left thigh, the embedded spear of ice just visible through the rent in his E-suit. The ice had numbed most of the pain and staunched the bleeding, but even so the blood loss had left him dangerously vulnerable to the cold. He heaved himself sideways, pulling his legs out of the water and hauling himself as far as he could go up the shelf, then wiped his visor and looked into the jagged wall of ice that had lain behind him.

The sight that confronted him was surreal. He could see Costas, yet it was an image that defied sense. He seemed to be lying within easy reach, yet was separated by a wall of transparent ice. With each tiny movement Costas seemed to fragment into a myriad shapes, refracted through numerous planes in the ice. Jack suddenly caught sight of Costas' face, the yellow helmet at first appearing grotesquely elongated but then compressing to some semblance of normality.

'I'm about a metre from you,' Costas said. 'When I recovered consciousness I was floating in a fissure. I tried to reach you, but this is how far I got. I'm as near as I can get to being frozen without actually being solid. It's all meltwater ice, from that crevasse above the longship. It should be easier to hack through than glacier ice. How are you with an axe?'

Jack suddenly saw a ray of hope. 'You know, it's my main occupation during the off-season when I disappear into the woods. When I tell everyone I'm writing. It makes me forget all this.'

'Good enough. Let's see what you can do. If you can break through, then the water from your side should get in and do the trick. The coil won't melt glacial ice, but it should keep this slush liquid. There's about a six-inch air pocket around me from my exhaust.'

'Where does the rest go?'

'Fissures and cracks above me. This ice may look solid, but it's really a mass of fallen slabs.'

Jack rolled over until he was lying face-down on the shelf. With his left hand he gripped the ledge to prevent himself from slipping into the slurry, and with his right hand he reached up and grasped the axe. He let himself go, sliding into the brash until he was kneeling on the bottom with the surface at waist level. He wrestled to remove his fins, drawing them up on their retaining straps behind his calves, then pulled the axe down with both hands and swivelled it so the bit was above him. Standing in the slurry, his tall frame bent low under the ceiling, he would have just enough room to wield the axe in short spans, though each heft would require extra effort as he struggled to maintain balance and momentum.

'Here goes.' He placed the axe blade on the ice just above

water level in front of Costas' face and took a short swing. The blade was dull but the metal still had the strength of a thousand years ago, and it was the force of impact rather than the cutting edge that mattered. As the bit struck it broke off a shard of ice and sent tiny fracture marks in a web from the point of impact, reducing his view of Costas to a meaningless mosaic. 'I can just do it,' Jack panted. 'Six inches less space and I wouldn't have the momentum.'

Slowly, deliberately, he began to hack at the ice, each blow striking off another shard, and each swing sending a jolt of pain through his leg. With the additional strain of holding up the weight of his cylinder pack above water, the exertion soon started to tell, and he began to breathe his trimix at an alarming rate. He tried to ignore the digital readout inside his visor and focus on the task at hand. He was deploying a standard woodsman's technique, cutting a wedge above and below his baseline. As each wedge deepened he struck off larger chunks from the space between, extending the hole until it was only inches from Costas and almost wide enough for him to get through.

As he lined up for the critical blow his legs suddenly buckled under him and he slipped back into the slurry, dropping the axe. He realized that he had not simply lost balance, that he had been toppled by some greater force. He righted himself and saw the surface of the water shaking violently, and heard distant groans and cracks. Suddenly the water began to rise, and Jack saw a dark fissure opening in the ceiling of the chamber.

'The air pocket's going,' he exclaimed. 'It's escaping upwards.' He heaved the axe out of the slurry and flung it against the cut one more time, but to no avail. 'The hole's already under water. I can't get any momentum.'

He slid back against the back wall of the chamber, the axe draped from his hand, and watched helplessly as the water level rose above his visor and reached the ceiling. Less than a minute after the crack had appeared, all that was left was the tumult of bubbles cascading upwards from his own exhaust, and that quickly dissipated through the crack after each exhalation. The temperature readout on his visor had dropped to minus two degrees, below the freezing point of the water. He realized with sickening certainty that the coil would never cope with the quantity of water now filling the chamber, that only the lower portion around the filaments would remain liquid.

The brash began to form in front of his eyes. He felt the water stiffen around his arms and head. It was happening again, a hellish torment he was fated to endure repeatedly, a nightmare relived. He stared wide-eyed as the ice began to encapsulate him. He began hyperventilating, as if his body was willing him to suck away his last reserve of trimix and lapse into blackness, a merciful oblivion in the face of the lingering horror that lay ahead of him.

'Your oxygen! Cut your oxygen hose!'

The voice snapped him back into reality. He instantly realized what Costas meant. He dragged his left arm through the slurry and pulled out the knife he kept in a sheath on his chest, bringing the serrated edge up against the two hoses under his helmet. For an appalling moment he forgot which was trimix and which was oxygen, the narcotic effect of nitrogen at this pressure playing tricks on his mind. His head was nearly immobile and he was unable to see down to the hoses. He shut his eyes and resolutely grasped the left hose, bringing the blade to bear just under the point where it fed into his helmet.

'What's left in your oxygen cylinder should fill the chamber long enough to clear the hole for another couple of blows,' Costas said. 'But for God's sake don't breathe it. Eighty per cent oxygen at this depth would mean instant death.'

Jack slashed the hose and a huge geyser of bubbles erupted into the chamber. The water rapidly lowered to chest level and he heaved himself up again, the severed hose dancing and hissing in front of him. He pulled the axe out of the brash and aimed it at the hole. With all his strength he swung against the ice, causing a large chunk to break free. He could see Costas pushing with all his might against the remaining barrier. Jack frantically pulled the floating chunk of ice aside and aimed another blow. Just then the hissing of his oxygen hose faltered, and the water level began to rise again, inexorably. He had one last chance. He lined up above the fracture line where the chunk had broken off, then relaxed completely with his eyes glued on the point of impact. He swung the axe back and brought it forward with all his might, causing a spray of brash as the blade skimmed over the rising water and slammed into the ice. Then he slumped back and began to pant uncontrollably, sending geysers of bubbles out of his exhaust as the water rose and submerged him again.

The corner of a fin appeared out of the ice. Jack felt a nudge against his body, and there was a commotion on the surface. *It had worked.* Another chuck of ice floated past, and a large black form emerged beside him like an inquisitive seal. Costas' eyes looked into Jack's. 'Am I glad to see you.'

'Thank God you lost weight,' Jack said weakly. 'I didn't book a double room.'

A spurt of red filled the water between them as Jack shifted in the confined space. 'How's the leg?' Costas asked.

'That's the least of my worries.' Jack peered at the water level above them 'Your oxygen,' he said urgently. 'Cut your hose and we'll have a few more minutes.'

'No good,' Costas said. 'My hose blew when the berg rolled. The shard of ice that cut it nearly decapitated me.' He struggled around until he was lying parallel to Jack, both of their heads now facing the ledge where the ice probe was embedded. The narrow confines of the chamber became even more apparent, barely large enough for the two of them festooned with all of their equipment. They were now completely submerged, slivers of ice from Jack's efforts floating around them, and Jack could see the filaments from the coil tangled below. Costas leaned down to pull his fins up his calves and then hauled himself behind the probe. 'It's flashing amber,' he said. 'The battery's nearly dead. If we stick around here we'll be on ice. Permanently.' He slid back down and struggled to remove something from the thigh pocket of his E-suit. 'Here, hold on to this for me.' Jack took it, then stared back at Costas.

'C-4 explosive?'

'You got it. Always carry some in case of emergency.'

'You're going to blow us up?'

'Beats the deep freeze.' Costas continued to delve in his pocket, then pulled out a miniature detonator transceiver. 'I'm certain we're inside the crevasse where Kangia and those Nazis saw the longship. The clear ice is meltwater that sealed up the crevasse. It's weaker than the surrounding glacier ice, and fragmented when the berg shifted. We might be able to widen the crack. It's the only chance we've got.'

'What's our decompression status?'

'Not good. Our depth seems to be dropping. There must be an internal water level in the crevasse above us, below the level of the sea surrounding the berg. Somehow it's filling up. At this rate we'll be in the danger zone in less than five minutes.'

'That's about how much trimix I've got left.'

'If we don't freeze up first. With the coil dead the water's already beginning to thicken. Time to get this show on the road.'

Jack suddenly shivered violently. The water was as cold as he had ever known, colder even than the deepest ocean depths. There was another ominous creak in the ice, and the crack above them closed in perceptibly. Costas rolled over and looked up, panning his headlamp along the silvery shimmer of exhaust bubbles that lined the ceiling. 'That's not what I wanted to happen,' he said quietly. A brief high-pitched alarm sounded from the probe, and the amber light went dead. 'Nor was that.' He rolled back and picked up the axe from the floor of the chamber, feeding it towards Jack. 'You've got a longer reach than me. The crack's widest above the probe. I need you to push the C-4 as high up as you can. It's already armed.'

Jack held the brown packet in one hand and the haft of the axe in the other. Costas sank behind him and heaved up against his legs, forcing another pulse of blood from Jack's thigh. Jack tried to ignore the pain and twisted his upper body so that his visor was up against the crack above the probe. With the rush of bubbles escaping through it he could only get a fleeting sense of its dimensions, but it was clearly a narrow chimney that extended high above them, a crack between the slabs of ice. He pushed the C-4 as far up as he could with his left arm, wedging it in the chimney. Then he pulled the axe up hand over hand and fed the wooden haft into the chimney, with Costas preventing him from sliding back. When he felt the haft meet resistance, he pushed up hard, dislodging the C-4 and thrusting it as high as he could into the chimney.

'Okay. That's as far as I can go.'

Jack sank down beside Costas, and the two of them struggled against the freezing brash until they were as far away from the ice chimney as they could get, pressed against each other in the opposite corner of the chamber. Jack everted the axe and fed it back under his straps, and both men reached down to slide their fins into place. Jack wrapped his arms tight around Costas, their faces pressed visor to visor. 'Wherever we're going this time, we're going together.'

'*Semper fidelis.*'

Jack shook his head. 'You never cease to amaze me. Latin too.'

Costas held up the transceiver between them.

'Good to go?'

'Good to go.'

A violent tremor shook them, accompanied by a shrieking and tearing sound that set Jack's teeth on edge. All around them the ice was lost in a blur of vibration. The cacophony was rent by a deafening explosion and Jack felt his body pummelled as if by a thousand punches. He pressed his visor tight against Costas, protecting the vulnerable glass from the shards of ice that were flying around them. Almost simultaneously their headlamps burst and they were plunged into a bizarre, tremulous darkness, broken only by the blurry green of the digital readouts inside their helmets. Something huge heaved against Jack's side and for an instant he felt he was about to be crushed, and then by a miracle it passed. He felt a rush of dizziness and realized they were tumbling, spinning round and round in a ferment of ice and water, utterly helpless as the crevasse rent asunder.

'We're getting shallower!' Costas yelled. 'For God's sake

don't hold your breath. Your lungs would blow in seconds.'

Jack's breathing began to tighten. In the swirling maelstrom there were no waymarkers, no visual points of reference. He forced himself to concentrate on the digital readout inside his visor, his arms clinging tight to Costas and their legs intertwined. Jack could just make out a depth reading of ten metres, and they were rocketing upwards. The figures gave him something to grasp on to, and he was dimly aware that the danger of air embolism was compounded by the risk of the bends, of decompression sickness. They were coming up way too fast.

Suddenly they were on the surface. It was light again, a steely, crepuscular light, and Jack could see beyond Costas to an awesome world of blue. They were floating in a vast cauldron of ice, at least the length and breadth of *Seaquest II*, with sheer white walls rising all around them. Jack felt dwarfed by the enormity of it. He arched his neck and looked at the source of light far above. It was a thin sliver of grey where the ice walls nearly joined, a first link to the world outside. The grey was streaked with black and light blue, and seemed to be rushing past at enormous speed.

'It must be one of those freak storms coming off the icecap,' Costas said. 'That's what pushed the berg.'

'A *piteraq*.'

They clung to each other as they bobbed around in the centre of the pool. Their decompression warning lights were flashing amber, indicating that they had pushed the envelope and were now in grave danger of the bends. Jack felt for any signs, a tingle in an elbow or a sudden surge of nausea, aware that the last six months away from diving might have reduced his resistance. He checked his trimix pressure gauge and saw the dial hovering at zero. 'I'm out of air,' he said. 'If there's any more diving we'll have to buddy-breathe.'

'Hook into me.'

Jack pulled the umbilical hose from the top of Costas' cylinder pack, and pressed the valve into an inlet under his helmet. With a sharp hiss his helmet filled up again with breathing gas, its makeup now close to atmospheric air as the computer adjusted the ratios to take account of their depth. Jack realized he had been running on empty, and he closed his eyes to concentrate on taking a few deep breaths.

'That should give us about ten minutes,' Costas said. 'I'd prefer to spend it ten metres deep to increase the decompression margin, but we don't have that luxury. We'll just have to wing it.'

The movement in the water had died down dramatically, leaving the surface preternaturally calm after the tumult that had ejected them from their icy tomb far below. 'The crevasse must have opened up when the berg moved, shattering all the meltwater ice inside it,' Costas said. 'Then the walls closed in again as the berg encountered resistance, probably the seaward edge of the threshold.' He looked around again, the scene now eerily still. 'I've got a bad feeling about this. Let's keep together.'

As if on cue, the silence was rent by a shattering concussion, and ice and water disintegrated in another shuddering blur. Jack became aware of a curtain of ice falling around them, jagged spears that sliced into the water like shrapnel. He concentrated all of his energy on holding Costas tight, knowing that if the hose that was his sole remaining lifeline were to rip out he would drown. He flashed back to the body in the ice, to his hallucination, then woke to a worse reality. They were dropping with sickening speed, sliding down a whirlpool of grinding ice, as if they were being sucked back to the frozen warrior and the place that had nearly been their nemesis. The water was falling away so fast that they were dropping through air, suspended half in and half out of the water, tumbling weightlessly against the chunks of ice that were splintering around them. Costas pulled Jack closer, straining against the centripetal force of the whirlpool, and pressed his visor hard against Jack's. 'The water's being sucked down as the crevasse opens,' he yelled. 'Hold on tight. I might be able to reverse the flow.'

Suddenly the water billowed up around them and they were immersed deep within it. For a terrifying moment Jack felt the air crushed out of his lungs by some force that was working against the vortex, propelling them back upwards. Then they erupted out of the water, bouncing on a plume of brash that threw them high into the cleft above the cauldron. They crashed into a wall of ice and slid upwards, each scrabbling desperately with one free hand for some kind of hold. Then they began to slide back downwards, out of control, until they hit a ledge that held them precariously on the wall. As they crouched dripping together on the icy platform, the plume of brash and spray dropped back into the seething cauldron at the base of the crevasse far below them.

'What the hell was that?' Jack panted, peering down a sheer drop of at least thirty metres.

'The C-4,' Costas said exuberantly. 'We were ejected from that chamber before I had a chance to blow it, but it came in useful after all.' He shoved the detonator transceiver into his thigh pocket. 'Right. I'm cold and hungry. Let's get out of here.'

'Better make it fast. Take a look at that.'

They peered down in horrified fascination at the ice chasm far below. It was beginning to narrow again, the walls compressing the slurry of ice and pushing it upwards. As the larger chunks were caught in the vice they exploded with a shattering resonance, sending lethal shards far up the crevasse. They knew that being caught in the maelstrom this time would mean instant death, their bodies shredded by the flying ice and then crushed as the crevasse caught them like a meat-grinder. Relentlessly, terrifyingly, the narrowing gap was closing in on them, advancing like some living thing, its deadly maw spewing a geyser of splintering and shattering ice, moving with alarming speed up the cleft even in the few moments they had been watching.

'This is it,' Costas yelled above the din. 'No second chance this time.' They swivelled on the ledge and faced upwards. The skylight at the top of the crevasse was about fifty metres away, the rushing streaks of grey now clearly visible on a background of blue. Suddenly the cloud parted and a dark shape appeared, blotting out the cleft, a blinding spotlight aimed directly at them. Then it veered away violently, trailing something that streamed out behind and whipped over the crack.

'It's the Lynx,' Costas shouted excitedly. 'They're trying to drop a winch.'

'I told them to stay away. They're pushing their luck against that wind.'

'They could hardly do nothing.'

'There's no way they'll get that cable down here. They must be waiting, hoping we can get to the entrance of the crevasse.'

Jack glanced down. The gap was now terrifyingly close, no more than twenty metres below them, the shards of exploding ice almost reaching the ledge. He looked up again. The crevasse was glassy smooth, offering no handholds. The euphoria at seeing the helicopter suddenly turned to cold dread. It was another nightmare, a return to his brush with death years before in the flooded mineshaft, where the end of the tunnel had been in sight but no matter how frantically he tried to swim for it he seemed to stay the same distance away.

Jack suddenly felt as if he were being pressed into the wall. He looked up again, then it dawned on him. 'The crevasse. Isn't it supposed to be vertical?'

'Holy shit. The berg's rolling!'

There was a huge lurch and everything went still. The cleft had seized up, no more than ten metres below them. Through the skylight they were looking directly at the promontory where they had visited the old Inuit the day before. Jack found himself thinking that it was going to be a perfect day, that the wind was leaving the land washed in sparkling light. Then he felt the dread again. They had to reach the crack or they would die. When the berg rolled again the skylight would drop underwater, taking them into the abyss as it toppled off the threshold, sealing their fates in an instant.

'The axe!' Costas shook him. 'The axe!'

Jack snapped back into reality. With his left arm still around Costas, he reached back and drew the axe from its straps. His hand was sticky with blood where it had brushed his thigh and the axe nearly slipped away, saved only by Costas' iron grip. They dangled the axe together down the slope, then flung it in a wide arc into the ice ahead of them.

'It'll hold,' Jack panted. 'Pull yourself up.' He tensed his body, his fins still planted on the ledge but his elbows and knees ready to find any undulation in the ice, anything that might stop him from sliding. They heaved up on the haft, then shook it frantically until it was loose. For a few seconds they would be totally without anchor, held only by the tension of their bodies against the ice. Costas looked Jack full in the eyes and nodded. Jack let the axe slide down again and heaved. It arched overhead, skimming the back of the crevasse, then slammed into the ice a metre and a half ahead of them. As Jack craned his head up to free the axe for another blow, he saw a black-clad diver dangling from a cable no more than a hundred metres beyond the berg, and realized that the noise he was hearing was the din from the Lynx's twin turboshafts.

There was another lurch, and a rumble from the cleft behind them. The noise of the helicopter was drowned out by an immense creaking in the ice. The walls of the crevasse narrowed. The axe was poised but there was no more room to swing it. Another lurch brought up a surge of brash from the cleft, washing over them, then everything happened at once. The skylight was lost in a ferment of water, a sucking whirlpool that rose up towards them, and suddenly they were sliding uncontrollably, plummeting towards the skylight as it angled into the abyss. Jack hit the incoming seawater with an immense crash, the axe still trailing behind him, then was pulverized by the force of the water cascading down from the maw of the crevasse. The icy brash that had so nearly been their nemesis pushed them out of the berg, ejecting them in a frenzied tumble just as the walls of ice crushed together and sealed the crevasse for the last time.

It was not over yet. Jack saw a vast wall of sculpted white advancing on them, extending as far as he could see in every direction. Already the crevasse was far below, marked only by a trickle of bubbles rising up the side of the berg, framing the black immensity of the abyss. As the berg rolled, Jack had the illusion that he was rocketing upwards, yet his body told him exactly the opposite. 'It's pulling us down,' Costas yelled, his voice contorted. 'Inflate your suit and swim for it!'

Jack pressed the inflator and began to fin hard, his left arm gripping Costas' shoulder. His depth readout showed they were hardly moving at all. They were still in the grip of the berg, being sucked down. He looked up and saw the sun shimmering off the waves, tantalizingly close. He felt the cold again in the pit of his stomach. Having survived the iceberg, they were about to die within sight of the surface. *This could not be happening.* He began to hyperventilate, to outstrip the oxygen remaining in Costas' cylinder. His breathing began to tighten.

'I'm ditching your tanks.' Costas was breathing heavily, a great plume of bubbles encircling his exhaust, and he finned furiously as he disconnected Jack's redundant hoses and flipped the quick-release buckle on his cylinder packs, sending the oxygen rebreather and the console backpack with its empty trimix cylinders plummeting into the depths. 'I'm doing the same to mine,' he panted. 'We've only got about a minute's air left anyway and it isn't doing us any good. Get ready to disconnect your hose. Stop finning now and when I say so take five deep breaths.'

'I'm holding on to you,' Jack said, his breath coming in short gasps. 'If you go down, I'm going with you.'

Costas disconnected his rebreather and it dropped out of sight. With his left hand he flipped the quick-release on his backpack and held it in place, and with his right hand he found the disconnect to the hose under his helmet. Already they were plummeting down, sucked deeper and deeper by the rolling iceberg, their chances receding with every metre they dropped into the abyss.

'Now!' Jack took five deep breaths, then yanked the umbilical. Simultaneously Costas released his hose and backpack. With Jack's left arm on Costas' shoulder, they began to swim determinedly upwards, taking wide, hard strokes with their fins, Jack still clutching the axe in his right hand. For a few moments he felt fine, his bloodstream brimming with oxygen, remembering to breathe out as he ascended. Then the toil of their escape began to tell, and he felt the first niggle of discomfort. They were rising steadily, a metre every couple of seconds, but they were still more than twenty metres from the surface. Any let-up in their finning and they would be dragged back down again. Jack started to suck on empty, his lungs instinctively heaving for more air, drawing every last dreg out of his helmet.

His legs began to falter, starved of oxygen. He was beginning to black out, overwhelmed by exhaustion. He was not going to make it. He stopped clawing his way upwards, and in a last conscious act struggled to free himself from Costas' grip, seeing his friend still going strong, desperate to give him some chance of reaching the surface alive.

Suddenly he felt an odd sensation, a jolting weightlessness. He had stopped finning but was still being impelled upwards. He was dimly aware that the berg had stopped moving. By instinct he found the dump valve to release air from his suit and stop him from rocketing upwards. Then he was on the surface, blinded by the light. He unlocked his helmet and ripped it off, gasping over and over again in the cold fresh air, his entire being focused on replenishing his life force. As soon as he could, he swivelled round and scanned the waves, shielding his eyes against the glare. After a few anxious seconds he caught sight of a tousled head bobbing in the waves about ten feet away.

'You okay?' he gasped.

'Well, at least that little swim solved our decompression issue.' Costas' voice sounded strange after the intercom, adenoidal with the cold. He was facing away from Jack, seemingly oblivious to their surroundings, completely focused on two gauges that he was holding out of the water. 'But there's a small discrepancy in the readouts. It's incredibly annoying. I need to do a little tinkering.'

Jack managed a small smile. He leaned his head far back, letting the sunshine play on his face. He could hear the helicopter descending above him, and heard the splash as the rescue diver dropped into the sea. He cracked open one eye and saw the glinting golden blade in the waves beside him, the prize he had refused to let go. Suddenly their extraordinary discovery in the berg came flooding back, and a burst of adrenalin rushed through him. He shut his eyes, his mind now coursing with excitement. A wave washed over him, a cleansing jolt of cold that left lines of salt water trickling over his lips. It tasted good.

11

'That's some ice axe you've got there.'

'Wait till you hear what else we found.'

James Macleod had just finished applying a compress to the gash in Jack's leg. His E-suit was slick with fresh blood, but the compress staunched the bleeding. Jack leaned back against the bulkhead, his face streaked with fatigue, and adjusted his flight helmet and headset. Between talking he was breathing deeply on the oxygen regulator that had been passed to him as soon as he had been winched into the cargo bay of the Lynx.

'You don't want to hear the odds Lanowski calculated against your survival.'

'No, I don't.' Jack was utterly exhausted, but felt he had to keep talking to tell them what had happened.

'When the *piteraq* hit we were completely shut down. Inuva told us they could be bad, but I had no idea what we were up against. Couldn't even get the chopper out of the hangar. It was terrifying, like banshees screaming above us.'

'We saw it from the crevasse.'

'When the berg rolled, all hell let loose. The displacement wave washed right up the shore and swept away the tent where we met Kangia. The local shaman was still there. As soon as we get you back on board *Seaquest II* the chopper's out on a search, but it's pretty hopeless.'

'Inuva?' Jack said.

'She's okay. She was with Lanowski.'

Macleod broke off to help the crewman acting as loadmaster to haul another dripping form through the open cargo door. Seconds later Costas was strapped into the seat beside Jack, pulling on his flight helmet and sucking gratefully at the oxygen regulator that had been handed to him.

'You okay?' Jack said.

Costas sucked a few more times and then lowered the regulator, giving Jack a doleful look.

'Oh. Let me guess.' Jack looked back with exaggerated sympathy. 'Your ice probe.'

'Months of research and development,' Costas said sadly. 'And that was the only prototype. I'll have to build the next one entirely from scratch.'

'No hurry as far as I'm concerned,' Jack said. 'I think I've just ticked diving inside icebergs off my list.' He turned back to Macleod. 'What was your contingency plan?'

'When we saw the berg had rolled three hundred and sixty degrees, we thought there was a chance. Lanoswki remembered the old crevasse above the longship. It was all his idea, modelling the likely rupture line, even calculating the explosive charge we'd need to blow it open.'

'You've got to hand it to the guy,' Costas murmured.

'So that's what Ben was doing,' Jack said.

Macleod nodded. 'Ben volunteered to take the charge down. He tried half a dozen times, but he couldn't get close enough to the crack. The wind was buffeting us and we had to fight to keep the chopper on station. Then he saw you inside the crevasse. He was trying to feed the cable in when the berg began to roll again.'

'You guys are heroes,' Costas said.

Macleod shook his head and smiled. 'We're just the shuttle service. I don't know how you did it.'

At that moment the loadmaster hauled a third figure through the door, and secured the winch hook to its davit. Ben ripped off his face mask and looked anxiously at Jack and Costas. He gave them a diver's okay sign, and they responded in kind.

'Okay, Andy.' Macleod slapped the bulkhead behind the pilot's seat. 'We need to get out of here before that thing finishes its roll. We're good to go.'

'Roger that.'

The others strapped themselves into the seats at the rear of the cargo bay. As the helicopter pitched forward and shuddered up to full power Costas jerked his hand to the axe lying across Jack's legs. 'By the way, thanks for saving me from the deep freeze.'

'I owed you. I seem to remember a little help a while ago inside a volcano.'

Costas looked warmly at his friend and nodded, his face suddenly lined with fatigue. Jack slumped back against the seat and breathed deeply from the regulator, feeling reinvigorated with every breath, knowing that the oxygen was cleansing his system of excess nitrogen. To his right he could see the immense form of the berg, seemingly as solid as a mountain, and to his left the sparkling shape of *Seaquest II*, far out in the bay. He was swept by the feeling of elation he had experienced on surfacing. For months since their return from the Black Sea he had been nagged by a secret uncertainty, that the prize no longer justified the risk, that he had lost the edge. Now he knew he was back where he belonged. He shut his eyes and was instantly in a deep and dreamless sleep.

'My apologies,' Lanowski said. 'I didn't count on a storm.'

'You gave us every warning,' Jack replied. 'It was my call.'

Jack and Costas were sitting on the foredeck of *Seaquest II*, slumped against the port railing where the helicopter had unceremoniously winched them down with Macleod a few minutes before. The ship was maintaining position in Disko

Bay about a mile west of the fjord entrance, and Jack could see the tip of the iceberg beyond the starboard railing opposite them. Even at this distance it was an awesome sight, and they had been reminded of its stupendous power from the helicopter when a massive slab of ice had calved off into the bay, sending another tidal wave sweeping up on to the shoreline where they had landed the day before to visit the old Inuit. They had been extraordinarily lucky that the berg had rolled a full three hundred and sixty degrees, that the huge force of the storm had tumbled it back to its upright position and left it perched precariously on the outer rim of the threshold. The next time it rolled it would flip over and stay that way, crushing any remaining air pockets to oblivion beneath hundreds of metres of freezing seawater.

Lanowski had been the first of the scientific team to reach them on the foredeck, joining the crew members who had guided down the helicopter winch and were now helping Jack and Costas to peel off their E-suits. They were quickly joined by Maria, whose look of relief turned to concern as she saw the blood on Jack's thigh. The ship's doctor was already on the scene, cutting away the bandage and spraying coagulant into the gash.

'It's not as bad as it looks.' Jack winced as the medic applied a suture, then held up a bloody spear of ice. 'Nature provided her own cold compress.'

'You were lucky,' the medic said. 'It just missed the femoral artery.'

'It's fantastic.' Lanowski was shaking his head and chuckling to himself, in a world of his own. 'While you were away Inuva and I worked out where the 1930s expedition must have found the ship in the icecap. Now I should be able to use my glacier-flow quotient to work out where the Vikings dragged the ship on to the ice for the funeral pyre. One of the tributary fjords to the north of Ilulissat, I'd say, where the icecap is more accessible from the sea.' He pushed his glasses up his nose and peered at Jack. 'Having such a closely datable horizon inside that berg is the greatest discovery of the whole expedition. It should provide independent corroboration for my flow theory, the first time we'll be sure of the rate of ice discharge over the last thousand years. Well worth your efforts. Congratulations!'

'We've just found a Viking longship, man,' Costas said in exasperation. 'One of the most sensational archaeological discoveries of all time. A little more exciting than the rate of glacial ice flow.'

Lanowski looked at him with unseeing eyes, his mind already far away in a world of figures and equations. He pulled out a pocket calculator and began furiously tapping at the keys, occasionally looking up and muttering under his breath. Costas shook his head in disbelief as the ungainly figure shuffled off without another word towards the deckhouse computer room.

'Talk about a one-track mind.'

'But a brilliant one.' Jack grinned across at the dripping

form of his friend. 'That's why we're a team. I couldn't do all that math.'

Jeremy appeared beside Maria, and she nudged him forward in front of Jack.

'We've translated the runestone that Kangia gave you, the one the Germans found in the crevasse,' he said diffidently.

'Brilliant. Let's hear what you've got.'

'It's west Norse, eleventh century, quite distinct from the runes used in England and Denmark at that time.'

'And?'

'His name was Halfdan.'

'We know. A veteran of the Varangian Guard in Constantinople.' Jack raised the object that had been resting on his knees, and Jeremy suddenly recognized it for what it was. He stared agape as Jack pointed to the runic inscription on the axe blade.

'Holy shit.' Jeremy suddenly forgot his restraint. 'They're identical to the Halfdan runes at Hagia Sofia in Istanbul.'

'He's our man.'

'Tall guy, early middle age, long yellow hair and beard,' Costas interjected. 'A little weatherworn and charred at the edges, but otherwise in pretty good shape for a guy who hasn't moved for a thousand years. We've just met him, halfway to Valhalla.'

'Huh?'

Costas jerked his thumb towards the entrance of the fjord. 'Inside the berg. He's on ice. We were over the central burial chamber when it rolled. The funeral pyre must have been extinguished when the ship fell into the ice, and the flames only licked at the edges. My guess is that runestone was resting on his body.'

A crewman pushed past the others and handed Jack a piece of paper. He quickly read it and then stared into the distance, a smile flickering across his face. 'I knew it!'

'What?' Costas said.

'A hunch I had before our dive. A pretty wild hunch, so I didn't share it. You remember the dendro date for the ship timbers, 1040 plus or minus a few years? For some reason all I could think about was Harald Hardrada's escape from Constantinople. If the sagas are correct, it took place very close to that median date, in 1042.'

'And?'

'I asked the IMU lab to run a comparison between the timber fragments we got from the chain in Constantinople and the wood Macleod's ice-corer brought up from the longship. The full checklist, species identification, tree-ring characteristics, fibre and cellulose specs.'

'Go on.'

'It's not just the same species, Norwegian oak,' Jack said excitedly. 'It's incredible. It's actually from the same tree. Planks cut radially from the same trunk.'

'Whoa. Steady on there.' Costas held one hand in front of him, trying to marshal his thoughts. 'Let me get this straight. You're suggesting that one of the ships Harald Hardrada used to escape from Constantinople with the princess and the treasure is the same ship we've just seen trapped in an iceberg off Greenland?'

Jack gave his friend an odd look and then started to nod.

'Of course.' Costas suddenly snapped his fingers and stared back at Jack. 'The repair work on the hull.' He looked up at the others. 'We found a section of planking which had been expertly replaced near the bow. It's in the photographs. I assumed it was collision damage with ice or rock, but it's exactly where the ship might have driven up against the chain across the harbour when they fled Constantinople.' He shook his head in disbelief and turned to Jack. 'So if this is one of Harald's ships, where's the treasure?'

'They're not exactly going to have put it in a funeral pyre,' Jack said. 'And we don't know the date when this happened. The Halfdan we saw was an older man, and he could have sailed here years after their Constantinople adventure, maybe seeking a new life for himself in the Greenland settlement. By then Harald would have been king of Norway and the treasure of his Varangian days secure in his stronghold at Trondheim.'

There was a percussive boom from the direction of the fjord, followed by an immense falling sound that reverberated across the still waters. Another giant slab of ice had calved off the iceberg, dropping out of sight into the depths and then emerging again like a surfacing whale to bob out into the bay.

'What about the longship?' Macleod jerked his head at the iceberg, a sense of urgency in his voice. 'We haven't got much time now. It'd be risky to go close again, but we could try another sonar scan.'

Jack lifted the axe from where it rested on his knees, twisting it until the sunlight sparkled off the gilding on the blade. He stared at it pensively for a moment and then looked at Maria, knowing they were both remembering their visit to the old Inuit the day before and her apprehension about Fenrir, the Norse wolf-god on the carved prow they now knew had been the spirit guardian of the longship.

'I took hundreds of pictures,' Jack replied. 'Enough for a full photogrammetric reconstruction. There's no way anyone's going near that berg again. When we found Halfdan he was partway to Valhalla. I think we should let him finish his voyage.'

'What about the axe?'

Jack weighed the haft again in his hands. 'I'll look upon Mjøllnir as a loan,' he said. 'It got Halfdan through all those wars alongside Harald Hardrada, and it's got us through a few scrapes. It's still got what the Vikings called battle-luck. Something tells me those old Norse gods are willing us on, and this is one of the best clues we've got. If Halfdan still had his treasured war axe from his days in Constantinople, then who knows what else the Vikings could have brought out here.'

'That reminds me.' Costas suddenly jerked upright and reached into the hip pocket of his E-suit. 'I pulled this out of the ice just when things went haywire down there. I'd completely forgotten.' He extracted the object and they could see it was another weapon, a dagger the size of a small hunting knife with a gleaming steel blade and a decorative handle. As he held it up and the blade glinted, the crew members who had been milling on the deck converged around the group, and there was a collective gasp of amazement.

'Let me take a closer look at that,' Macleod said. 'Something's not right.'

As Costas passed it over they could see what had caught Macleod's eye, and their astonishment turned to disbelief.

'A swastika,' one of the crew exclaimed.

Macleod turned the dagger over in his hands. 'Just as I thought,' he murmured. 'They did find the longship. Look at the pommel. A skull and crossbones, the death's-head symbol. This is a Nazi dagger, a weapon only carried by a sworn member of the SS.'

There was a stunned silence and then the woman in the crew spoke again, quietly. 'Could someone explain how a Nazi dagger got on a Viking longship inside an iceberg off Greenland?'

Macleod handed the dagger back to Costas and looked at Jack. 'I think it's time we told the crew the whole story.'

At that moment there was a sudden lurch in the deck, an unusual sensation in a ship with a state-of-the-art dynamic stabilizing system. The sea remained dead calm and covered with a steely-grey mist after the storm. Then someone shouted from the starboard railing. 'It's the berg! She's rolling!'

Everyone except Jack and Costas converged on the opposite railing to watch the mouth of the fjord. Even though it was more than a mile away, the spectacle was awesome, a breathtaking display of a force of nature no human agency could ever control. Through the mist they saw the huge front face of the berg drop off the underwater threshold and roll over the edge, the jagged eruptions of ice from the top of the glacier replaced by smooth undulations sculpted by the sea and streaked with black from the threshold. As the berg stabilized, Jack and Costas knew that the longship was now lost for ever in the abyss, its fallen warrior destined to sail south along the old Viking sea route to the New World and find his eternal resting place as the berg melted far out in the Atlantic. It had nearly been their tomb too, and Jack found himself gripping the axe hard as he and Costas rested against the bulwark and watched the berg float majestically towards the open sea.

Jack's leg throbbed, and he felt bruised all over. They slowly stripped off their E-suits, both men suddenly overwhelmed by exhaustion. He saw Maria and Jeremy having a heated discussion, as if she was trying to persuade him of something, and then they detached themselves from the group beside the starboard railing and made their way back across the foredeck, Jeremy trailing behind. Macleod joined them, and Jack peered up at Jeremy as they approached.

'You haven't told us what the rest of the runestone says.'

'I was coming to that.' Jeremy pulled a palm computer out

of his pocket, activated the screen and cleared his throat. 'Prepare to be amazed.'

'Go on.'

'There are five lines of runes altogether, scratched into the quartz slate by one hand. As I said, they're Norse and eleventh century, consistent with our warrior being the same Halfdan who scratched his name into Hagia Sofia in Constantinople.'

'Well, what does it say?'

Jeremy cleared his throat again. 'I've had to add some connectives to make sense of it, but here's the gist: *Halfdan died here of wounds received in the battle against the King of England near Yorvik. Halfdan will fight again for Odin at Ragnarok. Harald Sigurdsson his king made these runes the winter after the battle. The Wolf takes Halfdan to Valhalla. The Eagle sails west for Vinland.*'

There was a stunned silence. Jack stopped pulling off his E-suit and stared at Jeremy. 'Harald Sigurdsson. That's Harald Hardrada.'

'The Mappa Mundi inscription from Hereford suggests he was out here,' Maria said. 'Now we know for sure.'

Jeremy nodded. 'The *Wolf* must be the name of the ship in the ice. The *Eagle*, the other ship, sailed on for Vinland. That's the name of the Viking settlement in Newfoundland, the farthest Viking outpost in the west and the only one known in North America.'

'Wait a minute.' Jack's mind was suddenly reeling in astonishment. 'Yorvik was the Viking name for the city of

York, seven miles west of Stamford Bridge. The battle can only be Stamford Bridge in 1066, between King Harold Godwinson of England and King Harald Hardrada of Norway.'

'Correct.'

'But Harald Hardrada died at Stamford Bridge.'

'So the history books tell us,' Jeremy replied quietly. 'But remember there's no first-hand account of the battle. The events of that year were completely eclipsed by the Norman Conquest, and the Norman annals were hardly likely to extol an English victory. Most of what we know comes from a brief mention in the *Anglo-Saxon Chronicle* and from the *Heimskringla*, the semi-mythical history of the kings of Norway, written in Iceland almost two centuries later. The copy of the *Chronicle* we found in the Hereford library mentions it, but only in a few lines.'

'Plenty of scope for omission, even a cover-up,' Costas murmured.

'My God.' Jack slumped back against the railing, his face dripping with seawater and sweat. 'So Harald Hardrada survived Stamford Bridge. That changes everything. Somehow he and his remaining warriors made it out here, in the same two ships he had used to escape from Constantinople twenty years before. Remember the treasure of Michelgard, that incredible reference on the Hereford map? Harald must have had his treasure with him when he went to England, ready for a triumphal procession through York and London that never happened. Instead he sailed off with it after the defeat, taking it with him and his surviving followers far to the west, seeking a new land beyond the edge of the Viking world.' Jack lifted Halfdan's axe in his hands, then gave a tired but jubilant smile. 'I think we've just had another piece of battle-luck. I knew I was right to come out here.'

'You might like to have this, then.' Costas had been struggling in the depths of his E-suit inner pocket, and pulled out a small nodule of ice. 'I thought I'd dropped this when the berg rolled, so I didn't mention it. I found it loose above the burial chamber, near that Nazi dagger.'

He handed the dripping object to Jack, who rolled it in his fingers and then passed it to Maria. A lustrous gold band protruded from one side of the ice, and Maria eyed it closely. 'It's a finger ring, a Viking design,' she murmured. 'Twisted gold, like a miniature arm-ring or neck-torque. But I've never seen one with a signet like this.' She clasped the ice in the warmth of her palm and then began rubbing it, gradually revealing the gold beneath. After a few moments she held it up to the sunlight. 'I can see the surface of the signet. It's got an impressed design. It's . . .' Her voice trailed off, then she regained her composure. 'Jack, tell me I'm not seeing things.'

She passed the ring over and Jack stared through the ice that still clung to the signet. The form beneath was wavering, refracted by the sunlight into a myriad different shapes, but the outline was unmistakable.

'*The menorah.*'

He stared at the seven-branched shape, his heart racing with excitement. Something amazing was happening. First the ship in the ice had proved to be Viking, the funerary vessel of a Varangian warrior. A man who would have served with Harald Hardrada, whose last journey to the far side of the world took place in one of the very vessels Hardrada had used to break free from Constantinople, a ship which had sailed across the Golden Horn on the very spot where Jack and Costas had stood aboard *Sea Venture* only days previously. And now this, an extraordinary link to the greatest lost treasure of antiquity, something Jack assumed had disappeared for ever after Stamford Bridge.

'Don't get your hopes up yet,' Costas said quietly. 'This might not be all it seems.'

'What do you mean?'

Costas had sidled up alongside and was peering inside the ring, at the interior face of the signet. 'Like Maria said, tell me I'm not seeing things.'

Jack flipped the ring over and let out a gasp. It was a shape as familiar as the menorah, but could only be modern. They had been looking at it on the dagger only minutes before. It was a swastika.

Jack looked up slowly, his elation replaced by blank puzzlement. Maria glanced at him and then turned to Jeremy, her face set. 'The time is now,' she said to the young man firmly. She squatted down between Jack and Costas while Jeremy remained standing, fidgeting slightly and looking more than usually pale.

'Jack,' Maria said quietly, 'about that Nazi expedition. There's more you need to know. There are forces at play here far darker than we could ever have imagined. Jeremy's got something to tell you.'

room in the north range where he retreats for research and writing when he can get away from the Vatican.'

'Do we trust this guy?' Costas said, his voice sounding loud in the cloister. 'I mean, he's a bit of an unknown quantity.'

Maria stopped and turned sharply on him. 'You wouldn't be here if I didn't trust him.'

'Okay.' Costas saw Jack gesturing at him to back off. 'Sorry. It's just a hell of a long way to come.'

'He insisted that we meet him here.' Maria's voice was still curt, and she stopped and took out her cellphone. 'I'll join you. I've got to make an urgent call. Jeremy knows the way.'

That morning they had flown in the IMU Embraer from Greenland to Glasgow in Scotland, and then taken the waiting helicopter one hundred miles north-west to the island of Mull. It had only been twenty-four hours since Jack and Costas had escaped from the perils of the iceberg, and both men had slept soundly most of the way. On Mull they had joined the well-worn pilgrim route to the holy isle of Iona, taking the ferry across the narrow channel to Port Rònain, then walking up through the village to the abbey buildings in their setting of meadows with the sparkling blue sea beyond. As they gazed at the abbey Jeremy had explained that a building had stood on this spot since the time St Columba arrived from Ireland almost fifteen hundred years before, had survived Viking raids, the Reformation and abandonment, and was now once again a thriving monastery and one of the holiest sites in the British Isles.

They passed along the sunlit alley of the cloister to another small door, and ascended a wooden staircase to an attic corridor with windows overlooking the abbey. Jeremy knocked on a door and a moment later they heard the clatter of a bolt being unlatched and a chain withdrawn.

'Gentlemen. Welcome.' Father O'Connor ushered them in, then locked the door again behind him. He had discarded his Jesuit cassock in favour of the simple brown robe of a monk, and with his cropped white hair and the simple wooden cross hanging on his chest he seemed straight out of the Middle Ages. He looked pale and worn, older than when they had seen him three days before in Cornwall. The room was small, piled high with books and papers, and they could see where O'Connor had been working at a laptop on a desk in the corner. They picked their way over the floor and sat down on wooden chairs arranged in a semicircle in front of the desk. Above the small fireplace opposite, Jack recognized a scaled-down reproduction of the Hereford Mappa Mundi, and propped up beside it he could see a scanned copy of the exemplar for the map Jeremy and Maria had found in the sealed-off staircase in Hereford Cathedral, showing the extraordinary image of the New World in the lower left corner.

'Let's get straight to the point,' O'Connor said. 'It's been a long journey.'

'Thank you,' Jack said. He opened the bag he had been carrying and took out the Nazi dagger and the gold ring with the menorah symbol, and placed them on the desk in front of O'Connor. The older man glanced at the objects and flinched slightly, averting his eyes. But then he looked up, staring at Jack.

'First let me apologize to Jeremy for the burden I placed on him. I took him into my confidence over a year ago, when he first came to study the early runic inscriptions on Iona. I had been seeking a younger colleague, a scholar who could carry on the flame. I swore him to secrecy, but told him when we met in Cornwall that the time might come when we would need to reveal everything to you. Even Maria knew nothing until yesterday.'

'Whatever it is, you could have told us when we discussed the Mappa Mundi and the menorah,' Jack said testily.

'I had to be sure of you. Believe me, I am on your side and we have a common enemy.'

'I'm not aware of any enemy.'

O'Connor shifted on his chair, stared distastefully at the objects in front of him, and then leaned forward on his elbows. 'We'll begin with the Nazis. As you've probably guessed, you're not the first ones to hunt for the menorah.'

'I never did buy the idea that we were,' Costas said cheerfully. 'Stuff like that doesn't happen. Someone, somewhere will have been searching for it. People never forget lost treasure.'

O'Connor smiled thinly, and then looked grim. 'It's not as straightforward as it seems. And it's not a game. The best way to show you what we're up against is to tell you something about the characters on that *Ahnenerbe* expedition in 1938.'

'We know about Künzl, but we're still trying to identify the one with the armband.' Relaxing slightly, Jack took out copies of the photographs Kangia had given him and tossed them on the desk.

'I can help here,' O'Connor said quietly. 'Ever since the scandal over Pope Pius XII's failure to condemn the Nazis during the Second World War, the Vatican has been particularly sensitive on this issue. I've recently taken over as Vatican spokesman on the Holocaust. Officially we liaise with Jewish groups and apprehend surviving war criminals. Unfortunately most of those who escaped punishment are now dead, but we still try to tie up loose ends for the sake of history.'

'I can't imagine any of them making it past St Peter,' Costas said grimly.

'God will make the final judgement,' O'Connor replied. 'But most assuredly there is a special place in hell for those who murder children.'

There was a knock on the door, and O'Connor got up and stared through the spyhole before unlatching it and letting Maria in. She sat down in the empty chair beside Jack and they looked expectantly at her. She looked pale, distracted. 'I was right,' she said. 'I've just spoken to an old friend of mine who works for the Wiesenthal Holocaust Centre in Berlin.' Jack suddenly remembered Maria's Jewish background, her father's Sephardic roots. 'Our Nazi was a failed student at Heidelberg, with delusions of being a famous anthropologist. He joined the SS in 1933. After the *Ahnenerbe* expedition he volunteered for the SS-Totenkopfverbände, the Death's Head units. The ones who ran the concentration camps. His name was Andrius Reksnys.'

'Not German?' Jack asked.

'Lithuanian,' she replied.

'There were plenty outside the Fatherland willing to heed Himmler's call,' O'Connor said. Maria's cellphone chirped, and she looked apologetically at them and quickly slipped out of the door. O'Connor tapped his laptop and clicked through a series of websites. 'I know this man,' he said quietly. 'Here he is.'

He swivelled the screen so they could see and read from a scanned document, translating from German.

The Chief of the Security Police and the Security Service, Berlin, November 5, 1941

55 copies

(51st copy)

OPERATIONAL SITUATION REPORT USSR NO. 129a

Einsatzgruppe D

Location: Nikolayev, Ukraine

Addendum to Report No. 129 concerning the activity of the *Einsatzkommandos* in freeing places of Jews and finishing off partisan groups. SS-*Sturmbannführer* Andrius Reksnys personally executed 341 Jews. Revised total for the last two weeks: 32,108.

'*Einsatzgruppen*.' O'Connor forced out the word with revulsion. 'Himmler's mobile death squads. Responsible for murdering over a million Soviet Jews, among others.'

'How did this monster escape prosecution?' Jack asked.

'Usual story.' There was an edge of anger to O'Connor's voice. 'Shockingly few of the *Einsatzkommandos* were ever brought to justice. In the final Russian onslaught in 1945, Reksnys disguised himself as a *Wehrmacht* private and fled west, to surrender to the British. There were suspicions during his interrogation but nothing concrete. On his release in 1947, now named Schmidt, he recovered his son from an orphanage and went to Australia. Together they made a fortune mining opals near Darwin. Then in the mid sixties he sold his operation without warning, and disappeared.'

'And the son?' Jack said. 'Surely he was too young to have been in the war.'

'Pieter Reksnys was six years old in 1941,' O'Connor replied. 'But there's an eyewitness account from a Jewish survivor at the *Einsatzgruppen* trial, at Nuremberg in 1947, that spoke of a boy in Hitler Youth uniform accompanying *Sturmbannführer* Reksnys in his work. It's a chilling account, one of the worst of the trial. Apparently the boy loaded his father's Luger between each batch of executions, even carried out some himself. It was this account that eventually made the connection when Interpol became involved in the 1990s, and led to Andrius and Pieter Reksnys being tracked down to Mexico, where the son ran a drugs and antiquities cartel. He's now in his early seventies, and is still there.'

'Why so long?' Costas said incredulously. 'Why did it take so long to identify them?'

'Contrary to the Hollywood version, chasing down Nazi war criminals was never a priority in the West after the late 1940s,' O'Connor replied. 'The main intelligence agencies, the CIA, the British SIS, were completely wrapped up in Cold War espionage. They knew all about Eichmann and Mengele and the other Nazis who had escaped to South and Central America, but few thought they posed a threat. Only the Israelis put serious efforts to bringing any of them to justice.'

'And now we reap the rewards,' Costas muttered.

'Not entirely.' O'Connor opened a drawer and placed a plastic sleeve with a photograph on the table. 'You probably won't remember this. A footnote in the newspapers about eight years ago, but actually the highest-profile Nazi death since Eichmann.'

The picture was a shocking image of a dead man lying on his back in a pool of blood, his eyes and mouth wide open and his face contorted with pain. He was an old man, wearing a dark suit, with his right arm flung over his front; visible through the smear of blood was a red armband with a black swastika.

'He wore that armband in the privacy of his own home,' O'Connor said. 'An unreconstructed Nazi to the end. In case you haven't guessed, that's Andrius Reksnys. He was shot in the stomach to ensure a slow death, to give him time to be really frightened of where he was going next.'

'Mossad?' Costas said.

'There is liaison with the Israelis,' O'Connor replied quietly. 'But this was an independent operation.'

'What are you saying?'

O'Connor's face was blank. He spoke coldly. 'Andrius Reksnys was a henchman of the devil. All the efforts of international law had failed to bring him to account. He deserved to face the judgement of humanity, as well as God.'

'Are you saying the Vatican runs a hit squad?' Costas said incredulously.

'The Holy See is not just a spiritual beacon,' O'Connor said. 'For centuries our survival has depended on strength in the world of men, on the power to persuade the unwilling to submit to God. Look at my own order, the Jesuits. Or the Crusades. Or the Inquisition. For centuries the Vatican has overseen the most successful covert intelligence network in the world, and has never shrunk from using it.'

'The Crusades were hardly a glorious episode, even if the intention was righteous to begin with,' Costas muttered. 'I can't imagine the sack of Constantinople was quite what the Pope had in mind.'

'You'd be surprised,' O'Connor said. 'The Papacy has always had to resist being drawn too far into the secular world, losing sight of the spiritual plane that bonds together all Christians. By the time of the fourth Crusade, the Vatican had developed a real problem with the Eastern Church, schismatics who they regarded as heretics. It became a feud, and like all feuds led the antagonists to lose reason. Some apologists for the sack of Constantinople even twisted it into God's actual purpose for the Crusade, punishment for deviating from the true path.'

'The feeling was reciprocated,' Jeremy added. 'The Byzantine eyewitness Niketas Choniates called the Crusaders the forerunners of Antichrist, chief agents of his anticipated ungodly deeds.'

'The Holy See has always faced temptation from the dark side,' O'Connor continued. 'Those who struggle against the devil can so easily end up doing the devil's work. The Crusades were the ultimate challenge of the Middle Ages, and we did not always overcome. Monstrous tendencies have exploded into history in our moments of weakness. There are those among us who feel we owe a debt for failing to stem the greatest evil of all, the Nazi Holocaust.'

'So Reksnys' death has nothing to do with the menorah,' Jack said.

O'Connor paused, then got up. 'I fear I may have misled you. His death has everything to do with the menorah. Please bear with me.'

There was another knock at the door, and O'Connor ushered Maria back in. She sat down, fingering her cellphone. 'I've got news from Hereford,' she said, looking serious. 'Fantastic news. My team from the Oxford Institute has finished excavating the manuscripts from the sealed-up stairway. It's amazing, the greatest trove of Anglo-Saxon manuscripts ever discovered. It's like finding the Roman library in the Villa of the Papyri at Herculaneum, and it's going to be just as much work putting the pieces all together again.' She glanced at Jeremy, who was leaning forward in rapt attention. 'Unless you're in a hurry to return to the States, there's going to be a full-time job looking after all this.'

'Yes please,' Jeremy said.

'So why the glum face?' Costas said.

'It's what else they found.' Maria suddenly sounded tense. 'Right at the bottom of the stairwell, buried under all the paper and vellum. A skeleton of a man, a tall man, dressed in a monk's cassock. Hundreds of years old, medieval. His limbs were askew as if he'd been thrown there. And the back of his skull was shattered.'

There was a stunned silence, and O'Connor paced towards the reproduction of the Mappa Mundi on his wall, before turning to face them. 'It is as I suspected. In the spring of 1299, Richard of Holdingham, mapmaker, came to this very place, to the isle of Iona. He was accompanying his ailing master, Jacobus de Voragine, Archbishop of Genoa, on his final journey. Afterwards Richard went south to Hereford, to oversee the completion of the map he had started fifteen years before. There were errors in the inscriptions he wanted to correct. He had left an exemplar, a sketch for the Hereford monks to work from, and the illuminator had not been very literate. And now we know from his own personal exemplar, the one Jeremy and Maria found, that he wanted to add more, that he had a secret addition he wanted to make in the left-hand corner of the map, where the monks later added the inscription naming him as mapmaker.' O'Connor stopped in front of the fireplace, deep in thought. 'We know he spent his final night at Bishop Swinfield's palace at Bromyard, and that he walked the final road to Hereford in the guise of a pilgrim. After that he vanished from history. The corrections were never made. He was never heard of again.'

'You think he was murdered?' Maria said shakily.

'I have no doubt of it.'

'I felt so close to him,' Maria whispered, her voice shaking with emotion and her hands gripping her chair. 'I've studied him all my life, and I've never felt as close to him as I did that evening in the cathedral. It's almost like he was there.'

'A murder?' Costas looked dumbfounded. 'And what was this guy doing on Iona? Can someone tell me what's going on here?'

'Yes,' said O'Connor, pulling open a drawer. 'Listen to me.'

A few minutes later O'Connor sat back in his chair and let the others study the maps he had just been showing them. Rolled out over the desk was a large-scale map of northern Britain, and beside it he had placed a plan of the Battle of Stamford Bridge in 1066. On the large map he had traced a line from the Yorkshire coast near Stamford Bridge up to the northern tip of Scotland and down the west coast to the island of Mull.

'So Harald Hardrada came here to Iona, after the battle.' Jack's mind was reeling as he struggled to comprehend what O'Connor had just been telling them. He lowered himself back into his chair, and the others followed suit.

'He must have been in a hell of a state,' Costas said. 'Bad enough for the English soldiers who fought him to assume he was dead on the battlefield.'

'It was a miracle he survived the journey,' O'Connor replied. 'He was well looked after. There were about thirty of his warriors altogether, almost all of them grievously wounded, many former Varangian Guards. They were rowed in the two longships by loyal retainers. Some died on the way, some here on Iona.'

The pieces were beginning to fall together in Jack's mind. 'When Harald finally left Iona to sail west, there was a contingent left behind, loyal followers to await the return of their king.'

O'Connor looked at him shrewdly and nodded. 'They called themselves a *félag*,' he said. 'An ancient Norse term for a fellowship, a secret society.'

'And who were the *félag*?' Jack asked.

'At first they were a few of Harald's companions, wounded survivors of Stamford Bridge who came with him to the holy isle but elected to stay behind when their king sailed west. They were younger men, warriors Harald had nurtured since his Varangian days, men who still had ambition and fire within them to carry on the cause. They may have included several of Harald's own sons. Quickly they accrued others around them, never more than twenty in number. Their sworn intent was to keep the flame burning for the return of their king, to do all in their power to ensure that a true Viking once again ruled in England.'

'Not very realistic after 1066,' Jack said.

'They hated the Normans, and their French Plantagenet successors. Within a few generations the cause of the *félag* had become the cause of the English. Remember, there was plenty of Viking blood already in England, among those who called themselves Anglo-Saxon. The Viking king Cnut had ruled England in the time of Harald's youth, and there were huge swathes of the country where Viking raiding had led to settlement and intermarriage: in East Anglia, in Northumbria, up here in the western isles. So it was natural that the English, once the enemy of Harald's Vikings at Stamford Bridge, should unite with them in common cause against the Normans.'

'They can't realistically have expected Harald's return.'

O'Connor shook his head. 'It became a mystical underpinning, a binding force that made the *félag* one of the most successful secret societies of the Middle Ages. Those few original companions had sworn secrecy to their king, that they would never reveal his survival or his passage west, for fear that the Normans would try to follow or take reprisals. After a few generations, when the return of the king in this life became impossible, they began to look forward to joining Harald at the great Battle of Ragnarok, the final showdown in Norse mythology between good and evil. They would once again stand shoulder to shoulder with their liege, wielding battleaxes alongside him, vanquishing their foes and spreading fear as they had done in the glory days of the Varangians. Their sacred mantra, the oath that bound them in fellowship, became *hann til ragnarøks*, Old Norse for "until Ragnarok", until we meet at the end of time.'

'So the name Harald Hardrada passed into history.'

'Not quite.' O'Connor reached out to his bookcase, and handed a volume over to Jack. 'Geoffrey of Monmouth, *Historia Regum Britanniae*, History of the King of England. A medieval bestseller, mostly fictional.'

'And?'

'The book responsible for the romantic legend of King Arthur.'

'Good God,' Jack murmured. 'Of course. The once and future king.'

'Geoffrey was one of the *félag*, a couple of generations after Harald had gone. They were sworn never to mention the name of their king, but by the middle of the twelfth century the *félag* had begun to make inroads into English society. In the face of Norman oppression it became expedient to spread the fantasy of an ancient British king, a heroic leader who would one day return to free his people. Peel off the romantic fiction and you've got some hard facts.'

'For King Arthur, read Harald Hardrada,' Jack murmured. 'For the Knights of the Round Table, read the Varangian Guard.'

'It's what you said about Atlantis,' Costas added. 'Behind every myth there's some reality.'

'Yes, but people had been debating the Atlantis myth for ages,' Jack replied. 'This one's a bolt from the blue.'

He turned to O'Connor. 'So the *félag* wasn't all just mystical?'

'By no means. By espousing the English cause they easily gained adherents, and as the generations passed the *félag* came to represent the great and the good among those who claimed Anglo-Saxon and Viking roots. They had little hope of infiltrating the Norman aristocracy, so by the time the last of the original Varangians had died, most of the *félag* were churchmen, pagans in disguise. The Church was the one area where Englishmen of Anglo-Saxon and Viking blood could still wield power, and the *félag* used it to their utmost advantage. By the end of the twelfth century their influence reached as far as Rome, and the membership included churchmen in Europe with English connections. Jacobus de Voragine, Richard of Holdingham's master and one of the senior clergymen in Italy, was the bastard child of an English mother who claimed descent from King Cnut. On several occasions there were even members among the College of Cardinals in the Vatican.'

'So Richard of Holdingham was one of the *félag*,' Maria said, her voice subdued.

'He was the last of the true *félag*, of the continuous line from Hardrada.'

'True *félag*?'

O'Connor paused, clearly troubled. 'Early on there was a schism, a dark side. You can compare it to the struggle in the Church we've just been talking about, against the temptation of the devil. We don't know when it happened or who it was, but it was someone who had seen the menorah with his own eyes, one of the original companions who had chosen to stay behind. A Judas in the midst of the *félag*. The menorah had already been a secret symbol of kingship to Harald himself, worth far more to his prestige than its weight in gold, and after his departure it became elevated even further as a symbol of the *félag*, another part of the ritual that bound them together. But where some saw sacred cause, others saw gold. It attracted avarice, greed.'

'Like the Holy Grail,' Costas suggested. 'To some a mystical quest, an allegory for some great revelation about Christianity. To others a golden cup.'

'Exactly. To those who could not resist, the search for Harald's treasure became paramount, an obsession. Secretly they set up their own fellowship, their own *félag*, with the sole intent of finding the menorah. Those who remained true sensed the malign force in their midst. Precious knowledge of Harald's voyage had returned from over the western ocean, knowledge they were able to conceal from those who would use it with ill intent. The knowledge was only ever entrusted to one man, who would pass it on to the next appointed man, master to apprentice, as long as the line could be sustained.'

'I'm beginning to understand,' Jack said slowly. 'Jacobus de Voragine, Richard of Holdingham.'

O'Connor nodded. 'They were the last. Somehow the line had survived for over a hundred years following its greatest crisis, in 1170. In that year Thomas Becket, Archbishop of

Canterbury, was murdered by followers of King Henry II in his own cathedral. Becket's ascendancy had been the time of greatest power for the true *félag*, and his death was the beginning of the end.'

'Thomas Becket was a member of the *félag*?' Jack said in astonishment.

'And the holder of the knowledge,' O'Connor said. 'The knights who hacked him down were not only seeking vengeance for Henry II.'

'Did they get what they wanted?'

'He refused to back down, and in their rage they murdered him. They were reviled in England and joined the Third Crusade, ostensibly to seek absolution for their crime. They became known as the Knights of the Blooded Hand, for all these men had scars across their palms where they had cut themselves to form a blood pact. Their quest had gained its own mystique, its own rituals, though their allegiance to the cause of Harald Hadrada was a sham. They began to seek the other Jewish treasure that Harald had left behind when he escaped from Byzantium with his Varangian companions. The golden table from the Jewish Temple, the Table of the Shewbread.'

'But that was in Constantinople.'

O'Connor nodded. 'The knights were all butchered before they could get there, by Saladin and his Muslim warriors before the walls of Jerusalem. But another one did get to Constantinople, a generation later, in 1204.'

'That's the date of the Fourth Crusade,' Costas said. 'What

we've been looking for in the Golden Horn. The chain and everything.'

It was suddenly cold in the cell-like room, a chill breeze seeping through a crack in the window. Jack's mind was racing. 'Hang on. The Sack of Constantinople. That was Baldwin of Flanders. Are you saying . . .?'

'He was the one. As a young man Baldwin had been to Rome, and had seen the Arch of Titus in the forum. The arch had become a place of pilgrimage for the *félag*, a sacred shrine. Richard of Holdingham undoubtedly went there. They not only saw the image of the menorah, but also the other treasures being carried by the Roman soldiers. They knew what the golden table looked like. Baldwin didn't divert the Crusade to Constantinople by accident, just to do the Venetians' dirty work. But others, those of the true *félag*, knew Baldwin's intent, and got there in secret before him. There were still Varangians in the imperial guard at Constantinople, men for whom the name of Hardrada was hallowed, a legend from the glory days. They were persuaded to take the remaining treasure and sink it at a secret location in the harbour before the Crusaders arrived. All of the Varangians died in the siege, and the location was lost.'

'Eureka,' Costas murmured. 'Not bad for us. Maybe Maurice Hiebermeyer's got something to look forward to in the Golden Horn after all.'

'By the time of the Fourth Crusade, the schism in the *félag* had turned into an all-out blood-feud,' O'Connor continued. 'Retribution was sought for the murder of Thomas Becket, and the cycle began. Even those who still held the cause true lost sight of their nobility, and lived in fear of their lives. Like many secret societies they turned in on themselves, began to self-destruct. Richard of Holdingham must have known he was a marked man once he returned from Iona, once he had torched his master's body in the longboat in the hallowed *félag* ritual, sending him off to Valhalla at the very spot where their king had set sail. Their enemies knew that Jacobus must have passed on the knowledge to Richard before he died. There was no apprentice for Richard. His last act was to have been his record on the Mappa Mundi, his assignation of their secret to the future, to be discovered and deciphered by someone when the darkness had passed. And with the murder of Richard the line came to an end.'

'Do you think he relented in his final moments, when he faced death in the chained library?' Jack asked.

Maria looked at him, her face full of emotion. 'He had the spirit of Thomas Becket beside him. He must have known he was going to die whatever he did. I believe he was strong to the end. Fortunately his attacker must have failed to recognize the exemplar of the map for what it was, or maybe Richard had time to conceal it in the library in the moments before he was confronted.'

'He could never have guessed it would be more than seven hundred years,' Jack murmured.

'And I fear the darkness is still with us,' O'Connor said.

'Fine.' Costas was fingering the ring, and held it up between them with the symbol of the menorah clearly visible. He pointed with his other hand at the swastika on the dagger. 'And now to the really big question. How do we get from the medieval murder mystery to these bad guys in the twentieth century?'

13

J ack sat enraptured in the book-lined room of the old abbey, amazed at what he was hearing. Thoughts crowded in on his mind, and he struggled to separate them out. He had known they were on the trail of Hardrada since the revelation of the map, that an extraordinary thread tied their discovery in the Golden Horn of Istanbul with the longship in the ice off Greenland, but he could never have guessed that the holy isle of Iona was another link in the chain. And now O'Connor was telling another story, one that moved beyond the thrill of discovery to a world of darkness and danger.

'With the end of the Crusades, and the rise of the Ottoman Empire, any hope of finding the remaining treasure in Constantinople seemed lost,' O'Connor continued. 'To the west, all contact with Greenland was severed, and the promised land discovered by the Vikings was forgotten. By the time of the European voyages of discovery in the late fifteenth century, the last of the Knights of the Blooded Hand was long dead. Yet the myth endured, passed from father to son in the greatest of secrecy, by descendants of the *félag* across Europe and eventually in America. By the nineteenth century, all who received the story thought it fantasy, no more historical than the stories of King Arthur and the Round Table, and held on to their pledge only to sustain a romantic legend. Then it somehow reached the ears of a mad Austrian inventor obsessed with World Ice Theory.'

'We've heard about him,' Costas broke in. 'The reason why the Nazis went to Greenland.'

'So this character refounded the *félag*?' Jack said.

'One of his collaborators, a Lithuanian entrepreneur named Piotr Reksnys. Father of Andrius. A nasty piece of work.'

Costas grimaced. 'It runs in the family.'

'The timing was perfect,' O'Connor went on. 'The first decades of the twentieth century saw a resurgence of interest in the Vikings and Nordic heritage, in Germany and across northern Europe. After the insanity of the First World War, it became a movement to bolster the idea of racial supremacy among a people who had lost their way. Secret societies thrived, and began to attract the thugs and fantasists who dreamed of a new Reich in Europe. They led to the ugliest society of all, Himmler's *Schutzstaffel*, the SS, complete with fabricated Norse ancestry and rituals. The idea of a reconstituted *félag* fitted this baleful world perfectly, only unlike these other organizations the *félag* had some historical resonance.'

'And a different goal,' Jack said.

'The menorah,' O'Connor said. 'They had all the trappings of a supremacist society, but that was just for show. They were obsessed with finding the menorah.'

Costas picked up the ring. 'So what about this?'

O'Connor waved his hand dismissively. 'A sham. Reksnys made out that these rings were some ancient inheritance, forged from the gold in Harald's treasure, but they were not. They're typical fabrications of the period. Reksnys knew the Viking kings had been ring-givers, bequeathing gold and silver neck-rings and arm-rings to their faithful followers. Like the Nazis he was obsessed with the operas of Wagner, with the ring cycle, the *Nibelungenlied*, the legend of Ragnarok and the fall of the Norse gods. Reksnys revived the mantra of the old fellowship, *hann til ragnarøks*. They were *fostbrædralag*, sworn brothers, and they called themselves thole-companions, the old Viking name for oarsmen. There were to be twelve of them, and he even refurbished a castle in Norway and persuaded his initiates that it had been an ancient meeting place of the *félag*, complete with fabricated Viking armour and axes, supposedly left by their Varangian precursors. He even reconstituted the most extreme form of punishment used by the Norse, reserving it for members of the *félag* who had strayed from their oath of loyalty.'

Maria looked aghast. 'You don't mean the blood eagle?'

O'Connor nodded. 'Harald's ship was the *Eagle*. The guardian of the *félag* was the great eagle giant Hræsvdg. The blood eagle was to be performed on his behalf, like a sacrificial rite.'

'It was the Norse equivalent of hanging, drawing and quartering,' Jeremy said. 'Only without the hanging and quartering.'

'The outline of an eagle was carved on the back of the victim, while he was still alive,' Maria said quietly. 'Then they cut away the ribs and ripped out the lungs.'

'God almighty.' Even Costas was at a loss for words.

'They haven't used it yet on one of their own,' O'Connor said. 'But at the *Einsatzgruppen* trial one of the Jewish survivors spoke of a rumour that an SS officer had carried out something like this on a group of prisoners, using his ceremonial dagger.' O'Connor looked at the object on his desk with disgust. 'Even among the horrors of the Holocaust it was too much to believe, and there was nobody left alive to confirm it. But it would have been in Andrius Reksnys' area of operations.'

'I'm really beginning to love this guy,' Costas murmured.

'And there was one other feature, something that marked the *félag* out wherever they went.' O'Connor paused. 'They slashed their hands across the palm, a sign of blood fealty. They believed they were the Knights of the Blooded Hand, born again.'

'The SS, the *Ahnenerbe*, the search for lost Aryan civilizations, for Atlantis,' Jack murmured. 'It was all a perfect vehicle for the *félag*, a cover to reach their goal.'

O'Connor nodded. 'Andrius Reksnys, the son, was a fanatical Nazi. The picture the old Inuit presented of him is typical. A real sadist and bully. But he was an even more fanatical member of the *félag*, steeped in the obsession since childhood.'

'Why?' said Jack.

'Because it wasn't just mystical. There was a goal, a quest. They worked out that Harald Hardrada must have headed for Greenland. They studied the *Greenlanders' Saga* and *Eirik the Red's Saga*, which show that the Norðrseta, the northern parts beginning around Disko Bay, would have been the staging post for voyages further west. When they heard that the explorer Knud Rasmussen was planning an expedition to the Greenland icecap at Ilulissat, they leaped at the chance. By then Himmler had become obsessed with World Ice Theory and a lost polar civilization, and there was no problem authorizing an SS *Ahnenerbe* team to attach themselves to Rasmussen's expedition.'

'And Rolf Künzl? How does he fit in?'

'Totally innocent of the goals of the *félag*. He was the one who mapped out the voyage described in the sagas. He was the world expert on the Vikings in the West, the perfect companion for Reksnys. They used him. And when they knew he had found some clue in the ice, something he then concealed, he was doomed.'

'The runestone in the longship,' Costas said.

O'Connor nodded again. 'Künzl was quick-witted enough to know he had found something of momentous significance, and the fact that Reksnys was so desperate to get his hands on it was enough for him. Künzl loathed Reksnys and the Nazis with equal fervour. So he decided to pass the runestone to the old Inuit for safekeeping. Künzl had known nothing about the *félag*, but had begun to guess that he was dealing with more than just Nazi lunacy. He and Reksnys had fought in that crevasse, and from then on he must have known it was a blood-feud, a duel to the death. That was always the weakness of the old *félag*. The murders of Thomas Becket and Richard of Holdingham meant that their secrets went with them to the grave. In the thirst for vengeance the killers lost sight of their goal. After the war began, Künzl was safe as long as he was fighting with the Afrika Korps, but when he was arrested with the von Stauffenberg conspirators, Andrius Reksnys finally had his chance. He used his considerable expertise to try to extract what he could from Künzl in the Gestapo torture chambers. He failed, and in his rage he let Künzl be executed along with the others. He must have assumed that Künzl, the great scholar, would have left some written record, but he discovered that Künzl had destroyed all of his personal papers, and that all records of the expedition had disappeared from the *Ahnenerbe* headquarters early on in the war.'

'One question,' Maria said quietly. 'The menorah

would have meant everything to the Nazis. The ultimate symbol of domination over a race they were determined to destroy. They would have wielded it as the Romans had done in their triumph over the Jews two thousand years ago. What would Reksnys have done if he had found the menorah?'

O'Connor got up again and gazed pensively at the map. 'The search for the menorah was kept secret, even from Himmler. If Himmler had found out anything about the menorah and the *félag*, that the search was being concealed from him, then Reksnys would probably have suffered the same fate as Künzl. To answer your question we need to move to the present day. We're not dealing with neo-Nazis here. Nothing that banal. The *félag* is still with us, as strong as it ever was. And the menorah has even more potency today than it did in the dark days of the 1940s. They could hold the world to ransom for it. The Catholic Church, the Jewish state, the Arab states. Extremist groups of all persuasions.'

'Auction it to the highest bidder,' Costas murmured.

'So it's really about greed, not ideology,' Maria said.

'That was what drove the schism in the *félag* almost a thousand years ago,' O'Connor replied grimly. 'Greed and power.'

'So how do you know all this?' Costas blurted out. 'I mean, if it's all so secret, how does a Jesuit historian in the Vatican get access to this kind of information?'

'That was to be my last revelation.' O'Connor took a deep

breath, pulled up the right sleeve of his cassock and held his hand towards them, palm outwards. There was a collective gasp of astonishment. Diagonally across the middle ran a jagged white scar.

'The blooded hand,' Maria whispered. 'I thought that was just an old injury.'

'You can relax.' O'Connor let his sleeve down and slumped into his chair. 'I am no longer one of them. My grandfather was an American inventor who was part of the World Ice Theory circle, no less eccentric than its founder but probably slightly less mad.'

'My God,' Maria exclaimed. 'You never told me about this. I thought your family were all academics.'

'It was a strange period,' O'Connor said quietly, gazing at the floor. 'The world started to go insane a few decades before the First World War, and we're still not out of it.' He looked up, and smiled thinly at Maria. 'My grandfather was a scientist, but dabbled in a lot of fringe stuff like many academics at the time, and eventually let this particular obsession consume him. Like my father before me I was sworn into the *félag* in my youth, went through the whole initiation rite. I loathed it, hated the false rituals, and as soon as I found out about the Nazi connection I wanted out. I discovered my vocation as a Jesuit, and I could not reconcile it with membership of the *félag*. The *félag* has always professed to be pagan, to despise Christianity even while they worked within it. I believe they expected me to return to the fold, saw me as a useful future asset within the

Church. They agreed to let me go with a vow of secrecy. It is a vow I have now broken.'

'But you are not bound by their absurd rituals,' Jack said.

'Indeed.' O'Connor looked down, and then gazed directly at Jack. 'But I have stoked the fire of vengeance. Over the years I gathered all I could on Andrius Reksnys. I was merely contemptuous of the *félag*, but with Reksnys it was different. The more I found out about his murderous activities with the *Einsatzgruppen*, the more determined I was to bring him to justice, even if it meant breaking my vow of silence. The memory of Rolf Künzl drove me on. I took my creed from the old Varangian Guard, from the earliest *félag*, that our fate is predetermined, that Ragnarok is inevitable, so what matters is our conduct in this world. It was my sole inheritance from the old ways. Somewhat at odds with my Jesuit calling, but it linked me to the nobility of the earliest *félag* and gave me strength.'

'You can't have acted alone,' Jack said. 'Someone else shot Reksnys.'

'Once I was in the Vatican, I brought a small group of trusted companions into the fold. One is here in the abbey today. You may have seen him in the Church. Jeremy was to be another. We came close to assembling enough evidence against Reksnys, but not close enough. We were determined that he should experience horror before death.'

'You reawakened the cycle of blood-feud,' Maria murmured.

'Sometimes justice is best served by the old ways.'

'And the *félag* know who you are?'

'Earlier I told you that the Vatican had been penetrated by the *félag* in their heyday in the twelfth century. Today there is one again, one among my superiors who knows about the menorah, who has found out about your quest.'

'How?' Costas said.

'An insider.'

Jack felt a sudden chill of certainty. 'I know who it was. It's been niggling me since the Golden Horn. *Sea Venture*'s second officer, the newly appointed Estonian. He was listening in from the bridge when we first discussed the menorah.'

'He went AWOL two days ago,' Costas said grimly. 'We weren't going to bother you with it, but Tom York told me when I called him this morning.'

O'Connor nodded bleakly and continued. 'I knew the Holy See would do all in its power to prevent the location of the menorah from being revealed, but then I realized that there was more to it than that. The *félag* will do anything to know what we know, to thwart and destroy us and carry on the search themselves. And there is one we should fear most.'

'Who?' Jack asked.

'The grandson. Andrius Reksnys is dead, his son Pieter is holed up somewhere in Central America. The grandson is still at large. I believe he is now a sworn member of the *félag*. He's a thug. He inherited the family gene.'

'Like grandfather, like grandson,' Jack said quietly.

'The father, Pieter, is no better,' O'Connor said. 'Remember his early education on the Russian front. But he seems to be fully preoccupied running his criminal organization in Central America. The grandson's the one to worry most about. He's the warrior of the *félag*, the point man. He grew up steeped in all the rituals, and it has become his creed. He bought into what I rejected. He's used many aliases, most recently Poellner, Anton Poellner. Among the *félag* he calls himself Loki, the name of a particularly nasty Norse god. His absurd warrior creed led him to train as a mercenary, and he gouged a trail of blood through the Balkan conflicts. He honed his skills at a terrorist training camp on the eastern Black Sea, in Abkhazia.'

'I think we can guess where that was,' Costas said.

'When his grandfather was assassinated he went on a particularly murderous rampage in Kosovo, and let his guard down. He was arrested by the British SAS and convicted in the Hague as a war criminal. Five years ago he was sent to jail for life in Lithuania, the country he claimed as his homeland. They opened up a mothballed jail from the Gulag specially for him, a place where captured officers of the SS had been held for years after the war before being executed. Then about a month ago a new judge decided the evidence against him was insufficient, and he was released.' O'Connor's lip quivered in disgust. 'He was only a child when I left the *félag*, but I can still remember his face. His father had refused to cut his palm until the time was right, so Loki flew into a rage and slashed his own face with an

was locked in a room with those who confronted him. He confessed to me the evening before his murder that they had forced it out of him, our midnight discovery at the arch and our interest in the menorah. That puts me in the firing line. And it means you too, I'm afraid.'

'Do you know who is behind all this in the Vatican?'

'There's a kind of internal inquisition, run by one of the cardinals. It's always been there. But this is more sinister, as bad as it can get. I'm not certain who it is, but I have a pretty good idea. The *félag* has changed since I left it more than forty years ago. I know who some of them are. The war crimes judge who released Loki, for one.' O'Connor again gripped his chair in anger. 'All I can say now is he's shockingly powerful within the Vatican. He could squash me on a whim. I've got nothing to pin on him for certain but enough to put his activities in the spotlight when I go public about this. What I am sure about is that the hit on Alberto was not the Mafia. You can probably guess who I think it was, and he won't be stopping there.'

'Is there anything you can do now?'

'I believe I'm safe here for the time being. The holy isle still has some sanctity, even among the new *félag*. But this has become too big for us to deal with alone. Blood-feuds must be a thing of the past. We're talking murder here, plain and simple. And if they somehow get their hands on the menorah, if it still exists, then the odd murder will seem a trivial matter. The Middle East would ignite like it never has before if the greatest symbol of the Jewish faith was thrown into it. Nobody would come out unscathed, Jews, Arabs, the Catholic Church.'

'Have you got any documentation?'

'It's all here.' O'Connor patted the briefcase by his chair. 'Hard copy. I can't trust it to a computer. Loki is the key. He works alone, with horrifying speed. His masters are the great and the good, judges, senior churchmen, politicians. The days when the *félag* could all don helmets and wield battleaxes are long gone, however much they fantasize about it. There are no others like Loki. If we can stop him, then we buy the time we need.'

'Interpol?'

O'Connor nodded. 'I can pull strings. We have some friends in higher places. An international arrest warrant, a global security alert. But I need time, two days at least to assemble a dossier. It would backfire horribly if the application were rejected, but if the story of the search for the menorah still leaked out.'

'That gives us a deadline,' Jack said pensively. 'Two days or all hell breaks loose. It's a pretty tall order.'

'Something gives me faith in you.'

'Let me help you, Patrick.' Maria leaned forward on her chair, looking at O'Connor and then at Jack. 'I think I've done all I can for you on *Seaquest II*, Jack. I was thinking of staying here anyway and having another go at that runestone, to see if there's anything we missed. But this is way more important. Father O'Connor needs all the help he can get.'

'I could do with it,' O'Connor said. 'We've worked well together in the past.'

'You're welcome to stay with us, Maria,' Jack said. 'More than welcome. I should have made that clearer.'

'Jeremy can take over as expedition expert,' Maria replied. 'If there's anything more to do with Vikings and the New World, he's your man.'

'Okay,' Jack said, a flicker of anxiety crossing his face. 'Just make sure you look after yourself.'

O'Connor had one last thing to show them. He ushered Jack and Maria through the cloister and out into the grassy precinct in front of the abbey, leaving Costas and Jeremy behind in the cloister to reformat a new scan of the Hereford map that had just arrived. Through the early-evening mist that now shrouded the island, Jack glimpsed the rocky outcrops that rose beyond the precinct, an image unchanged since the days of the Vikings. O'Connor led them along the cobbled track of Sràid nam Marbh, the Street of the Dead, past Reilig Odhráin, the hallowed burial ground of kings. On the way Jack paused beside the great stone cross of St Martin, its weathered form still standing where it had been erected more than a thousand years before. He put his hand on the stone and felt the writhing serpents that had been carved into the granite almost two centuries before the Battle of Stamford Bridge, when the sea raiders of the north were still no more than a distant rumour to the monks on the island. He felt a frisson of immediacy, the same excitement he had felt on seeing the longship in the ice. Harald Hardrada had passed this way, had seen this cross. Jack suddenly had an image of the stricken king being carried on a bier towards the abbey, his wounded followers straggling up from the longships beached in the channel below. He felt he had been shadowing Hardrada all along, in the Golden Horn, in the icefjord, but he had never felt so close, so certain that the trail ahead was drawing them on to follow the great king into the unknown.

They walked in silence, lost in their own thoughts, digesting what had gone before. Half an hour later they reached the western side of the island, a wide bay fringed with golden beaches. O'Connor led them over a dune and found a place to sit, with Jack and Maria on either side. The mist had lifted to reveal a long vista off to the west, the deep orange rays of the setting sun searing their way towards the horizon. O'Connor lit a pipe, drawing on it a few times, then began to talk quietly.

'This is Camus Cùl an t'Saimh, the Bay at the Back of the Ocean,' he said. 'After days on the brink of death they brought Harald to this spot, fearful that word of his survival would leak out to the Normans. They brought his longships, the *Eagle* and the *Wolf*, and pulled them up on the beach. They filled them with provisions and placed Harald on his litter in the centre of the *Wolf*. Halfdan the Fearless, his oldest companion, lay grievously wounded at his feet, ready to die if his king began to wane.'

'*Wergild*,' Maria murmured. 'A man could forfeit his life to Odin to save the life of his master.'

'The monks helped them haul the ships into the shallows. Those of Harald's band who were still fit and able manned the thwarts, drawing the long oars through the tholes. The masts were set and the sails unfurled. From here Harald and his thole-companions sailed into history, watched by the monks of Iona and the small band of the faithful he had left behind to keep the fire burning.'

'Where did the ships go?' Maria asked.

O'Connor paused, took out his pipe and jabbed it towards the western horizon, then recited quietly from memory.

"But now farewell. I am going a long way
With these thou seëst – if indeed I go –
(For all my mind is clouded with a doubt)
To the island-valley of Avilion;
Where falls not hail, or rain, or any snow,
Nor ever wind blows loudly; but it lies
Deep-meadowed, happy, fair with orchard-lawns
And bowery hollows crowned with summer sea,
Where I will heal me of my grievous wound."

So said he, and the barge with oar and sail
Moved from the brink, like some full-breasted swan
That, fluting a wild carol ere her death,
Ruffles her pure cold plume, and takes the flood
With swarthy webs. Long stood Sir Bedivere

Revolving many memories, till the hull
Looked one black dot against the verge of dawn,
And on the mere the wailing died away."

'Tennyson, *Morte d'Arthur*,' Jack exclaimed, shaking his head in wonder. 'A pretty Victorian view of it, but if what you say is true, the romantic version of the Arthur legend goes right back to this spot.'

'Substitute Vinland for Avalon and you've got the promised land, the earthly paradise,' O'Connor said. 'The story of Leif Eiriksson's discovery of the New World would have trickled back to Harald's court well before his decision to invade England, and it would have intrigued such a well-travelled man. He'd been pretty sedentary for years, apart from the occasional war parties to Denmark and Sweden, and he must have had wanderlust. Maybe he'd been planning an expedition across the western ocean even before Stamford Bridge. He wanted one last adventure, one last great voyage of discovery, something to take him back to the glory days of his youth with the Varangian Guard. With his defeat at Stamford Bridge the voyage became an imperative. The reports would have suggested a land of great abundance, of lush meadows for pasturage and endless forests for shipbuilding, the two things the Vikings coveted above all else. And there was nothing to go back to Norway for. His prestige would have been shattered if he'd returned alive, whereas death assured his place among the heroes. The *Heimskringla* even records that his remaining army in

Norway swore eternal allegiance to him after news of the defeat had reached them, even after they thought he was dead.'

'And he had his treasure,' Jack said.

'Chests of it,' O'Connor said. 'They certainly weren't going to the New World in search of gold. They already had so much they didn't need any extra ballast. Silver coins, tens of thousands of them, Arab *dirhams*, English pennies of Cnut and Aethelred, coins from Harald's empire and beyond. Gold and silver neck-torques, arm-rings, precious heirlooms of his ancestors. And all of Harald's booty from his days with the Varangians in the Mediterranean, some of it melted down, some still intact. Priceless religious reliquaries and ancient jewellery. And to cap it all, the greatest treasure of Harald's reign, the treasure which had been ennobled by his exploit in escaping Constantinople, which had come to mean far more than its weight in gold.'

'The menorah,' Jack murmured.

'If Vinland is the site of L'Anse aux Meadows in Newfoundland, then it's pretty well due west from here, over more than two thousand miles of open ocean,' Maria said. 'So what's our longship doing way up in Baffin Bay at Ilulissat?'

'It's in the sagas,' Jack replied. 'Leif Eiriksson found Vinland by sailing first up the west coast of Greenland, then across to Helluland and Markland. These places correspond to Baffin Island and Labrador, and the staging point in Greenland must have been Disko Bay, at the narrowest point of the Davis Strait. Harald was following the best available navigational advice.'

'That's what Künzl must have worked out in the 1930s,' O'Connor said.

'So they overwintered at Ilulissat?' Maria asked.

'They were probably forced to stay by the pack-ice clogging up the sea. It would have been autumn when they arrived. The light gets poor, and ships get iced up by spray. Macleod said the slush ice begins to form in October, and when it hardens it can cut timbers like a saw. Overwintering would have been tough, but these were tough men used to hardship. They probably had some of the local Greenlander Vikings with them from the southern settlements, employed as guides and hunters. I wouldn't be surprised if they camped in the same bay beside the icefjord where we saw Kangia, among the ancient tent circles.'

'It would have been especially tough on the wounded,' Maria said.

'Many must have perished on the voyage, and in the camp. By the time Halfdan died my guess is the number was so depleted they were easily able to spare one of the ships for the burial, the *Wolf*, the ship you saw in the ice. There weren't enough hands left to man two ships.'

'So how did word get back?' Maria said 'Two centuries later Richard of Holdingham knew they had reached Vinland, was confident enough to sketch it on his map. The archaeology indicates that L'Anse aux Meadows was pretty short-lived, abandoned well before 1066, so it's not as if there were regular supply trips that could pass on reports.'

'Jack was right about the Greenlanders,' O'Connor replied. 'They were sympathetic to Harald, a fellow Norwegian, especially when they saw he had no intention of subjugating them and staying there. He swore them to secrecy, and the silver he gave them kept their trade with the Old World prosperous for generations to come. We know this because the *félag* sent out an expedition in search of Harald, several generations later. Eirik Gnupsson, Bishop of Greenland and one of the *félag*, convinced his flock that he was a loyal follower of Harald, and learned what I have just recounted. He was told that Harald promised to leave a waymarker in Vinland if he and his companions decided to sail further south. Richard must have been told this in the greatest secrecy, but nothing more. Eirik Gnupsson sailed for Vinland but was never heard of again. There was never another expedition, and the location of Vinland was lost to history. Even to the Greenlanders it became a kind of Avalon, a mythical promised land, ruled by the once and future king.'

'That reminds me,' Maria said. 'The story of King Arthur. What about his queen, Guinevere? The menorah wasn't the only thing Harald stole from Constantinople.'

'Ah. I was wondering when you were going to ask that.' O'Connor tapped out his pipe on the sand and smiled at her, their eyes meeting. 'Legend has it that Harald was tended by a woman, her hair cropped short, dressed in the tunic and trousers of a man. History tells us that years earlier

Harald had released the princess and returned her to Constantinople after he escaped. But we know your namesake was never kidnapped at all, that she was a willing participant. It was Maria who released Harald and his Varangian guardsmen from prison the night before their escape. She stuck with Harald through thick and thin, through his marriage of convenience to the Kievan princess Elizabeth, through all he needed to do on his road to kingship. She tamed him, became the true guiding light of his life. And in his ultimate bid for power, to conquer England in 1066, she accompanied him, to a kingdom where she would at last have been able to assume her birthright as a princess. Harald planned to install her as his consort, to crown her Queen of England.'

'Harald was fifty-one in 1066; she was maybe ten years younger,' Maria said. 'Were there any other women in the two longships, when they set off to Vinland?'

'Maria was the only one.'

'Not the best advanced planning for a new colony.'

'The Viking mentality,' Jack smiled. 'Steal what you need when you get there. And remember, they were probably half crazed with exhaustion and pain, unable to think straight. Most of them probably thought they were going to Valhalla.'

The orb of the sun began to sink into the sea in the west, casting an orange glow over the eroded folds of bedrock that protruded from the slopes on either side of the bay. They looked silently out to sea, absorbing the muted radiance of the evening. 'They say the holy isle is bathed in the bright light of angels,' O'Connor said. 'It's a light you see in places like this, where heaven and earth seem to meet, and in places where the crust of human endeavour has been peeled away to the bare rock beneath. The heart of the forum in Rome, the Temple Mount in Jerusalem.'

'Both places where the menorah has been,' Maria said.

'I've thought that,' O'Connor murmured.

Jack leaned forward, his eyes suddenly ablaze as he stared at the horizon. 'The menorah was here, with Harald, at this very spot,' he said. 'Ever since I saw Halfdan in the ice I've known we were on the trail, almost as if something were willing us on. All we need now is some clue, something more concrete about where they went after leaving the icefjord.'

O'Connor looked at Jack penetratingly, lighting his pipe again. 'Halfdan gave you battle-luck, remember? He passed on the flame. Somehow I think there's more ahead for you.'

They were beginning to get up when Jeremy came bounding along the sand, and they could see the burly figure of Costas straggling some distance behind. Jeremy came to a halt in front of them, flushed and excited, his ebullience back in full force.

'Well, what is it?' Jack said amiably. 'Something else you've been concealing?'

'Not exactly.' Jeremy was struggling to regain his breath. 'The Mappa Mundi. While you were in the berg. I knew it.'

'Slow down,' Jack said. 'Take your time.'

Jeremy sank to his knees and extracted a rolled sheet from

his carrying case, then took a few deep breaths and began to regain his composure. 'Sorry. But this has got to be the most exciting thing yet.'

'Well?'

'Those hours I spent in my cabin. Avoiding you all,' Jeremy said apologetically. 'Well, I was poring over a digital version of the map we found in Hereford, Richard's exemplar, twelve-hundred-dpi resolution. Something was nagging me, something I thought I saw when Maria and I first unrolled the map in the cathedral chamber.'

'Go on.'

'I had our imagery lab in Oxford do a multi-spectral scan. Take a look.'

Jack took the sheet and unrolled it on his lap. It was a blown-up image of the lower left corner of the Mappa Mundi exemplar, showing the extraordinary image of Vinland and the New World they had first examined in Cornwall a few days previously, with the one inscription referring to Leif Eiriksson and the other to Harald Hardrada and the treasure of Michelgard. Jack suddenly saw what Jeremy meant. 'There's another drawing underneath!'

'Here it is, isolated and enhanced. Costas helped me do it.' Jeremy handed him another sheet, and Maria and O'Connor craned over to look. It was a simple linear tracing, a deep U-shape with the line bending back down on either side and trailing off, and two irregular circles in front.

'It's Vinland!' Maria exclaimed. 'It's exactly the same as the image of Vinland on the map that superimposed it, only on a bigger scale. The U-shape is the bay, and Vinland is marked at the head of the bay on the superimposed map. I was at the Viking settlement at L'Anse aux Meadows in Newfoundland last year. The archaeological site is at the head of the bay, exactly where Vinland is marked here, and these are the promontories on either side that extend out into the Strait of Belle Isle. Those circles are the islets off the coast, Little Sacred Island and Great Sacred Island. They would have been crucial navigational waymarkers for the Vikings.'

'That's what's so fantastic,' Jeremy said.

'What do you mean?' Jack said.

'Take a close look at the larger one.' Jeremy passed him a magnifying glass. 'There, where there seems to be a smudge.'

Jack slid the tracing aside and looked again at the imaging scan. 'I can see a cross mark on it, a definite cross,' Jack murmured. 'And that smudge on the side. Are those letters?'

'Runes.'

Jack's excitement mounted. 'Translation?'

'There are two lines,' Jeremy said. 'Even with the image intensifier I can barely read them, but I'm pretty sure of it. The first line says *Haraldi konungi*, Harald the king. The second line has two words, gold and Michelgard, the gold of Michelgard. That's Constantinople, of course.'

'Good God.'

'Richard of Holdingham must have done this sketch to begin with, but then had second thoughts. It's too exact, it gives too much away. So he erased it and drew the more generalized map showing Vinland, with the Leif Eiriksson inscription. Then he thought again and decided to add a reference to Harald Hardrada after all, that he had been in these parts with the treasure of Michelgard.'

'The first sketch is telling us something,' Jack murmured. 'It's telling us something incredibly precise.'

'X marks the spot.' O'Connor smiled broadly, for the first time since they had seen him. 'This suddenly makes it all worth while.'

Costas suddenly appeared over the head of the dune, looking slightly flustered after his route march over the island. 'The chopper's returned,' he panted as he joined them. 'Macleod wants to know whether you'll be returning to *Seaquest II* or going back to Istanbul. They're standing by in Disko Bay awaiting instructions. They're scheduled to sail north to carry out research on the edge of the polar icecap, and some of the scientists are getting distinctly itchy feet.' Costas suddenly noticed the sheet of paper on Jack's lap, and kneeled down for a closer look. 'A treasure map. My favourite. Where is it?'

Jack gazed at Costas with a familiar gleam in his eye, and then pointed his finger at the glowing orb of orange on the horizon.

'Due west, about two thousand three hundred miles. You can tell Macleod to dig out the copy of the Viking sagas I left him. It tells you how to lay on a course for Vinland.'

O'Connor stood up. 'It's time for you to go, it seems?' He shook Jack by the hand. 'I don't know where my path will lead me,' he said. 'Just do one thing for me, will you, Jack?'

'You name it.'

'Find out what happened to the menorah.'

Jack flashed a smile and put his other hand on O'Connor's shoulder. 'We'll do our best. Things have gone pretty well since Halfdan lent me his axe. I think there might just be a little battle-luck left.' He suddenly looked deadly serious. 'And you must take the greatest care.'

14

Thirty-six hours later, Jack lay in pitch blackness on an earthen floor on the other side of the Atlantic, cocooned in a sleeping bag and insulated from the damp ground by a thermarest. He shifted his rolled-up clothes to make a more comfortable pillow and stared into the darkness. Beside him Costas was snoring loudly, and he could hear the occasional rustle from Jeremy beyond his feet. He had leaped at the chance of spending the night in a reconstructed Viking longhouse, a low-set, thick-walled structure built entirely of turf, on the very spot where Leif Eiriksson and his band of Norse adventurers had built their first crude shelter on the shores of North America a thousand years before. But for Jack it had been a restless night, plagued by ill-defined dreams. His mind was still full of the extraordinary account O'Connor had given them on Iona the day before, of a secret brotherhood that had spanned the centuries and come to be associated with the worst horror of modern times. Every time Jack dozed off, the same images crowded his mind, snarling wolf-gods and swirling eagles, the seven-branched candlestick and the dreaded swastika, images that no longer seemed like dislocated fragments of history but meshed together to tell a story full of potency and danger.

Jack awoke with a start to a steaming mug of coffee thrust in his face. Costas gave him a gentle kick and leaned his stubbly face towards his friend. 'Rise and shine,' he said cheerfully. 'We've only got the site to ourselves for the morning. The Parks Canada people need to open it for a tour group at noon.'

Jack grunted and quickly raised himself, pulling on his jeans and blue fisherman's sweater and lacing up his boots. He flinched as he rubbed against the wound in his thigh, his legacy from the iceberg. In the sunlight streaming through the low entrance he could see Jeremy rolling up his thermarest and packing his sleeping bag. They had arrived in darkness the night before, and for the first time Jack could appreciate the dimensions of the longhouse. It was elongated and low-set, built entirely of turf on a timber frame with a stamped dirt floor and a pitched roof. He could see how it might have accommodated twenty or thirty people, several family groups, clustered around hearths evenly spaced along the chamber. It would have been a damp, dark place, fetid and rank during the long winter months. He could understand why the Vikings always yearned for the open air and the sea, for the summer months tending their flocks and embarking on long voyages of raiding and exploration.

Jack took his coffee and stooped through the entrance to the world outside, shielding his eyes against the glare of the morning sun. On the grass a short distance away was the red and white form of the Canadian coast guard Sikorsky S-61N Sea King helicopter that had brought them to the remote northern peninsula of Newfoundland from Goose Bay in Labrador, the nearest airfield where the IMU Embraer jet had been able to land. Jack turned from the helicopter and looked at the site around him. The longhouse was one of three sod buildings reconstructed on the edge of the original Viking settlement, only yards from the meadow where three dwellings and a primitive smithy had been excavated by the Norwegian archaeologists who had discovered the site in 1960. They had found only low ridges where there had once been turf walls, ghostly imprints of post holes and fire pits, and a meagre handful of artefacts, but it was enough to prove conclusively that the Vikings had been here. Jack looked across the lush grassland to the seashore, and out to the rocky islets with their sparse vegetation framed against the northern horizon. The site had none of the splendour of an ancient tomb or a lost city, but it had been one of the greatest archaeological discoveries of all time, irrefutable proof that adventurers from the Old World had visited the Americas five hundred years before Christopher Columbus. It was the first known European settlement in North America beyond Greenland, the first place where iron was smelted in the New World. And now Jack knew they were poised to open a whole new chapter in the history of the site, an episode that could scarcely have been dreamed of before the Mappa Mundi find. As he finished his coffee he felt the darkness of the night lift from him, and he began to tingle with excitement.

'Hard to believe Iona lies more than two thousand miles to the east.' Jeremy's tousled head appeared through the entranceway, and he stood beside Jack rubbing his eyes and cradling a coffee. 'But it looks much the same, doesn't it? This would have been familiar terrain to the Vikings.'

'This must be home turf for you too,' Jack said with a twinkle in his eye.

'My mother was Canadian, from Nova Scotia,' Jeremy replied. 'Visiting this place as a kid was what inspired me to study Norse archaeology. It's amazing how few people come here, even though it's a UNESCO World Heritage site. Read some history books and you'd still think the European involvement with North America began with John Cabot in 1497.'

'But the Vikings didn't stick around.' Costas had caught Jeremy's words as he stacked their bedding outside the longhouse, and he came over to join them. 'I thought L'Anse aux Meadows was more an outpost, a seasonal camp.'

Jeremy nodded. 'If we go by the archaeology alone, this

place was occupied for a few seasons at most, then maybe visited sporadically for a few years after that. The three longhouses could have accommodated upwards of a hundred people, so maybe there was an attempt to establish a permanent settlement. There were women here too, and livestock. But it didn't last. We're talking around AD 1000, maybe a little later. Iceland had been colonized from Norway about the end of the ninth century, Greenland by Eirik the Red about a century later, so that's probably where the settlers here came from. The style of turf house is typical of Iceland and Greenland at that period. Leif Eiriksson was the son of Eirik the Red, as the name implies.'

'They were probably testing the boundaries of their world,' Jack reflected. 'The Phoenicians did the same. The furthest Phoenician outposts date from the earliest period of exploration, and were all short-lived. Mogador in west Africa, Cornwall in Britain. Attractive trading potential, but too far away and vulnerable to last for long. It looks like the same story here.'

'That's a good model,' Jeremy said, ruffling his hand through his hair. 'Excavations here in the 1970s revealed lots of evidence for woodworking, for preparing logs and planks suitable for shipbuilding. It's a little difficult to envisage now, but there were dense forests of spruce and birch reaching right up to these meadows. It would have seemed like a gold mine to the Icelanders and Greenlanders, who had no forests of their own and had to import large timbers from Scandinavia. They repaired their ships here and may even have built new vessels, but most of the timber was probably shipped back to Greenland and Iceland.'

'I'm baffled,' Costas said. 'With all that wood, plus great pasturage and fishing, why didn't they establish a permanent colony?'

'Scraelings,' Jack said.

'Who?'

'The Norse name for the native peoples, the Indians,' Jeremy replied. 'It means wretches, which says it all for the Viking attitude. There was quite a large population in Newfoundland at that time, and their war canoes and bows made them more than a match for the Vikings. The archaeology doesn't give us much to go on, but the sagas tell an ugly story. When Leif Eiriksson first arrived, relations with the natives may have been tense from the outset. Soon there were confrontations, violent clashes. The occasional murder by one side or the other may have turned to outright war, with more distant bands joining in and the Vikings soon being overwhelmed by sheer force of numbers. They probably had to direct all their energy to stockading this place, to building a wooden palisade around their dwellings. It would have been impossible to tend livestock or hunt and fish, and in their weakened state illness would have been rife. They would have been unable to fell trees and prepare timber for shipment back home, their main reason for being here. The sagas tell us that Leif's brother Thorvold was killed by an arrow, and that may have been the death knell for the settlement.'

'Sounds like the pilgrim fathers in America, at Jamestown,' Jack said. 'Hemmed in by hostile natives, plagued by starvation and disease.'

'There's an even darker story.' Jeremy took out a battered paperback from his pocket. 'These are the *Vinland Sagas*, passed down by word of mouth and written down in Iceland in the thirteenth century. They're difficult to read as history, sometimes contradictory and confused, but the discovery of this site proves they're based on real voyages. According to the *Greenlanders' Saga*, another of Eirik the Red's offspring, his daughter Freydis, organized an expedition to Leifsbúðir, "Leif's Houses", their name for the Vinland settlement. There were two ships, one with about thirty Greenlanders, the other with about the same number of Icelanders. Once they'd disembarked there was some kind of dispute, maybe involving women, some deep-rooted animosity, that led Freydis and the Greenlanders to run berserk and murder all of the Icelanders in one awful rampage. Freydis herself murdered the five Icelandic women, and probably their children as well. If it truly happened, the dark deed would probably have taken place at night inside one of these longhouses.'

'Blood-feud,' Jack murmured, remembering his troubled sleep. 'I hope that's not our most enduring legacy from the Vikings.'

'Do we have firm dates for any of this?' Costas asked.

'The radiocarbon dates look about right for the foundation of the settlement, around AD 1000, with the other expeditions recounted in the sagas taking place over the next fifteen years or so. Freydis's expedition may have been the last.'

'Until Harald Hardrada.'

'That's what we're here to find out.' Jack rubbed his hands in anticipation, and eyed the compact chart case that Jeremy had placed alongside their bags. 'It's time we looked at that map again.'

Twenty minutes later they stood on the foreshore a few hundred metres from the archaeological site. Behind them lay the gently undulating meadows that surrounded the Viking settlement, and on either side the low-lying coast swept round the tidal flats of the bay. Beside them two Canadian coast guard crewmen were readying a lightweight Zodiac inflatable boat they had carried down from the helicopter. Jack shielded his eyes and looked out to sea. The light was pellucid, with the clarity they had seen in the icefjord, and the breeze carried with it a vestige of the chill air that flowed off the ice to the north even in June. For a moment Jack found himself thinking of the iceberg far away in the fjord, wondering whether it would finally melt somewhere near these shores and put Halfdan to rest on the trail of his companions. He brushed the thought aside and focused on the low rocky mass visible a few kilometres offshore.

'Great Sacred Isle,' he murmured. 'That's what we came here for.'

'There's no doubt about the identification.' Jeremy was holding a copy of Richard of Holdingham's sketch, and comparing it to a photocopy from the local Admiralty Chart. 'From what Maria taught me, Richard was a painstaking scholar and would have transcribed the map as accurately as he could, probably copying from an original sketch which somehow made its way to him from Greenland.' He suddenly put down the sketch and rushed over to a nearby hummock, where a cloud of steam was rising from a small camping stove.

'So what exactly are we looking for?' Costas asked. 'Pottery, coins, the odd rusty battleaxe?'

Jack smiled at his friend. 'Not a chance. Eight years of excavation at L'Anse aux Meadows in the 1960s produced exactly four Norse artefacts. A bronze pin, a stone oil lamp, a spindle whorl and a gilded brass fragment. And that was for a community that may have numbered over a hundred, and was here for several years. The Norse picked up what they dropped and didn't throw away anything. If Harald Hardrada chose to leave something, we may find it. If not, we probably won't find anything.'

Jeremy came tottering over the grass carrying two wooden bowls and spoons, and thrust them at Jack and Costas. 'Carved them myself when I was a kid,' he said proudly. 'Exact copies of Norse bowls from Greenland. And the stuff inside's authentic too.'

Costas peered suspiciously at the congealed mass in his bowl, and patted it with his spoon. 'Looks old enough,' he said. 'And smells like a resin factory. I take it this isn't food?'

'My own recipe.' Jeremy affected to ignore him. 'Based on the analysis of Norse refuse sites. Coarse barley flour, ground peas and pine bark. A kind of gruel. Quite good really.'

'Where's yours?'

'Couldn't wait. Ate it already.'

'Right.' Costas sniffed his spoon, and took an experimental lick. 'God almighty. Refuse is about right.'

'It's all you're getting. The total Viking experience. No modern food allowed at L'Anse aux Meadows.'

Costas grumbled, and Jeremy turned to Jack, who had quickly polished off his bowl and was staring again at the map.

'This was the place of no return,' Jack said. 'If they really got this far, none of Harald's men ever made it back home alive. They were on a one-way ticket to the end of the world.'

'What about their guides?' Costas spoke through a sticky mouthful, his eyes fixed balefully on Jeremy.

'I doubt whether any of the Greenlanders accompanied Harald this far,' Jack replied. 'With only the one longship remaining after Halfdan's burial they would have had no way of returning, and even at Ilulissat they would have had to await rescue by the Norse hunters and fishermen who made their way up to Norðrseta in the summer.'

'Remind me,' Costas said. 'We're here because of the map, the depiction of Vinland with the reference to Harald Hardrada on the Mappa Mundi. How did the information that Harald had been here get back to England, to the *félag* and Richard of Holdingham all those years later?'

'From what O'Connor was telling us, that bishop who arrived in Greenland in the early twelfth century, the one who was a member of the *félag*, managed to coax an account of Harald's expedition out of the local Norse. The guides who had returned from the icefjord to the western settlement in Greenland must have told of Harald's departure for Vinland, and the story would have passed down through the generations. If the history of Iceland is anything to go by, the Greenlanders must have had a rich tradition of sagas, some of them passed on secretively. None of the sagas survived the mysterious disappearance of the Greenlanders a few centuries later.'

'What about that cross on the map, X marks the spot?' Costas said. 'If that really does mark something out there, how could the Greenlanders possibly have known?'

'Easy,' Jeremy said. 'The Norse left waymarkers, navigational signposts. They would have been essential to retrace voyages in such a huge area that was hardly explored. Some of the stone cairns around Baffin Bay attributed to the Inuit may in fact have been raised by the Norse. The *Greenlanders' Saga* even tells us how Thorvold, the one who was shot down by the Indians, raised a ship's keel as a marker on a cape somewhere to the north-east of here. It became known as Kjalarnes, Keel Cape.'

'So you're suggesting Great Sacred Isle was a known waymarker.'

'I think there was more to it than that,' Jack said. 'For the island to be singled out so precisely on the map suggests something more, something closely associated with Harald's progress. It's just a guess, but I wonder whether Harald promised his Greenlander guides before leaving Ilulissat that he would leave some mark of his progress. An obvious place for the Greenlanders to suggest was their own navigational waymarker for Leifsbúðir at Great Sacred Isle, a place Harald could easily find. The Greenlanders may never have ventured here to find out whether he made it, but the memory of Harald's promise lived on.'

'Let's see if it's waiting for us, then.' Costas handed Jeremy his finished bowl, then gestured towards his rucksack. 'Got any mead or beer to wash that down with?'

'Out of luck there, I'm afraid. But what I have got is just as authentic. It's a kind of sour runny yoghurt, made from cow's whey left in an open vat for a few weeks. Best served warm. If you'll just give me a minute with the stove . . .' Costas was already halfway to the beach, backing off with his hands held up defensively. Jack grinned at Jeremy and jerked his head towards the Zodiac. 'I think breakfast is over.' A few moments later they were zipping up the survival suits and lifejackets lent to them by the coast guard for the trip. They helped push the boat out into the shallows and then hopped aboard, sitting on the pontoons while one of the crewmen cranked up the outboard. As they chugged slowly out through the bay they turned and watched the low coastline receding in their wake.

'The tide's in,' Jeremy shouted over the engine. 'When it's out, this whole bay is dry land. The Vikings caught salmon by laying traps at low tide, then returning on the next low tide. Harald's men would have had no trouble stocking up with food.'

The crewman opened the throttle as they left the bay, and they moved from the clear shallows to the greenish-black sheen of the open sea. Ahead of them the island was suddenly lit by a brilliant shaft of sunlight, shining through a gap in the clouds that were beginning to fill the sky.

'A shard from Mjøllnir,' Jeremy shouted.

'What?'

'The Norse believed that lightning and shafts of light were shards struck off Mjøllnir, Thor's hammer,' Jeremy shouted. 'It's usually a good sign.'

'Not another Norse omen,' Costas replied. 'I'm beginning to dream wolf-gods and blood eagles.'

'Don't worry.' Jack grinned at Costas through the spray. 'You'll get over it. And you'll soon have your feet back firmly on the ground.'

15

Twenty minutes later they stood on the lee side of Great Sacred Isle off the northernmost tip of Newfoundland, doffing the survival suits which they left with the crewman beside the Zodiac. The island ahead of them was about a kilometre long and half a kilometre wide, and was made up of rocky outcrops interspersed with patches of bog and meadow. At various points it rose in low ridges that Jack was inspecting with a pair of lightweight binoculars.

'My favourite.' Costas sighed contentedly, and kicked on his hiking boots. 'A treasure hunt.'

'No sophisticated gadgets this time.' Jack lowered the glasses and glanced at Costas as he laced up his boots. 'The terrain's useless for geophysics, and what we're looking for probably wouldn't show up anyway. We're talking Mark 1

Eyeball. Anyway, it's the only way I've ever found treasure.'

'So what are we looking for?'

'Something on the highest point, or a prominent point on the seaward side. But your guess is as good as mine. A cairn, or courses of stones lying on the ground that look too regular and may be from a collapsed pile. But if it was a wooden marker like that keel in the saga, then we're probably out of luck.'

The three of them fanned out over about a twenty-metre swathe and began to work their way up towards the centre of the isle, Jack in the centre. The terrain was not difficult to traverse, but was an awkward mix of exposed rock and soggy gullies that reminded him of their walk across Iona a few days before. After scrambling up the first small ridge, Costas stopped suddenly and looked at the ground. Jack caught his movement and spun round. 'Got something?'

'It's about Harald's Vikings.'

'Go on.' Jack relaxed and looked at Costas expectantly.

'No women. I mean, apart from Harald's lady, and she was obviously out of bounds.'

'Maria said that. But remember they weren't planning a colony. In their own minds they were going from one battle to another, to their last showdown. Anything they found on the way, fine, but if not, they had a higher purpose. Plus they were hardly in a fit state.'

'Are you worried about her?' Costas said. 'Maria, I mean?'

Jack was silent for a moment, then replied, 'She can look after herself. It's O'Connor who's in the firing line.'

A little over two hours later they had scoured the entire island, and come up with nothing. Jack had dropped out of sight of the other two, and found himself wandering along the rocky foreshore on the west side of the isle. He was beginning to feel dislocated, and the memories of his troubled dreams the night before were flashing back through his mind. For the first time he seriously wondered whether they had come to the end of the trail. For the archaeologists who had followed the Vikings before, this bleak and forbidding site had been a scene of triumph, of euphoria that made even the tiny scraps of Norse remains at L'Anse aux Meadows seem as exciting as King Tut's treasure. Yet here the trail had ended. Nothing conclusive had ever been found further west or south, no evidence of Viking settlement or exploration.

Jack squatted down on the foreshore, found a flat pebble and skipped it far out into the sea, counting the splashes until it disappeared. Maybe this was truly the edge of the Norse world, the boundary of the afterlife. Maybe this was where they had found their mystical battle at the end of time, their Ragnarok. Ever since Iona, Jack had felt an extraordinary convergence with Harald Hardrada, as if Harald were his spirit-companion, just present on the other side of the boundary. Maria had told him the Norse believed that those with wanderlust followed the paths left by their ancestors, by their spirit-companions, and Jack had begun to feel that he was being drawn along by this other presence. Now he suddenly felt marooned, swirling in a mist of uncertainty, without even a hint of where to go next.

Maybe this was exactly what Harald himself had felt at this point. Jack thought again of the map, of the ship in the ice, of Halfdan's great war axe. It was not all fantasy. It really had happened. There had to be something more here. He pressed his hands against the solid rock of the island, willing it to give up its secrets. He remembered the axe again. 'Battle-luck,' he whispered to himself. Then he got up and strode resolutely back up the low ridges of the island, spotting the other two together on a slab of rock towards the lower eastern shore. He reached them in a few minutes, then passed them his water bottle before taking a swig himself. 'We've got an hour before the ebb tide begins and we have to leave. Any suggestions?'

'I've just been telling Costas,' Jeremy said. 'Something's been niggling me. Something about that map.' He took out Richard of Holdingham's map and placed it on the rock, then sat down and stared at it with his hands clasped over his head. Suddenly he jumped up exultantly. 'I've been stupid,' he exclaimed. 'What I said about Richard, how meticulous he was. Look closely at his sketch. It's not a cross, an X. It's the Viking symbol of Thor's hammer, the stem with two arms coming to a point at the top.'

'Cool.' Costas sounded deadpan. 'But how does that help us?'

'Let's say they found a rock of that shape, and put their cairn there. Maybe not the best place for a beacon, but that's exactly what the Norse would have done. It would have been an affront to Thor to ignore it.'

'We've just found it,' Costas suddenly exclaimed. 'Take a look around your feet.'

They looked down and realized the slab they had been standing on had a peculiar regularity in its shape. They would not have noticed it without prompting, but as they clambered around they could see from one angle a clear similarity to the Thor's-hammer symbol.

'Okay,' Jeremy said excitedly. 'What we're after is markings, probably runes. Look under any overhangs you can find, anywhere sheltered.'

He vaulted over the side of the slab and began working his way along the edge, scanning the worn surface of the granite intently. After only a few seconds he dipped under an overhang and they heard a muffled whoop of delight. Jack jumped down beside him, and Jeremy took his hand and pressed it against the underside of the slab. 'Can you feel it?'

Jack moved his hands over the rough, damp rock, and began to feel interjoined linear depressions, like gouged lines. 'Yes!'

'Do you have a torch?'

Costas moved alongside them and thrust a mini Maglite into Jeremy's hands. He squatted back under the overhang, and trained the light on the rock. 'Two runes,' he said. 'The first is the third rune in the Norse *futhark*, the sound TH. With only two runes here, I'd suggest we're looking not at the letters of a word but at the rune's symbolic meaning, which in this case is eagle.'

'Eagle,' Jack said excitedly. 'Could that mean Harald's ship?'

'The second one clinches it,' Jeremy said. 'You'd better take a look.' He heaved himself out and passed the light to Jack, who crouched down and took Jeremy's place under the rock. Jack trained the light upwards straight on to the seven-branched symbol of the menorah. He stared transfixed, barely breathing. He could scarcely believe it. Harald Hardrada himself must have been at this very spot, staring up at the marks his men had made, perhaps the last person to see this before now. The pitted rock of the ancient runestaves looked like the surface of the carved stones Jack had seen two days before on Iona, yet he had only ever seen the symbol of the menorah carved in stone on the Arch of Titus in Rome. The image he was now looking at seemed to defy all the conventional parameters of history. It was incredible. He had to blink hard to remind himself that he was thousands of miles away from Iona and Rome on the other side of the Atlantic.

When Jack re-emerged he had a broad smile on his face, and slapped Jeremy on the back as he shook his hand. 'That'll do nicely,' he said. 'Very nicely. Congratulations, Jeremy.'

'What do the runes mean?' Costas said.

'The *Eagle*, Harald's ship, plus the symbol of his treasure,' Jack replied.

'Harald was here.'

'Something like that.'

'So it really did happen.' Jeremy slumped down on the grass beside the rock, exultant but drained. 'This rewrites the history books completely. Vinland was not just an obscure outpost, but a place visited by the greatest king of the Viking age.'

'And he went further,' Jack murmured.

'What happened here?' Costas said, peering glumly at the low shoreline where it was beginning to spatter with rain. 'I mean, if this godforsaken place was such a paradise for the Norse, why didn't Harald stay?'

'The Norse were great believers in the spirit world,' Jeremy said. 'The barrier between their world and the spirit world was porous, easily transgressed. The wolf-god, the eagle-god, the evil god Loki, any of them could appear in the real world in various guises visible to those with *seiðr*, a kind of second sight. The spirits of the dead could haunt a place. Maybe Harald and his men could sense a malign presence when they arrived here.'

'You wouldn't have needed second sight,' Costas said. 'Even after half a century there'd still be all the skeletons, especially if they were trapped inside one of the longhouses.'

'Harald's men probably would have felt compelled to collect the bones and cremate them, and then burn and bury everything else they could,' Jeremy said. 'And these runes probably had a double meaning, a protective magic to keep the spirits of this place at bay, and safeguard Harald and his men for what lay ahead. They were a rune-spell, a *galdrastafir*.' He got up and reached under the overhang, tracing his fingers over the staves carved in the rock. 'One rune might be the eagle's beak, another the tooth of a wolf, another Thor's hammer.'

'And one might be the menorah,' Jack added quietly.

'The more I've seen it, the more I believe the menorah became Harald's own rune, not only a symbol of his prowess and achievement but also a kind of talisman, something wrapped up in his own destiny.'

'His survival at Stamford Bridge would have seemed little short of a miracle,' Jack said. 'As a Viking warrior Harald would have hoped for glorious death in battle, but the fact that he was spared may have suggested that an even greater battle awaited him. In their half-crazed state he and his men may already have crossed the boundary into the spirit world, and believed they were seeing portents of their own destiny at the final showdown of Ragnarok.'

'Remember what Father O'Connor said,' Jeremy replied. 'The Norse believed in predestination, that one's fate is fixed at birth. Maybe Harald felt his was still to come, and was being driven onwards. He still needed to find his greatest triumph, to die a death befitting the supreme image of the Norse hero.'

'Okay, guys, you've lost me,' Costas said. 'All I want to know is where he went from here.'

Jack nodded and looked serious. 'Well, one thing they would have been able to do here was replenish their water and food and carry out ship repairs. One of the first things the archaeologists found in the 1960s was a primitive smithy where local bog iron was smelted and made into rivets. And some of those wood chips found near the foreshore could have come from Harald's men making replacement hull timbers.'

'And then where? East or south?'

'West down the St Lawrence estuary would have been a tough haul against the river flow,' Jeremy said. 'And going any further in that direction they would have been terrified of reaching the edge of the world and plunging into Ginnungagap, the great abyss.'

'Not exactly the glorious end they had in mind,' Costas said. 'So we're talking south?'

Jack nodded, then turned round and squatted with his back to the rock while he took out a palm computer from his backpack. He looked up at Jeremy. 'It's my turn to apologize for concealing something. I'm already one step ahead.' He flipped open the screen and activated the computer, and Costas and Jeremy squatted on either side of him. After a few seconds the isometric image of a Viking longship appeared on the screen.

'Lanowski emailed this to me late yesterday evening, after you were both asleep,' Jack said. 'It's a 3-D image of our Viking longship in the ice, based on the photogrammetric data we acquired inside the berg. Assuming that the *Wolf* and the *Eagle* were sister ships, this gives a pretty good idea of what the vessel looked like that brought Harald and his men to Vinland.'

Jack scrolled around the image to give them different

isometric views, and zoomed in to reveal details. They saw an elegant vessel with a single mast and square sail, broad-beamed amidships, with the stem and stern rising symmetrically. They could see where each strake of the hull had been made up of several planks, the lower edge of each overlapping the outside of the one below and joined to it by rivets and clenched nails. The keel was deep, with steeply angled lower planks, giving the vessel good resistance to sideways drift. Below the gunwale were evenly spaced oarports, and at the stern a steering oar on a projecting boss, just as Jack and Costas had seen on the longship in the ice. Lanowski had left out the superb carving that had adorned the stempost, but flying from the stern was a white flag which on close inspection proved to contain the distinctive IMU logo and a spidery image of a seven-branched candlestick.

'My God,' Costas murmured. 'The guy's got a sense of humour after all.'

'After overwintering at the icefjord they would have needed to refit their ship for the voyage south,' Jack said. 'Remember she was a venerable vessel by Viking standards, the same ship Harald had used to escape from the Golden Horn twenty-five years before. They would have had their work cut out for them making her seaworthy again after having survived the trip from Iona, and then being laid up on the ice all winter.'

'What time of year are we talking about?'

'The palaeoclimatologists in Macleod's team have got

pretty excited about the ice-cores they took through the berg where the longship was trapped. Apparently the winter of 1066 to 1067 in Greenland was particularly harsh, presaging the Little Ice Age of the medieval period. It would have been May or even early June before the Davis Strait was clear of drift ice.'

'Once they'd decided to consolidate in one ship, the *Eagle*, they could have used timbers from the other vessel to make repairs,' Costas said.

'Exactly what Lanowski found when he studied the pictures,' Jack said. 'Cross-beams and even part of the keel had been removed from the stern area.'

'What about caulking material?'

'They could only have survived the winter by hunting and fishing on the ice,' Jack said. 'I'm convinced they had Greenland Norse with them, men they had taken on board at the western settlement of Greenland to act as guides. They would have shown Harald's men how to smear the timbers with seal blubber as protection against shipworms, and to make rope from walrus hide.'

'And they would have told them there was no hope in going north,' Costas suggested.

'In theory, the Vikings could have navigated the north-west passage through the Arctic to the Bering Strait, but there's no evidence they ever went west of Baffin Bay,' Jeremy replied. 'There's a smattering of Norse artefacts from Inuit sites as far north as Ellesmere Island, on the edge of the polar icecap, but they were probably collected by Inuit hunters from shipwrecks or from abandoned Norse settlements in Greenland. It's like the evidence for Franklin's doomed expedition to find the north-west passage in 1845, a tantalizing scatter of finds absorbed into another culture.'

'It's kind of spooky,' Costas murmured. 'Everywhere we go we seem to be on the trail of the Vikings, yet it's as if they weren't quite there. I think I'm beginning to believe in that spirit world.'

Jack jerked his head back towards the low shoreline behind them and the site of L'Anse aux Meadows. In his mind's eye he saw the Viking ship, sail furled, drawn up and keened over in the shallow tidal estuary. 'You can be sure they were here. And remember our longship in the ice.'

'So we agree they reached here in, say, late June of 1067?' Jeremy asked.

'Once the drift ice had gone and the weather had settled, it would have been a relatively easy passage across the Davis Strait from Ilulissat and down the coast of Baffin Island and Labrador to this place, following the route told to them by the Greenlanders,' Jack said. 'It's iceberg alley out there, but they could have mustered enough fit oarsmen for short bursts to keep out of harm's way. Chances are they had a steady and favourable wind all the way, behind them or on the quarter. Even in rough seas a vessel like this would have been able to ride out storms, supple enough to flex with the pitch of the sea, and with a high enough freeboard to prevent the hull sinking under the weight of icing. And the Norse were extraordinarily skilled navigators. They had a kind of sunstone, a refractive feldspar that would catch polarized light in overcast weather and tell them where the sun was, but mostly they navigated by their senses, by an intimate knowledge of the sea and stars. If Harald ever got caught in one of the perennial fogs off this coast, they would have kept on course by the smell of the land, the waft of the pine forests.'

'And you really think Vinland was their promised land?' Costas persisted, looking dubiously towards the shore again. 'It looks pretty bleak and forbidding to me.'

'That's not how it would have appeared to the first Vikings who came here. It had all the ingredients for the good life.' Jack paused, and looked pensively towards the mainland. 'But by Harald's time it had a darkness over it, a pall cast by Freydis's murderous crime. The Greenlanders would have known of it, and may even have warned Harald to stay away. Half a century after the events described in the sagas, Vinland may have acquired a sinister reputation, a place where people went but rarely returned. The Norse were the toughest adventurers around but were a pretty superstitious bunch, and for them this place was baleful, cursed. They would not have wanted to stay.'

'And there were the Scraelings.'

Jack nodded. 'By this stage Harald's men probably numbered well under a normal longship's complement of about thirty, maybe only half that. They would have known about the Scraelings from the Greenland Norse. To provoke any kind of confrontation would have been suicidal. They probably slipped into this bay unobtrusively, took the timber and iron they needed, tapped pine resin for caulking, killed a few deer for clothing and venison, collected as much fish and meat and wild fruit as they could. Their last act may have been to burn and level the settlement and then stop at this island to make their mark, before leaving Leifsbúðir for ever.'

'And then heading south,' Costas said.

'Down the coast of Newfoundland, across to Nova Scotia, maybe along the eastern seaboard of the United States,' Jack said. 'You remember the simulation programme Mustafa used to model the Black Sea exodus, the daily progress of the refugees from Atlantis? I had Lanowski use it to model the likely progress of a Viking ship along this route, factoring in everything we know about the longship, the likely season and the weather conditions in the eleventh century. Our new Canadian captain of *Seaquest II* knows these waters like the back of his hand and was able to add his invaluable expertise. They were like ancient Mediterranean seafarers, the Vikings. They measured their progress in daily runs, *dœgr*. With the Labrador current behind them and favorable winds, they would have been able to progress south. If they stuck close inshore and avioded the Gulf Stream, within three weeks they could have rounded the panhandle of Florida and been in the Caribbean.'

'The Caribbean?' Costas whistled. 'Incredible.'

'It's just conjecture,' Jack said. 'Wherever they got to, they would have needed to put ashore to replenish water and food, within a week or ten days of leaving this place. Let's say they encountered native peoples again where they put ashore, and were discouraged from trying to stay longer. Then another week or ten days and they were down opposite Georgia and Florida. The shoreline would have looked increasingly inhospitable, an unfamiliar terrain of tropical vegetation and dense scrub. But there would have been no easy turning back, against the currents and wind, with reliance on their sail and too few fit to man the oars for sustained rowing. With increasing desperation they may have continued south. It's pure speculation, of course, but they could even have sailed through the Florida Keys and into the Caribbean. If that happened, the prevailing winds could have blown them south-west, even as far as Central America.'

'That's a hell of a long way from Constantinople.'

Jack suddenly remembered his precious days with Katya six months before in Istanbul, the two of them absorbed in the labyrinthine past of the city, their discussion of how the back alleys of history could lead to the most extraordinary adventures of discovery. For a moment he felt a pang of regret, but then was overtaken by a surge of excitement. 'A very long way indeed,' he said. 'But look where we are now, how far we are already from their homeland. The Viking presence here at L'Anse aux Meadows is fully documented, corroborated by archaeology. Anything's possible.'

'Half crazed with thirst and exhaustion, some of them still crippled by their wounds from Stamford Bridge,' Jeremy murmured. 'It's an incredible image. They would have been terrified but exhilarated, fearful any moment of dropping over the edge of the world yet every day getting closer to Ragnarok, to the showdown where they would join Odin and Thor battle-girded for the last time with their great war axes. To us the tropics seem benign, but to the Vikings they would have been a vision of hell, a gathering aura of crimson that would seem to be drawing them ever closer to their destiny.'

Costas stood up and gazed towards the north-eastern horizon, through the strait towards the shore of Labrador and the open Atlantic. The cloud was building up, and a sea mist was beginning to shroud the coast. Suddenly he pointed to a white form that appeared in and out of the mist on the horizon. 'It's *Seaquest II*,' he said excitedly. 'And the Lynx is on the way.'

Jack looked out to sea. He had gambled a little bit of his reputation on persuading Macleod to call a halt to the icefjord project and sail south to meet them, in the expectation that they would be going somewhere further after L'Anse aux Meadows. Jack never normally exerted authority over his colleagues in the other IMU departments, and fortunately Macleod had developed a keen interest in the archaeology after having brought Jack to Ilulissat in the first place. But the conditions for taking ice-cores were rapidly becoming untenable as summer drew in, and there had been serious rumbles of discontent among the invited scientists. Jack pursed his lips and for the next few minutes watched as the dark speck of the helicopter became recognizable and the thud of its rotor filled the bay. It flew lazily overhead and then settled down on its pontoons in the shallows close to the Zodiac. After the turbine had powered down they watched the helmeted figures of Ben and Andy emerge and wade across to greet the two Canadian coast guards.

'Where do we go from here?' Costas said. 'Looks to me like the trail's wide open.'

'We need something more,' Jack said, his brow knitted. 'I'd hoped there'd be something extra, some small clue. But at least there's nothing for anyone else to go on. It means I can get back to Father O'Connor and give him the go-ahead to break his story to the press and Interpol. He and Maria should have finished compiling the dossier on the *félag* by now, and we haven't got enough here to justify delaying any longer. As long as the discovery of the menorah was likely, O'Connor's overriding concern was that we get there first and prevent it falling into the wrong hands. Now we must focus everything on stopping that character Loki. O'Connor's life may depend on it.'

'I don't want to be there when you have to tell Macleod to turn right round and sail back to the icefjord.' Costas squatted down to adjust his boots and leaned back against the grassy verge below the slab of rock. Suddenly there was a tumbling sound and a stream of Greek expletives. Where Costas had once been, all they could see were his boots emerging from a mound of turf.

'Are you all right?' Jack spun round and peered anxiously into the black hole that had formed beneath the rock. He and Jeremy began frantically heaving away the turf and stones that had trapped Costas' legs.

'Just the usual shattered pride.' The voice was muffled, and was followed by a silence. 'But I've found a new friend.'

As Costas' upper body came into view, they were met by an astonishing sight. In the small cavity in front of his face was a crouched human skeleton, the skull tucked down beneath the knees and the feet buried in earth. Hanging off the bones were the tattered remains of animal-skin clothing, and the scalp still retained patches of long white hair.

Jeremy crouched forward for a closer look. 'My palaeopathology's a little rusty, but I'd say we've got a male, maybe late middle age.'

'Scraeling?' Costas said.

Jeremy shook his head. 'The physiognomy's European. And this guy's tall, well over six feet. He could be one of the early English or French explorers, but I'd say these bones are older than that, really old. I'd say we've got ourselves a Norseman.'

Jack closed his eyes and swayed slightly. This could be it. He prayed that his luck would hold.

'Those are some pretty impressive scars on the bones,' Costas said.

'I've seen that before in Viking warrior burials in England,' Jeremy said. 'Battle injuries caused by axes and swords. Not the kind you'd get from an encounter with Scraelings, who had no edged metal weapons. This guy was pretty severely hacked about. There are some odd scars that may be later injuries, particularly those ring marks around his wrists, as if he'd been shackled. But all the battle wounds I can see look well healed, a long time before he died.'

Jack looked pensively at the skeleton. 'Are you thinking what I'm thinking?'

'Remember there were other Norse out here,' Jeremy cautioned. 'But it's possible, just possible, that we've got another of Harald's men, another one to add to Halfdan. The thing that baffles me is the age of the injuries. If he died on their voyage down from the icefjord, the slash marks from wounds at Stamford Bridge the autumn before would still be fresh on the bones. These ones had healed up years before, even decades.'

'And this isn't a burial,' Jack said. 'This guy crawled in here, and holed himself in with those rocks. That's why his bones haven't been scavenged.'

'This might help.' Costas' muffled voice came from under the rock, where he had squeezed his upper body into the space in front of the skeleton and was gingerly feeling in the darkness under the ribcage. He carefully prised out two objects, and held the larger one out. Jack took it without thinking, his mind still on the puzzling enigma of the skeleton.

'Well, what is it?'

Costas re-emerged to see the other two staring agape at the object in Jack's hand. It was a flat pendant, about the size of a small saucer, and was carved in a lustrous green stone, unmistakably jade. The curvilinear, undulating surface seemed abstract in design, but as they stared at it they could make out eyes, a beak, stylized wings.

'Holy shit,' Jeremy whispered. 'It's the Maya eagle-god.'

Costas crawled out and brushed himself off. 'Maya,' he said phlegmatically. 'Mexico, the Yucatán. Temples in the jungle, human sacrifice. Am I right?'

'Impossible.' Jack carefully brushed a film of dirt from two silver discs that formed the eagle's eyes. He stared at them, shook his head and passed the pendant to Jeremy. 'It's impossible. Tell me I'm not seeing things.'

'They're coins,' Jeremy said quietly. 'Okay. Let's be clinical about this. The one on the left's a Viking coin from England, a quatrefoil penny of King Cnut. Look, you can read CNUT REX ANGLO, with the crowned bust.' He flipped the pendant over. 'You can see the reverse on the other side. ARNCETEL OEO, minted by a man called Arncetel at York. Cnut ruled from 1016 to 1035, but his coins were valued for their purity and are found in hoards across Scandinavia to at least the 1066 period.'

'And the other one?' Costas said.

'That's Roman. Over to you, Jack.'

Jeremy passed back the pendant and Jack peered closely at the right-hand coin. 'It's a silver denarius of the emperor Vespasian,' he said. 'IMP CAESAR VESPASIANUS AUG. A particularly fine portrait head of Vespasian, warts and all, with a laurel crown.'

'You've just lost me again,' said Costas. 'Did you say Vespasian? The Roman emperor?'

'Old Roman bullion coins, gold and silver, sometimes found their way into Viking hoards,' Jeremy said. 'Looted from old treasuries, brought back as curiosities by the Varangians from the Mediterranean.'

Jack raised his eyebrows, then turned the pendant over. He brushed the reverse of the coin gently with his finger, and then stifled a gasp. 'Good God. It's a Judaea Capta coin. One of the coins issued by Vespasian after the Roman conquest of Judaea, in AD 70 or 71.' He angled the pendant towards the light and they could clearly see the seated figure of a woman in front of a Roman legionary standard, and below it the single stark word IVDAEA.

'Isn't this what we're after?' Costas said. 'I mean, the lost treasure of the Temple in Jerusalem?'

'I may be wildly wrong,' Jack said fervently, 'but I think we've got two coins from the treasure of Harald Hardrada. How they got into this pendant is a total mystery. Something extraordinary happened, something that brought this man back here years later, to a place he had first come to on Harald's ship. And yes, this is what we're after. It's fantastic. This coin may have been minted from silver vessels looted from the Temple along with the menorah. Who knows, it may even have been touched by the emperor Vespasian himself. It could be pure coincidence that Harald had this coin in his hoard, but I doubt it. Harald knew his history, had been to Jerusalem. In his own mind and those of his followers, anything associated with the menorah and the Temple treasure may have added lustre to his name. I really feel we're standing in Harald's footsteps now. This is our best find yet, maybe the closest we'll ever come to the menorah itself.'

'Maybe not quite the best find,' Costas said with a twinkle. 'Take a look at this.' He reached into the shadows under the rock and picked up the second object he had found with the skeleton. 'I think it's another runestone.'

Jeremy excitedly took the flake of rock and peered closely at it. One side had been crudely smoothed, and was covered with faint lines. 'Similar to the runestone found by the Nazis on the longship,' he murmured. 'Same basic *futhark* and time period, but different hand. The runes have really just been scratched on the surface, maybe the last act of this guy as he squatted under the rock.'

'Maybe that's what he came back here to do, to leave a record,' Costas said. 'Maybe he was keeping true to Harald's promise to the Greenlanders.'

'Anything legible?' Jack asked.

'It's easier for me to transliterate the runes into Old Norse, using the standard alphabet.' Jeremy whipped out a notebook, and they watched as he quickly penned a neat line of symbols across the page, occasionally backtracking to make emendations:

Þar var ørœfi ok strandir langar ok sandar. Rak Þá skip
Þirra um haf innan. Sandar hvitir viða Þar sem Þrier
fóru ok ósæbratt.

'I can't read the first line completely, but it has the word
dœgr, runs and the rune for the number twenty. I think it
means they sailed for twenty runs, along a coast with long
beaches and sands. Then their ship, the *skip*, was driven all
about on the inner ocean, *um haf innan*. Then they came to a
flat land, covered with forest, with extensive white sands
wherever they went, and shelving gently to the sea. The last
two lines are also unclear, but the first of them seems to say
a land of fire and light.'

'It's just like you said, Jack,' Costas exclaimed. 'Twenty
runs, twenty days, takes them along the eastern seaboard. It's
a coast with long stretches of beaches and sands, especially
when you get to Florida. Then the inner ocean. That sounds
exactly like the Caribbean.'

'Driven all about.' Jack spoke with mounting excitement.
'July, August, that's the beginning of the hurricane season.
They could have been blown right across the sea, lost all
sense of where they were.'

'Then the flat land, covered with forest,' Jeremy said.
'When I was a kid we sailed across to the Yucatán peninsula
in Mexico. That's exactly what you see. It's incredibly flat, a
limestone plateau only a few metres above sea level, covered
with dense scrub and jungle and surrounded by brilliant
white beaches.'

'And hot as hell in summer,' Costas said. 'A land of fire and light.'

'This is not just a wild guess. It's all beginning to add up.' Jack lifted the jade pendant, then eyed Jeremy intensely. 'And what about that final line?'

Jeremy let out a low exhalation and gazed back at Jack, his face flushed with excitement. 'I can make out three words. The first one is the standard Norse word for the underworld, the watery abyss at the edge of the world, *Ginnungagap*. The second is *Ragnarok*. The third I've never come across before in Old Norse. It's a proper name, a place name. *Ukilabnal*, or something close to that. It looks like Harald and his men reached their day of reckoning at this place, their final showdown at the edge of the underworld.'

'It didn't work out for our friend.' Costas jerked his thumb at the skeleton. 'I bet he wished he'd gone to Valhalla along with his buddies.'

'Does the name mean anything to you?' Jack asked.

'Oh yes.' Jeremy's voice was hoarse, and he could hardly get the words out. 'Anthropology 101. Luckily my undergraduate adviser forced me to keep my options open. Introduction to Mesoamerican Civilization.'

'Go on.'

'In the eleventh century, Uukil-abnal was the name of Chichén Itzá, the greatest ceremonial centre of the Maya, smack in the centre of the Yucatán jungle.'

'Well I'll be damned.'

Costas let out a sigh of satisfaction. 'At last.' He stood up, arched his legs stiffly where they had been pinned down and looked with distaste at the drizzle that was enveloping him. 'You guys with Viking blood may have some kind of yearning for all this misery, but it just leaves me cold.' He turned to Ben and Andy, who had been loitering nearby, and grinned broadly at them. 'Pack your bags, boys. We're going to Mexico.'

16

The first inkling Maria had that something was wrong came just before midnight. She was hunched over a laptop computer in a monk's cell three doors down from Father O'Connor's study, in the medieval cloister on the isle of Iona. They had decided to stay up late and get the job done, two long days after she had waved Jack and the others off in the helicopter. She had been glancing at the photograph pinned on the wall in front of her, the extraordinary image of the jade pendant with the two coins that Jack had emailed her from L'Anse aux Meadows the day before. She was itching to be back, to be alongside Jack again. For the third and final time she was working through the document that she and O'Connor had prepared on the *félag*, straining her eyes to keep focused on the screen. In a few minutes she would be able to copy the file to O'Connor and join him for a final proofread, and then they would email it off to his contact at Interpol in Austria. She was tired, as drained as she had ever been, but she was beginning to feel a glimmer of relief. They were not out of danger yet, but at least she had persuaded O'Connor to leave the monastery the next morning and accompany her back to the safety of *Seaquest II*.

The first sign had been a dull thumping in the corridor. No obvious cause for alarm, but Maria was edgy with exhaustion and nerves. She turned towards the door, slightly ajar, and the dark corridor beyond. It had gone quiet again. She had grown accustomed to the stillness of the monastery, but something was different. She felt a sudden chill, a presentiment of fear.

Then without warning the door swung open. A gloved hand reached in and snatched it, stopping it from crashing into the wall. Then a dark figure advanced on her with lightning speed, head held low. Maria had no time to react. One hand slapped her head aside and savagely twisted her ear, and another clamped her mouth. The table was hurled against the wall and a foot crushed her laptop. She was dragged violently backwards, through the door and into the corridor. The hand was wet against her mouth, sticky and warm. Her ear was twisted again and she was blinded by pain, her eyes watering, unable to breathe. Suddenly she was released and slammed face forward against the wall, her arms pinned behind her. Duct tape was slapped over her mouth and her wrists. Her assailant held her body tight to his and yanked her hair back. She could feel the coarseness of his skin against hers, the metallic smell of his breath.

For a horrifying moment there was no movement. Maria began to shake uncontrollably. Her breathing returned, in short, searing gasps through her nose. She felt claustrophobic, about to suffocate. Her assailant snorted, pushed her sideways until she nearly fell, then jolted her through an open door and held her tight again from behind. She felt his breath against her ear, the nauseating smell.

'Get a hold of that.' The words were snarled into her ear, the accent indefinable. Maria blinked hard to clear her eyes. She was in O'Connor's study. Through the blur she saw the candle on his mantelpiece, the copy of the Mappa Mundi on the wall behind. The flame was flickering on the ink of the Red Sea, and seemed to be throwing a red aura over the rest of the map. Maria felt light-headed, close to blacking out. She blinked again, desperately trying to clear the red tunnel around her vision. She saw the candle on his desk, the one she had lit for him an hour before. She looked down. Her breathing was coming in quick stabs. Then it stopped.

There was someone on the floor. She felt her knees give way, and her assailant pulled her upright, squeezing her until she retched.

She looked down again.

Father O'Connor.

Her heart lurched in horror. The candle cast a shadow over the floor, and at first all she saw was a dark form. Then she began to make out his head. His mouth was duct-taped, his eyes wide open. She struggled to make a noise, to speak to him, but her assailant stifled her nose. Surely O'Connor must see her, must realize she was trying to communicate. He remained still, his eyes staring. He was lying on his front, his head under his desk, his arms and legs splayed wide open. He was wearing his brown monk's cassock.

Then she realized. The colour on the map. The sticky wetness on her face. The metallic taste.

It was blood.

She looked at O'Connor again. Something was horribly amiss. The darkness on his back was not his cassock at all. Then she knew, with sickening certainty.

The blood-eagle.

She looked frantically from side to side, her eyes adjusting to the gloom. There was blood everywhere. Soaking the remains of his cassock, seeping out in a pool under his body, splashed and spattered over his desk and books, flecked in livid trails over the ceiling.

She looked again. She could see the gaping hole, the shape. From shoulder to shoulder, and down the back. The wings and the tail. On either side she saw things too awful to register. Lumps of bloody flesh. Rows of severed bone, a ribcage. Bulbous piles of organs, like offal on a butcher's bench.

Maria screamed, but no sound came out.

Her assailant jerked his hand under her chin and pressed his cheek hard against hers. She could just make out his face, could see the leering smile, the murderous, washed-out eyes, the smears of drying blood. He began to rub his cheek against hers, his stubble rasping her skin like sandpaper, pressing her again and again with the smoothness of a scar that ran from his eye socket to his jawbone, all the while panting heavily, grinning obscenely at the carnage on the floor. She could feel his arousal, smell the adrenalin. Her mind began to shut down, seeking oblivion in the face of horror.

'That was for my grandfather,' the voice whispered. 'O'Connor was conscious when I cut out his lungs. He knew what was happening. The blood-feud is finished. Now it is time for me to claim my prize.'

He kicked her legs from under her and dragged her back towards the door. The last thing she felt was the throbbing pain in her cheek, her own blood commingling with O'Connor's. Then there was blackness.

Jack skilfully manoeuvred the Zodiac towards shore, allowing the boat to slide down under its own weight into each trough and then gunning the engine until it stood at the crest of the next wave. Above them the sky was flecked with high, fast-moving clouds heading south, and they were buffeted by a strong onshore wind which had been gathering strength all morning, raising a rapid swell. The air had the same pellucid quality they had seen in the Arctic, but even the wind could not disguise the burning intensity of the sun as it bore down on them, the glare blinding to their unaccustomed eyes. Behind them the breakers over the reef-girt shallows underlined the sleek form of *Seaquest II*, which was maintaining position over deep water a mile offshore.

For Jack it was exhilarating to feel the spray of the sea again, after five days cooped up during the long voyage south from Newfoundland along the eastern seaboard of the United States and into the Caribbean. It was the same wherever he was, in the Arctic, on the Golden Horn, by the shore of Iona or Great Sacred Isle, an uplifting in his soul he felt every time he tasted the sea. He stood up, his left hand holding the throttle and his right hand holding the painter line from the bow, and motioned for the other two to slide forward and get ready. Just before entering the surf he killed the outboard and swung it up on its pinions. Costas and Jeremy leaped into the water on either side, holding the Zodiac against the surge and return of the breakers until it was pushed into an eddy beside a sandbar. They swung it round until the bow pointed into the waves and waited while Jack threw out the anchor. Once they saw he had things under control, they waded ashore, their black IMU wetsuits dripping with the warm seawater and their hair matted with spray.

They were on a low, narrow beach backed by a continuous line of thorny jungle, the twisted trunks and strewn fragments of dead coral and driftwood testament to the severe hurricane damage of the year before.

'Xerophytic scrub,' Jeremy panted. 'Welcome to the

Yucatán. Not really rainforest up here at all, but jungle in the true sense of the word.'

'Wasteland, you mean.' Costas ventured a few feet into the tangled undergrowth, then backed out quickly, brushing a spider's web and midges irritably from his face. 'Give me the Caribbean over Greenland any day, but how a civilization could have developed here is beyond me.'

'The key to the whole Maya thing was fresh water.' Jeremy led Costas along the beach until they came to the source of the sandbar, a channel of extraordinarily clear water about three metres wide that cut through the jungle and flowed into the sea. 'The place is riddled with it. Some of these rivers come underground, through amazing cave systems that originate far inland. I should be able to show you later on today.'

'You've spent time here?'

'Student field trips. Sweating in the jungle, measuring overgrown ruins, getting eaten alive.'

'You should learn to dive,' Costas said drily.

'That's what Jack's been telling me. He says you're an advanced technical diving instructor, one of the best. Maybe when this is all over.'

'A pleasure. Just don't get any ideas about diving inside icebergs.'

'I'll leave the thrill-seeking to you guys.' Jeremy grinned. 'I'd be in it purely for the archaeology.'

'What was that place again, the Maya name on the runestone with my friend under the cairn?' Costas wiped away the sweat that was beginning to trickle down his face.

'Uukil-abnal,' Jeremy replied. 'The name in the eleventh century for Chichén Itzá, the most famous archaeological site in the Yucatán. A fantastic overgrown city sticking out of the jungle. Pyramids and all that. I think that's our next stop.'

Jack came up after having anchored the Zodiac in the surf, and they began stripping their wetsuits to their waists.

'Nice beach,' Costas commented. 'But a little desolate.'

'Cortés came here in 1519,' Jack replied. 'But the conquistadors took one look and bypassed this place completely. They didn't conquer the interior of the Yucatán until years later.'

'I can see why.' Costas struggled out of the top of his wetsuit, then flinched as a gust of wind blasted sand against him. 'So you think Harald Hardrada was here?'

'Lanowski did a best-fit calculation for where the longship might have made landfall after being swept across by a summer north-westerly from the Florida Keys,' Jack said. 'We chose this particular spot because of the river. The Vikings would have been desperate for fresh water, and they would have been able to draw up their longship in the creek. Also the edge of the river's a likely place for a Maya track into the interior.'

'This may even have been a Maya beach landing, a harbour,' Jeremy added. 'Most of the major Maya sites are well away from the sea, but they were pretty competent seafarers. I've seen paintings showing large war canoes, easily the size of a Norse longship.'

'Not exactly what Harald and his men were hoping for,' Costas said.

'If they were apprehensive about the Scraelings, these guys down here would have had them shaking in their breeches, fearless Viking warriors or not,' Jeremy replied. 'The Vikings may have dreamed about that final showdown at Ragnarok, but once they saw the reality of what they were up against, they might have had second thoughts.'

'Probably no choice by this stage,' Jack said. 'Their ship would have been a wreck after the voyage, and they would have been starving. They were committed to ending it all here. My guess is they would have set off into the jungle.'

'I've been meaning to ask,' Costas said. 'That character Pieter Reksnys. The Nazi's son, Loki's father. Didn't he end up in Mexico too?'

'Apparently when O'Connor was a Jesuit missionary in Central America in the sixties, he knew all about Reksnys' whereabouts.' Jack raised his hand to his eyes, shielding them from the glare of the sun. 'But O'Connor was keeping a low profile, so he avoided an encounter. There was a price on his head in the *félag* even then. Apparently, when Andrius Reksnys and his son sold their opal mine in Australia they moved first to Costa Rica. It was a haven for Nazis on the run. Then when the Nazi hunt began to die down in the late 1960s, Reksnys senior moved back to Europe, to the remote castle in the Obersaltsburg where he was gunned down five years ago.'

'The dead old man in the newspaper photo, with the swastika armband.'

'Right.'

'O'Connor say anything more about that?'

'Not when I spoke to him,' Jack said. 'He won't reveal who they used, and we don't need to know. Maybe he'll change his mind. But he said no regrets. I think he felt it was his duty as a former member of the *félag* to make amends and see that justice caught up with Reksnys.'

'Fair enough.'

'The younger Reksnys, Pieter, the one who'd helped his father Andrius with those SS executions, had more than enough money to retire and devote himself to providing his own son with the same twisted view of the world. But like a lot of these characters he couldn't keep his fingers out of organized crime, especially in this neck of the woods, where virtually anything goes.'

'Drugs? Guns?' Costas said.

'He dabbled in them, but he came to focus more and more on the antiquities black market, eventually to the exclusion of everything else. It became his obsession, and was immensely lucrative. From the 1960s there was huge demand in America and Europe for Mesoamerican antiquities, for decorated pottery, gold, jade, stone carving. According to O'Connor, Reksnys had his eye on the Yucatán even before it began to open up to foreign investors.'

'He's here?' Costas said, looking out into the jungle. 'Right under our very noses?'

'This place was like an untapped gold mine. Even now the Mexican authorities have huge problems policing the area, especially in the tracts of jungle owned by foreigners like Reksnys. And just like the Mafia who run the tourist industry, guys like Reksnys have plenty of connections among the politicos and the police. It's as corrupt as hell down here. There are literally hundreds of uncharted Maya sites dotted through the jungle, to be picked over at leisure if the few clean police and the archaeologists can be kept at bay.'

'Any idea where Reksnys operates?'

'He's very elusive, lives barricaded away. But we know he owns a large area of jungle in the north Yucatán, between the coast where we are now and the inland site of Chichén Itzá.'

Costas whistled. 'Seems an incredible coincidence.'

'There's no way the *félag* could have made the connection with the Yucatán, except by pure guesswork. The only clue to this place we have is that jade pendant from L'Anse aux Meadows, and there's no evidence anyone found it before us. But if there is something here, if Harald and his men truly got here, then Reksnys may have come across it by pure chance. He's probably got more people working for him than there are archaeologists in the whole of the Yucatán. My hope is that if we do come up with anything, it's in one of the policed archaeological zones and not out here in the wilderness.'

'So the menorah would be right up his street,' Costas murmured. 'Not just as a sacred artefact for the *félag*, but from a professional point of view. He'd know exactly how to market it to the highest bidder.'

'That's the one thing that really scares O'Connor. And remember we're not just talking private collectors. Once again the world would have to contend with a Nazi influencing the course of Jewish history.'

'How's Maria getting along?'

Jack lightened up for a moment. 'Kicking herself for missing the L'Anse aux Meadows excitement, but planning to join us here unless we draw a blank. I'd be very pleased to see her away from Iona.'

'And back with us.'

'Too many males around here.'

'You know she's close to Father O'Connor.'

'I know.'

'I mean, very close.'

'I know.' Jack paused. 'I think it began after that conference in Oxford, before they showed us the Mappa Mundi.'

'Something else that malign force in the Vatican could hold against him.'

'O'Connor's been walking a tightrope in more ways than one. But Maria was always very discreet.' Jack paused again, and looked down. 'Anyway, she's one of my oldest friends. I knew her even before I had the dubious honour of meeting you.'

'It was destiny,' Costas said. 'Where would you be without

my technical backup? I've never come across anyone more hopeless with computers. And I'd be stuck inside some windowless prison in Silicon Valley, earning tons of money but having no fun.' He swatted a mosquito from his neck, and ducked his head as the wind blew up a swirl of sand that hit them like a blast from a furnace. 'No icebergs, no beach holidays.'

'And no murderous psychopath on your trail,' Jack replied. 'I just hope to God O'Connor gets to Interpol before Loki gets to him.'

'What's your fallback if everything goes belly-up?'

Jack gave Costas a harrowed look as they began to push the Zodiac back into the surf. 'I don't have one.'

Three hours later, after a jolting ride along a jungle track, they came to the entrance to Chichén Itzá, some sixty kilometres inland from the beach. The ruins of the ancient city covered a vast area, though only the central precinct had been cleared of jungle and restored. Grey limestone structures reared above the tree canopy ahead, but Jack knew that all round them lay ruins submerged in the undergrowth that had entombed the city in the centuries since its abandonment. Some of the images seemed startlingly familiar, pyramids and colonnaded temples, but others were not, sacrificial platforms, terrifying hybrid animal and human sculptures, images that seemed from another planet. It was eerie, as if something were not quite right, as if they were entering a film set of ancient Egypt or Mesopotamia where some attempt had been made at historical accuracy, but much had been left to the imagination of a designer rooted in some particularly lurid science fiction.

Jack was in the front seat of the four-wheel drive provided for them by the Mexican archaeological authorities, and as he opened the door he was greeted by an official who ushered them into the site. A few days earlier an earth tremor had caused concern about the stability of the ancient structures, and the site had been closed off to tourists while an evaluation was carried out. Jack thanked the official and found a shady place to unfold his map. He was joined by Costas. They were wearing shorts, T-shirts and jungle boots, but the summer heat was overwhelming and Costas was already dripping with sweat.

'Thinking fondly of our iceberg?' Jack asked, with some amusement.

'No way.' Costas puffed himself up, but looked doleful and hot under his panama hat. 'Remember, I'm Greek? Heat's in the blood.'

'Right.'

Jeremy walked over to them after talking in Spanish with the official, and pointed out a route on the map. 'I was forced to spend a summer here as an undergraduate on a field training project, before I saw the light,' he said ruefully. 'I'll try to give a balanced account, but I have to tell you this place gave me nightmares. The Vikings were therapy after this.'

'What kind of time period are we looking at?' Costas asked.

'The Maya were one of the great early civilizations, as you know,' Jeremy said. 'They flourished here around AD 300 to 900, that's from about the end of the Roman Empire to the Viking age. But by the mid eleventh century this place was ruled by the Toltecs, a warrior caste from the north. The Maya were still here, but they became the underclass, enslaved and brutalized. The Toltecs swept into the Yucatán around the time Harald was doing his stint in the Varangian Guard. A lot of what you see here isn't Maya, but dates from the Toltec period.'

They trudged along the path under the canopy of the jungle, passing the occasional iguana and a band of ring-tailed monkeys, their chattering competing with the raucous shrieks of toucans and evil-looking blackbirds. The heat was staggering, far more humid than Jack had experienced at archaeological sites in the Mediterranean, and he struggled to imagine people living normal lives in a place so far from the ameliorating effects of the sea. After a few minutes they came out into a wide grassy precinct surrounded by colossal stone buildings. It was an extraordinary sight, the quintessential image of ancient Mesoamerican civilization, dominated by an imposing temple that rose in stepped tiers like a pyramid.

'Don't try to tell me these people weren't influenced by the Egyptians,' Costas said, wiping the sweat from his face.

'That's the Kukulkan Pyramid, the focal point of Chichén

Itzá.' Jeremy led them past the pyramid as he talked. 'But that building over there is where most of the sacrifices took place,' he said. 'The Temple of the Warriors. You can see the stone altar at the top where the living victims were tied down and had their hearts ripped out.'

'Delightful,' Costas grunted. 'But I thought all that kind of stuff was exaggerated by the Spanish.'

'Nope.' Jeremy led them to the north side of the precinct, past a structure where Jack saw a carved stone glyph that looked strikingly familiar. Jeremy saw him hesitate and called back, 'The eagle-god. It's exactly the same as the jade pendant from L'Anse aux Meadows. I'm sure it came from here.' He stopped beside the next building, a wide stone platform about his own height, and waited for the other two to catch up. 'You asked about sacrifice. This one's my favourite. It's called the Tzompantli, the Platform of the Skulls. The rotting heads of enemies were exhibited here, and just in case you needed reminding they carved them round the edge.' They saw that the sides of the platform were covered with hundreds of leering skulls, their jaws gaping and eyes wide open in terror and anguish. 'To cap it all, you have to imagine that all the buildings here, the pyramid and the Temple of the Warriors, this platform, were painted red.'

'With human blood, I assume.' Costas traced his finger over one of the skulls and grimaced. 'I know we had our bad episodes, the Roman Colosseum, the Spanish Inquisition and all that, but genocide and mass-murder were never institutionalized, never part of our way of life. For these people it was normal. You're born here, you get sacrificed. There was something deeply dysfunctional about this society.'

'The Maya had quite a lot going for them,' Jeremy replied cautiously. 'Amazing architecture and art, phenomenal economic organization. States that would easily have vied with the early city-states of the Near East.'

'Four thousand years before the Maya,' Jack said.

'And the Maya had no bronze,' Costas added.

'Or iron, or wheels.'

'Right.' Jeremy smiled wryly. 'This society was the pinnacle of what was going on in the Americas before the Spanish conquest. But everything went apeshit when the Toltecs showed up. They were the horror warriors of ancient Mesoamerica, the SS of their day. Everything you've heard about the Aztecs, those accounts of mass human sacrifice recorded by the Spanish conquistadors in the sixteenth century, magnify that several times and put it back five hundred years. Imagine the heart of darkness, apocalypse now, this is the place. The Maya themselves weren't exactly averse to human sacrifice, but when the Toltecs arrived they turned this place into a death camp.'

'No wonder Reksnys settled here,' Costas murmured. 'He would have felt right at home.'

'The fact is, for medieval Europeans this place would have been their vision of hell,' Jack said. 'For the Vikings it would have exceeded their worst nightmares about the end of the world, about Ragnarok. For any prisoner brought here it would have been a one-way ticket to Dante's Inferno.'

'There's something else I want you to see,' Jeremy said, walking briskly on. 'Follow me.' They passed the Platform of the Skulls and out of the central precinct, and then followed Jeremy on a wide processional way down a shallow gradient through the jungle to the north. After about two hundred metres they scrambled down an irregular rocky slope and stood on the edge of an eroded platform. In front of them was a vast sinkhole, some fifty metres across and twenty metres deep, its rim overhung with lush greenery and the limestone walls receding inwards through a series of striated ledges. The pool at the bottom was a putrid green, covered with a dense layer of algae and fallen vegetation. There was no access point to the water, and they could see that for anyone unfortunate enough to slip off the platform there would be no escape.

'The Cenote of Sacrifice at Chichén Itzá,' Jack murmured. 'I've always wanted to see this.'

'Cenote?' Costas said.

'A Spanish word, from the Mayan *dzonot*, meaning Sacred Well, Well of Sacrifice,' Jeremy explained. 'I was telling you about it on the beach. The whole of the Yucatán was once a coral reef, then it became a limestone plateau during the Ice Age when the sea level lowered. Over millions of years rainwater percolated into the limestone and created a huge labyrinth of caves and tunnels, filled with stalagtites and stalagmites. Then at the end of the Ice Age, eight thousand years ago, the sea level rose again and the system flooded. Caves with ceilings that remained above water eventually collapsed, creating sinkholes like this one.'

'What about the earth tremors?'

'We're just south of a huge meteorite impact site, the Chicxulub crater, which underlies much of the north Yucatán.'

'The one that wiped out the dinosaurs?' Costas said, looking around him with mock alarm. 'Anything bad that didn't happen here?'

Jeremy grinned. 'The dinosaur disaster's true. The rim is marked by a ring of cenotes, many of them collapsed into sinkholes. Nobody really knows why, but the crater underneath has some kind of destabilizing effect on the limestone.'

'A cave-diver's paradise.'

'It's incredible,' Jeremy enthused. 'Divers have explored systems fifty, a hundred kilometres long. Some of them are underwater rivers that run out into the sea. Below the slime it's crystal clear, like swimming in an aquarium filled with spectacular calcite formations. But it's also lethal. It put me off learning to dive when I was here as a student. More divers have died here than almost anywhere else in the world.'

'The Toltecs would have approved,' Jack said.

'Let me guess,' Costas said. 'They sacrificed humans here as well.'

'The Well of Sacrifice was first dredged for artefacts in the

1930s, but then in the 1950s it was one of the first archaeological sites to be explored using scuba equipment,' Jack replied. 'There have been other expeditions. Cousteau came here. The deepest deposits are still unexplored, but masses of artefacts have come up, pottery vessels, gold, jade. Almost all of it was thrown into the well intact, ritually deposited. And they found human skeletons. Hundreds of them.'

'It's the same story all over the Yucatán,' Jeremy added. 'Cenotes were the source of fresh water for the Maya, but also entrances to the underworld. They sacrificed warriors, maidens, children. That little building over there is the *temazcal*, a kind of sauna where victims were ritually purified. The stone ledges we've just come down were spectator seating, where the Toltec élite could sit and watch.'

'I guess variety is the spice of life,' Costas murmured distastefully. 'Once you've seen a few thousand hearts ripped out back there at the temple, you might want a change of scene.'

An official appeared sweating and panting behind them on the processional way, waving a cellphone and beckoning for Jeremy to take it. Jeremy hesitated, knowing that he had been mistaken for the leader. He looked towards Jack, who smiled and gestured for him to go. As Jeremy clambered up with the official to find higher ground for a better reception, Jack turned back and peered over the edge of the platform. The pool looked strangely benign, but for a moment his breath tightened as he felt the terror of the victims a thousand years ago poised at the edge of the underworld.

'You say there's still stuff down there?' Costas wiped the sheen of sweat from his face, then looked questioningly at Jack.

'Most of the artefacts and bones higher up have been lifted, but there are still deeply buried deposits where you might find heavier objects.'

'Are you thinking what I'm thinking?'

'Your sub-bottom borer,' Jack replied with a grin. 'Maybe if things work out in the Golden Horn, we could approach the Mexican authorities and suggest a shift to operations here.'

'Do you think there's a chance?'

Jack rubbed his chin, and squinted against the glare off the rock. 'From what Jeremy's been telling us, this is the place where trophies of war might have been presented to the gods. Let's imagine Harald and his crew made it ashore somewhere north of here, then were captured.'

'God, I hope not,' Costas said. 'That would have been a major let-down after all they'd been through.'

'For the Vikings who weren't lucky enough to die in battle, there was only one fate. The warriors would have their hearts ripped out back there at the temple. Any retainers who survived might have been enslaved. Maybe your friend who somehow made the trek back to the cairn.'

'The scars on his wrists and ankles,' Costas said. 'Shackles.'

Jack nodded. 'Others might have been brought here to this very spot for sacrifice. A spectacular procession from the temple to the cenote, the climax of the ritual of victory. Just like a Roman emperor's triumph. Crushing the Vikings would have been a big deal for the Toltecs, victory over blond, bearded giants with their fearsome weapons of iron. They'd come here like foreign gods, and the Toltecs had vanquished them. The spoils of war would have been presented to the gods.'

'The menorah would have been a pretty spectacular sacrifice.'

'How much did you reckon it weighed? Three hundred, maybe three hundred and fifty pounds?'

'That's an awful lot of gold to throw away.'

'It is an awful lot.' Jack looked at the shimmer of green on the pool below them, then back at Costas. 'And the Toltecs did like their gold.'

Jeremy reappeared over the limestone ridge and began to make his way down towards them. He was tottering slightly, and he sat down heavily on a rock. They could see he was ashen-faced.

'The heat's getting to you.' Costas looked at him with concern, and passed over his water bottle. 'Drink this and let's get into the shade.'

'It's not that.' Jeremy's voice was hoarse, barely audible, and he let the bottle slip from his fingers. 'I just spoke to Ben. I'm afraid I've got some bad news.' He looked up at Jack, his face stricken. 'The worst.'

Jack felt a cold dread grip his stomach. He had tried to prepare himself. He had hoped they would beat the odds.

'It's from Iona.' Jeremy looked bewildered, blinking the sweat out of his eyes. His voice was barely a whisper. 'It's Father O'Connor. He's been murdered. And Maria's missing.'

17

Later, how much later she could not tell, Maria surfaced from a terrifying pit of darkness, her mind clawing its way out of some unremembered horror that had been dragging her down relentlessly. She seemed exhausted beyond belief, spent by her struggle against the faceless demon of her dreams, yet she felt weighed down by the heaviness that follows deep sleep. For what seemed an eternity she lay motionless, drifting in and out of consciousness, waiting for her body to respond. She sensed her breathing, felt the hardness of the surface beneath her, a crick in her neck. She was lying in a foetal position on her right side, her hands tucked between her legs. Slowly she opened her eyes. It was dark, but not as dark as her dreams. From the corner of one eye she saw a flickering, a candle.

The wall in front of her was covered with shapes, colours. She saw splashes of red.

Her breathing stopped. She went rigid. O'Connor's study. She shut her eyes tightly, yearning for that darkness again, anything to blot out a reality she scarcely believed, a horror she tried desperately to push back into her dreams.

She felt a burning pain in her left cheek. A light touch seemed to play across it, a hint of a breeze. Suddenly she shrieked and sat bolt upright, her heart pounding and the blood rushing in her ears, frantically brushing at her face as she scrabbled backwards. She hit a wall, her breath coming in ragged gulps, then heard the flutter of wings swoop over her and disappear above.

She raised her hand and felt a sticky wetness on her cheek, then looked up. The candle revealed a pointed ceiling, high-sided, made of small stone blocks covered with patches of plaster. It looked old, decayed. At the apex she could make out a line of darker shapes, hanging in a row.

They had been feeding on her.

She began to retch, folding her arms tight against her stomach and leaning to one side. She smelled the metallic breath again. She tried to throw up, retching over and over, desperate for something to expiate the revulsion she felt, the stain of death and violation that overwhelmed all her thoughts, that was all she could remember of what had gone before.

She gave up, tried to calm herself, panting. She closed her eyes, her bleeding cheek pressed hard against the damp wall, desperately seeking strength. She was pouring sweat, rivulets of it dripping down the caked blood on her face. She looked down. She was only wearing her khaki trousers and a vest, torn and soiled. Someone had stripped off her sweater. Her watch was missing. She was burning hot, feverishly hot. She suddenly felt terribly dehydrated, desperate for a drink, and began to lick the sweat and blood off her lips.

She pushed herself upright again, swallowed hard and forced herself to look around. Everything looked damp, covered in green slime. She was in a rectangular chamber about ten metres long and five metres wide. There was some kind of entranceway at one end, a deep cut into darkness.

She thought of the buildings she knew at Iona, the old chapel on the north side, the refectory. She quickly dismissed all of them. The floor where she was now was natural rock, limestone by the look of it, smoothed in places but nothing like the granite bedrock at Iona. In the centre was a circular slab of wood, like a lid, as if this were a well-house. The lid looked like an exotic hardwood, darker even than old oak. At the other end of the chamber was a mass of fallen masonry, clogging the space from ceiling to floor. From the white patches in the rubble she could see where stones had been recently removed, flung out on to the floor. Where the wall protruded from the rubble it was covered with wooden boards, a crude protective screen that extended for three metres or so towards the centre of the chamber opposite her.

Maria raised herself, pushing up against the wall behind, feeling woozy and unstable. She stood for a moment while a wave of dizziness passed, then hesitantly stepped to where she had seen the splashes of colour. The heat was stifling, like walking in a sauna. One thing was for sure, she was no longer in the western isles of Scotland. The walls looked as old as the monastery, but everything else told her she was almost inconceivably far removed from Iona. It was a possibility her mind simply refused to analyze any further.

She tottered across to the wall opposite. The single candle that provided the only illumination stood on a small flat stone in front of her. She picked it up, throwing shadows in a demented dance all round the chamber, then held it with both hands to stop it shaking. She peered at the wall.

Her jaw dropped in amazement.

She blinked hard. She knew her body was on its last reserves, that she had been without food and drink for hours, days. She could be hallucinating. She looked again.

The red splashes were truly there. They were blood. But they were not real blood, like in O'Connor's study. This was a different kind of horror. She saw blood spurting out of necks, blood gushing from bodies gouged open, blood spilling in a livid slipway down a stepped slope.

It was a fresco, a wall-painting of unimaginable barbarity, a mass execution. Naked victims were being led up one side of a high temple. At the top, one was splayed out and held down on an altar, the executioner's hands plunged into his innards, another figure holding up a ripped-out heart. Maria felt her stomach convulse again. The executioner was a fearsome giant, stripped to the waist, with a sloping, flat forehead and hooked nose, wearing a loincloth and an elaborate headdress. Above him were stylized symbols. Jaguars, birds, garish monsters. The one directly above the executioner looked suddenly familiar. Maria flashed back to the moment the nightmare began, when she had been in her study at Iona, peering at the picture of the eagle-god pendant Jack had sent her.

She blinked hard, trying to register what she was seeing. She took a few faltering steps back, the candle wavering in her hands. To the right she could see the victims assembled, like prisoners after a battle. The wall-painting was clearly a narrative, a progression of scenes in a story, going from right to left. She looked at the ceiling again. She tried to marshal her thoughts, to think like someone whose mind was highly trained. As if in another lifetime, she remembered her tutorials years before with Jack when they were under-graduates, on the history of architecture. Corbel vaulting. One major civilization had built all their vaults this way, had never learned to make an arch. One civilization, famous for its architecture, infamous for its cruelty.

She looked back at the wall. Corbelled vaulting. Narrative scenes from right to left. Fearsome warriors with flat foreheads. The symbols, glyphs. Human sacrifice on a temple altar, sacrifice on a prodigious scale. She began to think the unthinkable.

The Maya.

She staggered back, hit by a wave of dizziness, then rallied her strength and took a few steps to the right, until she was standing beside the wooden lid. She held the candle up against the wall. She was midway between two scenes, the first of the painting. The scene at the outset showed a naval engagement, long canoes full of warriors, one with a square sail. The next scene showed a bloody battle, this time on land. Warriors dressed identically to the executioner were battling other warriors, those who would soon become prisoners. All had sloping foreheads, but the vanquished were even bigger, giants. All were stripped to the waist. In the foreground were the dead of both sides, some dismembered, some in a river, seemingly underground. The victors were wielding clubs and maces, the vanquished swords and axes.

Maria stopped herself. *Swords and axes.*

She looked more closely. She began to tremble, and made herself steady the candle. The sloping heads of the vanquished were not foreheads, but the nose-guards of helmets. They were stripped to the waist, but wore leggings, not the kilts and loincloths of the victors. They were bearded. They were blond. They had broadswords, and huge, single-bitted axes.

Varangian battleaxes.

Maria reeled. It seemed as if she were dreaming the final chapter of the story that had possessed her for days now, a chapter so extraordinary it could only be fantasy. She wished Jack were here, next to her, his calm, reassuring voice telling her this was all the stuff of fiction. She looked back at the scene of sacrifice, to the altar and the executioner where the wall seemed to be oozing blood. She staggered back and sank against the other wall, shutting her eyes tight, desperately trying to wake up back in the cell at Iona, to feel the warmth and steady breathing of another beside her.

'Dr de Montijo. So good of you to come. The effects of the drug will wear off shortly.' A voice was addressing her, a real voice. 'You are in Mexico.'

Maria jolted blearily awake. 'Yes,' she said, the word coming out even before she had registered what was happening. 'I know.'

'How?' The voice sounded shrill, testy. Maria tried to get up, but slipped down the wall again to where she had been lying. She could see nothing, her vision blinded by a torch shining directly into her face. Her mouth was bone-dry, and her voice was a croak. 'I worked it out.'

The torch snapped down and she saw a short, wiry man standing in front of her, his black hair slicked back from his forehead. She guessed he was about seventy, his hair obviously dyed, though he had the physique of a man thirty years younger. He had washed-out grey eyes.

The truth dawned on Maria. She looked at him with sickening certainty, scarcely believing she was finally in his presence. Everything else, her appalling state, even O'Connor's death, was eclipsed from her mind. *He was the one*. She fought to control her emotions, to keep her cool. She was suddenly wide awake. 'Pieter Reksnys. I see your father taught you well. Lithuanian, I believe? The master race.'

A hand shot out and gripped Maria's neck like a vice, displaying lightning agility for a man of his age. He jerked her towards him and raised her up, holding her almost off the ground. Through the suffocating pain Maria sensed something familiar, a nasty tang to his breath, a familiar odour. 'Never speak of my father again, Jew,' he hissed. 'And don't think he was the only one who pulled the trigger back then. I had plenty of diverting entertainment with the children.' He dropped Maria and stood over her while she coughed and retched. 'I only wish my own son had been alive then. He would have done his grandfather proud.'

He kicked Maria over on to her back, ostentatiously wiping his shoe on the ground afterwards. Maria saw another figure advancing on her. His head was held low, his hands clenching and unclenching, his movements sickeningly familiar. He grabbed her by the hair and dragged her over to the wooden lid, kicking it roughly aside and shoving her over the hole underneath. She could see nothing but blackness, a yawning depth that brought with it a waft of cooler air, as if there were water somewhere far below.

'Don't worry.' She was yanked up against him, and she saw the ugly scar. 'I reserved the blood-eagle for your boyfriend. When I throw you down into the underworld you won't even die. At least that's what the Toltecs told their victims.' The voice was hoarse, ugly, less refined than his father's. He made as if to push her in, then pulled her back roughly. 'My kind of people.' He laughed, an insane, high-pitched cackle, then hurled her down on the ground. 'But now the *félag* has some use for you. Enjoy our little vacation hideaway while you can.'

'The true *félag* died out seven hundred years ago.' Maria raised her head and tried to stare at Loki. 'Harald Hardrada's men would never have admitted scum like you. They wouldn't even have considered you worthy of a blood-feud.'

Loki lunged at Maria, but Reksnys held him in check. 'Not yet,' he muttered. He turned to Maria, speaking with mock apology. 'My son still has these romantic notions. He thinks he's in the SS.'

'Too weak for that.'

Loki lunged again and once more Reksnys held him back, then his voice hardened. 'Our *félag* was a means to an end. No more, no less. And it looks like we will have the last laugh on Harald Hardrada.'

Loki snarled and turned abruptly away, headed quickly out of the entranceway at the side of the chamber. Maria crawled back against the wall. Reksnys tossed her a small water bottle. 'So now we have become acquainted. I need some expert assistance. You are going to help me.'

Reksnys took out a digital camera and pointed it at her. Maria began to lose all feeling, sinking to the floor, then looked up at Reksnys and remembered what he and his son had done. O'Connor had ensured that justice was carried out against Reksnys' father, had staked his life on it and had paid the ultimate price. She owed it to him to do everything in her power to see that the job was finished. And she owed it to herself.

She would be strong.

Jack stood pensively in the control room on *Seaquest II*, cradling a coffee and watching a cloudburst release a shimmer of rain far out to sea. The sky had an ominous grey overcast, the high clouds they had seen on the beach that morning having been replaced by a dark mass rolling in from the Caribbean. Where the sun shone through, curtains of light hung and twisted and mingled in the sky, like the northern lights they had seen in Greenland but heavy with the portent of weather to come.

'It looks like we're in for some rain.' The Canadian captain of *Seaquest II* came up beside Jack, peering out to sea through his binoculars. 'We're almost into hurricane season. As a precaution I'm closing down shop. We're moving further offshore and I'm battening down the helicopter in the hangar.'

Jack grunted. It was not the news he wanted to hear. 'Thanks. Do what you have to do.'

The captain left for the bridge and James Macleod got up from the computer console where he had been evaluating data from the icefjord. Everyone in the room was aware of

Jack, but had been keeping their distance. Some of them had been on the first *Seaquest* and could remember the loss of Peter Howe in the Black Sea, how Jack had taken the responsibility personally. Maria had been enormously popular among the crew and scientists alike during their sojourn in the icefjord. Even Lanowski was subdued, quietly passing Jack a series of printouts of the longship in the iceberg he had finalized from the photogrammetric images.

Macleod sidled up to the window beside him. 'How long do you think we'll be here, Jack?' he said quietly.

Jack turned and looked at him, his face drawn and distant, then stared back out to sea. 'I don't know, James. I just don't know.' He pursed his lips and put down his coffee. They had been back on board for almost six hours now, and there was still no word from Iona. All they had to go on was a brief phone message to IMU headquarters from O'Connor's colleague in the monastery, the man Jack remembered seeing briefly in the church. Apparently the police were keeping the scene completely under wraps, and there was a media black-out. But there was no doubt of the facts. Father O'Connor was dead, and Maria was missing.

'We have to assume she's been kidnapped.' Ben had been within earshot, and had moved up to Jack's other side. 'Until there's a body, that is.'

'I know.' Jack exhaled forcefully, then stood back from the railing with his hands on his hips, his usual demeanour returned. 'We have to keep on top of this. We have to assume we'll be hearing more soon. Until then there's nothing we can do. It has to be situation normal.' He looked at Macleod, his expression grim but determined. 'There's your answer. My plan after visiting Chichén Itzá had been to collate all possible evidence from the north Yucatán datable to the second half of the eleventh century, to the time when Harald might have been here. Wall-paintings, glyphs, structures. Anything that might provide a clue.' He gestured to Jeremy, hunched with his back to them over a screen in the corner, surrounded by open books. 'I put Jeremy on it the moment we got back.'

'He's taken it very badly,' Macleod murmured.

'He revered O'Connor,' Jack said quietly. 'And Maria's his mentor. For someone like him, that's like pulling the rug out from under your life.'

'He's got us now,' Macleod replied.

'He's a good guy,' said Jack.

Costas had been tapping at the workstation next to Jeremy, and leaned back on his chair as they looked over. 'Jack. Something to look forward to. I've jumped the gun and been in touch with the IMU guy for the Caribbean, Jim Hales out of Grand Cayman. You know he's an old pal of mine from the US Navy submersibles research lab. He was straight on to Mexico City and they've given us the go-ahead for Chichén Itzá. Amazing how that guy clears the red tape. Any time you want to talk about setting up a project in that cenote, I've got the contact numbers.'

'Sounds like a plan.' Jack caught Costas' eye, and knew they both sensed the need to keep positive, to look ahead.

'I'll put first claim on the sub-bottom borer after the Golden Horn's done. Jeremy, you in on this?'

Jeremy looked at them, pale and distracted. 'Huh? If Maria will let me.' He suddenly checked himself, and the room went silent.

'She will,' Jack said firmly.

Jeremy tried hard to keep a brave face. 'Anyway, I'm not sure if the Well of Sacrifice is where I want to do my first open-water dive.'

'Don't worry.' Costas stretched his hand over and put it on Jeremy's back. 'We'll do some coral first.'

A red light began flashing in the centre of the room. Ben looked at Jack, his face deadly serious. 'To the bridge.' The two men quickly made their way out of the control room and up the stairway, followed by Costas. The captain was busily engaged with the chief officer at the binnacle but immediately gestured to the chart room. 'Priority message on the security channel.' Ben was first in the room and snatched up the radio receiver, talking quickly and then putting it down. 'That was IMU HQ. There's been an email message. It's directed us to a secure site and given us a password.'

Costas was already seated in front of the computer at the chart table. 'Okay. We're on line. Address?' Ben read it out and Costas tapped the keyboard. 'Password?'

Ben hesitated, then glanced at Jack. '*Menorah*.'

Costas let out a low whistle. 'Well, that gives the game away.'

Jack's knuckles were white as he gripped Costas' chair, and his voice was hoarse. 'We guessed who we were up against. This confirms it.'

'It's addressed to you, Jack.' Costas leaned aside to let Jack read the short email that had appeared on the screen.

To: Jack Howard

You and Kazantzakis will arrive by Zodiac at 2300 this evening at the beach landing point you visited this morning. Bring cave-diving equipment. You will blindfold yourselves and await our arrival. Any attempt to involve security or make contact with an outside body and your colleague will be executed.

'Maria's alive,' Jack breathed. 'Thank God.'

'The beach landing point,' Ben murmured. 'Doesn't surprise me they knew where we were. Probably the Mexican police. If it's Reksnys, he'll have prying eyes everywhere along this coast.'

'And cave gear,' Costas murmured. 'What the hell's that all about? I'm not going cave diving while it's raining. All the air pockets will flood.'

'They must have found something,' Jack said.

'That password?'

'I truly hope not.'

'Maria's somewhere here, near us,' Ben said. 'They must have flown her in from Iona. Reksnys has a private jet, and his own runway in the jungle. It's one of the few things you can't disguise from satellite surveillance. And he must have known *Seaquest II* was on the way here even before they hit Iona.'

'My guess is the hit was a one-man show,' Jack said bleakly. 'Loki.'

'We've been sent a photo. Better prepare ourselves.' Costas clicked on an attachment below the message, and a picture began to download. It had been taken with a flash inside some kind of chamber with an irregular stone floor and old walls covered in green growth. As the image opened they could see a figure slumped on the floor, a woman. It was horrifying, an image of torture, the kind of picture that leaked out of Iraq and untold Third World hellholes. She was filthy, wearing a clinging vest partly ripped open over her breasts. Her dark hair was matted to her neck, and her arms were streaked with green from the floor. She had been trying to look at the camera but had flinched in the flash. Her eyes were puffed up and closed, her mouth flecked with white, and she had an ugly abrasion over her cheekbone which was oozing blood and pus.

Jack felt a lurching shock of recognition. '*Maria*.' He felt physically sick. His hands slipped off the back of the chair and he sat down heavily on the bench beside it. He looked at the image again. His horror turned to anger, to seething rage.

The captain appeared at the door. 'Message from Iona. There's a police forensics guy who's been allowed to talk to us.' He saw the screen, faltered.

'Coming.' Jack's voice was cold, emotionless.

Ten minutes later Jack was back in the control room. It was empty except for Jeremy, Macleod and Lanowski having left for the bridge deck a few minutes before. Jeremy was still at his screen, working quietly, busily printing off images from the web and bookmarking pages of Toltec art. Above him the window was flecked with the first lashings of rain, and Jack could see that the weather was deteriorating rapidly. He paused, feeling utterly drained from what he had just heard, looked again at Jeremy, then made his way through the consoles. He did not know how to break it. He pulled up a chair and flipped it round to sit with his back to the window, then looked intently at Jeremy's images.

'Good work,' he said quietly. 'I could never have interpreted this stuff. I didn't do Mesoamerican archaeology like you.'

'I've made one really interesting discovery.' Jeremy passed Jack a sheet of paper. 'You remember the ancient Aztec prophecy about the return of the god-king Quetzalcóatl? When the Spanish arrived in Tenochtitlán in central Mexico in 1519, the emperor Moctezuma thought Cortés was Quetzalcóatl. It's one reason the Spanish conquest happened so quickly.'

'Go on.'

'Well, Quetzalcóatl was a Toltec, a semi-legendary king. According to Aztec legend at the time of Moctezuma, he'd been exiled from their kingdom five centuries before, and promised to return from the land of the rising sun.'

'Five centuries before,' Jack mused. 'That puts it in the eleventh century, smack in our period.'

'Right. The land of the rising sun, due east from the Aztec heartland in the vale of Mexico, was almost certainly the Yucatán peninsula. There's some historical corroboration for this, because that's about the time the Toltecs invaded Chichén Itzá.'

Jack looked hard at Jeremy, began to speak, then decided to let him carry on.

'It gets really intriguing when you look at the Maya sources,' Jeremy said. 'What we know of the final years of the Maya comes mainly from the Books of Chilam Balam, the Jaguar Prophet, mostly written down by local scribes in the Latin alphabet after the Spanish conquest. The books were hidden away and jealously guarded. Each one relates to a different community in the north Yucatán, a bit like the Norse sagas in Iceland. One of the most extraordinary prophecies concerns the arrival of bearded men from the east.'

'Bearded men?'

'You follow me? A lot of scholars have dismissed this as a later embellishment. Some of the books weren't written down until the eighteenth or even nineteenth century. But another book's just come to light, in the Vatican archives in Rome, of all places. It looks like the earliest of them all, partly written in Maya script, apparently confiscated by the first Jesuit missionaries in the Yucatán in the sixteenth century. It contains the legends and prophecies of the Maya community north of Chichén Itzá. There's the same story of bearded men, but with a twist. In this one they have a king, and he fights a great battle with the oppressors of the Maya, presumably the Toltecs. Then he disappears into the underworld, and the Maya await his return. It may be the origin of the Quezalcóatl prophecy of the Aztecs, except in the Maya story he's called Wukub Kaqix, the monstrous bird-deity, the eagle-god.'

Jack glanced at a picture of the jade pendant pinned beside the monitor. 'Pretty standard image around here.'

'But also the name of Harald Hardrada's ship, the *Eagle*. In the Norse sagas there are some hints that when the Vikings burned their boats, went to war with no intention of returning, they sometimes cut off the stems of the ships and carried them forward like battle standards. It was a signal that they would fight to the death, that they were on a one-way trip to Valhalla. It was a way of striking fear into the hearts of their enemies. Maybe that's what happened here, and the local Maya saw it.'

'Fantastic. This is fantastic, Jeremy. This is just what we're looking for.' Jack suddenly leaned forward and put his head in his hands, all pretence at bonhomie gone. He could keep it from Jeremy no longer. 'There's something I've got to tell you. We've had news from Iona.'

'I know.' Jeremy spoke softly, and put down the book he had been holding. Jack gazed up at him. He looked a world older than the ebullient graduate student he had first met the week before. 'I knew from the moment I heard O'Connor had been murdered. He spoke of it, prepared me for it. I know what happened in Iona.' Jeremy paused, tried to speak, then the words came out as a hoarse whisper. *'The blood-eagle.'*

18

It was well past midnight, probably pushing one in the morning. It had already been dark when Jack and Costas had slipped away from *Seaquest II* and driven the Zodiac ashore, reaching the beach rendezvous point well before the appointed time. All Jack could hear now was the incessant drumming of the rain, the sound rising in a crescendo and falling again as each downpour swept over them. The humidity was stifling. He knew he was in a small vehicle, a four-wheel drive by the sound of it, hunched in the back seat beside Costas. For what seemed an eternity but was probably only half an hour they had been jostling and bouncing along a rough track, heading somewhere into the jungle from the beach. The injury to Jack's thigh was throbbing. They had followed their instructions scrupulously and waited blindfolded beside the Zodiac with their diving equipment. Their captor had come without a word, bustling them into the vehicle without revealing anything about himself, about where they were going. It was unnerving, but Jack felt reassured having Costas bumping along beside him cursing every rut and pothole.

Ever since receiving the email ultimatum Jack had known they would be on their own, that they would have to follow the word of Maria's captors and trust to luck. Whatever was in store for them, it seemed a fair certainty that it involved diving. And with the route they were now taking, somewhere inland seemed likely. Cenotes, underground rivers. The rain was beginning to prey on Jack's mind. With a storm like this, the floodwaters could be dangerously high, filling underground caverns with water. And this close to the sea, the freshwater currents that honeycombed the Yucatán could be treacherously strong, sucking the rainwater through the labyrinth of limestone channels and out to sea.

The vehicle ground to a halt and Jack snapped back to reality. He was pulled out of the door and led across uneven ground, slipping and sliding on wet vegetation. The rain was torrential, pounding his senses. Then he was inside some kind of shelter, out of the rain but steaming hot. Costas bumped up behind him, and he heard their gear being offloaded. Then he was pushed forward again. His blindfold was ripped off, leaving him blinking and reeling. Duct tape was crudely slapped round his wrists. He was somewhere gloomy, candlelit. He saw Costas a few feet to his left, and a man in front of them. Jack immediately knew who it was. Pieter Reksnys was the spitting image of his father Andrius, the man Jack had seen in the photo of the SS *Ahnenerbe* team in Greenland, the picture Kangia had given Macleod.

Kangia. The icefjord. It all seemed a million miles away, back before some boundary they had crossed to come here, to this place where hell and its demons suddenly seemed far more than just a medieval nightmare.

Jack looked around him. They were in a room, a stone chamber, maybe an old church. It was hot as a boilerhouse, and Jack was pouring sweat. The ceiling was high, corbelled. There was a circular hole in the floor. The wall beside him was painted, vivid flickers of colour revealed in the candlelight.

Then he saw Maria.

He had tried to prepare himself, gazed at the emailed photograph before they left *Seaquest II*, but the reality was still shocking. She was sitting against the wall opposite the mural, groggy, swaying slightly, her legs drawn up and her wrists taped together. Her mouth was duct-taped. Her face was streaked and swollen, and her cheek had a raw welt across it. Their eyes met.

Jack tried to control his anger. 'Did he do that to you?'

Maria looked at him imploringly, then shook her head, motioning to somewhere behind Jack. He turned round and saw the only other person in the room, the man who had picked them up from the beach. It had to be Loki. The same slicked-back hair, the spare, mean features, the washed-out eyes. Like father, like son. Loki grinned as he saw Jack looking at him, turned to the light, drew one finger hard down his cheek. Then Jack remembered O'Connor's description. The scar.

Costas had been staring aghast at Maria, and suddenly lunged towards Loki. The response was terrifyingly supple, quick and fluid like a hunting animal. Loki had Costas in a half-nelson and was pulling his head up and sideways, raising him effortlessly off the floor despite Costas' greater weight.

'Release him.' Jack heard Reksnys' voice for the first time, harsh, grating, an undefinable accent with a hint of east European. Loki obeyed his father and pushed Costas away. Jack stared at Loki. This was the ruthless killer described by O'Connor, an independent operator who relished working alone, yet he was totally subservient to his father. Rage was not his only weakness.

Costas picked himself up, ostentatiously grimacing with distaste, wiping his shoulder with the back of his hand where Loki had held him. Loki sneered and slunk back to lurk in the far corner of the chamber. Reksnys pulled out a pistol, instantly recognizable to Jack as a Nazi-era Luger, and aimed it at Maria's legs.

'First one knee, then the other. Then I work my way up.' His voice had an ugly edge to it. 'Or you cease being foolish.'

At first there was no reaction from Costas, then a surly nod. Maria had gone sheet white at the sight of the pistol, and was staring at it in a daze.

Reksnys turned to Jack. 'I want you to study that wall-painting. Closely.'

Jack looked at him stone-faced. Then he looked at Maria, who nodded weakly, mumbling through the tape over her mouth, encouraging him. He gave Reksnys a look of contempt and then turned to the mural.

It was two-dimensional, without depth. It had once been a dazzling explosion of colour, deep browns, reds and greens, on a yellow and blue background. He immediately grasped the narrative sequence, the victors and the vanquished. To the right he saw a mêlée of boats, elaborately attired warriors with sloped foreheads, paddled vessels with symmetrical endposts. One vessel with a square sail, different warriors.

A square sail.

The next scene was a ferocious jungle battle. Some of the fighting above ground, some in a fast-flowing river, seemingly below ground. Mutilated bodies lay everywhere. The victors carried *atlatls*, spear-throwers, and square shields with the figure of a war god. They were led by an eagle-warrior, a muscular giant wearing an eagle mask with a staring eye, with wings on his back and huge tearing talons on his feet. His warriors wore jaguar-skin headdresses, anklets and wristlets, heavy jade necklaces and earrings. They fought with clubs, and fell on their victims with enraged, terrifying eyes. Their opponents had round red shields, different headgear, different weapons.

Jack peered at the weapons again. He looked at Maria out

of the corner of his eye. She must have been transfixed by this scene, stared at it as she lay on the floor before they arrived. She must have seen what he had just seen. She nodded at him, almost imperceptibly. She had seen it. He turned back.

Now he understood.

Jack betrayed nothing in his expression. He moved on, to the left. Captives were on the ground, some lying on their backs, some kneeling. Some were shackled, men not attired as warriors, captured servants being led off as personal slaves by each of the victorious warriors. Jack thought of the Viking skeleton at L'Anse aux Meadows, of the man who had somehow made the trek three thousand miles north, who almost made it back to his own world. This was the nightmare he was escaping from.

The next scene dominated the painting. Jack saw hideous images of death, of mutilation. On top of a terraced platform stood a priest-king, wearing the mask of the eagle-god. He was passing sentence on those taken in the battle. On the lower step were captives being tortured, having their fingernails ripped out. A few steps up a prisoner raised his hands in vain for mercy, and another was splayed on the steps, fainting, bleeding profusely from his fingers. At the top a priest plunged a knife into the chest of a victim, gouging out his heart, his soul ascending heavenward from the altar in a bloody trail. A severed head rested on a bed of leaves, and others tumbled in a cascade of blood down the steps. All around were fires, flaming pyres of incense. The ritual was not restricted to the hapless prisoners of war. Below a skull-faced deity, Toltec warriors offered their own blood from self-inflicted wounds, gushing out all over their bodies. On a stone table beside the king were three richly bedecked women, shaven-headed, being offered a blood-letting implement by a servant. One woman was drawing a thorn-studded rope through a hole in her tongue. Beside her a nobleman was doing the same through his penis.

Jack turned away. Reksnys leered at him, enjoying his reaction. 'I found this building myself, years ago when I acquired this land,' he said. 'It's a jungle temple, a sacrificial chamber above a sacred cenote.' He jerked his head towards the dark hole in the centre of the floor. 'I scoured this jungle for years, searching for just such a find. What I have come across is truly remarkable. We in the *félag* guessed at such a thing, but there was never any evidence.'

'Evidence of what?' Jack said.

Reksnys ignored him. 'Our sources told us you were searching for the menorah.'

'Sources,' Jack said derisively. 'You mean you tortured it out of Father O'Connor.'

'O'Connor was very helpful to us,' Reksnys replied, his voice suddenly shrill. 'But not in the way you think. In the Vatican he had become less cautious. Breaking into the Arch of Titus was one step too far. He had a superior who reported everything he did. We already knew about that woman.'

He jerked his head towards Maria and then saw Jack's

half-smile and suddenly narrowed his eyes. 'That information is useless to you now. It is of no consequence whether I tell it to you or not, and I only share the story of my discovery with you as a fellow archaeologist.'

Jack looked from side to side. 'I don't see any other archaeologists here.'

Reksnys affected not to hear him. 'We heard you had reached as far as Greenland. Of course we knew about the longship in the ice, discovered by my father with the *Ahnenerbe* expedition in the 1930s. Shortly before he was murdered he told me the full story, how Künzl had snatched the runestone from him and tried to kill him with his own SS dagger in the crevasse. Fortunately my father had a photographic memory and could reproduce the symbols for a runologist in our pay years later, after the war.'

'I trust the photographic memory of all the women and children he murdered on the eastern front kept him awake at night,' Jack said icily.

'Only counting them.' Reksnys snorted, then carried on. 'Something made me remember this little temple, something about the glimpse I had years ago of that battle scene, the appearance of the warriors from the sea. When I found it, the temple was swallowed in the jungle and filled with rubble. None of the local Maya will come near the place. Some nonsense about an eagle-god, the return of the king. I remembered Harald Hardrada, the menorah. The cherished dream of the *félag*. It was just possible. I cleared out the temple myself, stone by stone.' He looked childishly pleased with himself. 'It has been a most satisfying hobby.'

'Don't play games with me,' Jack said coldly, looking back up. 'This is more than just a hobby. It's an obsession. And it's illegal.'

Reksnys scowled at Jack and snapped his fingers. Loki was on him in a flash, standing chest to chest with him, butting him back, the livid scar on his face turned towards him. Loki was clearly used to intimidating those weaker than him, but Jack stood a full head taller and stared down at him contemptuously.

'Enough.' Reksnys barked the command and Loki snarled, hands clenching and unclenching, his eyes turned to his father like a dog to its master. 'Time for that later.' Loki sloped off, and Reksnys turned to the mural. 'And now for the reason you are here.' He walked over and lifted the large wooden panel off the left-hand side of the wall, abutting the rubble. 'There.'

It was the final scene. A procession was leading away from the base of the temple. It was the only scene not soaked in blood, though the figures were even more garish, more extravagantly attired than before. Some were human, others supernatural. Musicians sang and beat time, with trumpets and gourd rattles. A turtle carapace split open to reveal a god, pouring liquid from a jar. Others emerged from the shell of a crab, the jaws of a serpent. Warriors and women weaved among rows of torch-holders. A jaguar ate a human heart. A company of mummers performed, writhing, snaking in and out, one dressed as a crocodile and another a crab, with giant pincers raised up high. A team of ball players with protective belts and kneepads jostled each other, one being led back towards the temple by a sacrificial priest. Above the procession were poles with human skulls skewered on them. Some were stripped bare, leering skulls like the sculptures at Chichén Itzá. Others were more recent victims, with hair and flesh still on them. *Yellow hair. Beards.*

In front of the pageant was a space which Reksnys had left covered by a protective cloth. But leading up to it was a line of white-robed women, with sloping foreheads and tied-back red hair, adorned with mountainous headdresses and green feathers from the sacred quetzal bird springing in hoops from their backs.

It was a triumphal procession. Another image flashed through Jack's mind, an image that seemed unbelievably far removed from the world of the Yucatán. The Arch of Titus in Rome. The procession through the forum. The triumph of Vespasian over the Jews.

He moved a few steps to his left, Loki's eyes following him warily. The final depiction was still partly buried under rubble, but was clear enough. It was an abstract shape like a cauldron, its rim marking the end of the processional way. It was the jaws of the underworld, gigantic, gaping, hungry for sacrifice.

Chichén Itzá. The Cenote of Sacrifice.

Reksnys moved up to the cloth and put his hand on the lower corner. 'I believe that is where we are now.' He spoke to Jack as if they were fellow archaeologists. 'The underworld, the end of the procession. We all know who the vanquished are. I believe the victory procession ended where we are standing now, at the entrance to this cenote below us.' He spoke bullishly, with the utter conviction of the ignorant. Jack caught Maria's eye again. This time she shook her head. Jack looked back. He realized there was nothing in the painting to identify the setting. It could have been one of dozens of Toltec ceremonial sites. The only connection they had with Chichén Itzá was the runestone inscription from L'Anse aux Meadows. And that was unknown to Reksnys, safely under lock and key on board *Seaquest II*.

'I uncovered what you are about to see a mere three days ago, just before the *félag* exacted its revenge on the one who had betrayed us. A happy coincidence for your colleague here.' Reksnys jerked his pistol towards Maria. 'We knew your ship was in the Caribbean, and guessed our paths were converging. I thought we might benefit from your expertise. It is the only reason my son did not practise his art on her as well.'

Reksnys stood with his back to the wall, then with one quick movement lifted the cloth up.

There was a stunned silence. Jack felt his jaw drop, then regained his composure. Something Maria had once said came to him, something from rabbinical lore.

Drawn by the divine finger. Drawn by a finger of fire.

It was the menorah.

Seven branches, seven shafts of yellow shining as if they

were aflame, shedding lustre like beams of light. At the head of the triumphal procession, raised in front of the Well of Sacrifice.

Jack looked at Maria, who was staring at the image in a trance, as if she were gathering strength from it.

Reksnys abruptly let the cloth drop back, concealing the image, and gave a coarse laugh. 'Shocked?'

'I noticed you didn't look at it,' Jack said coldly. 'Or couldn't.'

'I despise it. I have no wish to behold this object myself. It is a means to an end.' Reksnys nodded at Loki, who pulled Maria up and pushed her across to him. Reksnys kept her at arm's distance, prodding her with the muzzle of the Luger, a distasteful look on his face. Then he shoved the gun in the small of her back, aimed down. 'I know exactly how to do it. A slow, lingering death. Plenty of experience with her type.' He jerked his head towards the rebreathers and dive bags stacked beside the hole in the floor. He looked at Jack. 'You are the world-famous underwater explorer, no?' His voice was mocking, sneering. 'Now you and your friend will go down into the underworld and find what I desire.'

19

Jack hit the water with a resounding splash, the echo resonating off the walls of the cavern. Costas had preceded him and was already carrying out an underwater recce, the arc of light from his headlamp visible off to one side. Jack quickly released the carabiner on the rope and gave it a tug. The rope began to jerk upwards, and Jack followed the glint of metal from the carabiner as it rose up the thin shaft of light to the hole in the limestone ceiling almost twenty metres above. He and Costas had silently kitted up in the ancient chamber a few minutes before, donning the equipment Reksnys had ordered them to bring from *Seaquest II*. Jack had refused to divulge any of his thoughts about the wall-painting, and Maria had remained obstinately silent in the corner of the chamber even after the tape had been ripped away from her mouth.

Jack was convinced that the scene with the menorah showed the Well of Sacrifice at Chichén Itzá, not this place. Yet all the indications were that Reksnys was right to think that the tunnel ahead of them held some clue to Harald Hardrada's last stand. The location of the temple above the cavern, the depiction of the jungle battle with the river running beneath it, local Maya tradition.

There had been no chance to make contact with the security team, who had been on standby since he and Costas had left in the Zodiac two hours before. Jack knew the Lynx was in the air somewhere offshore, but Ben could do nothing until Jack and Costas had found some way of radioing in their co-ordinates and confirming that the situation with Maria was safe enough for an intervention. Jack had given Maria a reassuring look just before he donned his helmet, had been cool and collected as Loki had winched him down the hole. But his mind was in a tumult, coursing with adrenalin at the prospect of what might lie ahead yet desperately running through the possibilities if they were to return empty-handed. At the moment the options were few, and they were not good.

Costas' voice came through the intercom. 'There's an underground river running through the bottom of this chamber, about eight metres beneath you. The current's pretty vicious. Not exactly recommended cave-diving conditions.'

'Roger that,' Jack replied, floating on the surface and following the sweep of light below that marked Costas' progress. He tested his buoyancy compensator and ran a systems check on the computer that controlled his gas supply. They were wearing semi-closed circuit rebreathers, variable mixed-gas systems that enabled them to go to greater depths than either pure oxygen or air would allow. It was a precaution, as they had no expectation that the cave system would exceed the thirty-metre maximum typical of the Yucatán cenotes.

'Remind me about this calcium carbonate stuff,' Jack said.

Costas surfaced beside him, inflating the buoyancy wings on his backpack and adjusting the intercom on his helmet. 'Dissolved limestone,' he said. 'During the Ice Age, everything here was above water. That's when the stalagmites and stalactites that are now underwater formed. Then at the end of the Ice Age, the sea level rose and the caves flooded. Leave something above water in one of these caverns, and it'll get encased in stone. Drop it in the water, and it'll stay good as new. We're in fresh water down to about fifteen metres, when you hit salt water.'

Jack looked up at the thin shaft of light streaming in from the ceiling above, to the ugly face he could just make out peering down at them. The rope and sling that had been used to winch then down had now been pulled up again, to await their return. He thought of Maria, and took a deep breath from his rebreather. He gave an okay signal to Costas. 'Right. Let's get going.' They dumped air from their wings and dropped beneath the surface, Jack following Costas just above the current. It was cooler than the sea, justifying their full wetsuits, but refreshing after the torrid heat above. They both wore triple headlamps on their helmets, and the beams revealed an awesome scene as they panned them around. Stalagmites reared up from the base of the cave in clusters, overlying caves and grottoes. The water was crystal clear, as clear as Jack had ever seen, flickering with pastel colours. They dropped down and rode the back of the current, their arms outstretched and their fins extended behind to keep them stable. Seconds later they swept under an overhang into a dark tunnel, leaving the gloomy light of the entrance chamber behind.

'When it's not raining, this tunnel's partly above water,' Costas said. 'You can see the waterline on the walls beside us, with fresh calcium formations above it. It looks like there'd normally be enough space for a small canoe or raft.'

Costas took out a pencil-sized lightstick, cracked it to mix the chemicals and then dropped it into a fissure. Jack watched the green glow disappear behind him, and Costas took out half a dozen more. 'I'm assuming we'll want to come back this way,' he said. 'The current's weak near the ceiling, so it shouldn't be a problem.'

Jack rolled over and saw a canopy of rock with none of the tell-tale ripples from air pockets. They had come at least two hundred metres from the entrance, maybe more. 'Any guesses how much further?' he said.

'I reckon we're looking for another chamber, somewhere accessible from the entrance chamber. If this tunnel dips below the waterline, we're on the wrong track.' As Costas spoke, the passageway began to do exactly the opposite, rising up and opening out, and their beams reflected off the underside of a water pool that spread out above them as far as they could see. 'Hey presto.'

They surfaced and looked around, awestruck. They were inside another huge cavern, at least fifty metres across, extending in a great dome that reached up to the jungle floor. It was how Jack imagined the sacred cenote at Chichén Itzá had once looked, before the limestone ceiling collapsed. Unlike the entrance chamber, this one was pitch dark, with no visible opening to the surface. They swam slowly across the pool, their lights reflecting off fantastic shapes that dazzled them like sculptures in ice. Stalagmites rose out of the depths like subsea volcanic vents, some of them joining stalactites to form continuous columns like the pillars of some great cathedral. They could see the force of nature still at work, rainwater seeping through the limestone ceiling and spattering on the exposed formations, adding another sheen of minerals in a process that had begun thousands of years before human history first touched this place.

In the centre was an island, one that seemed to have been created entirely from calcium accretion. The surface was a bizarre array of shapes that looked like some fantasy citadel. Huge tendrils hung down over it from high above, the fossilized roots of long-dead trees.

As the slope up to the island became visible, Costas dropped down to the bottom, about eight metres below. He suddenly seemed to be swimming sideways, and Jack saw him grab a stalagmite and pull himself up the slope until the current had released him and he could swim free again.

'That was frightening.' Costas stopped about five metres below Jack, and was catching his breath. 'You'd never be able to swim against that. Take a look to your right and you can see where it goes.'

Jack peered across to a point directly opposite the entrance tunnel. He could see a shimmering disturbance where the underwater river swept through the chamber, exiting under an overhang near the base of the cavern about twenty metres away. It was a black hole, a forbidding place with no sign of natural light further on. Jack realized how close he had come to losing Costas. He closed his eyes and swore to himself. As so often in diving it was the casual decision, the deceptively benign conditions, that had nearly had fatal consequences. Jack had not given a second's thought to Costas' decision to drop down, yet the danger was as great as any they had faced in the iceberg, or back in the tunnels of Atlantis. And in cave diving there was rarely a second chance, no going back on a wrong move.

'Jack, I've found something.' Costas was a little further upslope, but his upper body was wedged in a fissure. Jack sank down beside him, keeping a wary eye on the current a few metres away. Costas emerged in a cloud of silt, and pressed an object at Jack. 'Get a hold of that.'

It was a human jawbone. A small one, a child's. It was brown with age, but perfectly preserved. Costas held the rest of the skull towards him, and Jack could see the eye sockets, the lines where the bones of the cranium had not yet fused. 'They're everywhere,' Costas said. 'Hundreds of them.' Jack looked around. Lying in the silt, piled at the base of stalagmites, grimacing out from under overhangs. Skulls, limb bones, ribs. He reached into the silt and pulled out a small jade pendant, shaped like the gaping jaw of some mythical beast, like the image of the underworld on the wall-painting in the temple. He glanced through the pellucid waters at the dark hole where the river disappeared, and felt a sudden chill certainty.

'Human sacrifice,' he said. 'The Toltecs must have lowered themselves and their victims through the hole in the ceiling just as we were, then paddled through into this chamber. This was the edge of their underworld, the closest they could get. When the current was strong, after a storm, they could have thrown their victims into the very maw of the underworld, watched them sucked into that black hole and out of earthly existence. This must have been the ultimate place of sacrifice.'

'We don't seem to be able to get away from that,' Costas muttered. 'I'm beginning to yearn for Vikings again.'

'You may just be in luck.'

'What do you mean?'

'Upslope, about three metres. At the edge of the island.'

It was another skull, larger than the others, with different wear on the teeth. It had been badly crushed, as if the victim had suffered a terrific blow to the face. But it was not the skull that had excited Jack's interest. It was what it was wearing.

A gilded metal helmet, cone-shaped, with a long nose-guard.

Jack's heart began to race. He wafted the bottom, raising clouds of silt. Maya pots, intact. More human bones. A shining disc, gold, covered with glyphs. A handle protruding from a gully, covered in gilt wire. A sword handle. Beside it a long wooden haft, a glint of metal at the end.

With mounting excitement Jack drew himself out of the water, Costas beside him. Both men quickly doffed their rebreathers and fins and stashed them on the edge. With their helmets removed they could hear the noise of the cavern, water dripping on the pool, the whoosh of bat wings, eerie sounds magnified and distorted by echo. They clambered up on to a level platform and surveyed the underground island. It was about ten metres in diameter, rising to a cone in the middle, covered in slick accretion. The centre was a gigantic single stalagmite, growing from the cavern floor beneath the ceiling where the fall of leached calcium had been greatest. Around it were stalagmites that had formed more recently as the shape of the ceiling had changed, some of them beneath the calcified tree roots which hung over them in a fantastic shroud.

Jack was carrying a torch, and swept it over the island before placing his hand on the stalagmite nearest to them. It was a peculiar shape, almost seeming to curve above them, on the face of it no more extraordinary than anything else they were seeing around them.

'My God.' Jack's voice was resonant, echoing.

'What is it?'

Jack stumbled back a few steps, then shone his torch up the stalagmite. He remembered what Jeremy had suggested when they had last spoken. His voice was taut with amazement. 'Remember our longship in the ice?'

Costas followed his gaze, puzzled, and then gasped. The top of the stalagmite was a bulbous shape that extended out from the curve. They were looking at the prow of a Viking ship, the details of its surface lost under a millennium of accretion but the shape unmistakable. It was an astonishing sight.

'They must have carried it with them from the longship,' Jack murmured. 'Erected it here, a last battle standard.' He shone the torch at the bulbous form on top. 'The *eagle*.'

'Look on either side,' Costas exclaimed. 'I could be wrong, but I think it's a shield wall.'

Jack saw a line of concretion about a metre high extended in an arc, facing the entrance to the cavern. Costas was right. The ridge was undulating with striking regularity, made up of identical semicircles each about the width of a man. Three on one side of the stempost, four on the other. They looked as if they had been iced over. Below them were long, square shapes that could have been timbers, perhaps crossbeams salvaged from the ship. Jack remembered Jeremy telling him about Viking defences built from ship's timbers. He looked over the wall, to the space behind where the defenders would have made their stand. It was the most astonishing sight of all. Against the rampart was the spectral shape of a man, propped up on his back, limbs spread out. It had been a skeleton, but was covered with such a thick layer of accretion that it seemed to be fleshed out again, like one of the plaster shapes of bodies from Roman Pompeii.

It was wearing a helmet. The conical shape, the nose-guard, just discernible in the accretion. There was a shield, emerging at an angle as if it had been mauled. He had been tall, at least Jack's height.

Jack stared, transfixed.

Could it be him?

He leaned back on the fossilized shield wall, his voice hoarse with emotion. 'On the wall-painting, that river below the jungle battle. I think that's where we are now. And I think this was where the final drama was played out. Harald Hardrada's last stand.'

'You think the enemy in the painting really were Vikings?'

'The image of the menorah clinches it.'

'So this was as far as Harald got from the sea.'

'Let's imagine a dozen of them, not many more,' Jack said. 'The size of the vanquished army on the painting was probably an exaggeration, a way of making the victory seem greater.' He paused, marshalling his thoughts. 'They make their way inland with everything they can bring, their weapons and armour, their treasure, what they can easily salvage and carry from the ship to build a shelter. Much like Cortés and his tiny band of conquistadors hundreds of years later, only with no intention of ever returning.'

'Then they bump into the locals.'

'The Maya are dazzled, think they're gods, saviours arrived to rescue them from the Toltecs. But word inevitably spreads to the Toltecs, to the overlord in Chichén Itzá. He dispatches an army, there's a desperate battle in the jungle. The few survivors seek a refuge, a final stronghold. Rorke's Drift, the Alamo. In the Yucatán, if that's what you want, you go underground. They discover the jungle temple, maybe they're directed here by the Maya. They make their way down the sacrificial route, on the underground river. They light their way with burning torches, maybe burn their timbers on the island. Viking warriors fully girded for battle, ready to defend their shield wall at the edge of the world, wreathed in fire. But I doubt whether the Toltecs would have been daunted. Once the Toltecs find out and follow them, it's only a matter of time before they're overwhelmed.'

'I hope for their sake none of them were taken prisoner.'

'The only one we know about is your friend from L'Anse aux Meadows. Probably a retainer, a servant. Jeremy told me the Toltecs sometimes took enemy servants as their own slaves, a way of stamping their dominance on the vanquished. You saw it on the wall-painting. Maybe he was a turncoat. Some of the Vikings would have been half crazed, starving. Maybe he told the Toltecs about this place. Maybe his escape years later and incredible trek back to L'Anse aux Meadows was some kind of atonement. We'll never know. But he wasn't the only one to survive. Judging by the painting, several of Harald's warriors suffered the ultimate horror, taken to Chichén Itzá for sacrifice.'

'With the menorah.'

Jack suddenly remembered the breathtaking image they had seen on the painting, the fiery radiance. 'Reksnys is wrong. I'm convinced the menorah isn't here. The Toltecs may have left the Viking weapons here as some kind of offering, but I think they took the menorah with them from the battle site. We know the Toltecs didn't offer all of Harald's treasure to the gods, because we have those two coins incorporated in the jade pendant from L'Anse aux Meadows.'

'Which leaves us with a problem.'

'Reksnys is going to be disappointed.'

'We can't go back empty-handed,' Costas said. 'At best we'd be buying time, but probably not much of it. Chances are we'd be back down that hole again, dead before we hit the water. As Reksnys himself said, Maria was only saved on a whimsy. As soon as he finds out we don't have the menorah, he'll get bored. These people are always like that.' He looked at Jack. 'He'll let his son's temper run its course.'

'They might try to follow us down here.'

'Loki might. There were a couple of old scuba rigs, gear Reksnys must have brought along before the chance came to use us, and Loki could easily follow the trail of lightsticks through the tunnel. But if he reaches the stage of going after us like that, he'll be in a rage. That'd be curtains for Maria.'

'Are you thinking what I'm thinking?'

'We don't have any choice.'

'These underground river systems always come up, somewhere,' Costas said ruefully. 'But it could be miles.'

they were in the tunnel, twisting round a bend, blackness all around. The tunnel seemed to meander and turn like a living beast, seeking out a route among the calcite obstructions. They were completely at the mercy of the current, trusting the flow to keep them from crashing into the limestone walls on either side. Jack forced his head forward until his body was in line with the tunnel, Costas to his left, and they both extended their arms in a desperate attempt to use their hands as foils. Bulbous shapes appeared out of nowhere, caught in the beam of their headlamps, then vanished behind them with only inches to spare. Suddenly Jack was aware of a fork ahead, a widening in the tunnel divided by a column, a white pillar they were hurtling towards at terrifying speed.

'The right-hand tunnel!' Costas yelled. 'I can see light!'

Jack swerved his hands to the right, craning his body to follow the main flow of the current. It was no use. At the last second he pulled his hands in violently to avoid smashing into the column and they tumbled into the left-hand tunnel, a narrowing pit of darkness with smooth walls like an ice chute. Jack bounced off Costas and felt an excruciating jolt in his thigh, from his injury in the ice. For a terrifying moment he was back inside the berg. 'Wrong turn,' Costas yelled. Jack clutched him, could see his face behind his visor, frantic. 'This is a side channel,' Costas exclaimed. 'The main channel was flowing up towards the surface. I saw light.'

The current in the channel began to eddy, then slowed down. Even so it was impossible to swim against, and they were being pulled down, inexorably. They clawed at the walls, to no avail. Suddenly everything was distorted, hazy, something Jack had last seen in the icefjord where the fresh-water runoff from the glacier had formed a layer above the seawater. It was shimmering, oily, the change in refractive index throwing his senses into disarray. He began to feel disorientated.

'Shit,' Costas exclaimed. 'That was the halocline. We're below sea level.'

It was as if they had passed through into another dimension, into some darker world. The calcium formations were gone now, and the view ahead was bleak, forbidding. The intense, directional beam of light seemed to narrow the shaft, increasing Jack's unease. The tunnel was elliptical, about five metres across, but the ceiling had lowered and a deep bed of gravel rose up from the floor. They were still going down, their lights boring a hole into the darkness. 'Forty metres depth,' Costas said. 'The Yucatán cave systems bottom out at about fifty metres, maximum. We've got to be going back up soon.' Jack looked at his depth gauge. Forty-six metres. Fifty-two metres. The ceiling and the floor had almost converged, and they were wedged in now, burrowing in the gravel to make space. Then they came to a standstill, in a cloud of silt. Jack aimed his headlamp into the slit ahead, a crack only inches above the gravel. It was a dead end. They were trapped.

Costas heaved himself back beside Jack, his rebreather clunking against the ceiling and his body grinding through the gravel. 'Something's not right,' he said. 'We were being pulled down by a current, and that's got to go somewhere. And this gravel pile curves down at the sides, shaped by water movement. There has to be an outlet.'

He pushed himself down the right side of the gravel pile, into a narrow channel at the bottom, and pulled himself ahead until only his fins were showing. Jack closed his eyes, then opened them again, concentrated on little things, the shape of a fossil in the limestone a few inches from his face. He looked down again to where Costas had disappeared. He could see that the crevasse was free of silt. Swept clear by the current. Costas was right.

'Jack. Follow me.' He did as instructed, digging his hands into the gravel and heaving himself down the side of the tunnel. He felt the flow of water, saw light ahead. 'It goes up,' Costas said excitedly. Jack followed, slowly, squeezing through a boulder choke. There was hardly any room to move, and he was reduced to wriggling, clanging his rebreather pack against the stone walls. The tunnel beyond was narrower still, like a drainage pipe, smooth and rounded where the current had worn it down but only about a metre in diameter. Jack had never been in a space so narrow. It was beyond claustrophobic. There was no way they could go back, with the current pressing against them, and any blockage in the tunnel now would seal their fate. Costas' fins were a few feet ahead of him. Jack checked his depth gauge, remained focused. He stared at the rock inches from his face, then at his depth gauge. Forty-one metres. Thirty-seven metres. They were ascending, slowly but surely. Then the tunnel took a sharp turn upwards and they were in a chamber, a vast space filled with shadowy forms, great columns that towered upwards like white-robed giants, beckoning them up from the underworld. Far above, Jack could see a shimmer of green, distinct from the white beams of their headlights. He closed his eyes again, a wave of relief coursing through him, his heart pounding not with fear but with exhilaration. He rose beside Costas through the chamber, the water so clear that they seemed suspended in mid-air like figures from some scene of apotheosis. Then they were at the top of the cavern, only ten metres beneath the surface of the water, butting up against a crack in the rock where they could see the light of dawn shining through.

It was not over yet. The crack was a narrow squeeze, barely wide enough for one of them. There was no other exit from the chamber.

'Why does this always seem to happen when I dive with you?' Costas said. 'Next time let's do some open-water diving for a change.'

'If there is a next time.' Jack looked down into the black chasm yawning below, then back up into the crack. He could see foliage, the wavering forms of trees overhanging the surface of the water. His heart was still pounding, but no longer with excitement. This was a ridiculous place to die.

'We'll have to swim for it,' Costas said. 'You go first.'

'No way. You'll have the tighter squeeze, and I can help push you through.'

Costas unstrapped his rebreather and dangled it down

beside him. He pulled himself as far as he could into the fissure, about two metres above Jack, then ripped off his helmet and dropped the rig. It went plummeting past Jack, disappearing into the darkness below. Jack pulled himself behind Costas and heaved up against his legs. Nothing happened. He felt suddenly helpless, appalled that he might watch his friend die only a few metres from the surface, holding his legs. Then Costas kicked hard, and erupted upwards. Jack paused to regain his breath, unbuckled his harness and dangled it beside him, took five deep breaths and then ripped off his helmet and dropped the rig. He heaved himself up through the rock, his eyes open to the blurry haze of daylight through the water, and pulled himself through. Another kick of his fins and he surfaced in a slurry of green algae, in a small pool under fronds of undergrowth.

Costas was panting on the edge of the pool, looking like the creature from the black lagoon. He wiped the slime off his face, submerged his head and shook it violently, then reared up out of the water and offered Jack a hand. 'You might want to do the same. Don't want to terrify the natives.'

After Jack was out and shaking himself off, Costas delved into the top of his wetsuit and extracted a slim metallic device, about the size of a pocket calculator. He tapped the front and pulled out an aerial, bringing the device to his ear.

'Sometimes you're a surprising bag of tricks,' Jack panted.

'Combined GPS beacon and two-way radio,' Costas said. 'All I need to do now is activate the mayday button and Ben'll have us pinpointed. I can try to establish a radio link and talk to him when we know what the situation is.'

They had surfaced beside a rough jungle track. It was still raining, alternately drizzling and pouring. Costas activated the compass on his device and quickly took a bearing. Ten minutes later they crept up the limestone dome that covered the cenote and approached the overgrown temple. The Jeep that had brought them was at the end of the track. Jack saw a boy, a local Maya, playing on the road, but he had not spotted them. They stealthily rounded the building and each took one side of the entrance, their backs flat to the wall, listening. They could hear nothing. Jack could taste the salt of his sweat joining the water on his face. He looked at Costas, nodded. They sidled into the chamber, keeping to the shadows, straining their eyes into the candlelit gloom. There was no sign of Maria or Loki. The only occupant was a man sitting with his back to them on a diving tank, cleaning a pistol. Jack gestured to Costas and returned to the entrance, vigilant. Costas crept up behind the man and put his arm round his throat, clamping his mouth. The pistol dropped with a clatter. Costas drew the man close and spoke with a snarl.

'Now. Where were we?'

20

Twenty minutes later the noise of rain was drowned out by the shuddering roar of the Lynx as it came to a hover overhead, sweeping the jungle floor with its downdraught. Two men were winched down through the dense foliage, followed by a red first-aid crate. Once they were safely on the ground, the Lynx tipped forward and disappeared back into the cloud. Jack ran over from where he had been sheltering to pull the box from the undergrowth, and then scrambled over to help Ben.

'We didn't know what to expect,' Ben shouted above the downpour, holstering the pistol he had been holding at the ready. 'When Costas radioed in the GPS co-ordinates we were only about three miles from you, flying a search pattern just off the coast. The cover story was an aerial survey for archaeological remains offshore. Jeremy came along as the only archaeologist on board. And because he insisted. You don't want to fly uninvited into Mexican airspace bristling with weapons, especially at night, so it's only me and my Glock. But now we've found you, the Lynx has gone back for a full security team and we've contacted the police.'

'Loki's gone,' Jack shouted. 'Ordered by his father to follow us down into the cavern. Taken Maria with him. Didn't trust us. But Reksnys is all yours.'

'I'll need to do a perimeter sweep, priority. Jeremy'll have to do prisoner detail.'

Jeremy pushed his way through the undergrowth from where he had landed, his glasses steamed up and kicking off a mass of vines. Jack led them through the tangle and out on to the rough track, then straight into the temple. At the entrance they shook off water and Jeremy wiped his glasses. Inside, Costas stood with the Luger aimed at a form lying gagged and face-down on the ground, his wrists and mouth roughly duct-taped. Jeremy bounded past them to the wall-painting and peered closely at the image of the menorah, now revealed, and at the battle scene. 'Vikings,' he enthused, his glasses steaming up again. 'You were right. Fantastic. And look. I'm sure that one's a woman.'

'Time for that later.' Jack nodded to Costas, who gave him the Luger while Ben kneeled over Reksnys and refastened his wrists with a plastic tie. 'Costas needs to help operate the winch, Jeremy.' Jack passed him the pistol. 'Can you handle this?'

'Six months in the ROTC at Stanford,' Jeremy said, taking off his glasses again. 'A misplaced sense of duty after 9/11. Not really my kind of thing.'

Jack nodded. 'Remember who this guy is. Remember what they did to O'Connor and Maria.'

'My grandfather brought one of these back from the war.' Jeremy replaced his glasses and took the Luger, pulling back the breech toggle to check the chamber and then releasing it. He kneeled down and shoved the Luger into the small of Reksnys' back, pulling his head up roughly and leaning behind his ear. 'My friend Costas tells me you threatened Maria with this. A long, lingering death.' He pulled Reksnys to his feet and pushed him towards the door, disappearing with him into the rain. Ben looked at Jack. 'I don't think we've got much to worry about there.'

'Okay. I'm going down to get Maria,' Jack said.

'Not alone.'

'No choice. There's no way we can retrieve the rebreathers now. Reksnys had two scuba rigs here as backup, and Loki's taken one. It looks like he used the octopus regulator for Maria, allowing her to breathe off the same tank. The rig we've been left with doesn't have an octopus, and anyway the tank doesn't have enough air in it for us to buddy-breathe to the chamber and back.'

'I could contact the Lynx and have gear airlifted in from the ship.'

'No time. We've pushed our luck as it is.' Jack heaved the air cylinder on to his back, and clipped together the stabilizer jacket on his chest. 'Loki's already going to be in a rage. He would have been better off staying up here, and he knows it. The guy's an independent. His father's an evil bully but an amateur by comparison. Loki's caught between blindly obeying, all the nonsense about the *félag*, and his better instincts. He's been forced to a place where he's not in control the way he likes. It's our chance. But it also means he's going to be volatile. And I need to act now. I don't want him to come back into the chamber below us and work out what's happened. Maria wouldn't last a second. If she's still alive.'

'You haven't got a weapon.'

'I'll improvise.'

'Torch?'

'Costas and I left chemical lightsticks to mark the route.'

'Good luck.'

Jack grunted as Ben looped the rope under his arms. Costas checked his air and weightbelt and then held Jack by the shoulders, looking him straight in the eyes. 'Battle-luck,' he said.

'Battle-luck.' Jack pulled down his mask, sat on the edge of the hole and then swung himself out over the dark pool far below. Costas and Ben immediately began winching him down. Jack was focused, his whole being intent on his objective. He hit the water with his regulator in his mouth and immediately began swimming underwater towards the tunnel, following the trail of lightsticks they had dropped on the cavern floor just over an hour before. The tunnel seemed less oppressive now, and as he looked ahead he saw the extraordinary luminosity of the calcite walls where they were lit up by the lightsticks, fantastic formations of stalagmites and stalagtites that loomed out of either side like abstract ice sculptures.

Ten minutes after entering the water he saw the pool of light ahead that marked the final chamber. The light was different, more intensive than the chemical illumination. He reached the edge of the chamber, the bubbles from his exhaust cascading along the ceiling above him, and cautiously surfaced in a small side chamber just high enough for his head to be out of the water. In the centre of the cavern he could see the bizarre calcium formations of the islet, about twenty metres in front of him. The light was coming from the opposite side of the islet and shone in a wide beam against the ceiling.

The bubbles from his regulator would be a giveaway. For a moment he cursed their decision to ditch the rebreathers in the underwater river. He would have to swim on the surface, hoping not to be spotted.

He took off his mask and clipped it to his jacket, then looked around for something to darken his face, something to absorb the glare if a torch was shone at him. He reached out gingerly and rubbed a flat surface just in front of him. He sniffed his hand, and crinkled his nose. Potassium nitrate. Bat droppings. He took another swipe off the rock and rubbed it all over his face, careful not to make a noise.

He inflated his stabilizer jacket, blowing air into the

mouthpiece to avoid the noise of the low-pressure feed from his regulator, then pushed himself off and began to swim slowly towards the outcrop.

He reached the midway point. He could feel the tug of the underwater river, far stronger now than it had been when he and Costas had decided to follow it. A light swung round, caught his face. He froze. It swung back again, and he resumed swimming. If he was caught now, he would have no chance. He assumed Loki was armed. Everything depended on surprise.

He reached the edge of the islet. He heard a voice on the other side, magnified and distorted in the chamber, but unmistakably male. A snarling, menacing tone. Jack slipped off his tank and fins and sidled along to a place he remembered from his dive with Costas, where they had seen the first extraordinary clue. He reached down into the shallows. It came away easily, unencumbered by accretion, as well preserved in the fresh water as the one he had found in the ice. He stood out of the water, dripping and black in his wetsuit, and pulled the object up with him.

A Varangian battleaxe.

Jack made his way swiftly up the knobbled contours of accretion, thankful he was wearing neoprene boots that gripped the surface well. He passed over the fossilized Viking shield wall, the arching shape of the ship's stem, the haunting form of the fallen warrior. From the top he looked down on the other side of the islet. Loki was there, no more than ten metres away. He was standing with his back to Jack, straddling Maria, who was lying on her back staring defiantly up. Loki was holding a pistol in his left hand, a Browning High Power. In the other hand he held a blade against her heart, a sword. It was the Varangian sword Jack and Costas had seen in the water beside the axe.

Jack felt a chill of horror. History had never really stopped in this place. He was witnessing something ingrained in the stone of the Yucatán, impossible to exorcize. A human sacrifice.

With lightning speed Jack swept down on Loki, swinging the axe hard, severing Loki's left arm in one mighty swipe. The pistol flew into the water still grasped in the hand, spinning together and disappearing into the blackness. Loki staggered, shocked, then spun round to face Jack, his face a contortion of surprise and rage. The stump was gushing blood. He dropped the sword, staggered, lifted his remaining arm to the scar on his face, then staggered back again, picking up the sword. He suddenly exploded into action, lunging at Jack in a terrifying blur of speed and flashing metal. Jack was nearly caught off guard, only just raising the axe in time. Steel impacted against steel, clashing, grinding, ringing, a sound not heard here for almost a thousand years. Jack's body quivered as he parried the blows, but he stood his ground. It was only a matter of time before his opponent would falter. Loki was already too weak to stop his body from following through the swing of the sword, lurching, swivelling as he struggled to regain his balance. He stood back again, in a frenzy of pain, snivelling and panting, goading Jack with the point of the sword, staggering back further towards the edge of the water.

Loki's rage had cast the shadow of his own downfall. He could have remained on the surface with his father, let his mind rule, retained his lethal efficiency.

Jack weighed the haft in his hands, just as he had done once before, when another long-handled, single-bitted axe had saved their lives in the iceberg.

Battle-luck.

He reared up and took two strides forward. As he swung the axe he thought he saw runes flashing in front of him, runes where Halfdan's name had been on the other axe, runes that began with the same Norse letter.

The battleaxe of a mighty king. Thunderbolt of the North.

The axe came slicing through the air and struck Loki on the side of the head, then spun off from Jack's hands and cartwheeled into the water above the underground river. Loki's head jerked back and then sprang forward, like a marionette. For a horrifying moment he seemed uninjured. Then the scar on his face parted, split wide open through his eye socket. Jack could see jawbones and teeth, grimacing horribly like the sculpted skulls at Chichén Itzá. Then there was blood, thick, oozing drops that splattered on to the rock below.

Loki took one step forward, then slipped on the blood, falling heavily, his head grating hard against the side of a stalagmite. He heaved himself up again with his one arm, and stood swaying, staggering. The side of his face was now completely ripped away, and his eyeball was hanging out. His breathing was harsh, erratic, and he was moaning horribly. Jack could see where the axe had bitten deep into his brain. Loki staggered one last time and fell back into the water with a crash, taking the sword with him. For a moment he was suspended in mid-water, his one eye staring blindly towards Jack, still alive, clawing weakly for the surface. Then he dropped deeper and the current took him, dragging him down into the darkness, out of sight, sucked into the underworld.

He was gone.

Jack slid down beside Maria and they lay by the edge of the pool. He was shaking with adrenalin aftershock. She clung fiercely to him. The commotion on the water died away, and the only sound was dripping, rainwater percolating through from above, the sound magnified in the cavern but soothingly rhythmic after the echoing clash of steel. As Jack's shaking subsided, Maria stared into the crystalline water inches from her face. She reached in and pulled something out, a smooth chip of rock free of accretion. They could see marks on its surface, scratches. They both sat up. 'It's a runestone,' Maria whispered.

'Can you read it?'

'It's crude, rushed,' Maria murmured. 'Like the last entry in the diary of a doomed expedition.'

'Try.' Jack sounded exhausted, his voice barely a whisper.

Maria paused, muttered a few words to herself, then read it out loud. '*Only Ulf, Finn and Halldor are left. The Scraelings have taken the outer chamber. Thor protect us. Hann til ragnarøks.'*

Jack felt stripped of emotion, too drained to respond. All he could do was reach out and touch the dripping stone.

'Maybe Harald himself scratched this, his last act before the Toltecs were upon him,' Maria said. 'It was Stamford Bridge all over again, only this time it truly was the end.' She looked back at the spectral shapes on the platform behind her, then towards the blackness in the water where Loki had disappeared. She gave an involuntary shiver. 'They got as far as they humanly could, right to the entrance of the underworld.'

'I can feel what they felt,' Jack murmured. 'We're on the edge of the spirit world here, the very boundary. Something wants me to go down that passageway, to follow Loki. It's like a malign force drawing me in, willing me to frame the challenge. I feel as close to Harald here as I've ever felt, really close.' Jack looked around at the flickering shadows on the cavern walls, then shook himself and raised Loki's air tank from where it had been left by the edge of the water to Maria's back. 'And I know this is not a place we want to be.'

'It's not over yet,' Maria said.

'You've got plenty of air. There's a line of lights back to the entrance. Piece of cake. I'll be right behind you.'

'I didn't mean that.'

Jack gave her shoulder straps a final tug. He splashed water on his face to rub off the black mess and sat down beside her. Maria began to talk, slowly at first, hesitantly, then in full flow, as if she were telling something she had never told before, but had rehearsed countless times in her mind. Over the next few minutes Jack heard a story more awful than he could ever have imagined, a story that made the monsters of the underworld seem as potent as they had to the Vikings, that seemed to shape the lurking malevolence of this place into a force too evil to leave unchallenged.

Twenty minutes later Jack heaved himself out of the well hole into the painted chamber. Costas squatted in front of him, breathless after operating the winch. Maria sat dripping on the stone floor a few metres away. Despite the heat she was shivering slightly, and Costas passed her a towel and an IMU jacket along with a bottle of water. As soon as he saw she was safe, Jack swivelled round and addressed Costas.

'What's our status?'

'The Mexicans are here,' Costas panted. 'Two guys in a Jeep about ten minutes ago. They're *judiciales*, plain-clothed guys. Pretty unsavoury, if you ask me. They said a helicopter is on its way. Apparently all this tract is Reksnys' territory, but we're well away from his main compound. It doesn't look like he trusted any of his own security people to be out here. A few locals live in the jungle, Maya, but they're on our side. As soon as more police arrive and the Lynx returns from *Seaquest II* with a full security team, we can relax. Ben's doing a wide perimeter sweep as we talk.'

Jack jerked his head towards the hole. 'You probably gathered our friend Loki won't be joining us.'

Costas raised his eyebrows. 'Permanently?'

'He's gone for a cave-diving endurance record. Without air.'

'The Toltec underworld,' Costas said quietly. 'Not a place I'd want to spend eternity.'

Jack drew Costas aside and huddled with him in the gloom at the rear of the chamber, talking intently. Costas occasionally looked at Maria, his expression increasingly grim. After a few minutes Jack gestured for her to join them. Costas passed her something wrapped in a cloth which she checked and quickly concealed inside her jacket.

Jeremy suddenly appeared at the entrance, breathless and frantic. 'Quick. For God's sake. Reksnys has escaped. He's got a local kid. He's threatening to kill him.'

'How the hell . . .?'

'The Mexican police cut him loose, then they both vanished, did a runner.'

'Shit.'

There was a sudden commotion outside and Reksnys appeared, pushing ahead a boy of about five, the distraught parents pleading in Spanish behind him. Jeremy forced the parents back out and Reksnys marched in holding a leather belt round the boy's neck. He paraded in front of them, his head held high and sneering, then dragged the boy like an animal to the centre of the chamber.

'I can break his little neck in a second. Just like that.' He snapped the fingers of his free hand. He seemed to forget his audience, and spoke with almost childish glee. Suddenly he looked around. 'Where's my son?'

'Went for a swim.'

Reksnys failed to take in what Costas had said, and drew the boy towards him. '*Cómo te llamas?*'

The boy was too terror-stricken to reply.

Reksnys jerked the boy up towards his face. '*Cómo te llamas!*'

The boy whispered tearfully, 'Daniel.'

'Daniel.' Reksnys let the boy drop and then jerked him back against him, the belt held tight round his neck. 'Interesting name for a Maya. When I was young, I knew some little boys with that name. Daniel, Doron, Menachem. And there were some little girls with them too. But not for long.' Reksnys sneered again, then eyed Maria suspiciously as she detached herself from the others and took a few steps to the wall, to the place where she had recovered consciousness after her nightmare trip from Iona. She stood facing Reksnys, her legs slightly apart.

'I think,' she said, 'you once found it a lot easier using this.'

Slowly, deliberately, she raised the Luger and aimed it at Reksnys' head, both hands clasping the butt, her left index finger brushing the trigger.

Jeremy stared at Maria, shocked.

Reksnys sneered again. 'You don't know how to use that.'

She flipped down the safety catch on the left side of the frame. 'Oh yes I do.'

'It's not loaded.'

'Jack?' Maria said, not moving her eyes.

Jack pulled out a small box with the words *Nine-millimetre Parabellum* printed on one side, and showed the half-empty interior. 'We found these in your pocket,' he said. 'Remember?'

Reksnys was contemptuous. 'Put the gun down or the boy dies.'

Maria began to recite words she had memorized when she was a child. '*Operational Situation Report USSR, No. 129a,*' she said quietly. '*Einsatzgruppe D. Location: Nikolayev, Ukraine. Addendum to Report No. 129 concerning the activity of the Einsatzkommandos in freeing places of Jews and finishing off partisan groups. SS-Sturmbannführer Andrius Reksnys personally executed 341 Jews. Revised total for the last two weeks: 32,108.*'

There was a stunned silence. Maria kept the Luger levelled at Reksnys' head. He remained stock still, staring at her with cold loathing, the rope taut and shimmering against the boy's neck.

'May the fourteenth, 1943,' Maria continued. 'A beautiful spring morning. The flowers were up everywhere, the birds singing. The last in line in front of the ditch were a young family, a father and a pregnant mother and four small children. Do you remember? Your father let you finish the little ones.'

'Impossible.' Reksnys spat out the word, looking conspiratorially at the others. 'This woman is mad. There were no witnesses. There never were.'

'It was your first batch,' Maria continued matter-of-factly.

'You were not very experienced with the Luger. Three days later the youngest child crawled out from among the bodies, a bullet lodged in her skull. A sweet little girl, weeping and helpless in the spring sunshine.' Tears were coursing down Maria's cheeks, but her voice was unwavering. 'A German *Wehrmacht* soldier found her, took pity on her. She stayed with his unit all the way back to Berlin, looked after by the Germans, men disgusted by what the SS had done. When they were all killed in action she was rescued by a British soldier. Years later she married a Spanish diplomat, had a daughter of her own. Last spring I took her back to Nikolayev, to lie once again in that lovely meadow, to be with her brothers and sisters, her beloved Mama and Papa. She said they had been missing her, had been desperate to find and protect her.' Maria swallowed hard, blinking away the tears but staring unflinchingly down the barrel. 'That little girl was my mother.'

'Nonsense.' Reksnys jerked the boy towards him, his eyes flitting to and fro, his voice suddenly demented and high-pitched. 'Don't believe a word she says. She is a Jew.'

The room was deathly silent. Reksnys suddenly looked unnerved, began to shake, his face pale and dripping sweat. He pushed the boy away. Jack grabbed him and bundled him towards the entranceway. Reksnys staggered back and then stood upright, attempting to regain his composure. 'You have the boy.' He passed his shaking hands over his hair, greasing it back. He was struggling to make his voice seem normal again, to sound conciliatory. 'Now is the time to end this nonsense. You have what you want. The police will never pin anything on me. We can all walk away. Where is my son?'

'On a one-way trip to hell,' Costas said.

'Where is my son?' Reksnys was uncomprehending, his eyes bloodshot and staring, panic-stricken. There was another silence, and he looked frantically from one face to another, then staggered sideways. 'No.'

Maria aimed down the barrel, slowly, deliberately, all the time keeping it levelled at his head. Her voice was cold, clinical. 'Kneel down. Face the wall.'

Reksnys lost all control. He fell to his knees, his lips shaking, his eyes transfixed with terror. A dark patch appeared on his trousers and spread down his legs. 'No. I beg you. Not this.'

'I am a Jew.' Maria spoke quietly.

There was a deafening crack. Reksnys' head snapped backwards and he fell on the floor, convulsing. A gush of blood arched out. For a moment he was conscious, his eyes wide open, his legs jerking horribly. Then he was still. The spatter of blood on the wall began to drip down, rivulets of crimson that picked out the faded colours of the sacrificial scene, trickling to join the blood pooling on the floor below.

Reksnys began to move again. They stared aghast. He seemed to be convulsing, jerking like a rag doll, moving towards Maria. She dropped the gun and collapsed, seemingly paralyzed. Jack grabbed her, pulling her away. Suddenly the ground shook violently. Jack could barely register what was happening. Then he remembered. Chichén Itzá. The earth tremor a few days before. Reksnys hadn't come alive again. Earthquake. A crack appeared in the wall, tearing apart the painting. An ear-splitting cacophony rumbled up from the cavern below. Jack was aware of a frantic rush to the entrance, of dragging Maria outside, of seeing the waters rise in a great surge behind him and recede back into the cavernous hole that was left where the temple had been.

Later he watched as Maria opened her eyes. He saw the water dripping on her face, saw sunlight streaming in through the tangled canopy above, heard birds screeching. He breathed in deep, savouring the draught of cool, clean air that followed the rain. He thought of Maria's mother, of O'Connor.

It was over.

21

It's twenty-three metres from the edge of the platform to the water surface, give or take a few centimetres. We'll need to rig a pretty elaborate gantry to get the machinery operational.'

'If they could do it in the 1950s, we can do it now. I'll trust your ingenuity.'

'As it happens, I've designed just the thing.'

Costas pulled out a large blueprint from a cardboard tube and unrolled it on the hot limestone, pinning down one corner with the laser rangefinder he had been holding. Jack resigned himself to a detailed technical exposition, but then was saved by the appearance of Jeremy and Maria at the end of the processional way.

'Lunch.' Jeremy vaulted down the rock carrying a cooler,

and ducked under the tarpaulin they had rigged against the sun. It had been two full days since the storm had abated, and the air still felt cleansed and fresh, but that morning the heat had returned with a vengeance and the humidity was stifling.

Jeremy opened the cooler and laid out the food and drink on the table as Jack came up. Costas was grumbling to himself on the ledge but gave up at the sight of food and rolled up his blueprint. They sat down, with Maria leaning back on the rock behind them.

'What have you got for me this time?' Costas said. 'Some Toltec delicacy? Pickled human heart perhaps?'

Jeremy spoke between mouthfuls. 'Nope. Just good old Mexican.' He turned to Jack. 'Tourists back this afternoon.' He swallowed, and took a swig of water. 'The tremor that hit us in the jungle barely even registered here, so they think it's safe. Too damn hot to work here anyway.' He tore off another chunk of bread, and gestured at the deep pit of the Well of Sacrifice, below the platform where Jack and Costas had been standing. 'We really going to do this?'

'Later this year,' Jack said. 'I'm sure there's some fabulous stuff still down there.'

'I've got it all worked out.' Costas was gleaming with sweat under his panama hat, his mouth full of food. 'Come over when you've finished and I'll show you.'

'I'd love to see Harald's last stand, the stuff you guys found,' Jeremy said. 'Back in the other cenote.'

'I don't think so,' Jack murmured. 'The entrance is

blocked by hundreds of tons of stone, and in the other direction you'd be fighting an impossible current. We've found Harald's last battle, his Ragnarok, and that's enough. Something tells me I'd be pushing my battle-luck to go back there again.'

'It's a dark place.' Maria shivered. 'You don't want to go there.'

'It's just a bunch of stalagmites anyway,' Costas said.

Jeremy peered dubiously at the green surface of the sinkhole in front of them. 'If you're thinking of sending me down into this one as an alternative, count me out. This place spooks me enough as it is.'

'You can at least come along on the expedition as food bearer.'

'Maria?' Jeremy craned his neck over the table to look at her. 'The Hereford library, I mean. Can I have leaves of absence in my contract?'

Maria put down her water bottle and gave a tired smile. Jack had been watching her carefully from the other side of the table. She had been asleep or resting almost the entire time since Reksnys' death. The medical team on *Seaquest II* had treated the abrasion on her face, which was now covered in white gauze. There would be no scar, which would have been an appalling legacy. Psychologically was another matter. Jack knew from his own experience that the loss of O'Connor would hit her hardest when she was back on home turf, with time to reflect. And two days before, Maria had stood with a gun aimed at the head of the man who had ordered that murder, and who had traumatized her long before she had met O'Connor. Jack had seen her in a new light since she had revealed the terrible truth of her family's past. He had met her mother years ago, when he and Maria were students together, had assumed she was Sephardic like Maria's father, had never guessed. Like many Holocaust survivors, her mother had found some way of locking the horror away in her memory, had only let it overwhelm her when she knew she was dying. It explained Maria's strength, but also her restlessness, her reluctance to commit herself to anyone. Exposing a trauma she had internalized all her life would change her. The showdown with Reksnys had brought some measure of closure, bringing her own blood-feud to an end, but it had been a shocking experience and had taken its toll on her. Fortunately the Mexican police had been all too happy to change sides when they saw who was winning, and Maria had been hailed a hero for saving the little boy's life. Only Jack and Costas and Jeremy had witnessed the final scene.

Maria gazed at Jeremy. 'The job's got your name on it, but any more time with these IMU guys and you'll be hooked for good.' She gave him another tired smile and then looked across at Jack. 'What's the latest on the menorah?'

'I've been thinking about the symmetry of history,' Jack replied.

Costas gave an alarmed look and straightened himself. 'Oh no. Philosophy. Time I got back to my blueprints.'

'No. Wait. It's important, maybe the key to the whole

story.' Costas sat down heavily while Jack marshalled his thoughts. 'It came to me when I saw that painting of the Toltec procession to the Well of Sacrifice, so incredibly similar to the Roman procession a thousand years before on the Arch of Titus. Think of all the different places we know the menorah has been, all the different cultures. The supreme symbol of the Jewish people, second only to the Ark of the Covenant. Then it's snatched by the Roman emperors, and becomes a prestige item for them as well. Then the Byzantines. Then Harald Hardrada and the Vikings. Each time it could have been melted down, but it wasn't. For the Romans it was a symbol of conquest, of superiority. For the Byzantines it was one of the hoarded treasures that linked them back to the old Rome, to the old virtues. For Harald Hardrada it was a symbol of his personal prowess, and then became something more mystical, almost a talisman. By then its original Jewish significance was lost, but it still had almost supernatural meaning, the power to shape men's destinies.'

Costas had been listening intently. 'The Fourth Crusade, the sack of Constantinople,' he said. 'That's it. All that stuff we were looking for, the ancient works of art. Some of it had prestige value like you said, transformed into a different culture. The Horses of St Mark's in Venice, originally an ancient sculpture but then the symbol of a medieval city-state, something its makers could never have dreamed possible.'

'You get my drift.'

'And the other stuff, the works of art ditched in the Golden Horn. No prestige value.'

'Or symbolism that was dangerous, unwanted. For the Crusaders, like the Vatican, the symbolic power of the menorah had come full circle, back to its Jewish origins. That's why we thought there was a chance of finding it in the Golden Horn.'

'So after the Vikings we move on to the Toltecs,' Costas said. 'I see what you're driving at.'

'The Toltecs were big on symbols of victory, symbols of prowess and dominance,' Jack said. 'Really big. Just look at the architecture of this place, the sculpture. And they loved their gold. Maybe they didn't offer the menorah to the gods at the end of that procession, but stashed it away, something to be brought out only for the most sacred ceremonies. Think about the emperor Vespasian a thousand years before, the triumphal procession in the Roman forum. Like the Toltecs he sacrificed his prisoners of war, the Jewish captives. He could have sacrificed their treasure too, melted it down to make a king's ransom in coin. Instead he locked it away in the Temple of Peace.'

'The Temple of the Warriors,' Jeremy murmured. 'That was the most sacred place of the Toltecs, but it sure wasn't a temple of peace. It was more like Wewelburg Castle in Bavaria, the headquarters of the SS.'

'Not exactly what Vespasian had in mind,' Maria said.

Costas was nodding enthusiastically. 'Thinking outside the box. I like it.'

'See?' Jack grinned. 'Not much different from engineering. You have your plodders, and you have your geniuses.'

'I take it you're referring to Jeremy.'

Maria was still deep in thought. 'So when the Toltecs die out, the menorah vanishes from history, just as we used to think it did at the end of the Roman Empire,' she said.

'The trail goes cold,' Jack agreed.

'Any leads?'

Jack looked at Jeremy, who gazed back blankly and then suddenly looked distracted. He delved with his free hand into a satchel on the table and pulled out a book. 'What you were saying. I've just had a brainstorm. It's something else I found when I was looking for clues in the Maya texts. I couldn't think of a link when I read it, but it's suddenly dawned on me. It's possible, just possible.'

'Not again.' Costas looked at Jeremy with mock horror. 'You're not going to spring another secret society on us.'

'Have no fear.' Jeremy finished his bread and wiped his mouth, then took a gulp of water. 'Remember how it took the Spanish years to conquer the Yucatán, a lot longer than central Mexico? The Yucatán was the first place Cortés landed, but he didn't stick around long.'

'No gold,' Costas offered.

'Right. But he may have missed his cue there, maybe missed the biggest treasure of them all.'

'Go on,' Jack said.

'You won't believe this, but the last of the Maya kings wasn't conquered until 1697. That's 1697,' Jeremy emphasized. 'And he was a direct descendant of the kings of this place, of Chichén Itzá.'

Jack looked stunned. 'But that's almost two centuries after Cortés!'

'I thought Chichén Itzá was already destroyed, abandoned before the Spanish arrived,' Costas interjected.

'Several decades before Cortés, in the fifteenth century.' Jeremy nodded. 'The Toltecs were already long gone, imploded in some awful bloodbath two centuries before. They were replaced by a more civilized Maya dynasty called the Itzá, the people who gave their name to the place. What happened here in the final days is shrouded in mystery, but when the Maya finally abandoned the temples, they left here for ever, disappeared into the jungle and wandered around for years like the lost tribes of Israel.'

'Maybe they had a collective breakdown,' Costas mused. 'Centuries living in a horrifying vortex of violence, all that terror and sacrifice taking its toll. They finally cracked.'

Jeremy laughed. 'Well, whatever happened, they eventually made their way to Lake Petén, more than four hundred kilometres south in what's now Guatemala. Impenetrable jungle, as far away from the Spanish as you could get. They paddled across to a remote island and established a new city, Tah Itzá. They lasted there for generations, undisturbed and unknown except to a few missionaries. Tah Itzá came to have a mystical reputation among the Spanish. To some it was a terrifying jungle stronghold, a bastion of fierce warriors who practised satanic rituals, a hell on earth. To others it was a place of untold riches that could only be reached after great hardship, a kind of Maya Shangri-La, or Avalon.'

'Back to King Arthur again,' Costas murmured. 'I doubt whether Tennyson would have ever dreamed of putting his Avalon in the Mexican jungle.'

'They could have had their treasure with them,' Jack murmured. 'They may have been a vanquished people, a shadow of their former glory, but they would have salvaged what they could from Chichén Itzá. Like the Israelites, they would have kept with them their most sacred possessions, their greatest wealth.'

'Maybe they associated the menorah with the eagle-god, with the return of the king,' Maria said. 'That reference Jeremy found in the Books of Chilam Balam suggests the Maya had some memory of Harald and the Vikings. Remember what Reksnys said about the local Maya today, their reluctance to go down into the cenote below the temple. Maybe Harald was transformed into a kind of mythical saviour-god, fighting for the Maya against their Toltec oppressors. Maybe two hundred years after Harald met his end some intrepid Maya salvaged the menorah from the Toltec inferno, and it passed into yet another culture.'

'If they hadn't already sacrificed it,' Jack said.

'Or melted it down.'

'What we know comes from a manuscript revealed in Mexico only recently, in the late 1980s,' Jeremy continued. 'It's an incredible story, the account of a Jesuit missionary, Fray Andrés de Avendaño y Loyola, who reached Tah Itzá in

1695. Avendaño was a man of exceptional intellect and physical stamina, with great moral strength and sense of purpose. He became fascinated by the people he was sent to convert, as concerned with their livelihood as with proselytizing. The early missionaries get a bad press out here, but without scholars like Avendaño we'd know virtually nothing of these people, and whole populations would have become extinct. Father O'Connor was part of that tradition.'

'I wonder if Patrick knew anything about this,' Maria murmured.

Jeremy opened the book. 'According to his own account, Avendaño arrived that year on the shore of Lake Petén accompanied by two Franciscans and ten converted Maya. From the east, across the lake, they saw a spectacular sight.' Jeremy read out a passage. '*A great wedge-shaped flotilla of canoes, all of them adorned with many flowers and playing much music with sticks and drums and wooden flutes. And seated in one larger than all was the king of the Itzá, who was the Lord Kanek, which means the star twenty serpent.*'

'Sounds awesome,' Costas murmured. 'Any gold?'

'What Avendaño saw was every Spaniard's fantasy about the New World, the kind of thing the conquistadors sold their souls for two centuries before but rarely ever saw. You can tell Avendaño was overwhelmed. His instincts as a Jesuit were clouded by that lust that drove the Spaniards to conquest, like a shark smelling blood.'

Jack smiled. 'Go on.'

'The last of the Maya kings came before them. Listen to

this. *He wore a crown of gold, and gold discs in his ears from which golden pendants hung down to his shoulders. He had bands of pure gold on his arms and golden finger-rings, and his blue sandals were covered with golden bells.'*

Costas whistled. 'He was weighed down with gold.'

Jeremy shut the book. 'Avendaño failed to convert the Itzá. Two years later the city fell to Spanish arms.'

'You say they brought their treasure with them from Chichén Itzá?' Costas said.

'That's the story.'

'That's an awful lot of gold, for a vanquished people.'

'Just a thought.'

Jack was nodding slowly. 'If the Maya were so secretive about their sacred texts, those Books of Chilam Balam that prophesized the arrival of bearded men from the east, then they could have concealed untold other treasures. With the Spanish hunting everywhere for gold, an island stronghold on a lake set deep in the jungle sounds about right.'

'And maybe it was just gold, pure and simple,' Costas said. 'All that prestige value, all the meaning the menorah had for the hated Toltecs, had fallen away. Once the Maya reached their hideaway, maybe they melted it down.'

'And then it comes full circle,' Maria said softly.

'What do you mean?' Costas said.

'Think about it. The Spanish conquer the last stronghold of the Itzá. They finally get their Maya gold. Only it isn't Maya gold at all. And what do they do with it? They're hardly going to sit on their jackpot in the jungle.'

'They send it home,' Jeremy said.

'They melt it down again, they coin it, they send it back in the treasure fleets to Cadiz and Seville,' Maria said. 'Hundreds of pounds of gold, a spectacular bounty. It goes straight into the coffers of the Spanish king. And to the other great power behind the conquistadors.'

'The Catholic Church,' Jack murmured. 'And some of that wealth filters back to the powerhouse of the Church, to the Vatican in Rome.'

'Hang on,' Costas said. 'You're losing me again.'

'Don't you see?' Maria's eyes were alight. 'If we're correct, the menorah was never lost at all. Three hundred years ago, the gold first cast in sacred form in ancient Israel returned to the lands of its earliest heritage, reformed as bullion and as holy artefacts for a new world order. Maybe it was staring us in the face all that time, in the gilded splendours of St Peter's, in the golden reliquaries of the Vatican treasury, in countless embellishments and artefacts in churches around Christendom that received largesse from the mother Church.'

'And maybe some of it even found its way back to Jerusalem,' Jeremy said. 'Remember the saga of Harald Hardrada, offering gifts of treasure to the Shrine of Christ in Jerusalem? The story that climaxed with the Crusades, of western involvement in the Holy Land, wasn't all one of plunder and greed. Maybe, just maybe, some of the gold of the Itzá found its way back in recent centuries to the shadow of the Temple Mount in Jerusalem, and is still there today.'

Costas suddenly looked crestfallen, and glanced at his blueprint on the rock beside the cenote. 'My sub-bottom borer. All my plans. Are we saying what I think we're saying?'

'All this is just guesswork,' Maria murmured.

'And we have nothing to prove Harald even got here,' Costas said. 'The wall-painting's gone, the site of Harald's last stand entombed for ever. Nobody would believe us.'

'We've got this.' Maria removed the smooth chip of stone from her shorts pocket, the runestone she had found inside the cenote.

'It doesn't actually mention Harald,' Costas said. 'And the stone's not local, it looks like a schist they probably picked up at L'Anse aux Meadows.'

'But we know,' Maria said.

'I'll go with the Maya theory.' Jeremy was still reflecting on the menorah. 'Better than trying to work out what to do with the menorah if we found it.'

Jack got up, walked over to the sacrificial platform and peered down at the impenetrable green of the water. Then he turned his back on the cenote and unclipped a radio receiver from his belt. 'The menorah may be in the Well of Sacrifice after all. Or we may have reached the end of the road. But before I even think about another project, I've got a small debt to pay to an old friend. Something to do with battle-luck.' He glanced at Maria. 'And we need to get out of here.'

22

Four days later, Jack was crouched near the stern of *Seaquest II*, muffling his ears against the churning of the ship's wake as he took a call from Maurice Hiebermeyer in Istanbul. After a few moments struggling to hear he got up and walked back to where Costas was standing beside Maria and Jeremy, who were sitting on a bench behind the ship's helipad.

'I read you.' Jack pressed the receiver against his ear. 'Set it all out and I'll see you in the Golden Horn tomorrow evening. And thanks for taking over the excavation, Maurice. Great work. I owe you one. Out.'

Jack snapped shut the radio receiver and weaved his way around the lines that had been laid on the deck to secure the Lynx helicopter after its arrival. *Seaquest II* was heading back to the Arctic to resume the scientific project at Ilulissat icefjord, and several of the scientists who had disembarked during their diversion to the Caribbean were being flown back on board. The ship was now less than a hundred nautical miles east of Newfoundland, and the final helicopter shuttle was due in later that afternoon. Apart from a deep swell, the sea was settled and the sky was clear, but as they ploughed their way north there was a chill in the air that seemed more pronounced after their days in the fetid jungle of the Yucatán. Maria and Jeremy were both wearing IMU anoraks and were huddled behind the bulwark out of the wind.

'That was Maurice Hiebermeyer,' Jack said. 'It's great news. They've finally got artefacts dumped after the siege of Constantinople in 1204.'

'Crusader gold?' Costas said hopefully.

Jack grinned. 'A colossal gilt bronze statue of the emperor Vespasian, with a dedicatory inscription showing it had originally been set up in the Forum of Peace in Rome after the Jewish triumph. It's not exactly what we had in mind, but then archaeology's like that.'

'It's what I wanted to hear.' Costas sighed contentedly. 'My sub-bottom borer has come up trumps. Anyway, as I recall there was quite a list of items looted from the Jewish Temple other than the menorah. We'll find them. Just have faith in IMU technology.'

'That might have to go on the backburner for a while,' Jack said. 'Maurice had been itching to tell me about a find from the Egyptian desert since we came back from Atlantis, and I finally relented. It's incredible.'

'Not another papyrus,' Costas said. 'The last one got us into enough trouble.'

'This one's Roman,' Jack said. 'Just a scrap, but it holds a fantastic clue.'

'Another treasure hunt?'

'Ever heard of Alexander the Great?'

Costas saw the familiar gleam in Jack's eye. 'Okay. My kind of archaeology. You can count me in. Just no icebergs.'

'Deal.' Jack grinned and turned to Maria and Jeremy, but his expression changed as he saw Maria's downcast face. 'I've been meaning to ask, Maria,' he said gently. 'Your Ukrainian heritage. I know the Jewish population were Ashkenazi, but any hint of anything further back? I mean, I'm just trying to understand your passion for the Vikings.'

Maria lightened up, and gave Jack a sad smile. 'After I put my mother to rest last year, I spent a few days in Kiev, went to the cathedral of Santa Sofia and studied the famous wall-paintings. The kings and queens who ruled Kiev in the Viking age, traders and warriors who came down the rivers in longships from the north. Blond, bearded, impossibly tall, the very image of Harald Hardrada and his court.'

'Varangians,' Jack murmured. 'The Rus.'

'Before my mother died, she told me something of her family, for the first time. A story of intermarriage far back in our past, of family legend that had us descended from Rus nobility.'

'Thought so,' Jack smiled.

'Looks like I'm the only one here who doesn't have a drop of Viking blood,' Costas said.

'Don't count on it. Halfdan's inscription in Hagia Sofia isn't the only evidence of Vikings in that neck of the woods. There's another runic inscription on an ancient sculpture in Athens. It looks like Harald and his boys had some fun in Greece too. They got pretty well everywhere.'

Costas was looking at a map he had sketched of their adventure. 'In the western hemisphere, anyway.'

Jack was serious again. 'I also just spoke to the IMU security chief in the UK,' he said, addressing all three of them. 'As a precaution, just before she was taken by Loki, Maria emailed the penultimate draft of the dossier she was helping O'Connor prepare to the IMU security chief. As we speak, Interpol are instigating a number of high-profile arrests. Apparently the *félag* were heavily involved in international crime, money laundering, drugs and arms, the antiquities black market. One of them was even implicated in an audacious robbery at the Roman site of Herculaneum in the Bay of Naples, right under the noses of the Italian authorities. It looks like our friend Reksnys wasn't the only one using the power of the *félag* to line his own pockets.'

'Seems a long way from the heroic ideals of Harald Hardrada,' Costas murmured.

'The modern *félag* had nothing to do with that.' Jeremy's voice had an edge to it. 'They were a criminal organization, pure and simple. They had about as much historical legitimacy as the Nazis.'

'Apparently the dossier you and O'Connor compiled was crucial, the missing link that allowed Interpol to tie all these characters together,' Jack said to Maria. 'And now that they're implicated in murder, I don't think we'll be hearing from the *félag* for a good while.'

'What about that shadowy character in the Vatican?' Costas said.

Jack nodded, and a flicker of concern passed over his face. 'That's the one exception, I'm afraid. Reksnys nearly gave it away when he was boasting about his informers back in the chamber, but he stopped himself. O'Connor suspected who it was, but wanted more certainty before telling us. His murder cut that short. That was Loki's one small victory. But whoever it is, you can be assured he'll be covering his tracks right now, keeping a squeaky-clean profile until the investigation dies down. Meanwhile we might uncover more in O'Connor's records, some clue to who it is.'

'I'm going back to Iona to finish the job.' Maria's eyes had clouded, and she forced a smile through her tears. 'At least Father O'Connor kept his honour to the end. You remember what he said about the Vikings? Your fate is predetermined, so what matters is your conduct in life, your uncompromising behaviour. So you can enter Valhalla and stand alongside the gods at the final battle of Ragnarok knowing you have kept your honour and that of your brethren intact.'

'He was one Hardrada would have been pleased to have had alongside him,' Jeremy said.

'Such a waste.' Maria looked down again, her voice hoarse with emotion. 'All that knowledge, all that humanity.'

'Scholarship is about continuity,' Jack said gently, putting his hand on her shoulder. 'About passing on wisdom to the next generation, knowing it can provide the basis for new discoveries, revelations you can hardly guess at.' He glanced at Jeremy. 'I think Father O'Connor did that.'

'Speaking of which.' Jeremy looked at Jack with a sudden burst of enthusiasm, and patted a package resting on his knees. 'I had this flown in via Goose Bay in Labrador on the last helicopter shuttle. I wanted to see the real thing with my own eyes before telling you.'

Jack smiled warmly. 'I thought we hadn't heard the last from you.'

'You remember that afternoon with the old Inuit, when we talked about the disappearance of the Greenland Norse in the fourteenth century? That haunting final account, about how the Scraelings had taken the entire western settlement?'

'Go on.'

'The Hereford library has really come up trumps. Big time.' Jeremy clutched the package, his face flushed with excitement. 'It's what Norse scholars have dreamed of for years, a discovery as fabulous as any of Harald's lost treasure. Found dumped with all the rest of the old stuff in that abandoned staircase.'

'Let's hear it,' Jack said.

Jeremy stripped the bubblewrap from the package and revealed the hoary leather binding of an old book. 'It's phenomenal.' He turned to Maria. 'The lost saga of the western Greenland settlement, *Vestribygð a Saga*. Written down in the fourteenth century.'

Maria drew in her breath with sudden excitement, and peered over Jeremy's shoulder as he carefully opened the medieval codex to the final page.

'Does it give any details of what happened?' Costas asked.

'It certainly does.' Maria had been scanning the lines while Jeremy was talking. 'By now you should be pretty familiar with this.' She pointed at two words in the centre of the page, and Costas peered down. '*Haraldi konungi*, our true king,' Maria said. 'Harald Sigurdsson.'

Costas whistled. 'Harald Hardrada! The Norse Greenlanders remembered, almost three centuries after he left!'

'And check out the symbol after his name.'

'Don't tell me. The menorah.' Costas grinned as they all peered at the symbol like a rune among the Latin letters of the text. 'We seem to have come full circle. Constantinople, Iona, the icefjord and Vinland, the Yucatán, and now back to the musty old cathedral library that started it all.'

'This closes one loop, but then leads off somewhere fantastic,' Jeremy said. 'Wait till you hear what the text says.'

Maria translated slowly as she traced her finger along the lines. '*Anno Domini 1332. The leaders of the Vestribygð determined to follow their true king Harald Sigurdsson to the Norðrseta, and across the sea to the west.*' She looked up. 'They were fleeing Church oppression, like the Crusader tax imposed on them in the twelfth century. The Norse Greenlanders were pagans at heart. To them Harald Hardrada was their true king, not some distant pontiff in Rome.'

'So where did they go?' Costas asked.

Maria continued, her finger further down the page. '*North to the great icefjord where Halfdan the Fearless set forth in his ship to Valhalla.*'

'Good God,' Jack murmured. 'It actually mentions Halfdan and the longship.' He glanced over at Costas. 'The iceberg wasn't just a dream after all.'

'Nightmare, more like.'

'They numbered one hundred and twenty people, men, women and children, and after packing their ships with provisions they set off north-west, never to be seen again. They were led by Erling Sigvatsson, Bjarni Tordsson and Eindride Oddson.'

'I know those names,' Maria said excitedly. 'They're on the Kingigtorssuaq runestone, found in the nineteenth century on an island north of the icefjord. The only other runestone found in Greenland until the longship discovery.'

'Sometimes the pieces really do all fall together,' Jack murmured, shaking his head in wonder.

'So you're saying Bjarni and these characters led the refugees from Greenland towards the north-west passage?' Costas said.

'That's what the saga implies.'

'Any chance they made it?'

'No reason why not,' Jack said. 'They were the hardiest seafarers ever. Look at where Harald and his depleted crew got to after Stamford Bridge. They almost circumnavigated the western hemisphere. If the passages through from Baffin Bay to the Beaufort Sea had been free of ice in the summer of 1333, then the Greenlanders could have made it.'

'Vikings in the Pacific in the fourteenth century,' Jeremy mused. 'So much for ancient Chinese voyages of discovery. The Vikings would have to take the cake.'

'I think you might want to get some of your anthropology colleagues out there to run a few DNA tests,' Costas murmured.

'It's a fantastic thought,' Jack said. 'All along we've been seeking Harald himself, his treasure. But maybe his greatest legacy was the survival of these people, the people in all the Norse world who were closest to his ways. His brief passage through their land may have been the beacon of light that saved them from a miserable end all those years later.'

'If that was his legacy, I can't help thinking it would have satisfied him as much as any of his great victories,' Maria said, looking at Jack. 'A way of ensuring that the best of his people lived heroic lives with honour to the end.'

Jeremy closed the book and slipped it into its protective wrapping, and then he and Maria stood up between Jack and Costas. For a moment all four of them stared out over the stern to the east, where the rays of the afternoon sun were playing far out across the swell of the Atlantic. To Jack the distant horizon of the Old World seemed to beckon him back, heavy with the radiance of history, yet the shores of the New World and the seas beyond now had an allure he would never have dreamed possible only a few days before. His mind flashed back to the Golden Horn in Constantinople, and a surge of excitement coursed through him as he thought of all they had done.

Costas was holding the jade pendant they had found with the skeleton under the cairn, and was peering at the two silver coins mounted in the eyes. After a moment he looked up at Jack, his expression slightly bemused. 'So this is all we get of Harald Hardrada's treasure?'

'One Viking coin, one Roman.' Jack's face creased in a smile. 'I think that's pretty good, don't you? By themselves no more than dislocated fragments of history, but together they tell a fantastic story, something I never would have believed possible before all this. We found Harald's treasure all right. Those coins are worth all the gold in the world.'

'One final question,' Costas said. 'The Byzantine princess, Harald's other treasure from Constantinople. Maria's namesake. Do you think she really was with him to the end? I fancy her surviving, becoming a fearsome queen of the Toltecs. That would certainly add some spice to history.'

'As if we needed spice after all this,' Jeremy said.

'You thought you saw a woman on the wall-painting, a Viking,' Costas said to Jeremy, who suddenly nodded as he remembered.

'For me, it's the legend of the Valkyries,' Maria said. 'Female riders from the spirit world who chose the slain in battle for Valhalla, who then served them in the great feasting hall. I think Maria stayed with Harald to the end, a warrior princess, his thole-companion. She would have accompanied him to the afterlife. It was the Viking way. I think she's up there now, feasting alongside him with the rest of his noble fellowship, the true *félag*.'

'Maria, Queen of the Valkyries,' Costas said, deadpan. 'From what I've seen, it suits you.'

Jack grinned. 'Time we sent someone else to join them.'

The ship had been slowing down and was now motionless in the water, the last tendrils of its wake sloughing off in the swell to the south. The captain came clattering down the gangway from the bridge and joined them on the deck. 'We're in position, Jack,' he said. 'Any time.'

Jack nodded, looked appraisingly out to sea and then turned to a blanket-wrapped shape on the deck behind him. He carefully unrolled it and a dazzling object came into view. It was the mighty Varangian war axe they had taken from the longship, Halfdan's prized weapon that had saved Jack and Costas from certain death in the ice. It was the first time Jack had held the axe since they had been winched away from their ordeal, and he felt a tingle down his spine as he grasped the oak haft and raised the gilded steel of the bit until it was level with his head. He slowly turned it from side to side, revealing the pendant shape of Thor's hammer, Mjøllnir, with the wolf's head in the apex, and above it the double-headed eagle of Rome and Constantinople, all picked out in gold. On the other side he brought his hand against the runic symbols of Halfdan himself, marks made a thousand years ago when Halfdan had served his beloved leader in the glory days of the Varangian Guard, in the greatest city the world had ever seen.

The others moved wordlessly towards Jack and clasped their hands around the shaft. 'Battle-luck,' Costas said.

'Battle-luck,' Jack repeated quietly.

Jack's mind flashed back to the Golden Horn only a few weeks before, to the extraordinary adventure that had brought them here. He thought again of Father O'Connor, of all he had done to keep the dark side of history at bay, of the terrible price he had paid.

A sea mist had begun to swirl around them, cutting off the ship and the grey swell from the outside world, as if they had been caught in a time warp. Just over the horizon to the west lay Vinland, the furthest outpost of the Vikings. For a fleeting moment Jack thought he saw the ghostly stern of a longship slipping into the mist, its curving stern carved in the snarling form they had seen in the ice. It was as if they were poised at the place where reality became myth, where the Viking world ended and the spirit world began, a journey into darkness and terror more awful than Harald and his men could ever have imagined.

Jack weighed the axe in his hands, then raised the cold steel and brushed it against his lips. Somewhere near here the last remnant of the iceberg would release Halfdan and his longship into the flow, the same stream that had taken his beloved king to the final showdown at the end of time. Halfdan would need to be girded well, fitted to stand proud alongside the companions of the battles he had fought when the Varangians had no equal in the world of men.

Jack paced forward and with one graceful movement lowered the axe-head behind him and swung the haft high in the air, releasing it at the last moment as the weight pulled him forward. The axe arched high over the stern and began to tumble, catching a sunbeam through the mist and disappearing in a dazzling tumult of light. It was like a wayward bolt of lightning, a swirling flash of energy from the age of heroes. Then it sliced into the sea and was gone, leaving only the barest of ripples, soon lost in the swell. Jack felt strangely light-headed, as if a weight had been lifted from his soul, and he leaned against the stern railing and gazed at the grey surface of the sea as the others came up alongside. He found himself mouthing the hallowed words of Old Norse, words that had lost their sinister overtones and spoke of a history more extraordinary than he could ever have imagined.

'Hann til ragnarøks.'

Author's Note

The Menorah. The magnificent gold lampstand from the Jewish Temple in Jerusalem, looted by the Romans in AD 70, remains one of the greatest lost treasures of history, ranked alongside the Holy Grail and the Ark of the Covenant. The only known depiction of the Temple menorah is on the Arch of Titus in Rome, the basis for the cover illustration of this book. The triumphal procession shown on the arch is vividly described by Josephus, a Jewish eyewitness and confidant of the emperor Vespasian. Among the spoils of the Temple was a lampstand made of gold: 'Affixed to a pedestal was a central shaft, from which there extended slender branches, arranged trident-fashion, a wrought lamp being attached to the extremity of each branch; of these there were seven, indicating the honour

451

paid to that number by the Jews' (*Jewish War* VII, 149–50).
Josephus says little about the fate of the Jewish prisoners –
he only describes the execution of their leader, Simon – but
he affirms that some of the spoils, at least, survived being
melted down: in his new Temple of Peace, Vespasian 'laid up
the vessels of gold from the Temple of the Jews, on which he
prided himself' (VII, 161–2). Other treasure provided
bullion for the famous 'Judaea Capta' coins, the obverse
showing a vanquished female Judaea beneath a Roman
standard, above the word IVDAEA.

There are no further eyewitness descriptions of the
Temple menorah. However, compelling evidence that it
survived – perhaps removed to a secret chamber, such as one
actually discovered in the Arch of Titus itself – is provided by
the historian Procopius (*circa* AD 500–62), in his first-hand
account of the spoils taken by the Byzantine general
Belisarius when he defeated the Vandals at Carthage in
AD 534. They included objects looted by the Vandal king
Giseric when he sacked Rome in AD 455, 'the treasures of
the Jews, which Titus, the son of Vespasian, together
with certain others, had brought to Rome after the capture
of Jerusalem' (*History of the Wars* IV, ix, 4–11). According
to Procopius, Belisarius brought the treasures to
Constantinople – present-day Istanbul – and displayed them
in the hippodrome for the emperor Justinian. Procopius
then claims that a Jew persuaded Justinian to return them to
'the sanctuaries of the Christians in Jerusalem'. The fact that
Procopius describes the arrival of the treasures in

Constantinople suggests that the account is authentic, as many of his intended readers would themselves have witnessed the triumph, but his story of their return to Jerusalem seems implausible and a typical embellishment to highlight Justinian's Christian virtues. There is no credible evidence that the menorah was ever again in Jerusalem after AD 70.

*

The Fourth Crusade. The lost treasures of the Jewish Temple may therefore have survived hidden away in Constantinople into the medieval period. The survival of many other antiquities in the city is attested by the list of objects destroyed or looted by the Crusaders in 1204, including the famous *quadriga*, shipped to Venice to become the Horses of St Mark's. Some of the Crusaders would already have been on pilgrimages to Rome, and it is possible that their leader, Baldwin of Flanders, had seen the extraordinary image on the Arch of Titus and had read Procopius. Contemporary accounts of the sack of Constantinople are overlain by pious justifications, but the truth may be that the allure of loot proved too great, and Baldwin desperately needed to find a way of paying the Venetians for shipping his Crusaders towards the Holy Land.

*

Harald Hardrada. Whether or not the Jewish treasures survived in Constantinople as late as 1204 is an open question. A century and a half before the Fourth Crusade, the fabled Varangian bodyguard of the Byzantine emperor had been led by the towering figure of Harald Sigurdsson, known to history as Hardrada, 'Hard Ruler', 'the Ruthless'. Harald was a Viking mercenary, the exiled son of a king of Norway who would return to claim the throne and become the most feared of all the Norse warlords. During his years with the Varangians he became a latter-day Belisarius, campaigning for the emperor in Sicily and North Africa and amassing a huge personal fortune. To the Saracens he was 'Thunderbolt from the North', and he succeeded where the Fourth Crusade would not: he entered Jerusalem, pacified the Holy Land, bathed in the river Jordan and gave treasure to the shrine at Christ's grave. The expedition to Jerusalem probably took place in 1036 or 1037, making Harald Hardrada the first and most successful of all the Crusaders, albeit on behalf of the Byzantine emperor rather than the Church in the West.

Back in Constantinople, Harald was allowed to take part in 'palace-plunder', helping himself to treasure as a reward for his endeavours, and then one night in 1042 he kidnapped the empress Zoe's niece Maria – whom he had wished to marry, but been refused by her aunt – and escaped with his Varangian companions in two ships over the great chain that bound the entrance to the Golden Horn, the harbour of Constantinople. The sole account of this escapade has Maria being returned to the city once they were safely out, but perhaps she did accompany Harald back to Norway and through the rest of his extraordinary life, including his marriage to the Kievan princess Elizabeth and his relationship with at least one other woman, Thora, which produced his son and heir Olaf. According to his biography, Harald had a 'daughter', oddly enough called Maria, who accompanied him on his last voyage and supposedly died suddenly 'on the very day and at the very hour that her father had been killed' (King Harald's Saga, *Heimskringla* 98).

Almost everything we know about Harald Hardrada comes from the *Heimskringla*, an account of the Norse kings written in the early thirteenth century by the Icelandic poet and historian Snorri Sturluson (1179–1241). Eagle and wolf imagery abound in the passages of verse included in the text. The *Heimskringla* and a few sentences in the *Anglo-Saxon Chronicle* provide virtually all we know of the Battle of Stamford Bridge near York, where a Norwegian army under Harald was defeated on 25 September 1066 by the English king Harold Godwinsson, who in turn was defeated a few weeks later by the Normans. Stamford Bridge was a catastrophe for the Norse, and to many signalled the end of the Viking Age; of some three hundred ships that had sailed to England, only twenty-four are said to have returned. The last description of Harald Hardrada alive is of him fighting 'two-handed' in the thick of the battle, perhaps wielding a great battleaxe of the Varangians, surrounded by his loyal bodyguard.

Two of Harald's Varangian companions who escaped with him from Constantinople were Halldor and Ulf, both

Icelanders. Another may have been Halfdan, whose runic graffito can be seen on a balustrade inside the church of Hagia Sofia in Istanbul. Fragments of the chain that crossed the Golden Horn still exist. Elsewhere evidence for Harald's exploits is elusive, but there is enough to give substance to the life recounted in the *Heimskringla*. In Jerusalem, near the Church of the Holy Sepulchre, I have seen a cross carved in the rock that seemed to have the shape of Mjøllnir, Thor's hammer, a symbol that remained potent for the Norse under Christian domination as far away as Iceland and Greenland, kept alive along with all the legends of Loki and Fenrir and Valhalla.

*

The Mappa Mundi. The wonderful thirteenth-century map described in Chapter 2 can be seen today in a purpose-built museum next to Hereford Cathedral, alongside the famous chained library. When I first visited the cathedral as a boy, the library was still in the muniment room above the north transept aisle, where archives and treasures were stored at the time the map was being drawn. The apparent absence of a spiral staircase in the north-east corner of the transept leading up to the gallery has always struck me as odd, so that is where I have placed the fictional discovery in this book. Richard of Holdingham was a true historical character, named in the lower left-hand corner of the map, though very little is known of his life. I have imagined him 'apprenticed' in the fictional *félag* to Jacobus de Voragine,

Archbishop of Genoa, also a true-life character. Richard's absence at the dedication of the map is indicated by the mislabelling of Europe and Africa, a glaring error that a scholar of his calibre would surely never have tolerated.

★

A *félag*, or fellowship, was a Viking institution, and could be a band of warriors owing allegiance to a lord, bound by oaths of loyalty. Sworn enemies could suffer the dreaded *blódörn*, the 'blood-eagle'. Snorri Sturluson, thirteenth-century biographer of the Norse kings, described how one victim had an eagle carved on his back by an enemy, who 'stuck his sword into the body next to the spine, cut away all the ribs down to the loins, and dragged out his lungs'. The idea of a secret *félag* in medieval England is based on the antipathy of the English towards their Norman overlords, and on the Norse heritage which remained strong in parts of Britain where the Vikings had settled. One area where this influence was clearest was the western isles of Scotland, and on the holy isle of Iona today you can see the gravestones of Viking lords among the early Christian relics of the monastery.

★

The fascination of the Nazis with the Vikings is well known. The ultimate Nazi *félag* was the SS, complete with the infamous double-*sig* runic insignia. The mission of the SS became the subjugation of eastern Europe, of the lands once ruled by the Viking kings of Rus and Kiev, where the activities of the SS *Einsatzgruppen* – some of their members locally recruited – included the murder of over a million Ukrainian Jews. The *Einsatzgruppen* 'Operational Situation Report USSR No. 129a', quoted in Chapters 9 and 22, is a fictional addendum to true-life Report No. 129, with the wording only changed to include mention of the fictional Reksnys and his death toll. The Nazi atrocity in this novel is based on my visit to the ravine of Babi Yar in Kiev, where thousands of Jewish families were stripped and shot, and on images and eyewitness accounts in the Museum of the Great Patriotic War in Kiev. Today Babi Yar is a beautiful children's park, surmounted by a giant stone sculpture of the menorah.

The SS *Ahnenerbe*, the 'Department of Ancestral Heritage', existed as described in this novel. In recent years, extraordinary new evidence has come to light concerning *Ahnenerbe* activities in the 1930s, including expeditions to South America and Tibet, where Nazi scientists carried out craniological measurements. They believed that remote populations might preserve evidence of an Aryan master race, one they associated with the legend of Atlantis and the bizarre *Welteislehre*, 'World Ice Theory'. Heinrich Himmler, architect of the SS, believed that the Aryan birthplace was Iceland, and *Ahnenerbe* expeditions were sent there in 1936 and 1938. The *Ahnenerbe* expedition to Ilulissat in this novel is fictional, as are its two members, but Greenland is only one step from Iceland and Himmler would undoubtedly have been intrigued by the accounts of the famous Greenlandic explorer Knud Rasmussen and his studies of Inuit culture.

★

The Ilulissat icefjord, a UNESCO World Heritage site along with L'Anse aux Meadows and Chichén Itzá, may provide one of the clearest indications of global warming today, and has been extensively studied by glaciologists and climatologists. The ancient Inuit site of Sermermiut, 'the place of the glacier people', exists as described in this novel, along with Kællingekløften, 'suicide gorge'. The description of the iceberg is based on my own experience at the Ilulissat icefjord, and diving under ice in Canadian waters. Divers have entered natural fissures inside icebergs, and the technology exists for the kind of penetration described in this novel.

Timbers, textiles and gilded metal can survive almost indefinitely in ice. The idea that a Norse warrior might be preserved in this way came from the extraordinarily well-preserved bodies of two members of Sir John Franklin's ill-fated expedition to the Canadian Arctic in 1845, exhumed from permafrost on Beechey Island in 1984. For the Norse, ship burials were a well-established funerary rite. The burning of a ship is famously described by the tenth-century Arab traveller Ibn Fadlan, who witnessed the funeral of a Rus chieftain on the river Volga in which a woman joined her lord on the pyre. Snorri Sturluson gives us another account in which a burning ship filled with weapons and bodies was cast out to sea after a battle, carrying with it the mortally wounded Viking lord who had supervized the construction of his own funerary pyre.

The image of the ship in the ice is drawn from the spectacular Gokstad and Oseberg ship burials in Norway, though Harald's fictional ship would have been a more practical design. According to Snorri Sturluson, the two ships in which Harald escaped from Constantinople were 'Varangian galleys', oared longships (King Harald's Saga, *Heimskringla* 15). The best evidence for Viking ship types comes from almost exactly the date of the fictional voyage in this novel, from a group of vessels sunk in the 1070s near Skuldelev, in Denmark, to restrict the entrance to Roskilde Fjord. One was a robust, deep-hulled vessel suitable for open ocean sailing. The feasibility of Norse voyages to the Americas has been amply demonstrated by modern experiments, including the sailing of replica ships to L'Anse aux Meadows to celebrate the thousandth anniversary of the arrival of Leif Eiriksson in the New World.

*

The northernmost Viking settlement in Greenland was Vestribygð, the 'western settlement', located some five hundred miles south of the Ilulissat icefjord. However, the region of the icefjord and further north, Norðrseta, was frequented by the Norse and vital to their economy. The only runestone found in Greenland comes from the island of Kingigtorssuaq, almost four hundred miles north of the icefjord, and can be seen today in the museum at nearby Upernavik. It was placed in a cairn by three Norse adventurers – Erling, Bjarne and Eindride – probably in the early fourteenth century. My own explorations along this coast suggest that remote sites may contain further evidence of Norse activity. It is an extraordinary fact that Norse hunters in this extreme environment – seeking walrus ivory, whale, polar-bear hides and narwhal tusk, the 'unicorn horn' seen on medieval maps – helped to pay for the Crusades, through a tax imposed after the Norwegian king Sigurd Jorsalfar, 'The Crusader', established an episcopal see in Greenland in 1124. The Church exerted a tenacious hold over the Greenlanders, and the impossibility of paying Church taxes may well have been a factor in the disappearance of the Norse from Greenland by the fifteenth century.

There can be little doubt that Norse explorers sailed around Baffin Bay and into Lancaster Sound, the beginning of the Northwest Passage to the Beaufort Sea and the Pacific Ocean. A scattering of Norse artefacts has been found across the Canadian Arctic, some undoubtedly taken by Inuit from abandoned Norse settlements in Greenland but others reflecting Norse contact and exploration. No Viking ship has yet been found in these waters, but an extraordinary discovery close to the polar icecap may suggest a shipwreck. At tiny Scraeling Island, a barren rock off Ellesmere Island – some eight hundred miles north of Ilulissat – an Inuit site has yielded more than fifty Norse artefacts, including woollen cloth, fragments of chain mail, ship rivets, knife and spear blades, a carpenter's plane, fragments of wooden barrel and a gaming piece. Radiocarbon analysis suggests a date from *Eirik's Saga* – though no evidence has yet been found. Today the site at L'Anse aux Meadows is maintained by Parks Canada, and you can visit the reconstructed longhouse next to the site of three dwellings and a smithy excavated during the 1960s. The evidence indicates a short-lived settlement established about AD 1000. The story of Freydis and her murderous rampage comes from *Eirik's Saga* and the *Greenlanders' Saga*, the two Viking written sources on Vinland, and it could be that the pall cast by this event dissuaded the Norse from continuing the settlement, along with the threat of attack from Scraelings – 'wretches', the native Indians – and the easier availability of timber along the coast of Labrador to the north.

★

The only authenticated Norse artefact discovered in the Americas south of L'Anse aux Meadows is a worn silver coin excavated from an Indian site beside Penobscot Bay in Maine. It has been identified as a Norwegian coin of King Olaf, Harald Hardrada's son and successor who had been with him in England in 1066, and it may date to the very year of the fictional voyage in this novel. No Viking coins have been found at L'Anse aux Meadows or in Greenland, and how this coin came to be lost almost a thousand miles beyond the furthest known Viking settlement is a mystery.

★

There is no evidence that seafarers from across the Atlantic reached the shores of the Yucatán in Mexico before the Spanish in the early sixteenth century. However, the Maya prophet Chilam Balam, 'Jaguar Prophet', is said to have foretold the arrival of 'bearded men, the men of the east'. The Books of Chilam Balam were mainly written down after the Spanish conquest, leading some to speculate that the prophecy was a later embellishment, but the possibility remains that it was genuine and based on a memory of foreigners who had arrived before the Spanish. Only one group of 'bearded men, men of the east' are known to have visited the New World before the fifteenth century, and that was the Norse; and the evidence suggests that Norse exploration west and south of Greenland reached its greatest extent during the eleventh century.

The fictional jungle temple with its wall-painting is based on a remarkable discovery in 1946 by two American adventurers in the Yucatán, at a place which became known as Bonampak, Maya for 'painted walls'. Inside an overgrown corbelled building they found a narrative wall-painting of extraordinary power, showing a jungle battle, the torture and execution of prisoners and victory celebrations, including white-robed Maya ladies drawing blood from their own tongues. The painting dates from the height of the Maya period, about AD 800, but another painting, in the Temple of the Warriors at Chichén Itzá, dates from the time when the Toltecs swept into power in the eleventh century. It shows canoe-borne Toltec warriors reconnoitering the Maya coast, a great pitched battle on land and the heart-sacrifice of the captured Maya leaders.

If you visit the ruins of Chichén Itzá today, you are likely to be told that the stories of human sacrifice were exaggerated by the Spanish, or relate only to the Toltecs, not the Maya, whose descendants still occupy the Yucatán. You can reach your own conclusion at the Tzompantli, the Platform of the Skulls, where you can look past the sculpted rows of decapitated heads towards the sacrificial altar on the Temple of the Warriors, and then gaze down the ceremonial way to the Sacred Cenote, the Well of Sacrifice. Many of the depictions of torture and execution in Maya and Aztec art pre-date the arrival of the Spanish, and the latest techniques of forensic science are, almost literally, adding flesh to the picture: archaeologists in Mexico have discovered that the floors of Aztec temples are soaked with iron, albumen and genetic material consistent with human blood.

In the Yucatán, the most telling evidence comes from underwater archaeology. The Well of Sacrifice at Chichén Itzá, dredged in 1904–11 and excavated by divers in the 1960s, contained hundreds of human skeletons – men, women and children – as well as a treasure trove of artefacts: gold discs, carved jade pendants, a human skull made into an incense burner, a sacrificial knife, numerous votive wooden figurines and other offerings. The story is similar at other cenotes in the Yucatán, including several in the ring of sinkholes that formed over a huge meteorite impact site close to the north coast. Many of these cenotes remain unexcavated and are vulnerable to looters. The fictional cenote in this book is based on my own experience exploring these sites, and especially diving in the spectacular caverns and passageways of Dos Ojos, 'Bat Cave', near the Maya coastal stronghold of Tulum.

The story of the last days of the Maya kings, almost two centuries after the Spanish conquest, is based on the account of Father Andrés de Avendaño y Loyola (*Relation of two trips to Petén, made for the conversion of the heathen Ytzaex and Cehaches*), who was eyewitness to this extraordinary scene beside the remote jungle lake of Petén in 1695 or 1696. A further fragment of this account came to light in 1988, and is quoted in Chapter 21. The true source of Maya gold, as described by Avendaño and found by archaeologists in the Well of Sacrifice at Chichén Itzá, remains a mystery.

*

The Old French quoted in Chapter 2 is the actual inscription visible in the lower left-hand corner of the Hereford Mappa Mundi. The Bible quote in Chapter 4 is an abridgement of Exodus 25:31–40, King James Version. In Chapter 5, the two quotes from King Harald's Saga, part of the *Heimskringla* by Snorri Sturluson, were translated by Magnus Magnusson and Hermann Pálsson (Penguin, 1966). The poetry in Chapter 13 is from *Morte d'Arthur* by Alfred, Lord Tennyson (1809–92). In Chapter 15, the sentence in Old Norse describing Harald's sea voyage is fictional, but the phrases that make it up are taken verbatim from the thirteenth-century *Eirik's*

Saga, describing the Norse voyages to Vinland. The Old Norse phrase Þar *liggr hann til ragnarøks*, 'there he lies until the end of the world', comes from the poetic *Edda* (*Gylfaginning* 34) also by the prolific Snorri Sturluson, written down some time in the early thirteenth century.

The quote at the beginning of the book is from Josephus, *Jewish War* VII, 148–62, translated from the Greek by H. St J. Thackeray (Loeb Edition, Harvard University Press).

The two silver coins described in Chapter 15 – and one of them in the Prologue – truly exist. They can be seen along with other images from this book at www.davidgibbins.com.

Now you can buy any of these other bestselling books from your bookshop
or *direct from the publisher*.

FREE P&P AND UK DELIVERY
(Overseas and Ireland £3.50 per book)

Atlantis	David Gibbins	£6.99
Wicked	Gregory Maguire	£7.99
Atlantic Shift	Emily Barr	£6.99
Never Fear	Scott Frost	£6.99
After the Mourning	Barbara Nadel	£7.99
Flint's Law	Paul Eddy	£7.99
Blue Water	Manette Ansay	£6.99
Eleven on Top	Janet Evanovich	£7.99
Guardians of the Key	Clio Gray	£6.99

TO ORDER SIMPLY CALL THIS NUMBER

01235 400 414

or visit our website: www.madaboutbooks.com

Prices and availability subject to change without notice.